THE PROTECTOR'S VENGEANCE

PETER WACHT

The Protector's Vengeance
By Peter Wacht

Book 3 of The Tales of Caledonia

This book is a work of fiction. Names, characters, places, and incidents are the product of the author's imagination or are used fictitiously. Any resemblance to actual events, locales, or persons, living or dead, is coincidental.

Published in the United States by Kestrel Media Group LLC.

ISBN: 978-1-950236-22-0

eBook ISBN: 978-1-950236-23-7

Library of Congress Control Number: 2021925717

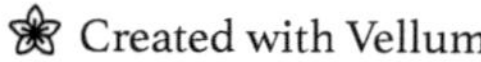 Created with Vellum

ALSO BY PETER WACHT

THE REALMS OF THE TALENT AND THE CURSE

THE TALES OF CALEDONIA

*Blood on the White Sand (short story)**

*The Diamond Thief (short story)**

The Protector

The Protector's Quest

The Protector's Vengeance

The Protector's Sacrifice

The Protector's Reckoning

The Protector's Resolve

The Protector's Victory

THE TALES OF THE TERRITORIES

A Fate Worse Than Death (short story)*

Stalking the Red Ruby (short story)*

Death on the Burnt Ocean (Forthcoming 2023)

Monsters in the Mist (Forthcoming 2023)

The Dance of the Daggers (Forthcoming 2023)

THE SYLVAN CHRONICLES

(Complete 9-Book Series)

The Legend of the Kestrel

The Call of the Sylvana

The Raptor of the Highlands

The Makings of a Warrior

The Lord of the Highlands

The Lost Kestrel Found

The Claiming of the Highlands

The Fight Against the Dark

The Defender of the Light

THE RISE OF THE SYLVAN WARRIORS

*Through the Knife's Edge (short story)**

* Free short stories can be downloaded from my author website at www.PeterWachtBooks.com.

YOUR FREE SHORT STORY IS WAITING

THROUGH THE KNIFE'S EDGE BY PETER WACHT

This short story is a prelude to the events in my series *The Sylvan Chronicles* and is free to readers who receive my newsletter.

Join Peter's newsletter and get your FREE short story at www.PeterWachtBooks.com.

SETTING THE STAGE

The Protector's Vengeance, Book 3 of *The Tales of Caledonia*, is set more than one thousand years before the events that occur in *The Sylvan Chronicles* and takes place in a separate land of *The Realms of the Talent and the Curse*. Caledonia, though a monarchy, functions more like a loose confederation of Duchies, much to the displeasure of the Crown.

It is during this time that some of the more adventurous and grasping members of the Caledonian nobility accept King Corinthus Beleron's territorial grants and begin to colonize the Territories far to the west on the other side of the Burnt Ocean. These Territories will eventually become the Kingdoms of *The Sylvan Chronicles*.

In Caledonia, as in the other realms, the ability to use the Talent sets apart the person gifted with this unique skill. But being able to use the Talent is only part of the dynamic. For if a Magus chooses to follow a darker path, the Talent becomes the Curse.

1

A GOOD MORNING

The silence of the early morning was complete but for the rapids rushing across the rocky riverbed toward the Silent Sea. Yet, with the sun still a distant thought, a tension that was almost palpable had displaced the sense of calm that should have accompanied the blanketing quiet.

"Are they close?" whispered Jerad Brexston, Sergeant of the Battersea Guard. A tall, burly man with a mop of dark curly hair, a frown of worry had replaced his ever-present smile. He patted his piebald warhorse gently on the neck, trying to keep the aggressive and agitated animal calm. "I have this sudden urge to urinate, and that almost always means Ghoules are about."

"You mean to say that your bladder serves as your primary warning against Ghoules?" asked the man sitting on his horse next to the Sergeant. He was just as tall, though not as handsome. The scar from the swipe of a three-digit sand cat claw trailed down his cheek to his neck on his left side, and although he wasn't very old, how he carried himself said otherwise. His hair and beard had turned a preternatural white, only a few streaks of brown still visible. But it was the sharp grey eyes that gave most people pause when first caught by the man's intense stare. There was a deadness there, a lack of emotion, which often sent a shiver of fear down a person's spine when meeting him for the first time. Though at the moment those usually cool eyes held a faint touch of amusement. "How is it that you're still alive?"

"I've wondered much the same, Protector," said Tarin Tentillin. The sharp-featured man wasn't as tall as his two companions, but he was just as imposing with his broad shoulders and chest. He was a fastidious man, his uniform always impeccable and clean and his hair and mustache, the tips waxed and curled at the ends, exactly as they should be regardless of whether he had ridden ten leagues without stopping or skirmished a Ghoule pack. "Some days he spends so much time in the latrine it seems that we are always under attack."

"It's not every time I urinate," protested Jerad. "It's just when I feel a tightness in my bladder like I can't control it, as if I'm going to wet myself. Once the fight starts, the feeling goes away."

"You should probably stop talking now, Jerad," said Bryen, who was a few years younger than the Sergeant despite his older appearance. For a brief moment his fingers touched the silver collar locked around his neck, the cold metal giving him a strange sense of comfort. It was a habit he had yet to conquer, and he wasn't even sure that he wanted to. "You're not helping yourself. Maybe you just have an infection. You do spend a good bit of time with the fairer sex."

"I'm just trying to explain how it works," said the Sergeant, not put off by his friend's comment. "And I don't have an infection. I always act honorably when I'm with the fairer sex. I just enjoy their company. I'm simply saying that my bladder has never failed me before."

"I guess that's a good thing for all of us," agreed Tarin, the Captain of the Battersea Guard looking to both sides and behind him to ensure that the men and women of the Southern Marches remained silent and motionless, worrying that if they failed to do so their ruse would be discovered at the worst possible time. He raised his fist as a reminder, several of his soldiers speaking soothing words to or stroking the noses of their horses in an attempt to keep their hot-tempered chargers still for just a few minutes more. "But it's not a skill that I would mention in mixed company, if at all. It doesn't necessarily place you in the best possible light."

"I'm simply explaining one of my unique talents that has proven useful in the past, much like the Talent that Bryen employs from time to time." The Sergeant of the Battersea Guard had an easygoing personality and was often the first to laugh at a joke, especially his own. But he was also tenacious, whether the fight involved words or steel. He never gave up anything easily, a characteristic that Tarin valued as his commanding officer, but also found exasperating at times.

Tarin couldn't help but smirk at his friend and subordinate's last comment. "I don't think that we can fairly compare your supposed talent regarding your bladder with Bryen's Talent. His Talent seems much more useful than yours."

"Make fun if you want," offered Jerad, not caring that his Captain and Bryen were challenging him. "I'm just saying that I believe the Ghoules are closer than we thought they would be at this time in the morning."

The Sergeant's eyes searched to both sides of the several companies of Battersea Guard hidden among the trees a few hundred yards from the northern bank of the Eastern River. The urge to vacate his bladder had intensified, almost painfully so, but he still didn't see any signs of movement within the wood. The gusts of wind from the previous night had died down, replaced by a stillness to the air that suggested the heat of the day would be oppressive at best. Even with the Ghoules' mottled green coloring and brown leather armor, which allowed the monsters to blend in perfectly with a forest environment, he should have caught a flash of movement by now.

Yet there was nothing. Not a single branch or leaf had moved. Still, his belief didn't waver, buoyed by the fact that not a sound drifted among the trees. The small animals of the forest that were usually skittering about before the break of day, foraging for a meal, had gone to ground. That could mean only one thing. The Ghoules were close. He was certain of that. His bladder was never wrong. It was just a question of when the creatures would appear.

"Where did these beasts come from?" asked Jerad. "I thought we cleared out the Southern Marches."

"We did," replied Tarin, his hand dropping to the hilt of his sword. He could feel it now as well. The sense that he and his soldiers were no longer alone among the soaring trees. "They probably came down from the western slopes of the Northern Spine or possibly even all the way from the Dark Forest."

"The Dark Forest," confirmed Bryen. "When I found these packs the first time they were still within that wood. The beasts avoided the Breakwater Plateau and stayed close to the Eastern River, bypassing Tintagel to the south. I've been tracking them ever since because Jerad is right. We did eliminate the Ghoules in the Southern Marches, at least for a time."

As he had done so frequently during the last few hours, Bryen took hold of the Talent, using the natural magic of the world to extend his senses and search around the troop. Nothing approached from the south or east. But he had identified the darkness coming toward them from the northwest during the evening the day before yesterday, and he had been tracking the Ghoules ever since. Three packs of Ghoules, which meant as many as thirty or forty of the beasts, along with at least three Elders. More than enough to be a real threat to Bryen and the other soldiers hiding in the wood.

"And for me that confirms it," offered Tarin, turning his

gaze toward Jerad. "I much prefer the Protector's Talent to your talent."

"Quiet," Bryen whispered. "They're coming through right now."

Hearing that Jerad lifted his eyebrows, giving Tarin a nod and a knowing look, as if to say that his bladder had been right once again and was just as useful as Bryen's Talent. The Captain of the Guard shook his head in aggravation knowing that his Sergeant would be insufferable for the next few days, but there was nothing to be done about it. Tarin raised his hand once more, five fingers spread. Then he closed his fist, the sign for his soldiers to keep themselves and their mounts still and silent because the enemy they were hunting drew near.

With the Ghoules approaching, Bryen checked his hold on the Talent, having used his unique ability to make it appear as if the soldiers of the Battersea Guard were a natural part of the forest. A Ghoule could look directly at where the troop was hiding within the grove and they would see nothing except for tall trees and a forest floor with only a few sparse bushes spread about, the lack of undergrowth resulting from the intertwined branches that blocked the sun from reaching the ground. If the soldiers moved, made any sounds, the illusion would fade and falter, and that's something that Bryen couldn't afford to have happen if his plan was to work. So far, so good, but he was beginning to think that he might have misjudged where he should have placed the soldiers at his back.

He could sense that the Ghoules were coming closer than he anticipated. Too close. And then the beasts were there, flashes of movement visible between the trees just off to their left. The men and women of the Battersea Guard stiffened, but they kept their movement to a minimum, some of the Ghoules passing by no more than a dozen feet from the concealed soldiers. Rather than worrying about the proximity of their enemy, the soldiers concentrated on keeping their horses calm and under control.

They had all fought the Ghoules before, and they knew the creatures' inherent advantages. The beasts were stronger and faster than humans. They often stood as tall as a mounted soldier. And because of their natural camouflage, fighting the beasts within the forest was akin to a death sentence. The soldiers' movement would be restricted by the trees, and they wouldn't be able to use their horses as effectively as they could have if they instead attacked the Ghoules in the long grass that led down to the river. But for that to happen, they needed the Ghoules to make it through the grove without the beasts noticing that they were loping right by their intended prey.

When he recognized the danger, Bryen slid down carefully from his saddle, Jerad taking the reins. The Protector moved slowly, taking several breaths between each step to his left to reduce the possibility that a passing Ghoule who happened to look his way actually would see him. Walking the twenty feet he needed to go seemed to take hours, but finally he was where he wanted to be with almost all of the Ghoules none the wiser. All but one of the beasts had walked by the deception that he had created. Yet all it would take to destroy the surprise was for this one Ghoule, an Elder, to walk through the illusion. Then the soldiers would be revealed. That was something that Bryen simply couldn't allow.

The Elder walked several dozen feet behind the other Ghoules, his brown robes flapping behind him, the beast barely visible within the forest because of his natural coloring even when Bryen looked directly at him. Rather than carrying a long, black spear that was taller than a Ghoule, his clawed hand grasped a staff made of black ash that allowed the beast to connect more easily to the Dark Magic gifted to him by the Ghoule Overlord.

With careful strides, Bryen slowly placed himself directly in front of the Elder. Waiting. Not daring to move so as not to give away his location. The Elder approached step by step. Thirty feet. Twenty feet. Ten feet. His clawed feet dug deeply into the soft earth of the forest floor. Five feet. The Elder Ghoule took one more step, then gasped in shock, a human appearing right before him as if he had simply coalesced out of thin air.

Before the Elder could shout a warning to his Ghoules, Bryen drove one of the Talent-infused blades of the Spear of the Magii into the creature's chest. The only sound that emerged from the beast was a soft gasp as the energy contained within the weapon burned through his core and then down into his arms and legs. In seconds, it was over. The Elder Ghoule slipped from the shining steel when Bryen tilted the double-bladed spear toward the ground, lowering the body silently to the earth, the charred figure barely recognizable.

Before the Elder's staff fell to the ground, Bryen grabbed it with his free hand. He regretted his decision instantly, a sharp pain sizzling up his arm, the Dark Magic contained within the staff rebelling against him, sensing the Talent that he controlled and immediately trying to fight it. Using that same Talent, Bryen clamped down on the Dark Magic, forcing it back into the staff. But even with the passage of only a few seconds it was already too late, the Dark Magic locked away within him calling to the power of the staff, seeking to join with it.

If this had occurred only a few months before, Bryen might have gotten flustered and made a fatal mistake. But he had learned how to separate the Dark Magic that was a part of him thanks to the Seventh Stone from the Talent and maintain the two energies distinctly, always making sure that he kept the Dark Magic locked away behind a barrier constructed of the world's natural magic. And he never manipulated the Dark Magic without the Talent encasing it, knowing that a single touch of the Curse was all that it would take to corrupt him, to allow the taint of the Dark Magic to flow through his veins so that over time the Curse would use him rather than the other way around.

He had Rafia and Sirius to thank for that. Although the Dark Magic of the Elder's staff threw him off balance for a moment, he recovered quickly. The Seventh Stone choosing to join with him had been an unsettling, frightening experience. But it did offer some advantages.

He was the Seventh Stone, and the Seventh Stone was him, and that meant that he could make the Dark Magic his own ... so long as he did it the right way.

As he had done several times before, he imagined a hollow tube crafted of the Talent connecting to the Elder's staff. Once firmly affixed within his mind, he allowed the Dark Magic held by the staff to flow through the cord, which pulsed a deep black as he drained the power from the weapon. Bryen knew that how he had visualized what he had done wasn't actually what had occurred, but the mental image made it easier for him to add with barely any risk the Dark Magic from the staff to the massive store that he already controlled, locking the Curse safely away within him. That task complete, he lay the useless staff in the dirt and turned his attention back toward the river.

"I ENJOYED SLEEPING with you last night. It brought back memories of better times between us."

The tall, thin woman stared at her companion, unsure of how she wanted to reply. Her curly, unkempt hair looked more wild than usual as she had slept with her saddle as her pillow, curled up near the fast-flowing water of the Eastern River. If the noise of the rapids at their backs wasn't bad enough, although she still hadn't decided whether the raging river or Sirius' snoring had been louder, she had found it exceedingly difficult to get a good night's sleep knowing that she was bait.

"We didn't sleep together," said Rafia Riverstone, who pulled a comb from one of the many pockets in her cloak and began to work through the tangles in her hair, realizing that it was a hopeless task before she had even begun but valuing how the familiar activity had a calming influence upon her. "Jokes at a time like this? I would think that you should be more focused on the threat that's coming at us."

Sirius grinned at her, which was rare. The old Magus tended to be grouchy at the best of times, acidic at the worst. Having spent the last few months in his company once again after a decade apart had made the memories of his mercurial temperament real, and she had wondered how it was that they had both survived the many years that they had spent together.

"I am focused, but we have a few minutes." The Magus rose to his full height, his long white hair sticking up in all directions as was its wont. He rubbed at the crick in his back, having found several rocks beneath his blankets and suspecting that he had missed a few more before he had bedded down for the night. He had slept on the unsparing ground since escaping Haven right before more of the Ghoules had arrived, and at his age all that hard travel was wearing on him. Though apparently that wasn't the case for the handful of soldiers around them who were already busy, even with the sun yet to rise. Sirius watched as one of the soldiers tended a small fire, having placed a pot for porridge and a kettle for tea over the flames. Two other soldiers were examining their horses' hooves, making sure that the steel shoes were in good shape, while two more packed away their bedrolls. No matter what the soldiers were doing, the hilts of their weapons were never more than an inch or two from their itchy fingers. "My dreams were particularly pleasant, bringing me back to our time together. It all put me in a good frame of mind."

"Will wonders never cease," chuckled Rafia.

"You don't have to be smart about it."

"How could I not be?" countered Rafia. "Ever since you arrived at Haven, you've been putting forward this idealized version of what our relationship was like when we were together. You seemed to have forgotten that for every passionate moment we had, there were just as many if not more moments of anger or sadness or disappointment."

"But that's what made it fun," offered Sirius. "We never knew what each day would bring."

"That's what made it so exhausting," said Rafia. "Yes, we had many good days. But there were also many more days where I wanted to stab you with a knife."

"That feeling was mutual," confirmed Sirius. "You almost carried through with it a few times."

"And that's the crux of the issue right there," said Rafia. "Sirius, you have created in your own mind this fantasy of our time together. But it was no better than those of other couples, and I would argue that because of our personalities it was often worse. We both have tempers. We both are strong willed and have strong personalities. Both of us believe that we are right most if not all of the time. And neither of us likes to lose, no matter the argument. Those are not good variables for a positive long-term relationship."

Sirius sighed. "You may be right. But I miss you, Rafia. I enjoyed spending time with you."

"And I with you," she replied with a smile. "But I wonder whether for you it was more of your missing the challenge of being with me. I know you well, Sirius. Perhaps too well. Whenever there's a problem to solve, you have to solve it. You can't help yourself. And I think you wanted to try to solve me."

"That's not true," huffed Sirius with a sigh.

"Is it not? Why did you show up at my door in Haven?"

"To help Bryen remove the Protector's collar from his neck. The boy didn't deserve what happened to him, and I wanted to make it right."

"He didn't deserve it, you're right," said Rafia. "But it wasn't just about removing the collar."

For a moment, Sirius simply stared at her, his mind working furiously for some other reason for going to Haven that he could offer in his defense other than the one that was most obvious. Nothing came to mind, so he had no choice but to give up.

"I was trying to solve a problem," he admitted.

"Yes, you were. And you did the same with me. You enjoyed the challenge of being with me because it required constant problem solving in order for us to maintain our relationship. You enjoyed that. I didn't. It wasn't long after we had gotten together that I yearned for more stability between us, for less conflict and fire and more calm and tranquility."

"Yes, I guess we both had different expectations and wants," conceded Sirius, his joviality now replaced by a more somber mood.

"And different ways of achieving them," added Rafia gently.

Before Sirius could continue the conversation, Rafia leapt up from where she had been sitting, placing her comb back in one of the pockets of her cloak and then pulling a short sword from the scabbard that she had lain against her saddle the night before for just such an occurrence.

"Guards! To arms!" she ordered.

The soldiers obeyed instantly, stopping whatever they were doing and sprinting toward the two Magii.

Several dozen Ghoules, shrieks and screams in their unintelligible language preceding them, burst from among the trees, sprinting toward their prey with a fiendish speed. The beasts had tracked this group of humans for days, and they were hungry.

～

"WHAT ARE THEY WAITING FOR?" demanded Sirius.

"They need to be certain that all the Ghoules are through the wood," said Rafia calmly.

At the same time, she released a bolt of white-hot energy from her palm aimed at one of the two Elder Ghoules. But the Elder had expected the assault, using the black mist spinning in front of him to deflect the energy into the trees. The Elder's success didn't bother Rafia. The two Elders, as well as all the Ghoules, were focused now entirely on her and Sirius and the handful of soldiers who had formed a semicircle with the Eastern River at their backs. The tight space didn't allow all the Ghoules to come at them at once, which was a good thing.

Because otherwise they would have been overwhelmed in seconds, and the Ghoules could then use the fire the soldiers left burning for their own meal. The knowledge of what that meal likely would be gave the soldiers with the two Magii an added burst of energy and strengthened their determination. They had fought the Ghoules often enough to know that the beasts not only enjoyed killing, but that they also enjoyed eating what they killed, their serrated teeth perfect for tearing flesh and crushing bone, the taste of human flesh particularly pleasing to them.

"Just as planned," said Rafia, a bloodthirsty smile breaking out on her face. She loved when a well-thought-out strategy came together. Almost as much as she enjoyed killing Elders.

The ground had begun to rumble and shake. At first, the Ghoules didn't notice the change, the noise and movement covered by the sounds of the whitewater behind the determined defenders. But then one Ghoule at the back of the pack turned, and then another, and then several more. They tried to scream a warning to their comrades, most of whom remained focused on the two Magii and the few soldiers opposing them, but it was too late.

A human with a glowing double-bladed spear charged from

the wood behind the Ghoules, followed by several companies of soldiers. The first line of cavalry didn't even bother to use their spears against the Ghoules, allowing the overwhelming strength and weight of their horses to do the deadly work for them, the massive warhorses slamming into the Ghoules, knocking them to the ground, trampling them, the soldiers following in the second line of attack using their spears to finish any of the creatures who might have survived.

The Ghoules tried to defend themselves, now caught between the charging Guard and the river, but the ferocity of the attack proved too much to withstand. Many of the soldiers had fought in the Battle of the North Road, as well as in the Raven Wood, the Deep Wood, and the Horseshoe. They had learned how to defeat these beasts with the Protector, and they were putting those lessons to good use now, maintaining a tight formation, using their horses as weapons, and not allowing the stronger and faster Ghoules to get in close to them through deft work with their spears.

With the Ghoules fully occupied, Sirius and Rafia turned their attention to the two Elders, who didn't seem concerned by the unexpected change in circumstances. At the same time, both Elders shot shards of black darker than the night toward the two Magii, who quickly raised shields constructed of the Talent in front of them, blocking the attempted strike. But the Elders didn't stop there, thinking that if they could kill the Magii quickly, they could then assist their Ghoules before they were overrun by the humans. With that thought locked firmly in place, the Elders maintained their attack, a black mist surging from their staffs of ash, their Dark Magic slamming against the shields of blazing white energy and muting the glow, the Curse and the Talent struggling for supremacy with the lives of those wielding the two distinct powers in the balance.

But the smaller battle within the larger battle was short-lived. Bryen, recognizing the danger presented by the Elders, nudged his warhorse away from the Ghoules and toward the Elder closest to him.

The creature was so intent on his fight with Rafia that he didn't even realize he faced a new danger until the horseman with the blazing spear was almost upon him. The Elder tried to recover in time, releasing his hold on the black mist that he had sent against the Magii, desperately attempting to turn his Dark Magic against this new threat before it was too late.

Because he was so close to his target, rather than use the Talent, Bryen twisted the spear in his hand so that the two blades were parallel to the ground. He saw the Elder's grin, revealing the beast's sharp teeth. Bryen used the Elder's hubris to his advantage. He knew that the beast assumed that the black mist surging around the top of his black staff would be more than enough to kill a soldier foolish enough to attack someone with his incredible power. But the Elder was badly mistaken.

Just as the Elder flicked his staff at Bryen, the black mist speeding toward him, Bryen swung the Spear of the Magii, simply flicking his left wrist. The glowing blade sliced through the Dark Magic like a warm knife through butter and then cut through the Ghoule's neck, the beast's head rolling to the ground as his body slumped to the long grass.

With only one Elder remaining now, Sirius and Rafia made quick work of the creature. While Sirius forced the Elder to focus on his defense by sending a stream of energy toward the beast, Rafia sought a more final solution. Raising her hands to her shoulders, she slashed them down toward the ground. In a flash, a bolt of lightning blasted down from the sky, destroying the last Elder so completely that only a cloud of black ash remained, twisting without rhythm until the wind picked up speed with a touch of the rising sun and captured the flakes.

Bryen nudged his horse toward Rafia, his head on a swivel

the entire time as he looked for any remaining threats. But there were none. The Elders were dead, as were all the Ghoules. The Battersea Guard had fought with an efficiency that had made their Captain proud, and Tarin already had ordered his troops to check all the Ghoules littering the ground around them, just to make sure that none of the beasts were playing possum.

"You really like doing that, don't you?" he asked the Magus, pointing with his spear toward the cloud of black ash that continued to swirl in the breeze, the blades no longer glowing as he had released his hold on the Talent.

Rafia nodded with a rapacious grin. "It's very satisfying."

"That I can understand," he said. "Not a bad way to start the day."

Tarin and Jerad both rode up, pleased not only by the fact that they had defeated their enemy so thoroughly, but also that they had done so with only a few serious injuries among their troops that Bryen likely could heal with the Talent.

"True," the Captain of the Guard confirmed, "but we still have a long way to go."

"Can't we just enjoy this for a moment?" asked Jerad. "We eliminated what looks to be three packs of Ghoules and three Elders. No deaths and only a few serious wounds."

Sirius stared at the Sergeant of the Guard, then nodded. "You're right. We can." Sirius waited in silence for all of five seconds. "All right, time to move on. We have more pressing matters to attend to."

Watching the exchange, Bryen could only smile, having gotten to know the old Magus quite well after all the time that they'd spent together during the last few months.

"Don't mind him," Rafia said, motioning toward the white-haired Magus. "He has a one-track mind, as you know. When there's a goal to be achieved, he finds it difficult to think of anything else."

"So I've noticed," Bryen agreed.

At the moment, Bryen's mind had split into several tracks, as he considered all the worries that troubled him. The threat presented by the Ghoules was bad enough. But what of the grasping King of Caledonia? How was he to deal with him? And were the ambitions of Marden Beleron tied somehow to the reappearance of the Ghoules?

It was a strange concern, he admitted, not knowing why a human would be so foolish as to seek an ally in the Ghoule Overlord, a creature bent on the destruction of the Kingdom. His Kingdom no less. Still, the thought refused to go away.

And what of Aislinn Winborne, a prisoner of the King? Would he get to the capital in time to help her? Could he even help her? And could he help his friends who had bled with him on the white sand?

So many questions and so few answers. Some people might have been bothered by the uncertainty of it all. But not Bryen. No, he was used to it. And when this was what life had to offer, Declan's words always ran through his mind.

"You must do what you must do."

He would. He would do what needed to be done. Live or die, he would do what needed to be done.

2

———

A MORE DIRECT ROLE

The howl mixed equal parts pain and terror, the victim's torment sharp and clear as it echoed off the surrounding peaks. The bestial noise was all too familiar, and it wasn't enough to stop the work.

It simply delayed it. The Elders on the northern side of the magical barrier that separated the Lost Land from Caledonia waited impatiently as the Ghoule trapped within the Weir slowly burned alive. Although the creature was immune to the Dark Magic that formed the Weir, it was vulnerable to the Talent that had been woven together with the Curse to form the barricade, and that scalding power slowly but inexorably charred the beast's flesh to a crisp and turned his bones to ash.

The Overlord, the leader of the Ghoule Legions, watched dispassionately from the southern side of the Weir, having crossed through without incident. The beast towered a head above the Ghoules working around him, his brown robes caught by the gusts of wind so common to the Winter Pass, the primary gap that ran north to south through the Shattered Peaks and offered the easiest access to the lands of men.

Even with the immense power of the Dark Magic that he

controlled, the Overlord could do nothing to help the Ghoule. He could only wait for the soldier to die. Then his Elders, clearly annoyed at the pace of the beast's death, could get back to the task at hand. Sending as many Ghoules across the Weir and into the lands of the humans as possible.

The Ten Magii who had constructed the Weir were fools, the Overlord believed. They had not understood the true nature of the Curse and how their use of that dark power would affect them. They could have used that power going forward, molding the Curse to them, allowing the Curse to mold them in turn. But they had not, frightened by what they would become and instead choosing to die because of their lack of knowledge and imagination.

Fools, indeed. But they had been smart enough to comprehend the value of integrating Dark Magic with the Talent. As a result of their fastidious work, the Overlord could do nothing with the power traditionally exercised by the Magii, as one of his soldiers had just discovered, and it was because of that energy, that Talent unique to so few humans, that the bulk of his Legions remained on the far side of the Weir, barred from their ultimate goal.

The Ghoule Overlord exercised complete control over the Curse, gripping the staff he carried a bit tighter as he thought about the responsibility and force that he wielded. Made of black ash, the staff was similar to those he gifted to his Elders but for the top. Theirs were nothing but knobs of polished wood carved into the shape of a diamond. His staff held the actual black diamond, the only one in existence and the true source of Dark Magic for him and his Ghoules. If he could obtain the Seventh Stone, he could enter the Sanctuary and link the Dark Magic contained within the black diamond with the Seven Stones. Then he could destroy the Weir once and for all, and his Legions finally, after centuries of waiting, would be free to ravage Caledonia.

But not yet. Although he could manipulate Dark Magic, make the power that flowed through his veins do things that no one else could even dream of, he could do nothing with the Talent without the Seventh Stone. For that he needed the Protector. Then he could erase the memory of his greatest failure.

The Ghoule Overlord remembered that ill-fated day when the Weir first appeared, marking the end of his first invasion of Caledonia. The humans, under the leadership of Arick Winborne, had pushed his Legions back from the Bay of the Dead, through the Dark Forest, and then to the very northern border of the Shattered Peaks and into the Lost Land. It had been a difficult and draining fight of many months, and, at first, the Overlord had worried that he had lost his chance to conquer the lands of the humans.

But then he had realized the value of what was happening. The value of the humans' temporary success. Although his Ghoules were retreating, they were not fleeing, and the humans' efforts were costing them lives that they could not replace while he could, as he had several dozen more Legions coming forward through the Lost Land that had not yet reached the Shattered Peaks. A second army, larger than his current one, of which the humans were oblivious. So he had allowed the humans to continue to push his forces to the north, weakening themselves, his Ghoules reducing the Caledonian Army's numbers day by day. Then, when the time was right, his second army would sweep down and roll over the humans like the landslides so common to the Shattered Peaks.

It was the perfect plan and would have guaranteed the future of his Ghoules, but he had waited too long. Just hours before he was about to send his new Legions into the lands of men, the Ten Magii crafted the Weir. The magical barrier stretched from the Burnt Ocean in the west to the Silent Sea in the east, and it rose from the lowlands of the Shattered Peaks to some point in the sky that the Ghoule Overlord couldn't identify. Peering through the Weir, the other side appeared no different than the one that he was on, although the image was distorted by the energy surging within the magical wall.

The Ghoule Overlord, even with the immense power that he controlled, could do nothing but manipulate the strands of Dark Magic that formed half the barrier, thereby allowing him to pass through the Weir if he did so carefully, keeping the Talent well away from him, a skill that he had taught his Elders that they were putting to use with mixed success at that very moment.

He could see the work that the Ten Magii had done to create the despised obstacle. The humans had woven the Dark Magic and the Talent together, strand by strand, to form a new substance. It had been accomplished with such skill that the Overlord couldn't determine where the weave began or ended. The Ten Magii had paid for their success with their lives, yes, but that was a small price to pay in the Overlord's opinion, because the Magii also had succeeded in crushing his hopes and dreams. For now.

The Overlord turned his attention back to the trapped Ghoule. The Talent within the Weir had latched onto the soldier, his Elders' work to create the narrow break within the barrier not to the standard required for success. Starting at the chest and then working its way to the beast's extremities, the energy infused within the Weir by the Magii slowly burned his body to cinders. The trapped beast's screams continued for several minutes, and then finally there was silence once again. Nothing remained of the Ghoule but for his leather armor and blackened steel spear, which had fallen to the ground within the boundaries of the Weir, joining the detritus of the hundreds of other Ghoules who had lost their lives attempting to pass through the barricade over the years.

"Nibli, to me!" shouted the Overlord in the guttural

language of the Ghoules, the mixture of hisses, grunts, and barks making the tongue unintelligible to humans.

The Elder sprinted away from the Weir, where he had been conversing with several other Elders about what mistake had been made that had allowed the last Ghoule to be captured in the magical weave. He kneeled before his leader, then rose quickly, transfixed as he always was by the mark of the black diamond carved into the Overlord's forehead.

"Master," Nibli replied, keeping his head down, knowing the possible consequences of angering the Overlord when he was already agitated by how slow the passage was progressing.

"Bring the Elders to me," the Overlord commanded. "We are losing too many soldiers in the crossing, more than a third already, and that is not acceptable. We must get more fighters across to have any chance at success."

"I agree, Master. But ..."

Nibli was about to continue, but the change in the Overlord's posture made him stop. He observed a small ball of black mist begin to form above the black diamond that rested atop the Overlord's staff. If Nibli had stepped too far, he would know soon enough.

"I selected you for this assignment for a reason," began the Overlord. "Of all my Elders, you are the most competent. You are the most likely to succeed in taking my packs into the lands of men and preparing the way for my Legions. Or so I thought."

"I am, Master. I promise you. I will not disappoint you."

"You already have, Nibli. Why are we having so much trouble sending my Ghoules through the Weir? The barrier is weakening. We should be able to get more soldiers through than we ever have before and at a faster pace."

Knowing that how he responded in the next few seconds would determine whether he would live or die, he decided that he would explain what he believed to be the truth, consequences be damned.

"The Weir is weakening, Master. That's the problem."

"How could that be the problem? That's what we want."

"In the past I and the other Elders could craft the portal through the Weir by manipulating the strands of Dark Magic that form the barrier so that the Talent would be pushed to the side, if only for a few seconds, just as you taught us. If the soldier was fast enough making his way through the gateway, he could do so without getting caught by the magic of man."

"I know all that," hissed the Overlord. "You are wasting my time."

"I am sorry, Master. But I believe that it is relevant. Before, the strands that we manipulated were cohesive, the weave of the Weir was consistent. And it still is, at least most of the time."

"But not all of the time."

"No, Master. Because the Weir is weakening, so is the consistency of the weave. Every time the Weir flickers, we lose control of the strands that we are manipulating. Some of the strands are fraying and snapping. If one of our soldiers is in the Weir at that time ..."

Nibli left the last unsaid, not feeling the need to complete the thought for his Master.

"Then the soldier is caught by the strand and there is nothing that we can do for him. And with the flickering becoming more prevalent because of the Weir's erosion, more of our soldiers are getting caught in the weave."

"Yes, Master."

The Ghoule Overlord nodded. It made sense. He should have realized it himself, but his thoughts were elsewhere. "So in the short term it makes our efforts to take our soldiers through the Weir more difficult, but in the long term it suggests that the Weir eventually will collapse on its own."

"Yes, Master."

"But we don't know when that will occur. One year. Five years. Ten years. Decades. So we have no choice but to continue with our efforts to hasten the destruction of the Weir, and to do so we will need to risk more lives."

"Yes, Master."

The Ghoule Overlord needed to give very little thought to what he believed needed to be done next. "So be it. We must get our Ghoules through the Weir, as many as we can as quickly as we can. Have the Elders intensify their efforts. We must have several dozen packs across if you are to do what is required of you. The loss of life to accomplish this assignment is acceptable."

"Yes, Master."

"So long as you succeed, Nibli."

The last was said with a menace that made Nibli hesitate before responding.

"Yes, Master. I will not fail."

"Good, Nibli. Good. Because your life depends on it."

The Elder nodded, then turned and trotted back toward the Weir to continue to oversee the other Elders in their attempts to bring more Ghoules through the magical barricade.

The Overlord was not surprised that the Weir had changed as it deteriorated, but he had been surprised that Nibli had the confidence or the foolhardiness -- he wasn't sure which -- to speak so bluntly to him. Perhaps this Elder would, indeed, achieve the task that he had set out for him. He could only hope. For not only was Nibli's life in the balance, but also all of his plans for the Ghoules.

Actually, that wasn't entirely correct. In the end, no matter Nibli's success or failure, all of the Overlord's plans came down to the Protector. The Overlord was intensely curious as to how and why the Seventh Stone had merged with the Protector. That was something he meant to explore once he had the human within his grasp. And he had to have the Protector. It was the only way that he could obtain the Seventh Stone and make it his own.

But he was worried. Because of the Dark Magic within the Seventh Stone, he should have been able to sense where the artifact was at all times. He had always been able to sense the Seventh Stone, the power it contained, the power that could be wielded with it, until those infernal Magii had hidden it away out of fear. And rightfully so, the Overlord conceded. Perhaps if he had located the Seventh Stone and acquired it, he could have put his plan into action centuries ago. But there was nothing to do about that now. Thinking of the past did nothing for his efforts to create the future that he wanted, that he needed, for his Ghoules.

The Magii had gotten lucky during the War of Expansion, as the Ghoules called their invasion of Caledonia. Success in that war would have given the Ghoules the new territory that they needed. Their land to the north of the Shattered Peaks had served them well for more than a thousand years, but not as it once had. Prey was getting scarcer. The Overlord was finding it more and more difficult to feed his Ghoules, and there had been but one direction to go if he wished to alleviate the strain and hardship that was becoming a part of everyday life for his creatures. Thus, his decision to invade the lands of men.

But the Weir had limited their options for finding new sources of food. The soft humans south of the Peaks would have served their purposes well, because to their north there was only the Frozen Waste, and that offered little in the way of sustenance. The Ghoules needed more space, more game, so that they could hunt. The only benefit to the Ghoules from their failed War of Expansion, and a poor one at that, was the loss of life. So many Ghoules had been killed that for a time the demand for food had been manageable. But no longer.

The Ghoules had grown in number once more as the years had passed, and for them to continue to do so they needed food and land not only to thrive, but also based on past history simply to survive. To obtain what they needed, they had to destroy the Weir, and then the fun would begin. Then, the Ghoules would conquer Caledonia and enslave the humans, making them no better than livestock for the Overlord's expanding Legions. Those not taken during the onslaught would be hunted as game. After Caledonia was theirs, the Overlord would lead the Ghoules to the Wyld and the other lands to the east and west. But first Caledonia.

He would wipe clean the blemish that had been their first attempt to conquer the Kingdom to the south. The Ghoules were the greatest race in all the lands. But they could not do as was needed unless they found more space to range, to hunt, to kill, to feed.

It all came back to gaining the Seventh Stone, and at the moment he could barely feel the energy contained within the artifact. His sense of its power was muted. It was there, and then it was not, which he found strange. Initially he thought that his inability to locate the Seventh Stone with the accuracy he once had resulted from his great distance from the artifact, but he knew that wasn't the case, at least not entirely. He should be able to sense the Dark Magic contained within the Seventh Stone quite easily, just as he could sense the Dark Magic used by his Elders or the humans he had gifted with the Curse.

He, the Overlord of the Ghoules, was the source of the Dark Magic that played through this world. He was the purveyor of it. He was the master of it. But he still couldn't feel the Dark Magic within the Protector as he should be able to, as he wanted to. A new thought struck him. What if the Protector learned how to use the Dark Magic of the Seventh Stone? Use it on its own or in conjunction with the Talent? Did that mean ...

A shriek of pain pulled the Overlord from his thoughts. He turned back toward the Weir, a growl of frustration escaping him. Another of his Ghoules had been caught within the weave of the barrier, and there was little that he could do. Nibli likely was right as he watched the Weir flash several times along its length, black to white to black to white again and again, then finally returning to the shimmering grey of the magical wall that he was most familiar with. Through it all the Ghoule stuck within the competing magics screamed in agony, his body slowly burning, a black ash falling to cover the rocky ground he had attempted to cross.

His anger at the loss of another fighter threatened to overwhelm him, to put him into a rage that he likely couldn't control, but there was no point in allowing that to happen. There was nothing that he could do about what was happening to his Ghoules. There was nothing that he could do about the Weir until he had the Seventh Stone. Until he had the Protector. Then he could open the pathway to Caledonia for his Legions.

The Overlord had trusted success to others so far, and that had not worked as well for him as he would have liked. Perhaps it was time to take a stronger hand in what needed to be done. Perhaps it was time for him to play a more direct role in the events to come, even if that meant placing himself and his secret ally at greater risk.

3

DAGGER IN HAND

The Tintagel Palace was constructed with open gardens planted down the middle of the sprawling citadel, linking the throne room at the eastern end to the main courtyard and gates that led into the city of Tintagel that were located to the west. The fortress had been designed to impress dignitaries and other visitors, as anyone seeking an audience with the Crown had to walk almost a half mile down covered paths with intricately carved columns supporting the sloping roofs made of slate tile. On each side sprang up a riot of colors provided by the flowers, bushes, and trees that were tended by a small army of gardeners.

Aislinn Winborne, the Lady of the Southern Marches, saw none of it. Instead her thoughts were on what she had accomplished less than an hour before, having just put on a display in the training circle that had enthralled the soldiers of the Royal Guard who had been training with her.

She had spent the better part of an hour dueling the Blademaster of Caledonia in the ring, starting with swords and then moving on to daggers. There was only one Blademaster in

Caledonia. By law there could be only one, the position earned by the greatest swordfighter in the Kingdom, who once achieving the rank through a bloody competition, was charged with training the Royal Guard.

Yet today, for the first time since she had begun working with him, Aislinn had touched the Blademaster several times with her sword, something that she had never accomplished before. In fact, it was something that none of the other soldiers who trained regularly with the Blademaster had yet to achieve. That's why, despite the dire circumstances she faced in the capital, she felt good about herself at the moment.

If only Bryen had been there to see it, she mused. Her Protector would have been proud. The Guards in the practice yard actually had stopped what they were doing to watch her duel with the Blademaster, many awed by the speed of the fight. They often struggled to follow the action, the movements between the two combatants blurred at times, the only contact between them confirmed by the occasional sparks that fell into the sand when their steel blades met.

The combat between the two had become more intense with each passing minute. And as the soldiers became more engaged in the fight, she began to hear shouts for the Vedra, the *Witch* in the old tongue. Apparently, the name bestowed upon her when she had dueled Marden in the Pit just a few weeks before had stuck, and that pleased her. Admittedly, she did lose her bout with the Blademaster. But she had expected that, and there was no shame in it.

At the conclusion of the fight, many of the watching soldiers had come up to her to offer their congratulations, impressed by her abilities. But even more important than her success in the training circle was the fact that all of these soldiers treated her with a respect and deference that should have been reserved solely for the King, but clearly wasn't. That, she believed, was her biggest victory since coming to Tintagel, her ability to win the confidence and perhaps even the allegiance of many of the Royal Guard. These soldiers saw past her long auburn hair, quick smile, and captivating dimples to the fighter hidden not too far beneath.

Definitely a good way to start the day, she confirmed to herself. Because so far, her sessions in the practice yard and her visit to the Colosseum were the only times of her forced residency in Tintagel that had proved useful. She had built a stronger relationship with Blademaster Jurgen Klines and many of the Guard who had become regular morning training partners as well as connected for the first time with Declan, Master of the Gladiators. She believed that she had built a sense of trust with both of them. But only time would tell if her efforts would bear any fruit.

Her success in these two critical endeavors were just the first steps to achieving her larger strategy. Her father remained a guest of the Crown -- a prisoner though not defined as such -- who was limited to his daily walks along the parapet, and she still had no idea how to remove the black steel collar affixed to his neck that prevented them from escaping the capital. If she didn't figure out some way to free her father from the magic Tetric had infused within the steel torque, she might, indeed, have to obey her father's demand that she escape on her own.

And though she didn't want to contemplate what acceding to her father's order would lead to, she understood that the time to make that decision could be fast approaching. Marden Beleron, King of Caledonia, and her betrothed, though she had yet to formally accept his proposal -- something that she desperately tried not to think about -- was becoming more and more aggressive about moving forward with their marriage, and her efforts at putting him off, though effective when she first arrived, were losing their shine. Clearly, Marden's patience was wearing thin. How much longer she could keep him at arm's length, she didn't know.

In fact, her last experience with Marden the night before had not only worried her, but it also had frightened her. For the first time since she had come to Tintagel months before with the goal of freeing her father, she had been summoned to Marden's private quarters. She had no choice but to appear, and she had hoped that bringing some of the soldiers she had come to trust would offer her some protection. But the members of the Royal Guard at the doors to Marden's lavish chamber had refused them admittance, only allowing her to enter.

She had done so reluctantly. What she had walked into hadn't surprised her, having heard stories of the late-night debauchery that Marden reveled in. As she had expected, many of his friends were there, lords and ladies from the various Duchies who spent more time in the capital than in their home provinces, drawn to the charismatic, engaging, and garrulous monarch, as well as the drinking and the milk of the poppy, the expensive drug Marden made readily available to any of his companions desiring it.

Aislinn had refused the multiple offers from the guests to imbibe or partake, all of them disappointed but not pushing her. She had little to fear from the young men who had tied themselves so closely to Marden. They knew who she was, who she was supposed to become. In short, they knew that she was Marden's, so she avoided the sometimes vulgar and offensive behavior that some of the other young women had to endure at the hands of the King's toadies.

But she couldn't avoid Marden himself. She had tried to make herself invisible, staying in a corner and hoping to sneak out as quickly as she could. But Marden had been waiting for her, and she realized quickly that the location she had selected along the wall had been a mistake, because it had allowed him to corner her. She had cursed herself for a fool for allowing such a thing to happen, something that she would never permit if she were in the training ring. And it was then that she realized that she should have viewed the conversation that she engaged in with Marden, which she remembered word for word, as a combat in and of itself. In the future, she would need to be better prepared.

"Finally, the love of my life has deigned to join one of my evening soirees."

"I had little choice, King Beleron. Your orders were quite clear. The soldiers you sent for me were quite insistent."

"Simply a request, my dear. Simply a request." Then, he had stepped in closer to her, forcing her to move back until she was up against the wall. "You look lovely tonight. So much more enticing than any of the other women here."

"Your words suggest that I am no more than something to be won over, King Beleron. Something to be acquired."

"And would it be so bad if I acquired you?" Marden asked, his grin broadening wickedly. "Think of the fun that we could have."

He meant it as a joke, but Aislinn clearly didn't take it as such.

"I am not one of your playthings, Marden. And I never will be."

She was about to say more, but she realized that circumstances might have progressed farther than she had judged initially. She could see his eyes clearly now despite the dim light. Bloodshot, and his pupils were dilated. Signs that he had been taking milk of the poppy for quite some time already that evening.

"Oh, but you are a plaything, Lady Winborne. You are the Kingdom's and my plaything both."

Marden had pushed forward then, pressing himself against

her with Aislinn having no way to escape as he pinned her against the wall. Surprised by his boldness, before she could stop him, he had crushed her mouth with his, kissing her hard on the lips. At first, she had been shocked that Marden had been so brazen, but then her anger had taken control.

She had pushed back against his chest, trying to force him away from her. But her resistance only had excited Marden all the more. He had begun pawing at her, starting with her hips and then moving his hands up to her chest. She had bit his tongue, drawing blood. Even though he was forced to pull back, she could tell that Marden barely felt the pain that he must be experiencing thanks to the deadening effects of the drug circulating through his veins.

Finally free from his mouth, she had tried to scream, but Marden's mouth covered hers again before she could take a breath. Her trying to defend herself had only made him more excited. With Marden becoming more aggressive, and knowing that none of the other people in the room would come to her aid, she had done the only thing that she could.

She had brought her knee up between Marden's legs hard and fast, her anger adding to the power of the blow. That had put a stop to Marden's actions quickly. He had groaned and then slumped, the pain debilitating even with the milk of the poppy in his blood as he had slid down the wall clutching his groin. Then she had stepped over the King of Caledonia, escaping him while he was curled up into a ball, whimpering and on the verge of throwing up.

She had to admit that though the beginning of her evening had been less than pleasant, how she had ended it had been incredibly satisfying. She had not seen Marden since last night, so she didn't know yet what repercussions there might be for her actions. Would he even remember it in his drugged state? But in all honesty, she really didn't care. She might be his bride-to-be, at least for now, but he would not have her. Never. And there was nothing that he could do to change that.

Aislinn was almost back to the fleeting safety of her rooms, her thoughts having turned to finding an excuse to meet with Declan again, when she was forced to come to an abrupt stop, her pleasure at her success in the ring draining away from her. As had become his habit, the King's Advisor appeared from between the columns that lined the path that led back to her chambers.

She should have expected that she would find him here. Since her arrival in the capital Tetric had trapped her several times, offering her a power beyond that of the Talent she already employed, a power that both terrified her and yet enticed her at the same time. During her last interaction with him, she had found it increasingly difficult to refuse the gift with which he tried to tempt her. The power he offered could free her and her father. But she understood the consequences if she accepted, so she had done her best since then to avoid him. That was proving more and more difficult since the King's Advisor kept appearing at the most unexpected places and times, as if he were always trying to catch her when she was distracted or at her weakest.

Her only solace during the last week was that Tetric had been away from the capital for several days. Where he might have gone and what he might have been doing, she didn't know. In her conversations with various people within the Palace she had pieced together that Tetric had headed north toward the Dark Forest, but why he had gone there no one knew.

"My Lady Winborne," began Tetric, offering her a perfunctory nod of his bald head. "Such a pleasure to see you again."

"Tetric," she replied tartly. "Unfortunately I can't say the same."

Not wanting to engage in conversation, she made to push

past him. But Tetric's clawlike hand latched onto her arm, locking her in place.

"Do you not have a few minutes to spare for me?" he asked pleasantly, even as his fingers dug more deeply into her flesh.

Aislinn stared at Tetric, her eyes blazing with hatred, but she was forced to look away, the black orbs of the King's Advisor having an almost hypnotic quality.

"It seems that I have no choice," she replied. "Release me."

"My apologies," said Tetric, letting go of her arm, though he took his time in doing so, clearly wanting to make a point. "We must talk again, child."

"We have nothing to discuss, Tetric. I have made my position clear." Free from his grasp, she took several steps back, feeling the need for the additional space. "It will not change."

"Oh, but we do, child. We have so much to discuss. We have so much to decide. But I fear for you, child."

"Why is that?" she asked, unable to stop herself even though she knew that any conversation with Tetric was fraught with deception.

"I fear that you are not making a good decision," he replied. "You are putting yourself, your father, your Duchy at risk."

Aislinn listened to the beginnings of the same argument that Tetric had been making for the last few months, but there was something different about him this time. Before, he had approached her with guile, as if he were trying to persuade her, to gain her agreement to his terms. But this time, that sense of temptation was gone, replaced by a hardness in him that hadn't been there before. An expectation of acceptance perhaps.

It was as if the weakness that she had sensed in him when she had first met the King's Advisor had been cut out, burned away, and in its place was a purpose as unyielding as the steel of her favored blade. That was unsettling enough, but even worse, his eyes had changed, becoming even more disquieting. They had always been black, but now the scleras had turned black as well. She stared into an abyss, and she was struggling to claw her way back from the edge, to pull free from his demanding gaze.

"I will not make this offer again, child," Tetric continued in a more exacting tone. "Remember, girl, what I gift to you is a power that few can ever hope to employ. A power that puts the Talent to shame. A power that few can defend against. A power that could shift the balance of your engagement with our illustrious king." He said the last with an undisguised contempt. "With a power like this, Marden would be the one to worry, because you could do whatever you chose to do, and he could do nothing to stop you."

"I have power enough, Tetric," rejoined Aislinn, feeling the pressure of Tetric's words weighing down upon her. What was he doing to her? She was finding it harder and harder to resist him. Was he using his Dark Magic to try to compel her and she couldn't sense it? But how could he ...

"No one can have enough power, girl," replied Tetric forcefully. "With the power I will give you, you can free your father. You can kill Marden. You can take the throne for yourself."

"I don't want what you offer me," replied Aislinn through gritted teeth, the feeling of being constricted becoming unbearable, her head feeling as if it were about to burst. She was having a difficult time thinking, a dense fog settling over her thoughts, hindering her ability to make decisions. It felt as if she were losing herself to a force that she didn't understand and that she couldn't control.

"What you want is no longer relevant, girl," hissed Tetric. "You had your chance to accept the gift that I offered you multiple times. Now, you will take it. You have no choice. You don't have the strength or the knowledge to fight me. You will take what I offer you."

As the pressure upon her intensified, becoming more and more painful, she noticed black spots flitting in her eyes. For a moment, she thought that she was going to lose consciousness. But then she realized what was really happening. Thin strands of black had appeared around her, flowing, writhing, connecting with one another. Tetric was spinning a web with Dark Magic. The strands were becoming larger, twisting into cords as they combined, the slowly forming net about to press down on her skin, and she knew that if she allowed that to happen, she would be lost. She would never recover. Tetric would gain what he wanted, and she would no longer be the person who she was. She would no longer have the chance to become the person who she wanted to be.

Fighting through the fog that was threatening to take over her mind, she had no choice but to ignore her promise to Marden and seize control of the Talent, the bright white energy of the natural world surging through her, burning away the fog, clearing her vision, and giving her a greater clarity of all that was happening around her. In an instant, she formed a shield around her body, the Talent preventing the net of Dark Magic from settling upon her, sparks of black and white erupting when the two powers met, shattering the shadows of the hallway.

Tetric's eyes flashed dangerously, never having expected Aislinn to break free from his hold so easily. For several minutes the nimbus of white energy surrounded her, the threads of black probing against her barrier, seeking a way through, but finding no path to strike at their target. Understanding that he had been defeated, at least for a time, Tetric released his hold on the Dark Magic that he controlled.

"That was a dangerous thing to do, girl."

"It was necessary," Aislinn replied, squaring up to Tetric, one foot slightly in front of the other, ready for whatever may come next. Confident that she could recall the Talent before her adversary could do anything to her, she released her hold on her natural magic as well, trying to adhere to the terms of her agreement with Marden for fear of her father's life. "I won't do what you want. I won't take what you offer. I'll die first."

"That might be necessary," hissed Tetric. "And such a shame if it proves to be the case."

The ease with which Tetric spoke of her possible demise chilled Aislinn. But even then, she was struck by Tetric's mannerisms. Not only had his eyes changed, along with several aspects of his personality, but his movements had as well. They were more sinuous now, smoother, almost animalistic, which she found both strange and unnerving.

"Such a shame if what proved to be the case?" asked a soft voice from behind Tetric.

The sharp-featured man who stepped from between the columns had a sword on his hip, but what drew the attention of both the King's Advisor and Aislinn was the dagger that he flipped casually in his hand, the weapon revolving through the air in an easy motion that was quite mesmerizing.

"You have no reason to be here, Blademaster," said Tetric, his eyes still on the dagger spinning in the air. "I suggest you leave."

"But I can't," replied Jurgen Klines, his often amused eyes hard now, lacking in emotion.

In Aislinn's opinion, they resembled Bryen's, the stoniness suggesting that taking a life, although unfortunate and not to be taken lightly, would be done without remorse if necessary. For Bryen that's what life was all about. Kill or be killed. And it seemed that the Blademaster had adopted the same philosophy.

"And why is that, Blademaster?"

"I need to return something," he replied with a nonchalance that belied his stance.

Klines stood on his toes, knees slightly bent, and though he continued to flip the dagger with his left hand, his right hovered over the hilt of his sword. If this conversation turned into a duel, he was more than ready.

"And what would that be?" asked Tetric, unable to stop himself.

"Why this dagger, of course," he said with practiced ease. "Lady Winborne left it at the practice yard, and I thought it best to return it to her as soon as possible. Best to have good steel in hand to keep the snakes slithering through the Palace in their place."

Tetric flinched at the insult. Unable to control his rising anger, he took two quick steps until he stood face to face with Klines.

"I question your loyalty," said Tetric. "Your allegiance to the King is not as strong as it should be."

"As I question yours," replied the Blademaster, his voice a whisper, barely heard in the cavernous hallway. "And just so we're clear, my allegiance is to Caledonia."

"The King will not be happy to hear that when I tell him," said Tetric. "It will be a pleasure to speak with him about it."

The Blademaster fought the urge to step back from the King's Advisor. Standing so close to Tetric made him uncomfortable. Not because he was frightened but rather because he was repulsed. Tetric had a habit of licking his lips between sentences, and perhaps because of a quirk of the light it appeared to the Blademaster as if the bald advisor was running a forked tongue over serrated teeth. But that simply wasn't possible.

"The King already knows it," Klines replied calmly. "If at some point it bothers him so much that he can't stand the fact that he must work with someone who can think for himself and does not have any tainted loyalties, then he can dismiss me. But until then, I shall continue to serve my Kingdom."

"Dismissal might not be enough. With your skill with a

blade and the respect you've earned among the Guard, more drastic measures might be required. Think on that."

The Blademaster leaned into Tetric so that their noses were almost touching.

"And are you the one to apply these drastic measures, Tetric? Because if so, I'd welcome the opportunity for you to try." Klines raised his eyebrows and crinkled his nose, as if he had just been struck by a bad odor, the veiled insult not lost on Tetric. "Perhaps we should both visit our good King this morning, Tetric. A conversation about loyalties is certainly in order. You can offer your thoughts on where my loyalties stand, and I can do the same with respect to yours. Because it's quite clear that your loyalties are to yourself and yourself alone."

"Very astute, Blademaster."

"Actually, no," disputed Klines. "It's obvious to everyone in the capital exactly where your loyalties lie, except perhaps the King."

Tetric stared at the Blademaster for almost a minute, not uttering a word. He could continue this conversation, even escalate it into something more, but he decided not to push the confrontation any farther. It wasn't worth it. At least not yet. But soon.

Instead, he turned his gaze back to Aislinn. "You will regret this, girl. You will regret not accepting my offer."

Then Tetric stepped back among the columns and disappeared into the shadows, leaving just as he had arrived.

Aislinn breathed a sigh of relief, realizing that she had been sweating through the entire encounter. Tetric always had made her uncomfortable, but never in a way such as this before, and that worried her.

"Thank you, Blademaster," she said, motioning to the blade still spinning in the air. "But I should let you know that the dagger is not mine. It must belong to one of the Guard."

"I know," Klines said casually, catching the hilt of the

dagger and quickly sheathing it in the scabbard on his thigh. "Actually, it belongs to me. I just thought that you might need some assistance. I have no doubt that you can handle yourself well against any who may oppose you, even that snake, but sometimes a little help doesn't hurt, and the Royal Guard protects its own."

Aislinn's smile lit up the darkened path. She nodded her head in appreciation, understanding the significance of what the Blademaster had just revealed to her.

4

ON THE MOVE

The sounds customary to the large majority of the Battersea Guard settling in for the night played through the grove they had selected for their camp, the trees rising right up against the fast-moving Eastern River. Bryen thought about the perimeter sentries as he listened to the familiar noises of harnesses jingling, horses whinnying, the clang of pots and pans, soldiers laughing and cursing, the crackle of the small fires. This evening at Tarin's order Jerad had doubled the number of guards and pushed them farther away from the cantonment so that there were multiple skirmish lines protecting the camp from any threats that might approach.

With the Battle of the Horseshoe just a few weeks old, Ghoules remained a distinct threat, although Bryen had confirmed several times now for the Captain and the Sergeant of the Guard that the closest Ghoule packs were on the northern side of the Dark Forest and the Breakwater Plateau. True, the beasts could cover more ground faster than any living creature on land, but even for these devils it would take them several days to travel the hundreds of leagues required to reach them. No, at the moment the primary danger came from the Royal Guard.

The soldiers of the Southern Marches were only a few days south of the capital of Caledonia. For Bryen to do as he hoped in Tintagel, secrecy was essential. Thus the requirement that they approach the city unseen. In fact, to increase their chances of success, the Guard would only be sleeping for a few hours that night. Then, around midnight, they would begin the march north, seeking another grove of trees to hide in before the break of day. Tarin believed that such an approach would allow them to avoid any patrols and get them to within a league of the capital without discovery.

Bryen hoped that the Captain of the Guard proved to be right. Too much was at stake only for them to be discovered because of an unexpected encounter due to bad luck or bad timing on the way to their objective.

It was that additional anxiety that kept Bryen from his bedroll. His mind wouldn't turn off, and he felt the impulse to do something to take his thoughts from his worries. Knowing that he would never be able to sleep in such a state, he had invited Rafia and Sirius to join him in a hidden glade just a quarter mile from the Guards' encampment for another training session in the Talent.

"Well done, lad," said Sirius. The tall Magus sat on the curling root of a tree. For the last hour he had been putting Bryen through his paces, having him use the Talent in various ways, increasing the level of difficulty with each assigned task, all the while keeping a sharp eye for any instance in which the Protector lost control over the Dark Magic coursing through him. So far, and not unexpectedly, the Magus had detected nothing to suggest that his young protégé was failing to keep the Curse under control. "Now see if you can take the offensive. Playing defense doesn't seem to suit you."

Since the training session had begun, Bryen had tested his

skills against Rafia, the Magus proving to be a difficult and clever opponent. She had forced him to construct various shields to deflect a series of attacks ranging from spheres of light no larger than a marble to spears of blazing energy to a white mist that threatened to freeze him in place, and even two bolts of lightning shooting down from the darkening sky, although Rafia had only used the last after confirming that there was no one around them for at least a dozen leagues. Bryen had discovered just recently that lightning was one of Rafia's favorite tools for fighting Elders.

"Leave him be, Sirius," said Rafia. "Learning to defend yourself with the Talent is essential. You can't attack if you can't defend."

"What does that even mean," disputed Sirius. "You're just afraid of what might happen when he comes after you."

Rafia grunted in reply, not feeling the need to respond. Of course she worried about Bryen attacking her. He was a skilled fighter, probably the most adept warrior she had come across in centuries, and he had demonstrated a mastery of the Talent that no other Magus ever could hope to achieve at such a young age and so quickly. Putting those two variables together was a dangerous combination for anyone challenging the Protector.

Hearing Sirius' request, Bryen grinned. In just the past hour he had learned a great deal from Rafia, but the old Magus was right. He preferred to attack, and he didn't hesitate to do so now.

He started with something that he had just learned from Rafia, using the Talent to craft hundreds of small orbs of light that he shot toward the Magus. He knew that play wouldn't be enough to distract her because he had figured out rather swiftly that Rafia preferred to attack just like he did, so that was only a part of his strategy. While the Magus formed a shell with the Talent that protected her and absorbed the spheres of energy that he had thrown at her, Bryen adapted Rafia's favorite weapon into something that he hoped would keep her on the defensive, if only for a few seconds.

Rather than calling down bolts of lightning, Bryen refined the concept. Pulling in more of the Talent, he focused his attention on a spot just a foot in front of Rafia. He couldn't break through her shield with what he was about to do, but that wasn't his intention. With a flick of his wrist, a shard of blinding energy blasted into the ground, the explosion of dirt and rock clattering against Rafia's shield.

Rafia found herself battling double vision as she struggled to clear the spots that danced in front of her eyes from the bright light. Exactly when she could see again, another eruption tore apart the ground in front of her, forcing her to close her eyes, but even then, the brightness of the blast flashed through her eyelids. And then another blast. And another. And one more for good measure.

Although Bryen had effectively blinded her to the point where she couldn't see what was going on without specks of black impeding her perception, she could still sense the movement around her through her use of the Talent. She realized quickly that she needed to adjust her approach if she was to have any chance at keeping Bryen away from her. Releasing her hold on the shield that had proven so effective against his first attack, she crafted two short swords from the natural power of the world, crossing the blades above her head. And just in time, as Bryen swung the double-bladed spear that he had formed with the Talent down toward the Magus, her swords thankfully catching the strike.

Clever boy, thought Rafia. He had taken a skill in the Talent that she had shown him, refined it to make it his own, and then used it against her. Employing the Talent to temporarily blind her was a stroke of genius. Not only was the Protector a worthy opponent, but he also was full of ideas, and she loved his creativity.

But she didn't have much of an opportunity to continue her train of thought. Defending herself became the priority, as Bryen continued his assault with an unrestrained ferocity.

"You certainly do like to get in close," said Rafia, not only pleased with Bryen for his ingenuity in how he was using against her some variations of what she had used against him, but also with herself for adapting so quickly and fending off the Protector's attacks.

Bryen twisted his grip on his spear, slashing for the Magus' right hip after she successfully blocked his first attempt to get past her defenses. Then, as soon as she blocked that attack, he tried for her left hip. And so it continued, Bryen slashing and cutting with his glowing spear, his movements tight and compact, often no more than a flick of the wrist, staying in tight to Rafia. His and Rafia's actions were so fast that Sirius often only saw streaks of white light as the double-bladed spear and two short swords came together repeatedly, becoming a single image of blinding white for a brief moment before separating and then connecting once again.

Bryen relished the fight, enjoying both the rapid and controlled maneuvers and the constant need to adjust his strategy. Rafia countered everything that he attempted, although there were a few instances when he almost gained the touch that he needed to end the combat. But perhaps most important to him was the fact that despite the tremendous amount of the Talent that he was drawing upon, the Dark Magic forced upon him by the Seventh Stone remained fairly quiet. It was there. Unavoidably there within him. But the Curse made no attempt to free itself from the bonds in which he had encased it, the bonds so critically important to ensure that he remained safe from the taint of its corruption.

That discovery pleased him even more. He felt liberated, no longer having to fear or worry about the Dark Magic as much as he once did. He believed that he had a better grasp of what he was doing now with the Talent after all his practice with Sirius and Rafia, better control, and keeping the Dark Magic locked away, protecting himself from its evil with a thin barrier of the Talent, had become second nature to him.

"It's how I was taught," Bryen replied, his voice cold and lacking emotion, his focus solely on his task, and that sent a chill through Rafia. "Declan believes that getting in close to your opponent is the best way to kill him."

Rafia nodded sagely. "A man after my own heart. I really do want to meet him."

"Why are you so obsessed with the Master of the Gladiators?" huffed Sirius, unable to keep the hint of jealousy from his voice. "If you're simply trying to irritate me, it won't work."

"It's not always about you, Sirius," Rafia called with a laugh, although she didn't have the opportunity to continue needling her former mentor. Bryen demanded her full attention, because once again, he had adopted a new strategy.

Just when Rafia thought that she had learned the rhythm of Bryen's assault, he broke the shining spear in two, the Protector now holding a glowing sword in each hand to match her own. Faster and faster they glided around the small glade, movements lightning fast, blades cutting and slashing, jabbing and thrusting, Bryen and Rafia dodging, ducking, and parrying each strike.

Despite his irritation at Rafia's last comment, Sirius couldn't stop his smile from forming as he watched the two Magii, one with centuries of experience, the other with barely a few months, holding their own against one another and putting on a display in the martial arts that he doubted anyone could ever hope to imitate.

Then strangely, without warning, the hovering light that Sirius had crafted with the Talent and placed above the glade to ward off the rapidly falling dusk flickered then dimmed to barely anything. At the same time, Bryen stopped his barrage of attacks, dropping to one knee.

"Bryen, are you ..." began Rafia, a look of concern crossing her face.

But the former Protector didn't hear her. The swords of light winked out. He closed his eyes tightly, his teeth clamped shut, every muscle in his body taut. In just an instant, the control that he had exercised over the Dark Magic within him had shifted to a point where he was about to lose himself to the Curse. The Talent that he had used to shield the Dark Magic, to keep it from touching him, was beginning to fray, and he had only seconds before it snapped entirely.

Never having expected such a quick change in circumstance, he fought it savagely, throwing as much of himself into the battle as he could, desperately trying to keep the fabric of energy in place. But nothing he did worked.

More of the Talent was being scraped away from the vault that he had created within his mind, and then the strands started to unravel. Fear threatened to overwhelm him as the Curse swelled within him, pushing against the barrier, incessantly, inexorably, the Dark Magic somehow knowing that in just a few heartbeats it would finally achieve its goal of ripping through the obstacle he had constructed to contain it. And when that happened, Bryen understood with a growing horror that he would be done for. If the Dark Magic didn't kill him, Rafia or Sirius would.

The two Magii watched with increasing trepidation, finally realizing what was happening to Bryen. All they could do was stand and watch, waiting to see how the internal fight would end, hoping for the best, but prepared for the worst.

Sirius was particularly perplexed. The lad had been doing so well through the entire combat, pulling in as much of the Talent as he needed to fight Rafia with no need to be concerned about the Curse. Why now? What had changed?

Bryen grappled with the urge to release his control over the Talent, realizing that giving in to the wish would mean his downfall. At the same time, another compulsion began to pulse within him. He experienced an almost unmanageable need to touch the Dark Magic within him, to release it, to use it. To make the tremendous power of the Curse his own. And despite his best efforts to maintain control over himself, he was weakening.

He could sense himself reaching for the Dark Magic, the barricade he had built thinning, then dissolving. All he had to do was reach out with a finger and it would disintegrate, allowing the Dark Magic to finally run free. To take him. Why was this happening? He was going against his own wishes, but he couldn't stop himself. A moment of despondency passed through him, making it even harder for him to continue the fight. He realized to his horror that he was losing the battle and that the end was coming.

"The Spear," he whispered desperately through gritted teeth. "Get me the Spear."

Rafia sprinted to where Sirius had been sitting, hefting the Spear of the Magii and running back as fast as she could.

Bryen saw her do it, but he didn't think that she'd get to him in time. The Dark Magic was ascending from the crypt within which he had buried it, preparing to consume him, preparing to make him its own. He was about to fall over the edge into the abyss, never to return. Who he was, who he had become, gone. Stolen from him.

With no time to spare, Rafia slid to a stop next to Bryen and placed the Spear of the Magii in his upraised palms. In a flash, the struggle within him faded. With barely a thought he rebuilt the wall that held back the Dark Magic and forced the Curse back into its cage. Satisfied that all was well within him once again, he used the spear as a staff, driving one end into the dirt and pushing himself to his feet. He breathed deeply, the last few minutes of his struggles against the Curse more tiring than the hourlong combat he had engaged in with Rafia.

As he slowly came back to himself, he replayed the last few minutes through his mind. He realized then that he hadn't been losing control on his own. No, he was being made to lose control. Something, or rather someone, had been pushing him, aiding him in his descent into the Dark Magic. Someone nearby.

Gripping the Spear of the Magii tightly, he pointed the topmost blade toward a swirling pool of ink at the edge of the glade, streaks of white energy shooting from the tip. But rather than striking the intended target, a spinning shield of shadow deflected the energy, the power of the Talent ripping apart several trees and sending thousands of splinters slicing through the air. Rafia, Sirius, and Bryen turned away and ducked, then looked back toward that pool of black that was darker than the night.

A massive shadow emerged from between the trees, the gloom fading away to reveal the Ghoule Overlord, who stepped arrogantly into the light of the small clearing. The creature grinned wickedly, his sharp teeth gleaming in the light, a small tornado of black mist whipping around the top of his staff of black ash, the black diamond pulsing in rhythm to the blinding white energy of Bryen's spear.

Shocked that the Overlord had appeared before them, Rafia and Sirius still reacted swiftly, taking in as much of the Talent as they could and preparing to release it at the leader of the Ghoule Legions. But they weren't fast enough. Before the two Magii could attack, a barrier of shimmering murkiness appeared, enclosing Bryen and the Ghoule Overlord and preventing Rafia and Sirius from intervening.

As a test, Sirius sent a streak of white against the wall of black, but he knew immediately that it was useless. The power of the Overlord was too great. The Talent simply sizzled for a few seconds upon striking the shield, the two magics dueling with one another, before the blast of white energy faded away, absorbed by the Curse. Though the barrier prevented the two Magii from engaging with the Overlord, they could still see and hear the exchange that took place within it.

"I see you, Protector," said the Ghoule Overlord in a deep voice. "I know who you are now. I know what you are." The Overlord stepped closer to Bryen, his black eyes suggesting a hunger that could never be sated. "You will be mine, boy. I will enslave you. Then I will take the Seventh Stone."

For a moment, Bryen was amazed by the clarity with which the Ghoule Overlord had spoken in the common tongue, the few Elders able to do so always struggling to form certain syllables or words. But then to his dismay he realized that the lord of the Ghoules had not spoken in the common tongue. He had spoken in his own language, and Bryen had understood him perfectly. Apparently another useful but disconcerting ability provided to him by the Seventh Stone.

"If you want me, come and get me," taunted Bryen. His grey eyes became even colder, and he began spinning the Spear of the Magii in front of him as if he were doing nothing more than waiting for his chance to step into the training circle.

"You have just experienced the power that I wield. You would do well to fear me, boy. You cannot challenge me. You cannot defeat me."

"So you say."

"So I know."

"Then prove it."

The Ghoule Overlord lifted his head at the last, staring down at this boy who dared to test him. This boy who was no more than another tool to be used.

"As you wish," rumbled the Overlord.

But before the beast could launch the Dark Magic spinning above the top of his staff, Bryen struck first. Pulling in as much of the Talent as he could, the blades on the Spear of the Magii so bright that the Ghoule Overlord could not look directly at them, the gladiator sprinted forward. At the same time, just as he had done when he dueled Rafia, he shot several bolts of energy from the tip of his spear that erupted at the clawed feet of the Master of the Ghoules, throwing up a spray of dirt and rock, the thunderous roar of each blast disorienting the creature.

That was all the time that Bryen needed to close with the beast, the Spear of the Magii slicing through the air, aimed for the Overlord's ribs. The creature recovered faster than Bryen had expected, raising his staff to block the blow. But then another blade was cutting toward the Ghoule, targeting his ribs on his other side. Once again, the Overlord deflected the slash with his staff. But Bryen wasn't done with him. The Protector was a whirlwind of motion, the two glowing blades cutting toward the beast's neck, then hip, then thigh, then gut, then neck again. Strike after strike, never tiring, Bryen was driven on by a cold anger hidden behind a calm and cool that was only revealed by the deadness in his eyes. Yet each time Bryen sought to make him bleed, the Overlord parried the attack.

At first the Ghoule Overlord thought that the boy had been a fool to do as he had done, attacking him so aggressively. But then the creature realized the genius of the move. Because the Protector had demanded so much of his attention, the barrier that he had thrown up to hold back the two Magii had weakened over time and then disappeared completely.

The two Magii had been waiting for that moment, and they were ready. White-hot energy streamed from Sirius' palms, aimed for the Overlord's chest, the beast having been able to extricate himself from Bryen's unyielding attack for just a few seconds. The Overlord raised his staff, the sizzling power slamming into a spinning mist of black. The old man was a formidable opponent, but he wasn't strong enough to defeat the Master of the Ghoules on his own.

The Overlord grinned, knowing that he could crush the old Magus at his leisure, make a lesson out of him. But then the beast realized that the woman was about to enter the fight. She had raised her hands to her shoulders and was slashing them down toward the ground. The Overlord heard a rumbling above him, and in response he quickly expanded his shield to block several bolts of lightning that surged down from a clear, nighttime sky.

As soon as he saw that Sirius was going to join the fight, Bryen had stepped back several feet, and then several feet more when he realized what Rafia had in mind. He turned away when the lightning struck, shielding himself with the Talent to protect against the rock and dirt that shot toward him.

Yet even with the roar of the lightning, Bryen had heard what the Overlord had said right before the power of the two Magii struck.

"Remember, boy. The Seventh Stone belongs to me."

When Bryen turned back around, the cloud of dust and dirt having drifted away on the faint breeze, he realized that the Ghoule Overlord was gone.

"You didn't kill him," said Bryen, who released his hold on the Talent. For some strange reason, he was certain that his enemy had escaped.

"No," replied Sirius, who came to stand next to the Protector, Rafia walking up on his other side. "But we did succeed in driving him away, at least for now."

"You know him," said Rafia. "And you were not surprised to see him."

"No, I wasn't surprised," admitted Bryen. "He was trying to control the Seventh Stone. That's why I struggled for a time. He was trying to control the Dark Magic within me. He almost won."

"But he didn't." Sirius patted Bryen companionably on the shoulder to emphasize his point. "That's what matters."

"I've met him before," continued Bryen. "I thought that it had been a dream, perhaps it was to a certain extent, but it had been just as real, even then."

Bryen motioned to the burnt scar that had been added to the three that already marred his cheek.

"That night on Haven," nodded Rafia.

"Yes. I should have told you."

"What's done is done, lad," said Sirius.

"But we do need to be more careful," said Rafia. "The Ghoule Overlord can sense the Seventh Stone. He can sense you. We always thought that was possible, but he just confirmed it. And to come here on his own, this far from his Legions, demonstrates how desperate the Overlord is to gain the power that you hold. He will not stop coming after you."

"Yes, he needs you," confirmed Sirius. "Once he captures you, he can take the Seventh Stone. And once he has that, you're no longer of use to him. He'll kill you, then probably eat you, because he'll have the power to do whatever he wants in this world."

Bryen nodded, expecting as much. Then he shrugged his shoulders, as if the danger of being eaten was an everyday occurrence. "Then I'll just have to kill him first."

5

─────

BACK IN THE CAPITAL

Talus Sharperson marched toward the throne room with a huge smirk on his face. He loved being in Tintagel. The energy of the city, the noise, the colors, the smells, the opportunity, the extravagance ... it all appealed to him. Sharston was just a village compared to the capital, barely a quarter of the size of Caledonia's largest metropolis and without most of the distractions that always pulled at him when he walked within its walls. But of all the differences between his home and the city that he preferred, perhaps most important for him was the fact that the pleasure houses here offered more variety and the chance to indulge his fetishes in private. He didn't feel constrained as he did when he visited the handful of brothels that could be found in his coastal town in which he was so well known.

The Duke of Sharston tried to cut a gallant figure, his clothes always of the highest quality, well cut, and reflecting the latest styles in Tintagel. He desperately wanted to avoid being placed in the company of some of the lords and ladies to be found in the farther reaches of Caledonia who, if he were being kind, could only be described at best as country bumpkins. But more often than not he wasn't kind. Rather, he preferred to be cruel, a characteristic that he believed was absolutely essential when governing the largest western province of the Kingdom that also served as a waypoint for the increasing number of Caledonians traveling across the Burnt Ocean and seeking to make their fortune in the Territories.

"Hello, my dear," said Talus, stopping near one of the many gardens that lined the covered walkway that led to the throne room.

He offered his hand to a beautiful young woman, expecting her to take it, kiss his knuckles, and then curtsy in recognition of his status as a Duke of Caledonia. Much to his surprise, the serving girl simply stared at him, not a clue as to who he was, her hands full of dirty linens to be taken to the wash, not used to speaking with anyone but the other servants while they were cleaning the living quarters in the sprawling Palace.

"My lord," the woman replied. She curtsied as best as she could while holding a pile of soiled laundry.

"Tell me, I am looking for a companion. Someone to spend time with while I am in Tintagel while meeting with the King on some important matters." Actually, he had no official business with Marden, but this young woman didn't need to know that. "I do hate to be bored, and you look as if you could do with a bit of fun."

The serving girl's eyes sparkled as she deciphered quickly what he was suggesting. He did have a nice smile, and he did appear moneyed what with the clothes that he was wearing. So perhaps this was an opportunity, she thought. A little fun and a little more coin wouldn't hurt her.

"I could, my Lord ..."

Talus quickly filled the opening the beautiful young woman gave him, seeking to push the door all the way open. "Talus Sharperson, Duke of Sharston." He even gave her a small bow, which was not necessary for someone of her standing, and flourished his half cape to add just a touch of flamboyance.

When Talus looked up again, he was startled to see that the serving girl was backing away from him, her face draining of color, a look of fear in her eyes.

"I'm sorry, Duke Sharperson. But I must be away. The Head Mistress is seeking me."

The serving girl was not opposed to spending time with a young, relatively handsome lord, but certainly not one with a reputation such as his. Stories of what had happened the last time he had visited the Palace when he sought to take advantage of the maids ran rampant through the servants' quarters.

Talus watched her go, not understanding why she was leaving him so quickly but giving it no further thought. In his mind there was no lack of women looking to spend time with an eligible, powerful, and wealthy lord such as himself.

Shrugging his shoulders, he turned on his heel and made once again for the massive doors that he could see far off in the distance that protected the throne room. Sighing, he resigned himself to the long walk that it would take to get to the far end of the hallway.

Finally, after almost a quarter hour had passed, he was there, the huge oak panels rising above him, the Guards on either side nodding in respect as they pulled the doors aside for him so that he didn't need to break his step. His smile only expanded when he walked into the throne room. The serving girl obviously didn't know who he was, but the Royal Guard did, and that returned the shine to his eyes.

His highly polished boots striking the white tile of the floor echoed through the hall. Surprisingly, the throne room was sparse in appearance, shadows playing across the walls thanks to the torches set in gold sconces with the primary source of light coming from the back of the chamber. Above the balcony from which the King could look down on his subjects was a series of intricately carved glass windows crafted into the shape of diamonds that during the afternoon, when the sun was dipping to the west, centered the rays of light on the dominant feature in the auditorium. The throne of Caledonia. Carved from a single block of black granite in contrast to the tiles of the floor and the white granite that covered the other three walls, the back of the throne rose more than ten feet in height. The seat of Caledonian power drew the eye of anyone entering the chamber, making the person sitting upon it the center of attention, which was its primary purpose.

Talus visited Tintagel as frequently as he could, partaking in all that the capital had to offer. This time he came for a specific purpose. He was in need of a new Champion.

For the last five years, Talus had been trying to replace his former Champion, who had been killed in the Colosseum by the Volkun. But his efforts had failed miserably, every man seeking to take the place of Stil Sheldgard unable to meet his expectations or his memories of the man he had molded into who he believed was the deadliest fighter in all of Caledonia. So he had decided on a different approach. He would purchase a gladiator to fill the role.

Recalling the combat between Stil and the Volkun still angered him. He had invested so much in his Champion. Stil was a mountain of a man, muscles where they had no right to be, no neck to speak of, and bald with a braided beard that extended all the way to his belt. Half the time he won his fights before they even began, terrifying his opponent without even having to raise his blade. Yet even with all that, Talus had wanted to make certain that his Champion couldn't be beaten, so he had gained some additional assistance from an unexpected place.

Nevertheless, after seven years of victories, of barely being touched by a blade, his famed Champion, undefeated and unstoppable, had fallen to a boy. To a gladiator younger than he was. The Volkun. Talus had wanted to kill that gladiator at the end of the combat, but Marden's father, Corinthus Beleron, had prevented him from doing as he deemed appropriate and what was well within his rights as a Duke of Caledonia. It took the passage of several years before he realized that perhaps how events played out had been for the best. He wondered if that gladiator was still alive. He had assumed that it was more likely that he had fallen on the white sand. Even so, the boy had been exceedingly fast, faster even than Stil, and he knew how to fight, so maybe he had survived these last five years.

If so, he would explore purchasing him. That would certainly get people talking, his replacing the Champion with the Volkun. But he'd need to be careful. He didn't want to do anything that would get the eyes and the ears of the court talking about him rather than the man who alighted upon the throne of Caledonia. In Marden's world there was only space for one person on his stage. Everyone else was a bit player. To upset that balance was dangerous, as had been proven many times over.

Talus tried to ignore the many other lords and ladies in the chamber, but he found it difficult. Just as always there appeared to be an inordinate number of beautiful young women spending time near the King, drawn to him by his easy smile, long black hair, and quick laugh, all of the pretties willing to ignore the spark of maliciousness that flickered in the back of his eyes from time to time.

"My King," said Talus, stopping in front of the throne and bowing deeply. "I wish to pay my respects."

"It has been too long," said Marden, pushing himself up from his seat and gesturing for Talus to rise. The King then reached out and grasped his hands, Talus unable to miss the strength of his grip.

"It has, my King. It is good to see you."

"Come," said Marden, gesturing toward the back of the throne room. "Let us walk and gain some privacy." The two young lords strolled out into the garden, and then turned to the left into Marden's private office, a large room that had once been a library but now served as a showcase of the history of the Beleron line, the trophies of war -- banners, weapons, flags -- lining the walls. The King motioned to Killen Sourban, Captain of the Royal Guard, who had been waiting just inside the doorway. "Could you bring in this afternoon's entertainment?"

Killen nodded, bowed, then walked out into the garden, intent on his task. The man's ice-blue eyes revealed little, but if Talus were to guess he would say that Sourban was looking forward to whatever was going to happen next.

"Entertainment?" asked Talus, not understanding.

"Nothing that concerns you, Talus," said Marden, who leaned back against a massive desk. "So how is life on the western coast?"

"Boring," replied Talus with a sigh, slouching down in a couch set opposite to the desk.

He and Marden were good friends, both of the same age and the same mentality. They were used to and relished their power and privilege, to what they believed they deserved, even though they had never earned any of it on their own. It had been given to them by the circumstance of their births. Moreover, both had assumed their places in similar ways. Talus had taken on his role in Sharston when his mother the Duchess passed suddenly, a rare wasting disease taking her in a matter of hours. So rare, in fact, that there had been whispers that she had been helped into the grave, but only whispers, as nothing had ever been proven and no one in the province had the courage to dig too deeply. Marden's father had died under mysterious circumstances as well. Some said that Tetric had aided King Corinthus' demise, but whether true or not, Marden didn't seem to care. The son of the former King was exactly where he wanted to be.

"Nothing of significance ever happens in Sharston," grumbled Talus.

"The same can't be said of Tintagel," said Marden slyly. "A new surprise every day."

"Really?" asked Talus, his interest piqued. "Do tell?"

"Nothing beyond the usual," Marden replied casually. "Plots and plans. Schemes and dreams. The same as always."

"Come now. You wouldn't have suggested if you didn't want to talk about it." Talus leaned forward eagerly, sitting on the edge of his seat. This was another reason why he so enjoyed being in the capital. The intrigue. The scandals. The fun.

"Nothing out of the ordinary," replied Marden. "I just need to put some of our illustrious Dukes and Duchesses in their places." The snideness of Marden's tone wasn't lost on the Duke of Sharston.

Talus laughed. "I heard about your engagement to Aislinn Winborne. Quite a coup."

"But not complete until the vows are said and the marriage is consummated."

"She's hesitating?" asked Talus.

"She and her father both," replied Marden. "They don't seem to recognize all that they gain by marrying into House Beleron."

"And all that they lose?" asked Talus.

"Unfortunately, they understand quite well what they lose," complained Marden.

"The Duke of the Southern Marches will accept your proposal," said Talus with absolute certainty. "He has no choice."

"He will," confirmed Marden. "He has no choice as you say. But that doesn't mean I don't need to make a point from time to time to remind the lovely Aislinn and her recalcitrant father that they do not exercise the power of the Southern Marches here in Tintagel. Here I rule. And that time approaches." Marden pushed himself off the desk. "But enough about that. Tell me why you're here."

"I will be visiting the games this Saturday."

"You always attend the combats in the Colosseum when you're in the capital."

"Yes, you're right about that," agreed Talus, conceding the point. "But this time, in addition to making some wagers on who will live and who will die, I hope to identify a few likely prospects to replace Stil."

"After all this time you're still focused on replacing your former Champion?"

"As I said, my King. I'm bored. I need some entertainment, and this is one way to do that." Talus got up from the couch, understanding that his time with his friend was coming to an end. "Would you care to join me?"

"I'll let you know," replied Marden, his attention drawn to the back of the room. "I have some more pressing matters to attend to at the moment."

Aislinn Winborne strode into Marden's private office, her head held high. Several soldiers followed after her, but they quickly stepped back when Marden nodded at them to leave.

"You requested my presence, Marden," said the Lady of the Southern Marches with an imperiousness that suggested that she was there of her own free will, and not because a squad of soldiers had accompanied her there. "What is this all about?"

Talus marveled at her beauty, but what attracted him even more was her arrogance. The Lady of the Southern Marches had a unique ability to look down her nose at you in a way that sent a shiver of delight through him. If not for Marden, Talus would have done all that he could to make her his bride. And then the real fun would begin.

"As sharp tongued as ever," said Talus with a chuckle,

unable to help himself. "A pity that your tone and your words don't match your beauty."

Aislinn turned her imperious gaze toward Talus Sharperson. She was frightened, having expected to be summoned after the previous night's incident and not knowing what Marden would have in store for her, assuming, of course, that he even remembered. But she did her best to hide that fear, in part with an acerbic wit.

"Funny. If only your thoughts were as sharp as the spikes rising from your head," countered Aislinn, raising her chin a bit more to give her just a touch more arrogance to her features.

For a moment, Talus didn't know what to say, his hand going to his head to touch his carefully maintained hairstyle. Then he realized he had been insulted. He was about to offer a scathing retort when Marden's laughter stopped him.

"Her tongue is as sharp as her sword," offered Marden. "Now if you'll excuse me, Talus. As I said, I have more important matters to deal with at the moment. My lovely bride and I need to discuss a few issues of a more personal nature. We will do that now, once we have some privacy."

Talus smirked, his mind automatically moving down the most salacious path possible. "Of course, my King." The Duke of Sharston headed for the door. "I will leave you to it."

With Talus gone, Marden turned his attention to his betrothed. "So, my Lady Aislinn. Shall we continue the conversation that you so rudely interrupted last night?"

A cold lump of fear settled within Aislinn's stomach. Marden was smiling. But his eyes held a cold fire that she had never seen before.

6

MAKING A POINT

"So tell me, Lady Winborne," said Marden Beleron, the King of Caledonia, hands clasped behind his back while walking slowly around his betrothed much like a shark circling its prey before it struck. "Why do you believe that you are different from everyone else? Why do you believe that you are above everyone else? What makes you so special?"

Aislinn stood in the center of the private office, her eyes focused on the doors leading out to the garden. She thought about making a break for it, of sprinting through the opening, onto the terrace, and then losing herself among the trees. From there she could find a way out of the Palace and be rid of this pompous, conceited, dangerous fool who played at King. But that was only a dream, a wasted thought. No matter what her father had told her to do, she could not leave him here. She could not consign him to a fate that might be worse than death.

So she forced herself to release her hands from tightly gripping the folds of her dress, a nervous habit she had yet to break. She assumed the posture expected of the Lady of the Southern Marches, back erect, head held high, hands serenely clasped in front of her, her eyes frigid and without emotion. Marden may control the board at the moment, but she would not be played.

"I do not believe that ..."

"Oh, but you do," cut in Marden, surveying her from head to toe with a lecherous eye. His voice was gentle, almost soothing, but his expression revealed the other things on his mind. Aislinn knew from her experience with him that this was only the beginning. Marden enjoyed drama, and he would build it slowly until he reached the climax that he wanted to achieve.

"I do not," she protested more vehemently.

"You do," disputed Marden, his voice harder. "You're doing it now. You've been doing it to me ever since you've gotten here. You have taken advantage of my kindness, my magnanimity. You have played with me, toyed with me, and not in the way that I would prefer." A lascivious grin broke out on the King's face, if only for a second as he appreciated his own humor, before he continued his controlled tirade. "You have put me off, looked down that perfect nose of yours at me, probably thinking that I do not meet your requirements. That I can never meet your requirements. But you misjudge. You do not understand the seriousness of your situation. You do not understand who you are now. You do not understand that you are no longer doing the judging."

"I am the Lady of the Southern Marches," replied Aislinn, "and I have acted as such."

"Yes, and there's the problem," said Marden as he continued to step slowly around her, hands still clasped behind his back, his eyes never leaving her. "You don't seem to understand."

"Enlighten me, Marden. What don't I understand?"

"That here in Tintagel, in my city, you are not the Lady of the Southern Marches."

Aislinn scoffed, not expecting such a comment. "Then what am I?"

"Who you are is less important than one simple fact," he replied.

"And that would be?"

"That you are mine," Marden shouted harshly, the crux of the scene having arrived. "Whether you know it or not, whether you believe it or not, you are mine."

"Say what you want, Marden. But I belong to no one."

"Then you're only fooling yourself," he replied calmly, the fire in his voice temporarily banked. "As soon as you stepped within the walls of my Palace, you became mine. What you want doesn't matter. What you think doesn't matter. What you believe doesn't matter." Finally, Marden stopped his pacing and turned to face her, his prurient grin marring his handsome visage. "Here, in my city, the only thing that matters is what I want. The only thing that matters is what I think. The only thing that matters is what I believe."

"Are you certain of that?" she asked strongly, though she heard a tremor of fear escape in her voice as she suspected the answer before the words even left her mouth. Her hands had returned to her skirts, twisting the fabric as her nerves threatened to get the better of her.

"Quite certain." Marden took a step closer to her. "I have been patient with you out of some small kindness that I feel toward you, hoping that you would ascertain not only the gravity, but also the inevitability of your situation. I had thought by now that this charade you have put on, this attempt to display your independence, your refusal to formally accept my proposal, would have ended."

"It is not a charade," replied Aislinn with what little heat she could muster, her fear and uncertainty growing. "I am the Lady of the Southern Marches!"

"You are whatever I want you to be!" screamed Marden, who took another step toward her, this time halving the distance. "You are whatever I require you to be! You are mine, and the sooner you understand that, the better off both of us will be."

Though terrified, Aislinn stood strong during the rant, her posture becoming even more haughty, her eyes narrowing disdainfully.

"I will never be yours," she replied quietly. "Never."

"Once again, you delude yourself," said Marden, his eyes blazing with anger. He took a third step toward her, now so near that she could smell the wine on his breath. Although she was exceedingly uncomfortable as he loomed above her, she refused to move back. "The last straw came last night. I did not appreciate what you did. What you did in front of my friends. But there was a value in it, once the pain subsided and I was able to think clearly again. Because I realized then that no matter what I did for you, no matter what I did to you, your perspective would not change."

"Then perhaps we should end this game right now, and we can both move on," suggested Aislinn.

"Always so quick to seek a way out," chuckled Marden. "I must commend you. But no. No, what you helped me to realize was that even though I could never break you, I don't need to. I just have to break your father. Once I do that, you will be mine. Whether you like it or not, you will be mine."

For just a few seconds, Marden's last comment caught Aislinn by surprise as she realized what he was telling her. But that was all the distraction that he needed. Before she could move out of the way, he lunged forward, grabbing her shoulders with his hands to hold her in place, and then he forced his lips onto hers. Shocked by the turn of events, she was frozen for just a moment, never expecting this to happen here and now, wanting to believe that the night before resulted from the influence of the milk of the poppy. But she understood instantly that she had only been fooling herself. Forcing himself upon her, this was who Marden truly was.

She raised her hands and shoved hard against his chest, trying to break free. But he was stronger than she had anticipated. Ignoring her struggles, Marden pushed down harder with his lips and pressed his body against hers.

Sensing the danger of her situation, she fought back ferociously. As he forced her lips open, she bit his tongue, drawing blood, but that only spurred him on again. Then she attempted the same move that had worked so well the night before, but Marden twisted his hip just in time to prevent her from bringing her knee up into his groin. It was only when she was able to raise her hands from where they were crushed against his chest and slap him hard across the cheek that he finally pulled back, but even then, it took three sharp blows to move him.

Licking the blood that trickled down his cut lip, Marden laughed, enjoying Aislinn's attempted resistance.

"I didn't know that you preferred it rough," he said, his eyes flashing dangerously. "But I must say that it excites me."

Marden leaned forward once more, trying to lock onto her lips again. This time, she was ready. Remembering something that Bryen had taught her during a training session, she didn't bother to avoid his smothering lips or attempt to push him away. Instead, she reached up with her left hand for his left hand, grabbing hold of his thumb, pulling back, and then twisting with all her strength. Caught completely by surprise by the pain that burned through his hand and then sizzled up his arm and into his shoulder, Marden screamed in agony, releasing his grip on Aislinn as he tried to spin his way out of her grasp.

He reached blindly for her, his free hand grabbing hold of her other arm, but the pain she was causing him was too much, and all he succeeded in doing was tearing free a good portion of her sleeve. No matter what he did, the burning intensified. Aislinn simply moved with him, refusing to release his thumb until she was ready to do so. She didn't shove him away until she was certain that he had learned his lesson, Marden coming to a stop when he slammed into his desk.

Marden shook out his injured arm for several seconds, massaging his thumb. When he turned back around, still flexing his fingers and rubbing his left arm, Aislinn had expected to see anger and a desire for revenge. But Marden only appeared amused and even more aroused.

"You really are quite the siren," he said. "Your lips tell me one thing, your actions something else entirely. Getting to know you better will be a great deal of fun."

Marden pushed himself off the desk, stepping close to her again, but not so close that she could reach him easily. He had known that she was good with a blade, but had not realized that her martial training had covered fighting skills that did not require steel.

"I take it that you learned that from your Protector. I've been told that during your time training with my Guard, you've taught my soldiers a great deal, and I can only assume that the gladiator your father purchased for you was your instructor."

"I learned many things from my Protector," Aislinn confirmed, though her voice betrayed her uncertainty and concern.

She wasn't sure where Marden was going with the conversation. Perhaps he was only buying time for the burning in his arm to stop so that he could try to take advantage of her again. If so, he was in for another hard lesson. Based on her experience, the sizzling pain that she had inflicted on him would continue for at least another hour, and then it would slowly transition into a dull ache that would stay with him for days. A fitting punishment for what he did to her, in her opinion.

"So I've heard," replied Marden, still rubbing his injured

arm, shaking it out every few seconds in an attempt to quell the throbbing, but enjoying little success. "My spies in Battersea tell me that you spent a great deal of time with your Protector."

"I had no choice," replied Aislinn with a scathing laugh. "The magic of the collar requires the Protector to be in close proximity to his charge, as you well know."

"Yes, but I received reports suggesting that you and your Protector were closer than you needed to be. Much closer."

Aislinn finally realized where Marden was leading this conversation. She chose not to reply. Let him think what he wanted.

"From our kiss just now you come across as someone unskilled in the amorous arts," said Marden, his tone almost professorial, as if he were seeking to solve a mathematical problem or a theorem. "But I'm not convinced. From what I've heard of you and your Protector, I believe that you're quite skilled. You're simply hiding it. Regardless, I mean to find out if I'm right."

"Believe what you want. It's of no matter to me."

"Perhaps, perhaps not," said Marden. "Even if your Protector were here, it would have no impact on the future that awaits you. Better just to give in, to make the best of the situation. You are mine. That will not change."

"I believe we covered this already," Aislinn replied with some heat, her eyes blazing with anger. "I am no one's."

Marden chuckled scornfully. "Still you fight it. As I said, you will be whatever I want you to be. You are now in a position no better than that of your Protector. And your Protector was a slave, no more. I saw him fight on the white sand once. Against Talus' Champion, in fact. A fighter, yes. The argument could be made that he was even a warrior, and perhaps one of the best gladiators to ever appear in the Colosseum. But nothing more than that. Not a Duke. Not a King. Just a gladiator. And still a slave fighting for his life. Even as your Protector, still just a slave, fighting for his life."

"Bryen is more than you will ever be," countered Aislinn. "He's more than just a fighter. And he is no longer a slave. I freed him before I came here."

Marden nodded, finally understanding why her Protector had not come with her to the capital. "Maybe he is more than just a fighter now that he is free, but in my opinion, he is still no more than a slave. Of course, your Protector isn't here. Bad luck for you, good for me."

Before Marden could continue the conversation, he heard a murmur of voices at the door to the chamber, and then Tetric appeared with Kevan striding just a step behind him, though the Duke of the Southern Marches' gritted teeth and stilted walk suggested that his obeying the King's Advisor was not entirely his choice, but rather resulted from the power of the black collar that encircled his neck.

"Tetric," acknowledged Marden. "Once again your timing is poor. I was just getting to know my bride-to-be."

"What have you done, you wretch!" roared Kevan, taking in his daughter's ripped sleeve and her disheveled appearance, the Duke's anger immediately shifting away from Tetric to the King. Kevan lunged for Marden, but he managed only a few steps before he froze, stiff as a board, Tetric using the collar to keep him in place.

Marden laughed at seeing what had happened to the Duke, his soon-to-be father-in-law. He so enjoyed watching the Dukes and Duchesses who thought that they were so much better than he was realize that the power they wielded was ephemeral and that their place in the world could only be guaranteed by him.

"Be careful, Kevan," warned Marden, as he came to stand right in front of him, no more than a knuckle separating the two. Marden had no doubt that if Kevan could, he would wrap his hands around his throat and strangle the life from him. But he couldn't move. Not unless Tetric permitted it. That thought brought a wicked grin to his face. "As I said before, you are no longer in Battersea. You are in my world. And in my world, you will do as I say."

Clearly Kevan wanted to reply, but the strength of the magic that Tetric was using wouldn't allow for it.

"Release my father, Marden," demanded Aislinn. "He doesn't deserve this."

"It's not a matter of what is deserved," corrected Marden, "but rather what is necessary. And in this very moment, it is necessary that you both be taught a lesson." Marden then turned his piercing gaze directly on Aislinn. "And you, my dear. You must understand what will happen if you continue to fight me. What will happen if you continue to disobey me."

"You don't need to do this, Marden," said Aislinn, her look of horror showing that she understood what he planned to do next.

"Oh, but I must, my dear. I must, because of you. Because of your stubbornness." Marden then turned away from her to focus on her father. He wanted to make sure that he didn't miss a second of what was about to happen. A thrill ran through Marden when he took in the sweat that had formed on Kevan's brow and had begun to trickle down his forehead, the Duke's efforts at freeing himself from the magic holding him all for naught. Yet still Kevan tried. Marden was impressed by the sad demonstration, but the Duke was still a fool, just like his daughter. "Tetric, my bride needs to be taught a lesson about her father's new place in my world. Our kindness and flexibility have failed to change his and his daughter's view."

"Yes, a lesson does sound in order," agreed Tetric in a deep but raspy voice. "How extreme a tutorial did you have in mind?"

"Let's work our way into it, but it must convince my father-in-law that he is no longer the Duke of the Southern Marches.

He is simply a chip to be played in a larger game. A piece, no more than that. But it still must do more than that. Please show the Lady Aislinn what will happen to her father if she fails to adhere to my demands."

"With pleasure, my King," replied Tetric.

Using the power that he had infused within the blackened steel, Tetric sent a tiny jolt of energy through the bond. The response was immediate, Kevan's eye's bulging as the pinpricks of fire hit him. With Tetric still holding him in place that was the only way that the Duke could express his suffering.

"Stop this, Marden," pleaded Aislinn. "You have no cause."

Marden ignored her, his attention focused unerringly on the Duke of the Southern Marches. "A good start, Tetric. But perhaps you could give Kevan a bit more control of himself. Seeing only a limited reaction eliminates much of the fun of the experience for me."

"Of course, my King. As you command."

Tetric sent another jolt of energy through the bond, this one stronger, and at the same time he released his control over his captive. The Duke of the Southern Marches collapsed to the ground, every muscle of his body seizing up as the dark power shot through him, the pain so intense that all he could offer was a silent scream.

"Much better, Tetric," said Marden, a charge of pleasure surging through him as he watched Kevan writhe on the tile. "Thank you. One more time please."

Tetric nodded, sending another surge of power into the collar that intensified Kevan's agony.

Still, Kevan refused to surrender himself to the pain, fighting every second of it, his eyes locked onto Marden, the source of his torture. Although he had lost control of his body, he had not lost control of himself. Marden had not broken his will, nor would he. Not now. Not ever.

"This can all come to an end, my darling," suggested

Marden, his gaze still fixed on her father, taking a great deal of pleasure from his suffering. "Once we are wed, there will be no need for this. You will finally have me, and I will have you ... and the Southern Marches."

With a nod from Marden, Tetric allowed the power that he had sent into the collar to fade away, and for several seconds there was silence in the chamber but for Kevan's labored breathing as he remained flat on his back, his muscles still twitching uncontrollably. Then, with a steel will, the Duke of the Southern Marches forced himself to his knees, then pushed himself to his feet to stand shakily in front of Marden.

Kevan ignored the King of Caledonia and turned his tired gaze to Aislinn. She stared into her father's eyes. She saw the pain there, but also the defiance. She knew then that her father could never be broken, and no matter how much it hurt her to watch what he had just suffered, she promised him with a look that she wouldn't break either, even for him.

"You will never have the Southern Marches so long as I live," said Kevan, his voice soft but sure.

"It might come to that," replied Marden.

"What's the meaning of this?" demanded the Blademaster, his voice filled with contempt. "You requested my presence, King Beleron, but I never expected to see something such as this. Your father would be disgusted."

Tetric took a step toward the Blademaster at the insult, but Marden waved him back, the King grinning like a boy at the reaction he had obtained from the normally taciturn Jurgen Klines.

The Blademaster had received word that the King required his attendance more than an hour before. But he never made it a point to rush to do Marden's bidding. He didn't believe that the son deserved the same respect that the father had earned, at least for a time. But then he cursed his own arrogance. Perhaps if he had gotten here sooner, he could have prevented what had happened as he took in the battered state of the Duke of the Southern Marches and the Lady Winborne's torn clothing.

"Perhaps, but then again, my father is no longer with us, so what does it matter?" replied Marden smoothly. He noticed that Klines' hand had shifted to the hilt of his sword, a finger of steel showing.

"Sheathe your sword, Blademaster," ordered Tetric, stepping in front of the King. "If you don't, it will go badly for the Duke and you."

"Yes, Blademaster. You must be careful. Otherwise, I will allow my trusted Advisor to show you the penalty for disobeying me."

For just a moment the tension in the room thickened, Klines staring at Tetric without fear. Aislinn guessed that he was calculating whether he could get his blade to the Advisor's throat before the Advisor could strike him with whatever power he controlled. She assumed that the Blademaster had determined that the numbers didn't work in his favor as Klines dropped his hand.

"Now let's begin again, Blademaster. I didn't request your presence here. I ordered it."

"And here I am, King Beleron. May I ask what you need of me?"

"I have no need of you. But I did want to make a point."

"And what would that be, King Beleron?"

"The point to be made is exactly this," replied Marden. He stepped close to the Blademaster, his courage bolstered by the fact that Tetric stood right behind him. "The point is that I am the King of Caledonia, and I can do as I please when I please."

The Blademaster examined the King, nodding the entire time as if he were having a private conversation with himself.

"Have you ever considered, King Beleron," the Blademaster

finally said, "that there are other ways to rule that might be more effective than the one that you've chosen."

Klines knew that he could say more, but he didn't see the point. He didn't think that his current monarch had the desire to listen to anything other than what he said himself.

"I have chosen the most effective way to rule, Blademaster. My way. Remember that. My way is what will determine your future here, Blademaster. My way will determine whether you have a future here."

Klines stared hard at the King. He understood that the boy was trying hard to intimidate him, but in actuality Marden was simply irritating him. He could continue this useless dialogue, if only to irritate the King a bit more, but there were more important matters that required his attention.

"Of course, King Beleron," nodded Klines in a muted, barely acceptable form of respect. "I understand you perfectly."

"Good," replied the King. "Let's make sure that we don't need to have this conversation again. It will not go as well for you a second time."

The Blademaster ignored the King, not feeling the need to respond. "It appears that the Lady Winborne has met with some distress and could use some time to regain her composure ... and change her clothes." He said the last with some heat, his anger and scorn apparent. "With your permission I will escort the Lady Winborne and her father to their chambers."

"You may, Blademaster," said Marden, thinking for a moment if he wanted to extend his fun a bit longer, but then deciding against it, believing that he had accomplished his goal.

"Thank you, King Beleron." The Blademaster offered a bow of respect to Duke Winborne, directing him to the door with his hand. Aislinn followed her father, nodding her thanks. But the words that pursued her stopped her in her tracks, a dagger of ice piercing her heart.

"One last thing, my dear," said Marden. "There really is no reason to wait until the Council for us to enjoy the benefits of wedded bliss, so I have moved up the date of our wedding. It will be in a week's time. Make sure you're ready."

7

———

BUILDING CONFRONTATION

Along with his reputation as the most accomplished swordfighter in the Kingdom, Jurgen Klines was known for several other characteristics that earned the respect of most and the scorn of just a few.

One was his focus on details. During his training sessions with the soldiers of the Royal Guard, he was meticulous to the point of being hated. If a soldier put a foot just an inch out of place when lunging or did not twist his wrist just so when defending against a downward cut, Jurgen Klines took them to task, and he made them keep at it until they got it exactly the way that he required. He demanded perfection, knowing that it could not be achieved, but still he believed that the search for it was worth the effort in that it would help to keep alive the soldiers he trained.

Another was his penchant for the truth. He expected and demanded complete honesty from those he worked with and would take issue with anyone foolish enough to offer excuses or lie to him. He explained regularly to the soldiers he worked with that success in a fight depended as much on trusting your comrades as on your own skill with a sword, spear, or battle axe, and you couldn't trust your comrades if they didn't trust you.

And one more was a passion for practice. Klines' father, who was a well-known Caledonian general during the time of Aurelius Beleron, had taught him the blade. Once his father had shown Jurgen all that he knew about fighting with a sword, he had told his son in no uncertain terms that now the rest was up to him. If he wanted to improve his skills, he needed to practice. Every day. Whether he wanted to or not. And if he didn't want to practice, Jurgen would likely die at some point in the near future because eventually he would come across an opponent who had spent more time practicing with a blade than he did. Klines had taken his father's advice to heart, making it a part of who he was, and he did all that he could to instill the habit that had been so ingrained within him within the soldiers he viewed as his responsibility.

Jurgen also had a dispassionate approach to battle. There was a time and a place for emotion. As a soldier, it was unavoidable, the tremendous highs of defeating another person seeking your death balanced against the gut-wrenching lows of watching your comrades die right next to you, with you unable to save them. Therefore, the need to lock away any sentiment that could influence your decision-making and affect your ability to fight. After the battle, you could find some way to release the passions that built up within you, but never during the fight. Never when your life and the lives of those around you depended on a cool, calm, and collected approach.

Yet now, having left the Lady Winborne and her father safely in their chambers, the Blademaster was finding it difficult to live up to his personal code. His emotions roiled within him, what he had discovered shaking him to his very core, although he refused to show it. His greatest desire at that moment was to return to the King's private office and teach the privileged brat a lesson. He had no respect for anyone who treated a woman in such a way or who condoned abuse and torture for his personal benefit and pleasure.

And there was the rub, wasn't it? He had never expected that it would come to this, but having watched and interacted with Marden since he had assumed the throne upon his father's death, Klines realized that his hopes that the boy would grow into a more reasonable, better man had remained simply that. Hopes. Foolish hopes, never to be realized.

Marden was who he was. He was going to do what he wanted to do. He wasn't going to change. There was no need for him to do so. Marden had learned at a young age that he could be who he wanted to be, do what he wanted to do, with few consequences. The Blademaster had seen the signs even then, a mean streak and rapaciousness that rarely could be sated, all hidden behind a veneer of good-natured humor, a dazzling smile, and good looks. But the mask could hold for only so long, because inevitably Marden's true nature rose to the surface, just as it had done a few minutes before.

The Blademaster realized that he had been a fool to hold onto a naïve wish. He was upset. Angry. Not only with his King, but also with himself. He had known what was going to happen, but he had done nothing to prevent it. He shook his head in irritation. He could torture himself with that realization and failure later. Now he needed to focus.

The most obvious next step was to place more soldiers of the Royal Guard outside the rooms of the Duke and his daughter. His Guards. The soldiers who had come to know and respect the Lady of the Southern Marches and would protect her, even from their peers, some of whom might feel a stronger connection to the King. That thought immediately brought to mind a less obvious next step, one having to do with allegiances. His allegiances in particular.

The Blademaster was loyal to Caledonia. Not to the Crown, but to the Kingdom. To some, that was a distinction without a difference. They would say that the Crown was the Kingdom and the Kingdom was the Crown. There was no separation between the two. But he argued against such a limited perspective. Caledonia was more than the Crown. More than just one man. And he taught the soldiers who trained with him why he believed that was the case. Loyalty was required of them, demanded of them, for they served a critical purpose. To protect Caledonia. But what did that mean when the primary threat to Caledonia came from the Crown? What was he supposed to do when the greatest danger to his Kingdom came from the man who ruled it?

His already confused thoughts were muddled all the more by what he had learned of Aislinn Winborne during her time training with him and his soldiers in the circle. He barely knew the Duke of the Southern Marches, having only heard of his reputation for fairhandedness and meeting the needs of his people. But he wasn't sure what to make of his daughter when she had first appeared in the practice yard. He knew she was promised to Marden, a marriage made of politics, which was not uncommon. But he had unfairly assumed that the Lady Winborne was like all the other hangers-on who frequented the royal court in Tintagel, a woman intent on assuming her place next to the King of Caledonia, seeking to enjoy the power and privilege that would come her way as a result of her position. He had discovered quickly that Aislinn Winborne was not what he had expected. Far from it, in fact.

She was honest and straightforward. She treated the soldiers of the Royal Guard with respect. Not as tools to be commanded, but as people to be valued. She drove herself to be the best and expected those working with her to try to do the same. In short, she was a fighter. She was a leader. And she reminded him of his late daughter.

He understood what the Lady Winborne was doing during those training sessions. She was attempting to create allies in a place where she had no friends. Where she was nothing more than a kept person. A pawn to be played in the larger game of Caledonian politics. He had permitted it, because there was a quality that he saw in Lady Winborne that he did not see in Marden Beleron. A quality that he couldn't necessarily describe but knew was essential to serving as a successful monarch. Perhaps it was compassion. Maybe kindness. The right word always seemed to elude him. Nevertheless, not only had she built a following among the Guards who trained with her, but she had also created an ally in him.

And he had failed her. He had not been there when she needed assistance. That thought felt like salt being sprinkled onto an open wound. His allegiance remained to Caledonia, but he understood as well that if he were to remain true to himself, if he were to remain true to his Kingdom, then more drastic action might be required. Because he had deduced that he could not maintain his allegiance to Caledonia if he continued to support Marden Beleron. And he could not be true to himself if he did not assist Aislinn Winborne.

Some might define the conclusion that he had just reached as treason. He thought of it as no more than common sense.

It was then, the Blademaster finally having worked his way through the dilemma that had burdened his soul for the last several months, that Killen Sourban, Captain of the Royal Guard, appeared, striding toward him down the long hallway with an arrogant step that never failed to set Klines' teeth on edge.

"You are a fool, Jurgen," said the cold-eyed Captain, his high-pitched voice difficult to connect to the tall and broad fighter who blocked the Blademaster from continuing down the covered walkway.

"So I've been told by you many times, Killen. Now step aside. I have more important matters to attend to than to waste my time speaking with you."

Sourban ignored the Blademaster, settling in place like a massive boulder coming to rest after rolling down a mountainside.

"Your current business is with me."

The Blademaster stared at Sourban with a look of disdain, his right hand settling onto his belt so that he could draw his sword with greater ease if it proved necessary to do so.

"What business would that be?"

"You threatened the King. I am responsible for his protection. Clearly you don't respect me if you are so blatant in your disregard for the House Beleron. I can't allow you to make a fool of me. An example must be made."

"You have nothing to fear in that regard," replied the Blademaster with some amusement. "You make a fool of yourself quite well on your own."

The Blademaster's words struck the Captain of the Guard like a slap across the face, his cheeks turning a mottled red, his rage barely contained.

"Be careful, Jurgen. You walk a fine line. I will allow you to apologize because of the history between us. If not for that, you would already be dead, bleeding out on the stone we stand upon."

The Blademaster tried not to snort with laughter. Killen was nothing if not unimaginative in terms of how he approached the world. If he couldn't use force or a blade to eliminate a problem, then he was stymied. That was the limit of his strategic thinking. But he was good with a blade. That fact could not be ignored and could be blamed on Klines, who had trained him as a soldier in the Royal Guard.

At first, the Blademaster had taken a liking to Killen. He had shown a skill and a willingness to work that appealed to Klines. But it hadn't been long before Sourban revealed an uglier side that worried the Blademaster. He enjoyed not only beating his opponents, but beating up on them, embarrassing them, seeking to make them appear the fool.

Instead of ending a combat quickly if he could, and he usually could, he would draw it out, often going beyond the bounds of what was acceptable in the practice yard. Sourban took particular pleasure in playing with his training partners, and the number of soldiers with broken bones and often worse injuries increased in relation not to Killen's skill, but to his temper and sadistic nature.

The Blademaster spoke to him about it several times, but with little success. He should have pursued it further, should have done something about it, but Klines had been distracted. Killen had taken an interest in the Blademaster's daughter.

Klines had learned when his daughter was quite young that telling her that she couldn't do something only increased her desire to do exactly that. So he had kept his mouth shut, allowing his daughter to handle Killen's advances as she saw fit.

He was relieved to discover that Arisel had little interest in the hulking soldier, his behavior and personality doing him in from the start. But no matter how many times Arisel rejected Killen's advances, he kept trying. Until one day Killen cornered her in the corridors by the practice yard, demanding to know why she refused him. Taking after her father, Arisel had been blunt and to the point, citing a plethora of reasons for why she had no desire to be with him. He had walked away from her in a rage.

The next day Killen seemed to have forgotten the whole thing, having turned his romantic attentions toward another woman of the court. Klines had assumed that the episode was over. Then a week later his daughter had been found dead. Murdered with the signs of an attempted rape. The constable never discovered who had committed the crime, and Killen had never revealed anything either in word or action that suggested that he was the one responsible, but after that every time Jurgen looked into the large soldier's cold, remorseless eyes he believed that there was a spark in the back that confirmed Klines' suspicions.

Even with the constable's failure to identify the culprit, the Blademaster was more than ready to take matters into his own hands. But he was not a cold-blooded killer. There needed to be some proof linking his suspected felon to the crime. Yet there was none to be found.

Klines thought that he had buried the rage that accompanied the loss of his only daughter when he had been forced to bury Arisel. But apparently not, because it all came back to him in a rush. Today seemed to be the day for him to rethink many of the precepts that he believed. Perhaps it was time to rethink as well how he had responded to the loss of Arisel. Perhaps it was time to follow his heart rather than his head. Killen's next action almost decided it for him.

"Are you listening, old man?" roared the Captain of the Guard. "You will apologize, or you will die by my blade!"

"Is that a promise, Killen?" asked the Blademaster in a tight whisper, his eyes flashing with a dangerous light. "You know, I think you might be right. It might be time to cross swords once again."

"You don't have it in you anymore, old man. You aren't what you used to be with a blade."

"That's your opinion. I would disagree. Shall we see who is right?"

Catching the deadly intent in the Blademaster's eyes, Sourban began to realize that the intimidation that he used to his advantage so frequently elsewhere was having a deleterious impact upon him now. The Blademaster was a thorn in his side, a constant reminder that he had not gained all that he had wanted in his life. But was he ready to challenge him now?

Doubts began to seep into his thoughts, weakening his

resolve. Killen chose to attempt a strategic retreat, still not realizing that he wasn't very good with strategy.

"There is little need for me to challenge you, old man. You aren't long for this world. Not if you continue to impede the King. It's foolish to act with him as you do. You are not his equal. You are his servant. Your sole task is to obey. He has only so much patience, so if you continue to push, he will push back."

The Blademaster ignored the threat, his hand now resting comfortably on the hilt of his sword.

"You can always hope, Killen," replied Jurgen with a wicked smile. "You need to remember as well that I also have only so much patience, and right now you're testing it. If you continue to push, you might get what you want sooner than you think." The Blademaster then stepped in close to the mountain of a man, his eyes flinty, his words as hard as the stone of the floor. "Just make sure that you're ready. Though you talk a good game, your blade is lacking. You may be the Captain of the Guard, but remember. I am the Blademaster."

8

NOTHING VENTURED

Jerad stood at the very edge of the wood, which extended for several leagues to his east and west. The forest wasn't very wide, the farmers having cut back along the edges of the grove to expand their fields, but what remained was dense with few trails. It was exactly the kind of hiding spot that the Sergeant of the Guard had hoped to find. A glimpse of the capital, an open view in all directions so that they would receive plenty of warning if an armed force came toward them, and land in front if they chose to fight, and several ways to escape through the forest if they chose not to. The question was for how long this many companies of the Battersea Guard could remain undetected this close to the Caledonian capital.

The gloom of the early morning hung over the countryside, a land of rolling hills and small valleys that wove their way toward a bluff upon which the city of Tintagel rose. Still just a dark smudge until the sun made its appearance in the east, the high wall upon which a few faint torches could be seen the only distinguishing feature at this distance of a few leagues. All was quiet, just a few plumes of smoke rising into the sky from the chimneys of the farmsteads dotting the landscape, no one on the roads, and, most important, no Royal Guard patrols heading to the south.

"You have nothing to fear," said Rafia, the wild-haired Magus seemingly reading his thoughts. "No one knows that we are here. No one will know unless we give ourselves away."

Jerad nodded, satisfied by her response because he knew her skill. Still, he was worried. If all went to plan, they would achieve their goal with barely any bloodshed. But then again, when did anything ever go according to plan?

"That will be the trick, won't it?" mused Jerad.

The soldiers of the Southern Marches had made camp deep within the forest. No fires were permitted. Noise was to be kept to a minimum. Several picket lines had been established to prevent any surprises and offer a defense in depth. And so far, all was well. Yet Jerad still felt uneasy. He thought that King Beleron would have expanded his patrols upon taking the Duke of the Southern Marches, worried that an attempt to rescue his prisoner might be made, but apparently not. Then again, perhaps he was giving the King of Caledonia too much credit.

The Sergeant, lacking his usual smile, turned and walked away from the fringe of the wood, Rafia staying at his shoulder.

"No need to look so grim, Jerad," said Rafia, who had used the Talent to blend the Battersea Guard into the woodland, creating a shield of magic that reflected what anyone who looked at the forest should see rather than what was actually there. "To anyone on the outside, it will simply appear to be a forest. And if someone actually enters the grove and comes toward you, the magic that I have set will attempt to turn them in a different direction, and they will believe that it is their own idea to do so. Just remember, there are no guarantees. Someone could stumble across the boundary that I've established, and if they do and the magic doesn't turn them, they will see you and your soldiers. You can't permit that."

"I understand, Magus. Have no fear. If someone wanders where they shouldn't, we will handle matters appropriately."

As they continued deeper within the forest, Jerad's eyes flicked to both sides, picking out where he had set the sentries. He nodded to himself, pleased. The soldiers were focused, alert, and well hidden. No one would catch sight of them unless the Guards revealed themselves, and if they did, it would be for one reason only.

"Don't kill anyone if you can avoid it," Rafia said. "Better to let the magic do the work for you."

"Of course, Magus," said Jerad, who finally smiled when he stepped into the large clearing that the Battersea Guard had made their own. The Magus certainly did seem to have the capacity to track his thoughts. He wove his way through the camp before coming to a stop near the center, where Tarin was conversing with several soldiers and confirming the duty schedule for the day. "But the safety of the Guard must and will come first," he continued, "and we must ensure that you, Sirius, and Bryen have the time that you need to accomplish your tasks in Tintagel. We will do what is necessary to make that happen."

"I understand, and I agree," said Rafia. "Just keep your soldiers back from the border of the shield and all should be well." The Magus scanned the busy encampment, her eyes finally coming to rest on her two traveling partners. Sirius sat on a log finishing a quick breakfast of bread and ham, clearly enjoying his sandwich. Bryen calmly stood near him, balancing himself against his double-bladed spear. As always, his grey, guileless eyes hid whatever the Protector might be thinking. "Now if you'll excuse me, young man, I'm going to grab a bite to eat before we head for the capital."

Jerad nodded, giving the Magus a slight bow of respect, before walking across the campsite and then into the woods, wanting to check the soldiers on the south side. He would then work his way around the pickets in a slow circle, just to make sure that all was as it should be, before breaking his own fast.

"Did you get me one as well?" asked Rafia, nodding toward the sandwich that Sirius was about to finish.

"I didn't know that you were hungry," protested Sirius between bites. "I'm sure that there's more to be had. We just need to find the quartermaster."

Before Rafia could let loose a string of curses because of Sirius' perceived lack of manners, Bryen pulled a bundle out from his pack and handed it to her.

"I wasn't sure when you'd be back, so I asked for an extra one for you."

Rafia smiled dazzlingly at Bryen as she unwrapped the savory package, and then took a bite.

"Thank you, my boy. You certainly do have better manners than this one."

"I would have gotten you a sandwich if you had asked me," protested Sirius. "But you didn't ask."

"Why should I need to ask? Why didn't you simply assume that I would want something to eat this morning as well? We won't be in Tintagel until early afternoon. Of course I'm going to want to eat something before I go."

"My mind was on other things," said Sirius, irritated by the direction the conversation was taking.

"From what I can tell the only thing that your mind was focused on this morning was stuffing your face."

Bryen closed his eyes, allowing the escalating argument between the two Magii to wash over him. How these two ever survived an intimate relationship for several decades, he couldn't understand. Using the trick that Declan had taught him to prepare for his combats in the Pit, Bryen centered himself, blocking out everything else that was going on around him. A calm settled over him that allowed for greater clarity of thought, something that had been lost to him during the last few days as he experienced a jumble of emotions triggered by several questions that circulated through his mind.

Would the strategy that he, Rafia, Sirius, and Tarin put together allow them to achieve their goal of freeing Duke Winborne and Aislinn? Would he have the chance to test his skills against the King? Assuming that he was able to reach the gladiators without incident, how would they respond to his proposal? What would Declan think? How would Aislinn react if he saw her again? All those questions and so many more with no answers as they approached Tintagel. Curiously, the possibility of leading a revolt against the Crown paled in comparison to his worry regarding the King's Advisor.

Why that was the case, he didn't know. Tetric was the cause of many of their current troubles, having taken the Duke, which had then set off a series of connected events, the most prominent being Aislinn's decision to follow her father with the hope of finding some way to release him. But Tetric had been a troubling presence for Bryen ever since his duel with Stil Sheldgard, the former Champion of Sharston. Like everyone else who had watched that combat from the royal box, Tetric had been shocked when Bryen had won and turned the white sand red with the Champion's blood.

Bryen knew the eye-opening result had captured Tetric's interest, the King's Advisor intrigued by the Volkun's success. Thinking about it now, Bryen could understand why. In speaking with Declan after the fight, they had both agreed that the Champion had been aided in some very remarkable ways that gave the imposing brute some distinct advantages. Such as the fact that what should have been a deep slash across the man's belly that released his guts turned out to be no more than a shallow cut. Or that despite the multiple strikes with which Bryen had hit his adversary, shredding the man's leather armor, the blows had little effect upon him. Further, the musclebound fighter was faster and had greater stamina than any warrior could legitimately hope to have. Until, that is, Bryen had unleashed unconsciously the Talent flowing within his veins, his Talent-infused blade destroying whatever sorcery had been embodied within the champion.

His and Declan's suspicions were confirmed when Tetric appeared in the practice yard the next day, the King's Advisor amazed that most of the wounds that Bryen had suffered during the bout had healed already. Upon that discovery, the next few days had been a never-ending series of tests, Tetric seeking to figure out how the Volkun had killed the Champion, and because of his interest both Bryen and Declan assuming that the King's Advisor was the one who had somehow imbued the man with the unique abilities that had allowed him to fight unharmed and undefeated for seven years.

As each day passed, Tetric had grown more and more frustrated. The King's Advisor likely suspected why Bryen could heal so quickly and why he had succeeded against a man who could not be killed with a standard steel blade. But he could find no evidence to support his conclusions. And then some other matter or scheme had seized the attention of the King's Advisor, and he had not returned to the Pit, Bryen not meeting Tetric again until the Advisor visited Battersea after the gladiator had become Aislinn's Protector.

Bryen always wondered why Tetric had never discovered that he could use the Talent. How had he hidden his ability from the Advisor? Did it involve belief, or rather the lack thereof, in that Bryen had never guessed that he could apply the natural magic of the world? Had he secreted his ability in the Talent for so long, even from himself, that Tetric couldn't identify it, the Talent buried so deeply that it only could be revealed through more consistent and conscious use? Or was it something else entirely? He remembered his last conversation with Tetric in the Broken Citadel before he had snuck off to the Aeyrie with Aislinn and Sirius.

"I sense a strength within you, but I don't know what it is. There's something not quite right about you, boy."

"So I've been told," Bryen had replied. "Many times." Tetric hadn't appreciated his attempt at humor.

Bryen doubted that Tetric's interest in him had diminished, as had been made plain during their time together in the capital of the Southern Marches. But then again, perhaps Bryen's concerns were misplaced. He would be entering Tintagel with two Magii at his side who could more than hold their own against anything the King's Advisor threw at them, and thanks to his training with them, now he could do so as well. Now that Bryen understood more about himself, if Tetric still wanted to explore what was off about him, he was more than happy to share, although he doubted that the King's Advisor would enjoy the experience.

"How do you put up with this?"

Bryen opened his eyes, taking a moment to come back to himself and confirm where he was. Tarin Tentillin stood next to him, observing the verbal sparring that continued between the two Magii.

"You get used to it," said Bryen. "They usually tire themselves out after about ten minutes or so."

"Much like a screaming toddler," nodded Tarin.

"That I wouldn't know."

"Perhaps someday you will, Protector," chuckled Tarin.

"I usually don't think so far ahead, Tarin."

"I can understand why," replied the Captain.

As he and Bryen started to walk toward the northern boundary of the camp, Sirius and Rafia trailed after them, Rafia finishing the last few bites of her sandwich, the argument between the two Magii having settled into a series of grumbles and grunts that apparently still served to irritate the both of them. But at least they were quieter now as they prepared to leave the grove and make for the road that would take them to Tintagel.

"So just let me confirm what we're about," said Tarin. "Since I rarely engage in treason."

"Of course," replied Bryen, feeling magnanimous as his mood shifted. The anticipation of what he was about to do had ignited his fears and his worries. Now that he was finally on the move, that unsettling feeling of anticipation had been replaced by a sense of purpose. His concerns had begun to melt away as his mind shifted to what he needed to accomplish during the next few days.

"You need to connect with Duke Winborne and the Lady Aislinn, without anyone the wiser, in a city swarming with the Royal Guard."

"Yes."

"You need to distract the King and Tetric so that you can help the Duke and his daughter escape."

"Yes."

"And just to make things easier, while achieving those two objectives, you also want to free the gladiators from the Colosseum and use that uprising as the distraction that you need to get the Duke and his daughter out of the city."

"Yes, that's right."

"And if all goes well, you'll also attempt to topple a royal line that's ruled for three hundred years."

"Yes, that about sums it up."

Tarin just nodded his head, his grin showing his amusement. "Simple."

"Simple."

"While in the Pit, I think that you may have been hit one too many times in the head, lad. Your sense of reality is leaving you."

"Probably," replied Bryen. "But nothing ventured, nothing gained."

"Another of Declan's favorite sayings?" asked Rafia, who had been listening to Tarin and Bryen's conversation now that her argument with Sirius had sputtered to a close.

"How did you know?" Bryen asked.

Rafia laughed throatily. "Oh, I am really looking forward to meeting the Master of the Gladiators."

The small group fell into silence as they approached the reflective shield that Rafia had constructed. The two Magii walked through first, the only way to tell that they had breached the barrier the slight shimmering that was revealed when they disturbed the magical deception while passing through.

"Protector," called Tarin.

Bryen turned right before he walked through as well, looking at Tarin with a question in his eyes.

"I'll see you on the other side," said the Captain of the Guard.

Bryen smiled and nodded. "I'll see you on the other side."

9

———

FOREGONE CONCLUSION

The lavish corner suite on the highest floor in the Tintagel Palace had once belonged to Corinthus Beleron, the former King of Caledonia, serving as his living quarters and private office. Upon the monarch's death, his son, Marden, had planned on making his father's rooms his own, desperate to take on the mantle of power and the associated trappings and privileges that he believed he so thoroughly deserved. The same day his father had died, Marden had sent workers into the suite to knock down all the walls and create a massive, open space. It wasn't a fear of assassination that guided his decisions. No, it was his nighttime proclivities and voyeuristic tendencies which demanded it.

The new King had lasted less than a night in his new, more expansive chamber, bursting out from behind the doors in the early morning hours and raving that the spirit of his father had visited him, claiming that he had been murdered and ordering his son to ensure that justice be done. Whether Marden Beleron spoke the truth and actually had been haunted by his father's ghost, or it was the result of partaking in too much of the milk of the poppy, no one in Tintagel Palace could say for sure. It was an old keep, first constructed more than a thousand years before, and looking back at the bloody and often treacherous history of Caledonia, it would not be surprising if, in fact, spirits wandered the halls.

Regardless, Marden had demonstrated little desire to spend time with his father when the old man was alive, even less so after the old King died. So the new monarch had returned that same morning to his own quarters on the far side of the keep, more than a quarter mile away from where he had discovered his father's ghost.

Marden's misfortune had proved a boon to Tetric, who was more than happy to make the rebuilt chamber his own, the larger space giving him an opportunity to expand his experiments and other work. With night having fallen and just a few burning candles placed in the sconces along the walls, the huge room was barely any brighter than the darkness that had settled over the city, shadows dancing across the walls as a slight breeze found its way through the few open windows.

In many ways, the large chamber was very similar to the one that Sirius had created for himself in the Broken Citadel. Almost every bit of available space was covered. Books, scrolls, and tomes were scattered across shelves, chairs, and tables, and once those surfaces were smothered, piles of texts and paper had appeared on the floor. For those resources most important to Tetric's current projects, he had pushed two tables together in the very center of the room.

Tetric blamed Sirius for many things, but at least he gave the annoying Magus credit where credit was due, particularly with respect to the influence Sirius had exercised on Tetric regarding how he approached his work. Determined. Focused. Driven. Always to the distraction of all else. It was the first trait that Sirius had instilled within him when the King's Advisor had begun training with the Magus. Yet as the dark of the night became deeper, many of the candles burning down to their stubs, the razor-sharp concentration so critical to Tetric's success escaped him. The bald-pated, stick-thin Advisor stood near the center of the chamber, his eyes open but seeing little, his mind a kaleidoscope of disconnected thoughts. He was distracted, but why that was the case eluded him. And he hated that.

Tetric had always savored his ability to master his surroundings, his fastidious and infuriating mentor teaching him that control over your environment was the starting point for gaining control over all else. And since that lesson, for Tetric it had been all about control. Control over himself first and foremost. Control over others his overarching objective. In every aspect of his life, he wanted to exercise control.

But he had found that to be more and more difficult the last few months. He didn't feel as if he was exercising much control over anything in his life. Rather, it seemed that something was exercising control over him. Tetric also realized that during this time he had begun to change. In the beginning, he barely noticed it. But during the last few weeks tiny alterations in his personality had become more prominent, more fixed, more dominant, and worryingly so.

Tetric reveled in the power that he had developed and learned on his own. He had acquired it through hard work, dangerous work, as he took chances and cut corners that others with his skill and background refused to do. That, in itself, had made the risks that he had assumed all the more exciting, and though he had grown in power to a level where few in the Order of the Magii could challenge him, he was not satisfied. He was never satisfied. Never fulfilled. No matter how much power he had, he always wanted more. No matter the work required. No matter the hazard. No matter the cost.

Which was why he found the sinister, tantalizing power given to him by his ally even more enticing. More intoxicating. More seductive. It was a power that he believed no one else in

Caledonia had or could make use of. At least no one who was human. Initially, his worries over the risk scarcely troubled him, his focus instead on learning the gift bestowed upon him. But as he began to wield the power, he became more concerned. He had discovered that his efforts at controlling this power were more difficult than he had expected. In fact, he suspected that rather than him mastering the power, the power was instead mastering him.

That belief seemed strange to him, even foolish. But he knew in his heart that he was right. He was finding it harder and harder to control the Dark Magic circulating within him, the Curse instead steering his thoughts and his decisions. So all he could conclude was that the Dark Magic was leading him down a specific path of its own choosing. And despite his desire to exercise control in all things, in this he had no control.

He first noticed it while he was in Battersea. He had been applying as much pressure as he could to the Duke of the Southern Marches, trying to convince the arrogant fool to allow his daughter to return with him to Tintagel. It was a foregone conclusion, the Duke the only one yet to realize it.

Tetric knew that he should have stayed in the backwater city and continued to cajole the Duke, but something invaded his thoughts, a strange urging that he didn't understand, and he wound up taking Killen Sourban and the soldiers of the Royal Guard through the Waste to the Aeyrie.

Tetric felt compelled to break into the Aeyrie even though he had failed when he had attempted to do just that more than a decade before. At that time, two Magii were charged with protecting the tower.

What were the names of those two Magii? His mind fixated on that question for just a second. He should know, shouldn't he? He had been in the Order the same time that they were. In fact, he had known them well. But he was having a hard time recalling who they were. He was certain that they were husband and wife.

It didn't matter now. He had the Ghoules kill them when they left the Aeyrie for Tintagel.

For several seconds he forgot what he had been thinking about, then it came back to him, though the effort to regain command over his own mind was like looking for a light through a dense fog. And then unbidden flashes of memories of him and his brothers drifted through his consciousness. Why these remembrances?

Shaking his head to clear it, Tetric's mind returned to his memory of the Aeyrie. He had tried to enter as he had so many times before when he was a member of the Order, placing his hand on the translucent stone exactly where the hidden door was located, but nothing happened. He had tried again, thinking that perhaps he had been doing something wrong since it had been so long since he had been there. Still no success. The door wouldn't reveal itself. Again and again he tried, each time with no success. And each time he failed his anger grew.

Not knowing what else to do, and his fury threatening to get the better of him, Tetric had called upon his Dark Magic. The Aeyrie, unresponsive for so long, the stone dormant and silent, had responded immediately to the Curse. Refusing to accept Tetric and recognizing what the former Magus had become, the spire crackled with an energy that forced Tetric to remove his hand, as he feared that the power surging across the stone would scour the skin from his palm. The Aeyrie then began to change color, pulsing a bright white that sizzled with the power coursing across its surface.

Tetric stepped back from the spire. It wasn't until he was at the very edge of the glade that the blinding energy that protected the Aeyrie winked out, the stone returning to its original state. Tetric had been astounded, never knowing the

Aeyrie had such a capacity. He considered approaching the spire once again. But for what purpose? Once he was a Magus, but no more, and somehow the Aeyrie knew that and had responded accordingly, seeking to protect itself.

Tetric remembered that he had feared then as he did now what would happen if the Ghoule Overlord didn't get what he demanded. But in that very moment he feared even more the possibility that his attempt to enter the Aeyrie and the tower's surprising response had sent a warning to the members of the Order. Although he welcomed the chance to challenge Sirius, his reckoning with his former mentor past due, he couldn't put his personal desires above those of his master, at least not yet. So he had returned to Battersea frustrated and angry, resigned to playing out the stratagem that he had initiated and that he hoped would in the end allow him to gain the artifact he so desperately needed.

Just as quickly as that memory surfaced, it disappeared, his mind once again a jumble of disparate recollections. Yet he couldn't be certain that these remembrances were his own. Trying desperately to exercise some type of command over himself, he tried to think back to when he was a child, learning for the first time how to employ the Talent. Nothing. Then he tried to recall his training with Sirius, which had been a major part of his life for years. But again, nothing. No matter what he tried to recall from earlier in his life, it was all missing. Those reminiscences once had been so clear. So vivid. So important to him. And now they were simply gone.

Tetric felt a headache coming on, a more frequent occurrence during the last few months. Then a memory settled within him, but he knew instantly that this impression wasn't his own. He stood atop one of the mile-high sandstone pillars in the Trench, the dark rock covered in green moss and a purple and white heather, a thick fog blocking his view to the ground, peaks of the many other spires surrounding the one he stood on poking through the clouds. He knew with an absolute certainty that he had never been here before. He had never set foot in the Trench. But he knew as well without a doubt where he was, and strangely, the remote location seemed very familiar to him.

He looked down into a bowl-shaped depression that was the Sanctuary. Six pedestals were arranged in a hexagonal pattern around the hollow, six of the Seven Stones -- emerald, ruby, black opal, white pearl, sapphire, jade -- shining brightly from their positions atop their pedestals, the energy contained within the Stones blasting up into the sky and then out to the east and west to form the Weir. A seventh pedestal, placed in the center of the arrangement, held the Seventh Stone, a fist-sized diamond that pulsed with a blinding white light and then flashed with a black darker than the night every few seconds.

He had never been here before. He had never set foot in the Trench, much less within the Sanctuary. But with a frightening clarity he also understood that everything that he was looking at was accurate. That if he actually did visit this place, this is what he would see. This was where the Ten Magii had sacrificed themselves in order to construct the Weir.

As he stared at the platform upon which the Seventh Stone sat, a craving surged within him. The desire to take the Seventh Stone for his own. An urging that he was powerless against. He imagined stepping down into the manmade crater and reaching out with his hand to grasp the blazing diamond. But rather than feeling a burst of pleasure at attaining the artifact, he recoiled in horror. The hand that had grabbed for the Seventh Stone wasn't his hand. It was a scaled claw of mottled green, the four fingers more like talons, capable of tearing through flesh.

For a fleeting moment he enjoyed a surprising lucidity that had been all too rare since he had returned to Tintagel from Battersea. With a sickening certainty, Tetric realized that he wasn't seeing the world through his own eyes anymore. It was as if he was becoming this other creature, or rather this other creature was becoming him, and that realization terrified him. Because there was only one beast with the power to do what was happening to him, only one monster with the skill and ability to use him in the way that he was being used.

He stared out the window, needing the fresh air and catching the glint of the moonlight off the Colosseum, the structure rising at the very end of the mile-long promenade that Marden was constructing to connect the stadium to the Palace. When he finally looked away, his thoughts became a jumble once again. He couldn't focus. He couldn't think. He couldn't even remember what had run through his mind just seconds before. He couldn't remember why he was there. He couldn't remember what he was doing. And why had he been so afraid? What had worried him so?

A painful cold blasted through Tetric's chamber, shaking him from the prison of his own mind and sending him into a fit of uncontrollable shivering that continued long after the icy temperature had dissipated. Hearing a hiss at his back, Tetric realized that he was no longer alone. Bowing his head in subservience, the King's Advisor faced the huge beast who had walked out of a portal of swirling black mist. The Ghoule Overlord, the creature who sought to conquer the Kingdom, who desired nothing more than to release his Legions upon the humans of Caledonia, had appeared right in front of the former Magus.

"Master, how did you do that?" asked Tetric, shocked by the power employed by the Ghoule Overlord to make his unexpected appearance in the Advisor's private chamber. "The power required to connect two places separated by several hundred leagues ... I didn't know it was even possible."

"Anything is possible, Tetric ... for me."

The words came out as a hiss, the Ghoule Overlord struggling with several of the syllables required to speak the common tongue. But most of what the Overlord said was clear enough for Tetric to understand his Master's meaning.

"I did not expect you here, Master," said Tetric, trying to recover quickly from his initial surprise, his shivering, originally brought on by the biting cold exuded by the Dark Magic used to create the portal and having continued because of his fear of this monster, finally having abated. "All is going well. The King will take his bride in just days. I don't understand why you take such a risk when our plans move rapidly to completion."

"That is not why I am here, Tetric."

The Ghoule Overlord's black eyes blazed with a disturbing energy, drawing Tetric in, not allowing him to look away.

"What do you mean?"

"I have given you more than you deserve, Tetric, and yet progress has been slow. Scarcely detectable. I have given you more power than I have ever given any other human. And still ... nothing. You have not yet gained what I seek. What I need. What I require."

"It is only a matter of time, Master," replied Tetric. "I promise you that." Then the former Magus tried to shift the direction of their conversation, knowing that if his Master continued down the current path, it would place him in a poor light. "Is it wise for you to be here, Master? If you are discovered, everything that we've worked toward could be for naught."

Tetric's nervousness had increased with each passing second, not only because of the unanticipated appearance of the Ghoule Overlord, but also because of the consequences if they were discovered together. None of the soldiers of the Royal Guard, even those pledged to him, would look kindly on his alliance with the Ghoules.

"You have nothing to fear, Tetric. No one will discover us. No one will know that I am here."

"Why are you here, Master? As I said, all is going well. Our stratagem will bear results shortly. Of that I have no doubt."

The Ghoule Overlord shook his head sadly, then chuckled softly, revealing his sharp teeth.

"Your efforts to find the Seventh Stone have failed, Tetric. You have wasted time. You have wasted effort. We have gained nothing."

"How could they have failed?" demanded Tetric, some part of his former fiery self still trying to break free from the chains that had been forming around him ever since he had accepted so greedily the Dark Magic given to him by his Master. "Everything is moving into place as it should. It's only a matter of time before we attain what we want."

"You were a fool to try to break into the Aeyrie. The Magii know what you did. They know what you want. You alerted them and in so doing confirmed for them our goal."

"They knew already," protested Tetric. "To think otherwise you'd be a fool."

"Are you calling me a fool, Tetric?" asked the Ghoule Overlord, his voice having gone dangerously quiet.

"No. No." Tetric replied quickly, a quiver of fear in his voice. He realized that with just a few thoughtless words he had trod on dangerous ground. "Of course not, Master. I didn't mean any disrespect. I was simply stating a fact."

"Why do you think that I gave you the black collar so that you could take the Duke of the Southern Marches from his province?"

"To further Marden's plans," Tetric replied, not understanding the purpose of the question. "Marden gaining more power at the expense of the other Duchies aids your plans as well."

"To a certain extent, yes. But there was more to it than that.

A more subtle purpose. Do you know that purpose, Tetric? You, someone supposedly so skilled in deception and subterfuge, must have figured it out by now."

Tetric grimaced, reluctant to admit his lack of understanding but having no choice but to reveal the truth. To not do so, to lie to his Master, would have severe consequences.

"No, I don't know," he mumbled.

"Come now, Tetric. You pride yourself on your intelligence. On being smarter than everyone else, including the Magii who expelled you from their Order for your many transgressions. You must have some idea why."

"No, I don't know," he said again, the words leaving an ashen taste because they acknowledged his own failure.

"Because I saw the looks shared between the boy Protector and his charge, the Duke's daughter."

"Why is that important? And how did you see?"

"Because I knew, looking through your eyes, that the boy Protector would come for her."

"How could you know that?" asked Tetric, but then the gravity of his Master's words struck him. He was beginning to understand what was happening to him. He should have realized sooner. But he had ignored it, thinking that it might result from his use of Dark Magic. He knew now that he had been wrong. Wrong about so many things. And he feared that the cost for all that had been given to him was about to come due. "How could you see that?"

"Because I know everything that you are thinking. Your mind is mine. I see everything through your eyes. What's more, what you fail to comprehend, I understand. The Protector is coming. There is no need to search for the Seventh Stone, Tetric. The Seventh Stone is coming to us."

"The girl's Protector has the Seventh Stone?" If that was the case, and the Protector was indeed on his way to Tintagel, that would certainly simplify his task.

"Not quite, Tetric," said the Ghoule Overlord, shaking his head to register his disappointment with the King's Advisor. "Rather, the boy Protector is the Seventh Stone."

"How is that even possible?" demanded Tetric, momentarily stunned by what his Master had just revealed.

"I must admit, I do not know. But I know what I can sense. I know what the Seventh Stone has become, what the boy has become. The two are one. So instead of continuing to search for the Seventh Stone, I will allow the Seventh Stone to come to me."

"I'll be ready for the boy," Tetric nodded, trying to reclaim his role in the proceedings. "I'll make sure that I take him, take the Seventh Stone. I promise you, Master, he will not escape."

"Of that I have no doubt," replied the Ghoule Overlord, a wicked grin twisting the corners of his mouth, his forked tongue flicking out and across his serrated teeth several times. "It is a critical task, one that can't be left to you. You have failed me too many times already, so I cannot take the risk that you will fail me again. This is a task that only I can manage."

"You?" asked Tetric, failing to keep the incredulity from his voice. "But you can't do anything here. You'd be found out ..."

"But I can," interrupted the Ghoule Overlord. "As I said, I see and hear all through you. We are connected in a way that you never considered could be possible, that you can't comprehend. We were two. We were separate. But just like the boy Protector and the Seventh Stone, you and I will become one."

Reaching out with the speed of a striking snake, the Ghoule Overlord grasped Tetric's head with a large claw, holding the human in place. Although Tetric struggled to break free, he didn't stand a chance, his efforts barely affecting the creature as the huge Ghoule called on his Dark Magic, the black mist forming above the top of his staff of black ash, then spinning faster and faster as it burst forth from the black diamond set in the wood, forming a fog darker than the night, the cloud of evil submerging both the Ghoule Overlord and his captive. For several minutes the jet-black mist twisted around the chamber, hiding what occurred within it. And then just as quickly as it had formed, the murk dissipated, revealing only Tetric. The Ghoule Overlord had disappeared. Or rather the beast remained, but his body was gone.

The Ghoule Overlord extended his arms to the side and then reached for the ceiling, stretching his limbs as if he was trying to work out the kinks from a long sleep, moving his body for the first time in years. He was new to this weak, human shell, and he knew that it would take time to adjust. Nodding in satisfaction, his staff held tightly in his hand, the Ghoule Overlord walked to the open window and looked down upon the city. Tetric appeared to be no different than before, but a new intelligence sparked in the back of his eyes, a predatory intelligence, an inhuman intelligence.

For just a second, a growl of irritation escaped the figure standing by the open window. The former Magus was making one last attempt to escape his prison, but the Ghoule Overlord crushed it mercilessly. Tetric was still there, or at least his essence was, locked away in the back of the Ghoule Overlord's mind. The former Magus was screaming in rage, stuck in a void with nowhere to go, no way to escape, no way to warn others of his plight. His Master had completed what he had started months before, imprinting Tetric with his own thoughts and memories, desires and wants, preparing the way for this final act as the Ghoule Overlord claimed Tetric's body for his own.

The Ghoule Overlord looked once again at the city stretching out before him. He would pull back his Ghoules and allow the Protector to come here. He would permit the Seventh Stone to come to him. Then he would take the Protector. And once he had the boy, he would draw the Seventh Stone from him. That task done, he would take his time with the boy. He would enjoy eating the Protector's flesh, gnawing on his bones, gaining some retribution for all of the difficulties this one, irritating human had caused for so many of his Ghoules.

Even so, this Protector was a worthy opponent, so he would honor him. He would make a bone knife of this one, a weapon to symbolize the effort that he had expended to locate what he and his Ghoules needed so desperately. Because once he finally gained the Seventh Stone, Caledonia was doomed. The Ghoule Overlord would destroy the Weir. He would release his Legions. He would finish what he had started a thousand years before. And he would wipe the descendants of that cursed Arick Winborne from the Kingdom.

10

LAY OF THE LAND

"It seems that all the information that we've gathered on our travels west has been accurate," said Rafia.

She, Sirius, and Bryen walked at a steady gait toward the western approach to Tintagel and the one the farthest away from the Palace. The Traitor's Gate had been named for Aldridge Roo, a lord from the western coast who had led an uprising against the Crown more than five hundred years before. His attempted overthrow of the ruler at that time had failed miserably, and it was through that gate that Roo had first been brought into the city and then paraded through its many neighborhoods until his ignominious end at the Palace, his normal finery replaced by a noose around his neck. Rafia hoped that their taking the same route as Roo didn't bode ill since they had much the same in mind now as did the long dead lord from the west.

She forced that momentary concern from her mind, turning her attention to more immediate matters. Rafia had been away for so long, and rarely visited the Caledonian capital to begin with, that she doubted that anyone would recognize her. But she couldn't say the same of Sirius, who visited on a more regular basis, and of course Bryen, the Protector having spent ten years of his life on the white sand. So in an attempt to maintain their secrecy, they all wore hooded cloaks to hide their faces and Bryen had broken down his very obvious and distinctive double-bladed spear into its component pieces, the two blades now strapped across his back in leather scabbards.

"I can't say that I'm surprised," said Sirius, the Magus regularly blowing out of the way with puffs of air the long wisps of hair his hood crushed down onto his head. The unkempt mess threatened to cover his eyes, and he was quickly becoming annoyed. "But I am surprised that the pace of decay in the capital has accelerated so quickly in just the last few months."

"It's to be expected," replied Rafia. "If Tetric is pulling Marden's strings as we suspect, then it was inevitable."

During their travels along the Eastern River and then north toward Tintagel, Tarin had sent out scouts to every village and hamlet they came across so that they could get a better lay of the land, always making sure that the Battersea Guard remained out of sight. The Captain of the Guard had worried that they'd be caught against the riverbank by one of the larger patrols conducted by the Royal Guard as soon as they had left the Southern Marches. But much to his surprise, no one living in that part of the Kingdom had seen a patrol that far from the capital in months. Apparently, the Royal Guard was focused almost entirely on maintaining order in Tintagel.

Not unexpectedly, that development had led to an angry undercurrent in the countryside, townsfolk and farmers becoming increasingly worried because of the stories circulating about Ghoules coming out of the Shattered Peaks and the Northern Spine, terrorizing villages and towns not only in the east, but also as far west as the settlements just south of the Dark Forest and even within a few leagues of the capital.

To make matters worse, conditions continued to deteriorate in Tintagel. Food was becoming scarcer because of farmers' unwillingness to risk the roads without the protection of the Royal Guard. Garbage and other filth were piling up in the alleys as the Crown had stopped paying its contractors. With the increasing risk of disease, many of the better off merchants and craftspeople were leaving the city in droves for the villages to the south that dotted the Bay of the Dead. And rather than address the growing problems by providing much-needed services to the populace, Marden instead had increased the number of days during the week that the gladiatorial games would be hosted, meaning more combats and more opportunities to distract from the rising threats to life and livelihood both within and outside of Tintagel.

The scouts had confirmed that and more in a village just two days' ride from Tintagel. The Royal Guard no longer patrolled more than a league beyond the capital, leaving the villages, towns, and farmsteads to fend for themselves. The Guard's concern was no longer keeping the roads safe and protecting all the people of Caledonia, but rather dealing with the rumblings of unrest within the city, having already stepped in several times in the last few weeks to quash a handful of riots that had broken out near the silos that stored the grain and other staples that so many citizens of Tintagel relied on for survival.

What Tarin and the others learned didn't surprise them, but it did leave them all both disturbed and hopeful. They were unsettled that life in the capital had worsened so drastically so quickly, but it also suggested that the Protector's mad idea might not be so mad after all.

Bryen and his companions had worried that the information they had gathered outside of Tintagel might be overblown, a common occurrence when stories were shared across cups of ale and beer, but Bryen realized as he, Rafia, and Sirius entered the capital that, if anything, the stories probably were too understated in their talk of dissent and discord. With the charged atmosphere within the walls, it didn't seem that it would take much to set off a conflagration that could lay waste to most of the city.

"Quiet," whispered Bryen, who had kept his own counsel as the two Magii continued to discuss all that Tarin and his scouts had discovered, their conversation becoming more animated. "Let's try not to draw attention to ourselves before we even walk through the gate."

The Magii thought initially to rebuke the Protector for interrupting them, but then they sensed it too. The unease and disquiet that hung over the city, a miasma of fear and worry. The sense that something big was about to happen, something dangerous and potentially explosive. So they kept their mouths shut and their heads down as they walked through the Traitor's Gate and past the Royal Guard. The few dozen soldiers stationed there were quiet, almost unnaturally so, their heads on a swivel and their eyes scanning around them as if they expected to be attacked at any moment.

And perhaps there was cause for their concern, as the residents of Tintagel stared at the armed men sullenly, exhibiting as much distrust toward the soldiers as the men at arms displayed toward them. It was as if the people of the city were seeking to blame someone for their escalating problems, and with the King hidden away in his Palace, their ire was turning toward the City Watch and the Royal Guard, the most obvious and accessible representatives of the Crown.

Bryen, Rafia, and Sirius headed deeper into the city with the few other travelers walking with them, as there were clearly more people leaving the city than entering. The farther they went into the capital, the quieter and more subdued it became. The many markets in the squares had disappeared and with them the vibrancy and energy that had infused the metropolis. The stalls common to the larger boulevards were vacant and many of the shops boarded up. When they passed the smaller streets and alleys, they not only saw but also smelled the squalor of the desperate and the destitute. Along the way more and more soldiers of the Royal Guard appeared, patrolling the main streets and manning checkpoints at key avenues and in the squares that used to be home to the merchants and tradespeople.

"Are you sure about this?" asked Rafia. "It might not be worth the risk."

"We should be fine," replied Bryen, acknowledging the Magus' worry. They were still several blocks away, but he could already hear the noise emanating from the Colosseum created by thousands of people stuffed onto wooden bleachers, the arena constructed of gleaming white stone becoming larger with every step that he took. "No one will notice us with the combats taking place today, and it will give us a chance to see if anything has changed with respect to the workings of the Colosseum. If not, then our plan just might work."

"And if circumstances have changed?" asked Sirius, who knew from past experience that things rarely stayed the same no matter how much you hoped that they would.

Bryen gave the old Magus a grin and a quirk of his eyebrows. "Then we adjust and do what we can with what we have available to us. No one said that this was going to be easy."

Having reached the main thoroughfare that led to the Colosseum, they could hear the shouts of the spectators more distinctly, the crescendo rising up and out of the open-aired arena. The presence of the Royal Guard was even more obvious here with soldiers spaced evenly around the structure. Leading away from the Colosseum were the beginnings of new construction that extended down the long promenade toward the Corinthian Palace. Just as they had been told, good King Beleron was building a monument to his family and himself rather than providing the basic services required by those living in the large city.

After paying the fee, which had increased since Bryen had last fought in the Pit, they entered the stadium to watch the combats, climbing up the steps toward the top of the stands so that they could lose themselves in the crowd. Once they had found some space on an already crowded bench, an angry glare from Sirius making several of the grumbling spectators scoot farther down the slab to give these slightly frightening newcomers some room to sit, they settled in to watch the afternoon's duels.

Rafia and Sirius focused their attention on the lack of soldiers within the Colosseum. It seemed that the Royal Guard was more concerned about what could happen outside the stadium rather than within it, which boded well for what the Protector had in mind.

Bryen, on the other hand, couldn't tear his eyes away from the white sand. He had never experienced the combats from the stands as a spectator before. It felt almost surreal, like he was in the midst of an out-of-body experience. A small part of him still believed that he should be down there in the Pit, fighting the giant centipede that scrambled after a hastily retreating gladiator, and he felt guilty because he was glad that he wasn't, having become sickened long ago by the wanton bloodshed and anguish meted out on the white sand.

The centipede truly was a rare beast. If he remembered his lessons from Declan, the creatures were only found in the Flats, a rough and uninhabited terrain to the north of Murcia. The animals were incredibly difficult to capture, as the centipedes burrowed deep within the earth when they wanted to escape, creating a landscape of underground tunnels that would become a deadly trap for anyone foolish enough to pursue them. How many men might have died to bring this single specimen here Bryen didn't know, but it certainly served as additional evidence that King Beleron was desperate to divert his people's attention from their everyday lives, to give them something, anything, that would take their minds off all that Bryen had seen as he had made his way through the garbage-strewn streets to what had been his home for more than a decade.

He watched with rapt fascination as the animal, longer than most men were tall, skittered across the sand with blazing speed, adjusting its positioning so that the gladiator, a stout fellow with a neck thicker than a tree trunk, never got a clean strike at its armored hide. Instead, the muscle-bound man struggled to keep the centipede to his front, and each time he failed to do so, the crowd gasped and cheered as more blood spilled onto the white sand, the centipede's sharp pincers, both as long as a short sword, slicing into the man's flesh.

Bryen started to lose himself in the fight, playing out in his mind how he would have fought a beast such as this. The centipede's belly was its weak point, so he would have devised a strategy where he could cut off some of its legs and try for the animal's underside.

Then a flash of red down by the gate that led to the gladiators' compound caught his attention, a braided ponytail visible just behind the steel mesh. Lycia. Bryen was certain of it. She was still alive. That realization warmed his heart, as he had worried about his friends when Duke Winborne had taken him from the Pit. He was certain as well that Declan was down there next to Lycia, likely having already concluded how the combat would end.

A ground-shaking roar from the spectators brought Bryen's gaze back toward the white sand, the gladiator stumbling away and clutching at his hand, the centipede having snipped off several fingers during its last attack. The injury and spurting blood incited the onlookers to an even higher level of blood-lust. The crowd sensed that the combat had turned, the gladiator backing off with his injured hand clutched tightly to his side, waving his sword weakly in a sad effort to keep the centipede at a distance. Bryen agreed with the crowd. It was only a matter of time now.

After watching just a few minutes of the combat, Bryen had surmised that the gladiator hadn't been at the Colosseum long enough to take in Declan's instruction or he had simply chosen to ignore it. Bryen had seen it happen before. It usually occurred with soldiers sentenced to the Pit. They had been trained to fight, it was their profession, and they believed that there was no need for additional instruction. To them, fighting was fighting. But Bryen had learned through years of hard experience that fighting in the Pit was more than just fighting. It was an art. Bloody and raw, but still an art. Whatever might be the case with this gladiator, Bryen could tell that he was too fresh and rigid for this unforgiving environment and the centipede too deadly.

In seconds it was over. The gladiator overextended himself, missing when he tried to stab the centipede in the skull, the beast dodging out of the way easily and cutting through the man's leather armor and into his belly with its razor-sharp pincers. The dying gladiator collapsed onto the floor of the Pit, a large pool of blood coloring the white sand red.

"I'll see you on the other side," Bryen whispered to himself, offering some small condolence to the fighter who had died for the pleasure of others.

Hearing his words, Rafia gripped Bryen's arm tightly in a comforting fashion. She had a small inkling of what might be going on within him in that moment.

"Are you alright?" she asked, her concern clear in her voice.

Bryen closed his eyes to center himself, then took several deep breaths. "Yes, thank you. I've just never seen the games from this perspective before."

"It can be strange," the Magus said, nodding in agreement. "Coming back to a place like this where you gave so much of yourself. More than you wanted to give. Where you saw your comrades die." Rafia gripped his arm again, making sure that her eyes caught Bryen's. "But you are no longer a part of this place. You are free of the Pit."

Bryen nodded, accepting her words, but not really believing them.

"You are never free of the Pit," he whispered. "It is always with you, every second of the day."

Then he turned his attention back to the sand, watching the centipede settle itself against the wall directly opposite from the gate the gladiators used to enter the Pit, its gaze never wavering. The animal understood that the fight wasn't over, that even with one enemy eliminated more would come.

It wasn't long before one of the gates leading to the gladiators' stockade opened, the crowd roaring with pleasure as two new fighters prepared to step out onto the white sand to test their luck against the giant centipede. A booming voice aided by the acoustics of the arena rang out to be heard above the din of the throng. A surge of heat rushed into Bryen's chest, his anger and hate swelling as heart-breaking memories rushed through him. Beluchmel, the Master of the Colosseum, had assumed his role as the master of ceremonies. Bryen would welcome the chance to have a private word about all the suffering the man had inflicted upon his friends and comrades. Beluchmel was more than happy to send a gladiator to his or her death against some dangerous, exotic beast if it meant filling his pockets with more coin.

"You have seen the speed and strength of the giant centipede," said Beluchmel from the speaker's box, his voice carrying easily to every person in the Colosseum. "The beast has already murdered one gladiator. But what will it do against our two greatest warriors?"

Beluchmel waited almost a full minute as the anticipation built among the crowd, the cacophony increasing in intensity. Bryen ignored the drama, shaking his head in irritation at the word Beluchmel had used to describe the death of the gladiator. *Murdered*. The animal had no choice. On the white sand the only rule was kill or be killed. The centipede didn't want to be there any more than any of the gladiators who walked out into the Pit.

"What will the giant centipede do against our undefeated champions, brother and sister, the greatest fighters to grace the white sand since the Volkun? What will the centipede do against the Crimson Giant and the Crimson Devil?"

Bryen felt a sense of relief when the tall, red-headed gladiators strode out onto the white sand, urged on by the chants of the onlookers. His friends had survived the past year. He was both pleased and proud. He could see that both fighters were focused intently on their opponent, watching it with a close eye. The animal remained where it was, not moving, keeping the wall against its back, though the beast tracked Davin and Lycia as they approached.

Bryen remembered the first time the brother and sister had stepped into the Pit. After they had arrived at the Colosseum, Bryen had spent less than a week training them before they were forced to fight a giant scorpion. Davin had thought at the start of his training that his larger size and strength would serve him well on the white sand. He had learned quickly after sparring with Bryen, and having to pick himself up off the ground a few hundred times in just a few days, that though size and strength could benefit you, speed was the key to success in the Colosseum.

Lycia had accepted that stricture immediately and had soaked in everything that Bryen had taught her. Before walking through the gate leading to the Pit for that first combat, both had tried to appear confident, but Bryen could tell that they were on edge. So much so that both had thrown up against the white stone of the Colosseum before walking out onto the white sand. And then, as they did now, Davin moved to the left,

Lycia to the right, seeking to divide their adversary's focus and attack from two directions at once.

The two red-haired gladiators advanced toward the giant centipede cautiously, not feeling the need to rush. They had watched the previous combat and had seen how fast the animal moved. Better to let the beast tire itself out rather than take any unnecessary risks simply because the crowd demanded that blood cover the white sand.

The centipede seemed content to wait as well as it remained against the wall, the seconds passing slowly, then in a burst of movement, the animal shot toward Lycia, its skittering legs pushing it through the sand at an astounding speed. But Lycia was ready. Using her preferred twin short swords, she side-stepped the attack and slashed down with the blade in her right hand, the steel skimming across the centipede's armored back. She didn't presume that her attack would pierce the centipede's hide, but she did expect the animal to ignore the blow and then twist back toward her, just as it had done to the now deceased gladiator, the man's body still face down in the white sand. So she was ready when the centipede curled its body and lunged for her face.

Before the pincers could slice into her flesh, the Crimson Devil raised the blade in her left hand, sliding the steel painfully between the animal's pincers, almost cutting one completely off. Before the enraged centipede could continue its attack, Davin was there, stabbing with his preferred spear toward the animal's soft underbelly. The centipede was fast, but not fast enough. Contorting its body into an arc, the beast avoided the worst of the gladiator's stab. But Davin's aim was true enough to slice across the centipede's soft black flesh, opening a long gash that disabled many of the centipede's legs on its right side. Shrieking in anger and pain, the centipede scrambled away from its two opponents in an uneven run, putting its back against the wall once again.

Bryen watched the fight intently. Both Davin and Lycia looked exhausted, and they obviously were carrying injuries from previous combats. Still, he knew that his friends would win. Just as when they fought the giant scorpion so many years before with the expected efficiency of seasoned gladiators, they would kill the centipede. But it would be a harder task than it needed to be, the increased number of combats forced upon them during the week obviously taking their toll.

As the Crimson Giant and the Crimson Devil stepped farther away from one another, they moved toward the animal carefully, swords and spear held at the ready. The centipede hissed angrily, leaping first to the left toward Lycia, but pulling back before engaging, and then charging toward Davin, rising up almost to the tall gladiator's full height, its pincers searching for the soft flesh of the gladiator's neck.

Just as quickly as the animal reared up, it dropped back down, hissing in pain, the slice Davin had inflicted on the animal slowing it down, the wound obviously more serious than originally thought. Neither Davin nor Lycia had any desire to kill the centipede, but they knew that they had no choice. So with some reluctance, before the centipede could slide back toward the wall, Davin drove the point of his spear through the centipede's carapace and into its brain, putting the animal out of its misery.

Lycia took a deep breath, thankful to have survived another combat, her wounds from her fight just a few days before still bothering her. Normally, she would have raised her swords to the sky to acknowledge the crowd, but this time her focus was on something else. Something that surprised her.

Strange as it may seem with thousands of people in the stands, she felt as if she were being watched. She scanned the crowd, trying to identify from where the feeling that had settled within her stomach came from, a nervousness she rarely experienced while on the white sand. She was certain that the eyes upon her and her brother were familiar, but as she looked up into row upon row of screaming spectators, the farther up she gazed the harder it became to identify individual faces. They all transformed into a blur of color and swaying motion.

Not understanding why she was feeling this way, she turned to her brother. He glanced at her with a questioning expression. He had sensed the same thing that she did. Neither knew the cause of the unusual premonition, this sense of being watched in the midst of a huge crowd, but it didn't seem like a threat. There was a familiarity to the gaze that suggested that they might know who it was, but there was no way that they could confirm their suspicions from the Pit.

Then again, perhaps they were simply tired. They were fighting more and more frequently every week, until each combat ran from one into the next. And because of the schedule, Davin and Lycia were not being given the time that they needed to rest or heal. They were barely noticing the beasts they were required to fight, the exotic animals more a diversion for the crowd. Shrugging his shoulders, as if to say his sister was right, familiar eyes were upon them, but that there was nothing they could do at the moment to discover why that might be the case, he trudged off the sand toward the gladiators' gate, Lycia sheathing her swords and following him.

As the two gladiators walked out of the Pit, Bryen saw that old habits die hard. Declan stood at the gate waiting for them. The Master of the Gladiators always greeted his fighters when they survived a combat, and he was always there to offer a nod of respect when they didn't and the attendants had to carry the body to the potter's field. Declan was rarely in a good mood, his visage often betraying his emotion, and it was clear from the storm cloud on his face that his mentor and friend hated what the King had forced upon his gladiators.

Nodding to his companions, Bryen rose and walked down the steps to the main concourse, having seen enough. Rafia and

Sirius followed, though a good distance behind as they realized that the Protector wanted some space to think through everything that he had witnessed. As he exited the Colosseum, Bryen checked the positioning of the Guards one more time. Most of the soldiers remained on the outside of the arena rather than inside. That would certainly work to his advantage with the plan that he had in mind, but he needed to remain cognizant of the fact that the barracks for the Royal Guard was located right next to the gladiators' compound. Yet even with all of the soldiers stationed in the city, although it complicated what he wanted to do, that didn't mean he had to adjust his strategy.

Before he accepted that determination, he wanted to see whether Marden had increased the number of soldiers patrolling the perimeter of the Tintagel Palace. With the unrest within the city, he wouldn't put it past him. If nothing else, Marden had demonstrated during his brief reign that his own interests always came first. So Bryen began to walk past the new construction and down the promenade that led toward the seat of Beleron power in Caledonia. It wasn't long before Sirius and Rafia caught up to him.

"Is it as you expected it would be?" Sirius asked Bryen.

"No, actually it wasn't," he replied. "Security is laxer than I thought it would be within the Colosseum. That could help us, though we'll still need to be quick if we're to have any chance of success."

"How do we connect with Declan?" asked Rafia. "Was he the one standing by the gate leading out to the Pit?"

"Why are you so interested in Declan?" demanded Sirius in a whisper.

"Because," she replied impatiently, "if Bryen is going to engineer the event that will give us the opportunity to free Duke Winborne and Aislinn, gaining Declan's assistance is essential."

"That may be, but you seem inordinately curious about him."

"Are you jealous, Sirius?" That thought pleased her for some reason, making her feel like a young girl rather than a Magus centuries old.

"I am not jealous," he protested. "That would be preposterous."

"Don't worry, Sirius," comforted Rafia with a sarcastic smile. "There may still be a chance for us. But you're making that more and more difficult by the day. So set in your ways. Reluctant to discuss personal issues that we need to talk about."

"I wasn't suggesting that. I was simply stating that you seem to be bewitched by the Master of the Gladiators and you haven't even met the man."

"And that's why I want to meet him."

"Ha!" shouted Sirius, who quickly lowered his voice after glancing around to make sure that no one had paid much attention to his outburst. With all that was going on in Tintagel, no one had noticed and no one had cared. "I'm right," he said in a forceful whisper. "You are interested in him."

"Oh, Sirius, I do so enjoy it when you're jealous."

"I am not jealous!"

"Are you two done?" asked Bryen, who was beginning to lose patience with the childish antics of the two Magii. "Can we move on to more important issues?"

"Of course, Bryen," said Rafia. "My apologies. Now how will we be meeting Declan? I am so looking forward to it."

She added the last for Sirius' benefit, enjoying the scowl that her words elicited.

"We are not meeting Declan," said Bryen, ignoring the wounded look that Rafia gave him. "I am. Tomorrow."

"But why not us?"

"You two are both too obvious. You stand out. If Declan sees you before he sees me, he might disappear. And I can't get to him in the gladiators' stockade."

"What do you mean we stand out?"

Rather than respond, Bryen simply looked at Sirius with a raised eyebrow. "Do I really need to explain?"

Sirius and Rafia glanced at one another. They both wore multicolored robes that hurt the eye if you stared too long and had slightly distracted expressions. Their hair stuck out in all directions, and they appeared a bit ragged because of all the travel, their clothes dusty and dirty, even torn in a few places.

Rafia nodded sagely, finally seeing what Bryen was saying. "You're right. But I still want to meet Declan."

11

DAGGER IN THE BELLY

"Stay safe, Master of the Gladiators. The streets are becoming more dangerous by the day."

"I'll do my best," replied the grey haired gladiator in a gruff voice. "It can't be any worse than fighting in the Pit."

The large soldier laughed. Declan didn't know the man's name, but he did recognize him. He was one of the soldiers who had accompanied Lady Winborne and the Blademaster when they visited the Colosseum. It seemed that when he could his friend Jurgen Klines was replacing the soldiers guarding the gates to the gladiators' stockade with men loyal to him rather than those loyal to Killen Sourban, the Captain of the Royal Guard. Why Klines felt the need to do that, he didn't know. But Declan could guess. He was well versed in the politics of the capital.

"Maybe, maybe not," murmured the soldier. "At least on the white sand you'll see the blade aimed for your gut. Out here, you won't know until your life is bleeding out onto the cobblestones."

Declan nodded, unable to argue the point, then strode through the gate and turned left, pushing his way through the milling mass of people crowding the streets and making his way around the Colosseum to the far side. Although his thoughts were elsewhere, the Master of the Gladiators remained vigilant, always aware of his surroundings as he wound through the multitude toward the only market still functioning in the city, recognizing that the soldier's opinion about the risk of walking the streets now wasn't too far from the truth. He didn't think anyone would accost him, not with his stout frame and menacing glare. But more and more people were finding themselves in desperate straits these days, so better to prepare for the worst and then be pleasantly surprised if it never happened. Although in his experience the worst occurred all too frequently.

Declan smiled to himself, but just briefly. He really was set in his ways. What he had just told himself, he had relayed to his gladiators thousands of times during the last two decades. As he stepped into the square that fronted the barracks of the Royal Guard, a touch of nausea settled in his stomach. He never liked visiting this square, usually doing his best to avoid it, but he didn't have a choice. Not now.

Distinct markets were located in various squares throughout Tintagel. There was one for farmers and their produce, another for blacksmiths and their offerings. There was a bazaar for artisans to display their crafts, another for performers to amuse the crowd. And so it went, each profession having their own mall to display their wares or their abilities. But no more. As the conditions within the capital worsened, all the other markets had closed, until only one remained for the few vendors still willing to risk the dangerous roads and a restless populace to sell their products and goods.

For centuries this plaza had been home to the slavers' market. He hated this square with a passion. Twenty years before he had been sold from the block that still stood near the entrance to the barracks. As he had learned over the years, although the Crown claimed that slavery was illegal in Caledonia, it was still a much too common practice when it met the needs of the King. Pushing down his distaste, Declan took a moment to scan what was on display among the few stalls scattered around the plaza, his hopes dropping as he saw the empty countertops and sparse offerings.

Although a slave himself, Declan was permitted to walk the city when he chose, leaving the gladiators' compound regularly in search of better food and supplies for the men and women who shared his fate and depended on him for their survival, which for all was a weekly exercise. The Crown provided a stipend to feed and house his fighters, but much of that never made its way to the people who lived and died on the white sand, Beluchmel always taking a large cut for himself. So to supplement the meager rations and supplies he was given, Declan bet on the combats, always putting money on his own gladiators. More often than not, they survived, which meant that he won, and with his extra earnings he bought what little that he could to help his combatants live until their next fight. But this was getting more difficult to do because of the lack of available food and inflated costs.

The pickings were slim, but he was able to find several sacks of apples and pears that had not yet rotted, some runty onions and potatoes, and a haunch of beef that hadn't gone bad. At least he thought it was beef. He couldn't tell for certain, but he also wasn't in a position to be picky, even with the exorbitant prices. After arranging for his purchases to be delivered to the gladiators' stockade, he was about to continue his wanderings when he felt as if he were being watched. It was the same hint of warning that had served him well more than once during his time in the Royal Guard.

He could head back to the compound, his hidden observer unable to follow him, but Declan was more interested in learning more about his tracker. So as he left the market, he moved into the city center. He started on the main thorough-fare that paralleled the promenade that led toward the Palace, stopping every minute or so to look at what a street vendor might be selling, even buying a meat pie that he hoped was rabbit, though he couldn't be sure, and he didn't want to think too deeply about what else the meat could be with the resurgence of rats in the city. Each time he halted, he scanned his surroundings surreptitiously, hoping to locate the source of his unease without alerting his tail. But no such luck. No one in the swirling crowd stood out to him. He needed to change his approach if he was to have any hope of identifying his pursuer.

Finding a break in the crowd, Declan walked down one of the narrower streets that led away from the main boulevard, passing more boarded up businesses than open ones until he entered a residential neighborhood and began looking for what would suit his purposes best. Still sensing a peculiar presence somewhere around him, he stepped into a small alley that ran behind a block of townhomes, then ducked behind a corner.

"You really are a difficult man to catch." The words were said quietly but strongly by a tall shadow standing right next to him, the voice deep and sounding familiar to Declan.

But he didn't give that trace of recognition much thought, instead turning to his right and placing a tree-trunk sized arm against the shadow's chest and pushing him up against the brick wall.

"Tell me why I shouldn't drive my dagger into your gut this instant."

The shadow tilted his head down, noting the sharp steel pricking his belly. "Because if you do, I'll do the same to you."

That tingle of familiarity upon hearing the shadow's words ran through Declan once again, his mind finally attempting to solve the problem. At the same time, Declan looked down, seeing a dagger pressed into his gut. Then it came to him as he recognized the voice. How could it even be possible?

"Bryen?"

"In the flesh."

Declan reached up and pushed back the hood, revealing the gladiator's smiling face. He then sheathed his dagger and pulled Bryen into a fierce embrace. Almost a full minute passed before he finally let go.

"What are you doing here lad? It's not safe."

Bryen sheathed his own dagger, then looked up and down the alley just to make sure that no one had followed either of them into the cramped space. Satisfied, he turned his attention back to Declan.

"Looking for you."

"Me?" Declan certainly enjoyed seeing his former charge, but he didn't understand why Bryen would risk coming back to where he had been enslaved for a decade just to see him. "Lady Winborne said that you were no longer her Protector. I thought that you would have taken advantage of your freedom and be a good distance away from here."

Bryen ignored the mild castigation in Declan's voice.

"What did you think of the Lady of the Southern Marches?"

"Determined. Strong-willed. Very certain of herself."

"Yes, that certainly sounds like the Lady Winborne," Bryen said with a soft laugh.

"And a bit frightened as well, though she hid it well."

"Based on what she's dealing with, that I can understand."

"She had some kind things to say about you," Declan said. "Fighting Ghoules and assassins. You'll have to tell me of your time in the Southern Marches and what it was like to serve as a Protector."

"That will take more time than we have right now."

"I expect so," said Declan. "It is good to see you, lad."

"And you, Declan. I've missed you."

"I doubt that."

"Come now, Declan. I've had no one looking over my shoulder to make sure that I stay on the straight and narrow."

"In speaking with Lady Winborne, it appears that she filled that role in my absence," said Declan. "Besides, I don't know how to take that last comment. Should I feel good about myself or insulted?"

"Take your pick," Bryen replied with a mischievous grin.

Declan smiled broadly, realizing that he was in a good humor for the first time since Bryen had been purchased by the Duke of the Southern Marches. Bryen had a unique way of needling him, and he'd missed it. He'd missed him.

"Now that you've gotten your teasing out of the way, you still need to answer my question. What are you doing here, lad? As I said, it's not safe."

Recognizing that time was short and that they could talk in more detail later, Bryen provided Declan with a brief review of where he had been and what he had been doing, choosing to leave certain things out as they would only lead to more questions that he didn't have the time or the desire to answer at that moment. He then turned the conversation to the matter that had pulled him back to the Caledonian capital, despite his better instincts yelling at him to stay away from Tintagel.

"Is she worth it, lad? After what her father did to you, why would you even give this a thought?"

"Is her father worth it? In my opinion, no. Not after what he did to me."

"But the Lady Winborne?"

Bryen shrugged his shoulders, having a hard time admitting to Declan what he was struggling to acknowledge to himself.

"She freed me from the Protector's collar, at least as well as she could. That's a debt owed. Apart from that, she doesn't deserve what fate holds for her."

Declan stared at the gladiator with an intuitive look. "That's the only reason?"

Bryen sighed, knowing what Declan was suggesting. But he wasn't ready to walk down that path.

"It's the right thing to do."

Declan continued to stare at Bryen for several seconds more, then he nodded.

"It's ambitious, son. Some might even call what you have in mind insane."

"Some already have," confirmed Bryen, Tarin in particular coming to mind. "But it is necessary."

"For this to have any chance of success, you would need an army."

"Well, in all honesty, I was hoping that you could help me with that."

"They're not soldiers."

"No, they're not. But they would have a real incentive to fight. As you've told me many times, everyone dies, but not everyone dies with honor. Even if we lose, is it not better to fight and die for your freedom rather than fight and die to amuse a crowd?"

"You have a point," said Declan, not surprised that Bryen had used his own words to persuade him. It was one of Bryen's unique talents. "How do you expect to make this happen so quickly?"

"I was once told that there is power in a name. Perhaps it's time to make use of it."

"Are you willing to risk your life and the lives of others on that?"

Bryen took his time before answering, knowing the import of his response. "My life, yes. Others, no. That will be for them to decide. I can promise them no more than an opportunity, and a slim one at that. It will be up to them to decide if they want to take the risk."

Declan looked at the young man he viewed as his son, realizing all that would need to be done to put the initial pieces of

Bryen's plan in motion.

"You really are serious, aren't you?"

Bryen stared at his friend and mentor, then gave him a brief nod.

"Blast it, lad. You are serious."

"Deadly."

12

—————

A PERSONAL INTEREST

"Are we lacking in grain, Killen? Or other basic foodstuffs?" Marden asked the question while he picked from the large tray displaying more than a dozen delectables set on the table in the center of his expansive, luxurious suite. Wearing just a robe that often flapped open at the worst possible time, at least in the opinion of the Captain of the Royal Guard, the King of Caledonia popped a grape into his mouth and then began spreading a soft cheese onto a piece of bread, adding some ham when he was done to make a small sandwich. His third in just the last few minutes, in fact. His activities from the night before had left him thirsty and famished, so he poured himself another glass of wine as well. "I find that hard to believe." He motioned toward the tray in front of him to emphasize his point.

"Some of the staples, yes, my King," replied Killen Sourban. The Captain of the Royal Guard understood that though Marden thought otherwise, his liege was disconnected from his people, spending most of his time in his Palace and only leaving the safety of the fortress to visit the Colosseum. In fact, the last time the young monarch had left the boundaries of Tintagel was during the first year of his rule, when he went on a tour of the Kingdom and visited the major Duchies and cities in Caledonia. Sourban remembered that getting him to do even that had been like pulling teeth. "Corn. Potato. Onion. Rice. Other vegetables, meat as well. Meat in particular. Even chicken. Everything is becoming more and more difficult to find. So the need for grain has increased, as has its price. As a result ..."

"The commoners are finding it harder to purchase food. Yes, yes, I know, I know. I'm well versed in economics. I understand the concepts of supply and demand."

"Of course, my King," replied Killen, nodding his head in apology, though his ice-cold blue eyes suggested that it was a gesture with little meaning, done simply to appease the King of Caledonia, who at the best of times revealed a mercurial temperament. "I didn't mean to imply otherwise."

Killen let his gaze wander through the rest of Marden's overlarge chamber, his King's preferred location for conducting the business of the Kingdom. The young ruler seemed to have an aversion to doing things the way that his father did, even down to where the work was accomplished. In addition to staying away from the deceased King's former chambers, now inhabited by Tetric, Marden avoided the throne room like the plague.

It appeared to Killen as if Marden sought to steer clear of any place he thought the ghost of Corinthus Beleron might appear after his supposed experience the first night of his reign. Killen didn't believe in spirits. He believed in steel. But he couldn't say the same for his monarch, Marden's father still tormenting him three years after his demise.

A rustle of movement to his side drew Killen's eyes. Turning his head, he saw the shapes of several women sprawled on the massive bed set against the far wall, flashes of skin peeking out from beneath the blankets. More of Marden's conquests. Killen doubted that the women would wake for hours, having glimpsed the wine pitcher by the side of the bed and the flowers scattered around it. Marden favored the root of the poppy, a drug that was both expensive and difficult to acquire. The women brought to his suite often didn't have a choice in whether they imbibed the drug, and as a result these young ladies would be asleep for a while longer unless forcibly awoken.

"There are more reports of unrest in the city, Captain," said Marden, licking his fingers clean as he began the same process again so that he could craft a fourth sandwich. "I was told last night by someone whose name escapes me that there was a riot the day before near the grain silos."

"Yes, my King. The Royal Guard removed the rioters in a matter of hours. All is quiet for now."

"That's good to hear, Killen. Any of the Guard injured?"

"Just a handful, my King. None seriously."

"And my people?"

Killen found it hard keeping the smirk that wanted to twist his lips from forming. Marden had no real sense of his people, as he liked to call them. How could he since he spent all of his time behind the walls of his castle?

"Several dozen killed, unfortunately. But it was unavoidable. Despite multiple warnings, the rioters refused to heed the orders of the Guard." Killen shrugged his shoulders as if to say that his soldiers had done all that they could to prevent from occurring what was being described in the streets as the Grain Massacre. The incident had only served to exacerbate the fury of the people, as Marden called them, toward the Crown. "If nothing else, I have no doubt that in the future, the people will respond more sensibly the next time your Royal Guard commands them to disperse."

"Yes, I hope they will. But who can say, Killen? Who can

say? Hunger can affect a person's decision making in strange ways."

"True, my King," replied Killen, finding the comment strange because he doubted that Marden during his privileged life had ever gone hungry for more than an hour. "Are you suggesting that I open the silos? Disperse the grain?"

Killen didn't really care about the commoners, even though he used to be one of them. He had been raised in an orphanage, doing odd jobs as a child for some pocket money, then working his way through various professions. Tanner. Carpenter. Blacksmith. As well as a few that were less reputable. And then finally soldier. The one that best suited his skills and his inclinations. He rose within the ranks of the Royal Guard quickly, taking in every word his mentor at the time, Jurgen Klines, had offered him. But he hadn't always listened to Klines. He had taken the Blademaster's advice with a grain of salt, allowing his own aspirations and desires to guide him.

In particular, he had learned through his experiences that once you moved up in the world, you never looked back, because you would never like what you saw if you did. So he didn't. Where he came from wasn't relevant to him. He only cared about where he was going. Because of that, he did worry about unrest in the city, as it could affect his plans.

Although he didn't agree with everything the Blademaster had taught him, he did believe and practice one of the first things Klines had told him, that control was essential. Control over himself. Control over his environment. The riots demonstrated how you could very easily lose control, and he couldn't allow that to happen, since his success relied upon exercising control at all times. He didn't like surprises, and with that in mind he likened the city to a tinderbox just waiting to be set ablaze. He definitely didn't want that to happen. At least not yet. Not unless it worked to his advantage.

"No, Killen. There is no need. Not yet."

"But, my King ..."

"Not yet, Killen!" ordered Marden, his voice a shout that failed to disturb the unconscious women, none of whom stirred. The King turned his gaze away from the tray of food to Killen, the Captain noticing his bloodshot eyes. Killen assumed that Marden was still feeling the effects of the poppy root, which would explain his good mood despite the early morning hour and his quick changes in temper. "We will wait until my people are a little hungrier. Then we will do as you suggest. When they really need the grain, when they are desperate for the grain, we will give it to them, and they will know that it came from me. I will be their savior, the protector of my people."

"Of course, my King," replied Killen resignedly, choosing not to point out that many of the people living in Tintagel were already facing miserable circumstances.

"In the meantime, we will give the common folk the diversion that they need. We will host the gladiatorial games three times a week now rather than two. That will take their minds off their struggles for a while longer."

"My King, adding the combats on Wednesday has done little in your efforts to distract the people," replied Killen in a soft, placating voice. He knew that his argument was wasted breath, but he had to try. "The price to attend the games now has become too much for most. Many people can't afford to buy food. If they can't afford to buy food, they can't afford to buy a ticket to the games. They want to feed their families. They care little for what happens in the Colosseum. Only the rich will attend the combats, and because of that the crowds are dwindling. Many of the well-off have already left the capital with more doing so every day. Even with reports of Ghoules coming down from the Shattered Peaks, they feel the need to risk the roads and find a safer location beyond the walls of Tintagel."

"The Ghoules are of no consequence," Marden scoffed,

barely listening to what his Captain had to say. "If the beasts are foolish enough to attack Tintagel, then we will deal with them. They will scamper back to the Lost Land once the Royal Guard takes the field. We must focus first on securing the capital, beginning with the threats within the walls."

"Thus my suggestion, my King. If we release the grain now, it will make it easier for the Guard to ensure the city is secure. We can then send several companies back onto the roads and into the countryside to ensure the Ghoules return to the Shattered Peaks."

"The Ghoules are not our primary concern at the moment, Killen," said Marden testily. "And I expect the stories of the Ghoules are overblown." He couldn't dispute his Captain's logic. But he didn't want to reveal all that he knew after having spoken with Tetric. The Ghoules were a problem now, but he didn't believe that they would be for long once they achieved their purpose. And better to allow them to do what they came to Caledonia for rather than meet them on the field of battle when the Royal Guard was concentrating on a more immediate danger. Better to give the Ghoules the space they needed and allow them to leave on their own just as Tetric had suggested. "I know my people, Killen. I know what they want. And they want spectacle. Talk to the Master of the Colosseum and make it happen."

"Yes, my King," replied Killen, knowing that his attempt to change his ruler's mind had been doomed from the start.

"But you are right to be concerned about the unrest," nodded Marden. "Increase the number of Royal Guard in the streets. That will settle things down."

"My King, that is an excellent idea, but I fear that may only incite the people more." Sensing his chance, Killen decided to take it, realizing that he needed to handle what he was about to propose next very delicately. "Particularly, my King, since some of the unrest is coming from certain members of the Royal Guard."

That shocking statement caught Marden's attention. The King dropped the sandwich that he had been biting into, his bloodshot eyes blazing with a maniacal fury.

"You've lost control of the Guard?" demanded Marden. "How could that even be possible?"

"No, my King," Killen replied quickly, realizing instantly that the hook that he had just thrown had caught Marden right in the mouth. Now he just had to reel him in. "The Guard belongs to you, my King. But there is a very small segment of the Guard whose loyalty has come into question."

"I don't understand, Killen. The Guard belongs to me. The members of the Guard are hand selected, loyalty to me the most important factor. And now you're suggesting that same loyalty is in doubt. I ask again, how could that even be possible?"

"Jurgen Klines, my King."

"The Blademaster? That's impossible. His loyalty to Caledonia is beyond question."

"Yes, my King. But you saw it yourself, I'm sure, when last you spoke with him. And I'm told that he is spending a great deal of time with the Lady Winborne, perhaps discussing things with her that he shouldn't. Teaching her how to fight." Killen waited just a moment before offering the final piece that he believed would take Marden down the trail that he had laid out for him. A path that would eliminate Killen's greatest rival and largest concern. "The Blademaster's loyalty is beyond question. To Caledonia, my King. But not to you."

Killen's final remark made Marden stop short. He was beginning to understand now. As his mind worked through the problem that Killen had raised, Marden realized that the Captain of his Guard had raised an important and potentially worrisome distinction.

"The Blademaster has served Caledonia for decades. He once filled your position, in fact."

"Yes, my King."

"But you believe that he can no longer be trusted."

"My King, I believe that based on what I have seen and heard, I have no choice but to wonder about his loyalty to you."

"That is a serious charge, Captain."

"It is not a charge, my King. Simply a concern."

"A fair point, Killen."

"One other matter, my King. There are reports from our scouts of large bands of armed men moving about the countryside. There have been stories of burned villages near the Dark Forest, but we have not yet been able to confirm these tales."

"Are we certain that these are not Ghoule raiding parties?"

"Yes, my King. That has been confirmed. I doubt the Ghoules would have the courage to come this far south."

"Bandits?"

"No, my King. The scouts have not been able to get close enough to identify them, other than to confirm that they are soldiers. But I suspect ..."

"Jurgen Klines."

"Yes, my King. He has connections in the Royal Guard and beyond. Spreading stories of unrest in the countryside, inciting a riot, perhaps even an insurrection ... none of this would be beyond his reach."

Killen thought to say more, but he held back, knowing that Marden's insecurities and fears were his best ally at the moment. So though it pained him, he kept his mouth shut, hoping that the false tracks that he had lain would lead the King in the desired direction.

"Yes, yes indeed, Killen. You make a good point."

Marden thought about the puzzle that his Captain had set out before him for quite some time, following the path diligently from one point to the next. The sigh of resignation that Marden emitted announced that he had made his decision.

"Arrest the Blademaster, Killen," Marden finally commanded. "But don't kill him. I want to speak with him and get to the bottom of this before I take any action."

"Yes, my King." Killen tried not to smirk, not expecting to have manipulated his monarch so easily. "On what charge?"

"Treason against the Crown."

Killen nodded and turned for the doors, prepared to execute Marden's command immediately.

"And one more thing, Killen."

"Yes, my King," said Killen, turning back toward Marden.

"This charade with my betrothed must come to an end. Since I assume the Lady Winborne will be with the Blademaster, please inform her that we will be wed on the morrow. I will not permit her to delay our nuptials any longer."

"Yes, my King."

13

CHOICE TO BE MADE

A light rain fell in Tintagel, a welcome change in Declan's opinion to the scorching days of the last few months. But the weather also highlighted the challenges that the Master of the Gladiators had struggled with for decades. He sat in a large open room in the building that separated the two barracks for gladiators and housed his small office, his private quarters -- no larger than a cell just like any of the other gladiators, and the storage rooms that held everything from food to practice gear to weapons. He had moved his preferred chalkboard that he used to teach his fighters tactics up against the wall behind him, because on the far side of the chamber a steady drip had begun as droplets of rain found their way through the gaps in the broken or missing roof tiles to splatter against the rough wooden floor.

Having unwillingly made the gladiators' compound his home for the last twenty years, it was a small inconvenience, knowing that the problem would be worse in the two dilapidated structures set aside for the gladiators where the thatch on the roof was old, worn, and sparse. Sleeping in a light drizzle was nothing compared to the fall downpours that were only a few months away. But perhaps that annual inconvenience would no longer be a concern depending on how the next few hours went.

"What have we done wrong, Declan?" asked a large gladiator who was almost as tall as Davin and twice as broad. The man had muscles in places that Declan didn't think people should even have muscles. But the man was more than just a muscle-bound fighter. He was smart and patient, which had helped him to survive on the white sand for almost three years, a record for most gladiators.

Before responding to the question, Declan surveyed the gladiators gathered in the cantonment. Slightly more than two hundred men and women had crammed themselves into the hall, the handful who were missing unable to be moved from their beds because of the wounds they suffered during their combats the day before. Still, there should have been more. The requirement that the gladiators fight twice a week and against more fearsome and rare beasts or overwhelming odds in order to excite the crowd was taking its toll, as there were more than a dozen fighters missing from their ranks, all of them having colored the white sand red yesterday, their bodies unceremoniously dragged from the Pit. At this pace, within a few weeks all the gladiators would be dead.

"You've done nothing wrong, Dorlan," replied Declan, the quirk in his lips suggesting that he was mildly amused. "Why do you think you've done something wrong?"

"The only time we ever have a talk like this is when one of us has done something wrong."

"And as I said, Dorlan, no one has done anything wrong."

"Still seems a bit strange," said the large gladiator, several of his peers nodding their heads or offering grunts in agreement. Dorlan was speaking for most of them. They had grown accustomed to their routine, and this meeting was not part of their routine. It made them uneasy.

"You're overthinking things, Dorlan," suggested Declan.

"I doubt that," said a musical voice from just behind the large gladiator. "Dorlan can barely keep one thought in his brain at a time. He's not overthinking, he's simply trying to think."

"That's enough, Kollea. It's too early in the morning to have to deal with your humor. I'm not ready for your jokes and quips."

"You were certainly ready last night," countered Kollea, the diminutive, wiry gladiator smiling broadly and giving Dorlan a wink that set his face afire and led to some good-natured ribbing from the assembled gladiators.

Everyone knew that Dorlan and Kollea, a dark-haired gladiator who, despite her petite size, swung a short sword with more skill than most of the fighters around her, spent more time together than apart. She was also more tenacious than a starving dog in search of food, a whirlwind of a fighter who preferred to attack from the start and keep her opponent on the defensive throughout the combat until she could finally drive her steel into her adversary.

"Enough, children," said Declan, his latent smile now replaced by a frown, his patience, never good to begin with, already waning. "We need to have a talk, and we don't have time to waste."

"Just like Kollea didn't waste any time finding Dorlan last night," said a voice from the back of the room. "She got him faster than she got her blade into that mercenary from the Territories yesterday."

The comment drew another round of laughter until Kollea stood up and turned toward the back of the room, her face betraying her anger, which was never far from the surface.

"I put that mercenary down in less than a minute," she clarified, completely missing the humor. "I doubt any of you could have done any better."

"Enough!" roared Declan.

Under most circumstances, he would have allowed the give and take to continue, believing that it was a necessary part of surviving as a slave to the Crown. When you were required to risk your life on the white sand, you had to enjoy those rare moments of levity that could be found in the gladiators' stockade. But the issue that he was about to raise likely would lead to a difficult conversation and a momentous decision. The additional stress had led to his rising temper and lack of patience.

Silence quickly descended in the meeting hall, the only sound coming from the drip of the rainwater puddling on the floor on the far side of the room. Even Kollea, who had such a difficult time controlling her temper, sat back down without another word after a calming glance from Dorlan.

"What's going on, Declan?" asked Lycia, her voice composed and calm. She could tell that something was bothering the Master of the Gladiators.

"The Volkun is in the city," he replied in a soft voice.

His brief statement led to an immediate uproar among the gladiators. Almost all of them knew the Volkun, had trained with him, a few had even enjoyed the privilege of partnering with him in the Pit. Despite his youth, the Volkun was a legend, the greatest gladiator to have ever graced the white sand, other than Declan perhaps. Then the flood of questions and comments struck.

"The Volkun?"

"The Wolf is back?"

"I thought he was dead."

"I thought he was enslaved by some backwater duke."

"He couldn't be back. He died in Roo's Nest."

"He didn't die in Roo's Nest. He died in Murcia."

"He wasn't taken to Murcia. He was taken to the Three Rivers."

"It wasn't the Three Rivers. It was the Southern Marches."

One gladiator ignored the chatter around him, a huge smile breaking out on his face. It was good to hear that his friend was still alive. Davin had feared the worst when Bryen had been taken from the Colosseum in chains.

Seeing Davin's smile, Lycia tried to process what she was feeling upon learning of Bryen's return. Shocked, excited, uncertain, but also not surprised. Now yesterday's feeling while in the Pit made sense. She was certain that the unknown observer in the crowd during her and her brother's midweek combat who had set the skin on her neck tingling was him.

Her thoughts inevitably drifted to one of the last times they had spent together. The physick had finished tending to their wounds. They had remained sitting there on the bench, their shoulders and knees touching, as they enjoyed a companionable silence. In that moment Lycia had felt a strange connection between her and Bryen, and she believed that he had felt it as well. He had reached for her then, his hand caressing her cheek. They were so close together that all she could see were his grey eyes. But before she could finish her memory, she was startled from her reverie by the silence that had fallen once more within the gladiators' barracks.

Not bothering to shout again, Declan had raised his hands, the quiet quickly returning because of their interest in what the Master of the Gladiators had to say.

"The Volkun lives," said Declan once all the eyes in the room had returned to him. "That I can assure you. I spoke to him when I went to the market. He asked that I broach a topic with you."

Declan's last comment set off another uproar, the questions from the gladiators coming fast and furiously.

"Why did he come back?"

"What's he doing here?"

"What was he doing before he came back?"

"Why would the Volkun come back if he was free? Was he free? Or was he still a slave?"

"What could he possibly want with us? He made it out of the Pit."

The questions continued for several more seconds, Declan's irritation increasing with each one asked as he listened to dozens of variations on the same theme. Why was the Volkun here? What did he want?

Before he lost his patience once again, Declan raised his hands, but the questions kept coming, the gladiators ignoring his request for silence. Using the voice that he had perfected as a Sergeant in the Royal Guard, he quickly smothered the discordant discussion that had taken hold of the room.

"I can't answer your questions," growled the Master of the Gladiators. "And even if I could, I wouldn't. Your questions are for the Volkun to answer. I will tell you why he's here and what he has in mind."

Declan then spent almost a full hour outlining Bryen's proposal, reviewing several key points multiple times so that there was no confusion. What the Volkun suggested was straightforward, almost elegant in its simplicity, and exceedingly dangerous. It essentially assured the deaths of most, if not all, of the gladiators. After another hour of questions, it appeared that all of the gladiators were satisfied.

"Whether you're willing to participate in what the Volkun has proposed," concluded Declan, "is for you, and you alone, to decide."

A deathly silence descended on the gladiators, many clearly considering what the Master of the Gladiators had just explained to them, a few others simply not wanting to be the ones to blame for breaking the charged quiet. Even Kollea, who usually made her decisions rapidly and without concern for the consequences, seemed lost in thought.

"And you, Declan?" asked Davin. "What will you be doing?"

Declan stared at the red-haired gladiator for a good long while, the suspense and tension building within the cramped barracks.

"I've been here for twenty years. I've seen hundreds of good men and women die for no good reason other than fighting for the pleasure of the crowd, fighting to entertain people who themselves don't have the courage to walk the white sand as you do." Declan pushed himself out of his chair, hands on his hips, staring down at the wooden floor for a brief moment before raising his head and revealing a set of eyes that burned with an intensity that those who knew the Master of the Gladiators rarely saw. "I'm tired of looking at grey and white day after day. I'd rather see the red of my blood staining the white sand of the Pit than spend another day staring at the white stone of the cursed Colosseum. I plan to fight. There's no other way out of this prison. Either we die in the Pit or we die trying to get out of the Pit. I prefer the latter. But I can't make you do what you don't want to do. As I said, the decision is yours and yours alone."

Declan's comment elicited grumbles of agreement and nodded heads from the assembled gladiators, hearing the truth in his words. Recognizing the sentiment spreading throughout the room, Declan nodded himself, pleased with the outcome of the discussion despite the danger and risk involved. He knew where the gladiators stood, having expected just such an outcome. Desperate men and women rarely hesitated when no matter how desperate the act it still contained a glimmer of hope.

"So be it," said Declan. "Fortune favors the bold."

"I thought fortune favored the brave?" challenged Davin.

"I've heard that fortune favors the strong," offered Dorlan. "That makes more sense in my opinion."

"It's hard to keep it all straight, what with all of Declan's sayings," suggested Davin. "There are so many to remember."

That brought a murmur of assent from many of the other gladiators, as well as an elbow in Davin's ribs from his sister.

"Davin, this is not the time," Lycia whispered. "You're not helping."

"I'm just trying to get clarification," he protested.

"You're being difficult because you can be difficult."

"That's unfair," said Davin. "I'm being difficult because I want the right answer."

"Are you two done yet?" demanded Declan, shaking his head in exasperation. Sometimes he felt as if he spent most of his time looking after a bunch of rambunctious and ill-behaved children. "There isn't always one right answer. You should know that. Regardless of what I've said, fortune favors the brave, the bold, the strong, it all means the same thing."

"Are you sure about that?" asked Davin, his voice betraying his uncertainty. "It seems awfully convenient for you to have reached that conclusion."

"Davin, you're lucky I like you. If I didn't ..."

Before Declan could finish his thought, Davin cut him off, recognizing that he had taken the argument as far as he could.

"Regardless of what the saying was or should be, I say that fortune is with us now," offered the tall gladiator in a strong voice. "We don't know how it will end, but we will never find out if we don't take a chance. I'm in. I fight with the Volkun."

"We know Bryen," said Lycia. "We trust him. I fight with the Volkun."

Davin and Lycia both stepped forward to emphasize their joint declaration, which prompted Dorlan, Kollea, and several other gladiators to rise from their seats and shout their approval. And then all of the gladiators were out of their chairs, screaming at the top of their lungs as if they had just survived another combat in the Pit.

They understood the reality of their situation. They understood what their future held. A bloody death. That was it. It was just a question of when. At least this way they could choose how they would die.

"If I'm going to die," said Dorlan, the massively built gladiator talking in an eerily quiet voice, "I'd like to die on my own terms." Murmurs of assent swept through the barracks. "We fight with Bryen. Live or die, we fight."

14

———

COMING HOME

"You've come at the right time," said Beluchmel, the large man waddling toward the massive, barred gate that led into the gladiators' compound. "I have several lords and ladies, as well as a few merchants, coming tomorrow who have the same interest as you."

"Really?" asked the robed woman with dark, curly hair, her thick strands obeying only the strong breeze that blew through the colonnade that circled the Colosseum.

"Others are in need of a gladiator as well?" asked the man traveling with her, while a third man stood silent behind them.

"You'll get first pick," promised the Master of the Colosseum, who ran a white cloth across his bald pate, the short walk from his office on the other side of the stadium a challenge even with the cool temperature of the early evening. He stopped in front of two large steel doors, pounding a meaty fist on one. A small grate slid open.

"Now?" came a gruff voice on the other side.

"Now," confirmed Beluchmel, and then to ensure the response was quick, he added, "by order of the King." The steel grille slammed shut, grumbles and curses drifting from the other side, but also the sounds of the gears beginning to move as the soldiers worked to open the gates to the practice yard. It was a slow process for a reason, the Royal Guard wanting to ensure that any attempt to escape by the gladiators would fail. Thus the design of the stockade as well as the cumbersome mechanism used to open and close the primary entrance. Then again, the cowled figure at the back of the small group thought, the individual who had designed the stockade had never considered how these and the other safeguards could be turned against the jailers.

"Have gladiators already been acquired from the Pit?" asked the man with a vacant expression who stood next to the woman, his hair no better than hers, wispy grey strands dancing at the slightest touch of the breeze. "I hoped that we would be the first. It would give us something to rub in the noses of those high and mighty fools who look down upon us."

Beluchmel almost salivated at the words. It was as he had thought when this couple had first stepped into his office. Rich and likely not all there in the head. The perfect people to do business with, as he could take advantage of them without them even being aware that he was doing so.

"Not since the Volkun, the greatest gladiator of the last decade, was taken by Duke Winborne more than a year ago," answered Beluchmel, who pushed his way through the steel gates before they were fully open. "After that almost every lord and lady in the land wanted their very own gladiator."

Why anyone would want a gladiator, Beluchmel didn't know. He viewed them as no better than animals. Trained to fight. Sentenced to death. It was just a matter of time before they fell on the white sand. He had heard that the Duke had made the Volkun a Protector, but that was just a rumor. He really didn't care. But he did care about the fact that when Duke Winborne purchased the Volkun, he had lost out on the sale. Sixty golds taken from his hands and given to

Declan instead. The unfairness of it all still stuck in his craw, and there had been nothing that he could do. He couldn't stand against a Duke and a very irritable Captain. But perhaps with these two and the others expected tomorrow, he could more than make up for that loss and put that memory behind him.

"Do you think we could find a gladiator like the Volkun to buy?" asked the white-haired man.

"I'm certain that we can," replied Beluchmel. "Just keep in mind that the price will differ based on the gladiator. If you select one with a well-known reputation, the price will be higher. Much higher."

"Of course, of course, my good man. We would expect no less."

"Just be certain that you know what you want," said Beluchmel. "There are many to choose from, and once the purchase is made, our transaction is done. The gladiator is yours."

"What do you mean by that?" asked the woman, who followed after the massive man, his size hidden by the large silk robes that he wore.

Beluchmel stopped for a moment to survey the three walking with him, suddenly feeling uncomfortable, as if something about them had changed in just the last few seconds, but he couldn't put his finger on it. His greed quickly overwhelmed that brief touch of concern. He sensed that he could easily get his price from the older couple once they had selected the gladiator they wanted. It was the third member of the group that caused him the greatest worry.

The tall man who trailed behind the couple hadn't said a word since the three had appeared in his office less than an hour before. He carried twin swords in scabbards hanging over a shoulder. But beyond that he could tell little of the man. The hood of his cloak covered his head, and all Beluchmel could see were a few sharp features that peeked out of the shadows of his cowl.

That, in itself, didn't concern him too much. He assumed that the guard simply preferred to keep his identity to himself, a common desire for many of the people he did business with over the years. No, what bothered him about this tall man was the air of menace wrapped around him. For just a moment, he thought that he caught a flash of cold grey eyes from beneath the cowl. The last time that he had looked into a pair of eyes like that, he believed that he had been about to die. So it took some effort for him to pull his gaze from the tall man who had yet to step through the gates and turn his attention back to the woman, who smiled brightly at him, her hands continually pushing loose strands of hair behind her ears.

"All of the men and women here at the Colosseum would be excellent choices," replied Beluchmel, who walked ponderously into the stockade. "All are excellent fighters. I'm simply suggesting that if your desire is to use a gladiator for some other reason, I suggest that you pick wisely. Some of the people coming tomorrow are looking to use gladiators in ways that are not traditional. In ways that do not play to their strengths. In my experience, that could be a mistake, but that's a mistake for them to make if they so choose. These gladiators are good at fighting and killing. Beyond that, don't expect too much."

"If you're so concerned about these men and women and their unique and perhaps somewhat frightening predilections, why are you so willing to sell them?" asked the older man, who strode after the woman through the gates.

"I'm not concerned about them," replied Beluchmel. "They're good at fighting and killing, just as I said. Use them that way and you'll be fine. It's the lords and ladies who have other interests in mind, the owners of the pleasure houses that are interested in acquiring a gladiator, who might be in for a surprise or two, that's all I'm saying."

"Good advice," replied the woman. "Thank you."

"I'm just here to help you," said Beluchmel, his voice dripping with a false sincerity. "If you're looking for someone like the Volkun, I can help you do that. And as I said, you're here at the right time. Good King Beleron refused to allow the sale of any more gladiators when the Volkun left the Pit, but he's had a change of heart in recent weeks. So we should take advantage of his largesse while we can."

Rafia turned a keen eye toward Sirius. She had no doubt that King Beleron's decision to allow the sale of gladiators would prove a financial windfall to the Master of the Colosseum, who would deftly skim a certain portion of the revenue earned for himself. Bryen had explained how it had worked while he had been in the Pit. The Crown provided a small allowance for the gladiatorial games, and it had been a constant struggle for Declan to feed, clothe, and house his gladiators with the meager amount of money that eventually made its way to the Master of the Gladiators after it had worked its way through Beluchmel's fat, greedy fingers.

She also had no doubt as to why Marden was permitting Beluchmel to put gladiators up for auction. He needed the money. It was as simple as that. Without a constant stream of funds, the King would find it difficult to maintain his Royal Guard and the many vanity projects currently under construction throughout the capital. Also, he likely assumed that for every gladiator sold, he could find five more people to enslave. With the unrest brewing in the city, there was no lack of possible candidates for the Pit wallowing in the dungeons beneath the Corinthian Palace. Just thinking about it made her sick. The greed. The inhumanity. The selfishness. But she was not above taking advantage of it herself if it meant that they could achieve their larger objective and perhaps prove to be more than just a thorn in the side of the covetous King Beleron and his Advisor.

"Coming lad?" whispered Sirius, who took a few steps through the gates before looking back at the tall figure who had yet to move, his feet apparently rooted to the ground.

The old Magus understood the discomfort that the Protector likely was experiencing. He was walking right back into the prison that had held him for almost half his life. For just a few seconds, Sirius worried that their plan would fail before they could put it fully into play, Bryen hesitating to enter the gladiators' compound after finally having gained his freedom. But then the Magus saw a brief nod from the hooded figure, who strode through the gates and caught up to Sirius, both now trailing Rafia, who was being guided by Beluchmel to the building in the center of the stockade that separated the two broken-down barracks that housed the gladiators.

Bryen had not expected that he would find it so difficult to return to the gladiators' stockade. He had grown up here. He had friends here. People he cared about. People who cared about him. People he had bled for and people who had bled for him. Still, even with all that, for several minutes he felt as if he couldn't breathe, anxiety and fear sweeping through him. He had only been gone from the Pit for a year, but it seemed much longer than that to him. He had missed his friends. He had not missed what it meant to live next to the Pit.

To release himself from the paralysis that affected him, Bryen put into practice what Declan had taught him to do every time he was about to walk into the Pit. It seemed appropriate for the current situation. He closed his eyes and took a deep breath, seeking to center himself, to push out all the distractions, mental and sensory, until his mind was focused once again on the task at hand, clear in its purpose, his fears and concerns, his memories and doubts, locked away to be dealt with at another time. With that accomplished, a spark returned to his eyes and a familiar, comfortable warmth surged within him, flowing from his chest into his limbs. He was ready.

For whatever was to come, for whatever the result would be, he was ready.

"Why is it so quiet?" asked Rafia, Bryen and Sirius now right behind her.

"Dinner," replied Beluchmel. "It's about the only time during the day that you won't see gladiators out here in the yard practicing their skills. Declan, the Master of the Gladiators, runs them hard. But it seems to benefit them. The ones who listen, anyway. The ones who don't, they don't last long on the white sand."

"He sounds ruthless," said Rafia, trying to keep Beluchmel talking and slightly preoccupied.

"He is," replied Beluchmel with a grunt. "Grouchy on a good day, intolerable on all the others. He can be difficult. He is difficult. It's his nature. Allow me to apologize for any insults he may offer to you now. But have no fear, he has no say in the sale of gladiators. I will handle the transactions myself and make sure that you pay a fair but not exorbitant price."

Rafia fought to keep the smirk that threatened to appear on her lips from forming. Beluchmel's act might work on others, but not her. The large man was interested only in the money to be made. He would say and do whatever was needed to ensure that he obtained the golds that he wanted. Having mastered her initial instinct, she transformed the burgeoning smirk into a smile.

"Our thanks," replied Rafia, her eyes sparkling as she placed a hand on the large man's forearm, giving him a few pats to demonstrate her confidence in his abilities. "We appreciate your help in this endeavor. We will rely on your expertise and knowledge."

"I am pleased to help," answered Beluchmel, an oiliness seeping into his voice. He could smell the money to be made off these two old fools.

Normally, he loved the haggling that was a part of this or

any other transaction in Tintagel. But Beluchmel thought that perhaps with these two he could simply name his price. He was already thinking about a starting figure based on the gladiator selected when the old man, who had remained silent for so long, finally spoke up again. His words made Beluchmel stop before he entered the dark doorway that led to Declan's office.

"I'm sorry, but I think I might have misheard," said Beluchmel before he pushed his bulk through the doorway. "What did you ask?"

Sirius stepped up next to Rafia, his eyes, initially subdued and even empty at times when he had first introduced himself to the Master of the Colosseum, now sparking with cunning and intelligence.

"I was curious as to how much it would cost to free all the gladiators."

For a moment, Beluchmel simply stood there, a frown creasing his forehead, as if he didn't understand the question. Then he began to laugh, the rumbling guffaw starting in the back of his throat and then spreading to the rest of his body, until he gripped his huge belly in merriment. When he was in control of himself once again, he shook his head, demonstrating his appreciation for the humor.

"Surely you jest?"

Sirius stepped up close to the huge man, his eyes now consumed by a dangerous intensity. "I wasn't trying to be funny. I was being serious."

Beluchmel tried to back away a few steps, but he had nowhere to go, the collapsing walls of the building keeping him in place.

"You can't be serious," said Beluchmel, stuttering the first few words because of his rising fear.

"Completely serious," said Rafia, who pressed up against Beluchmel on his other side, so that he was now cornered.

"You can't do that," Beluchmel gulped. He had taken these

two older people to be no more than easy marks, the tall man simply a guard. But he was beginning to realize that perhaps he had made a mistake. He was beginning to sweat more heavily, and not because of the short walk around the Colosseum, his robes sticking to his many folds of flesh, and his nerves threatening to get the better of him. "I can sell you one gladiator, maybe two at the most. But I have other clients that I must deal with. And I've received nothing from the Corinthian Palace that would allow me to do more than that this evening." Trying to regain control of the situation and himself, Beluchmel laughed, but this time it came out as no more than a nervous titter that appeared strange for such a large man. "Besides, even if the Crown permitted it -- and as I said I do not have the authority to sell you all the gladiators -- the price would be more than it would take to purchase a Duchy. You could never afford it."

Sirius stared deeply into Beluchmel's eyes, watching as the greed that had been there was replaced by a nervousness that quickly gave way to fear. He laughed then, a mirthless chuckle, which seemed to infect Beluchmel with another bout of tittering laughter that came to an end as soon as Sirius abruptly stopped his own. An uncomfortable silence descended upon them as Beluchmel tried and failed to decipher what was going on behind the old man's now piercing gaze.

The Master of the Colosseum glanced up at the surrounding walls, but realized that he was on his own. The few soldiers lining the three staggered parapets built around the compound were paying no attention to what was going on within the stockade now that all the gladiators were in their barracks. Instead, their attention was drawn to the shouts and occasional screams that carried over the walls from time to time, a common occurrence in the capital during the last few months as conditions for most of its inhabitants had worsened.

"You know, you're right," said Sirius, finally breaking the quietude. "It would cost too much to purchase all the gladiators. Let's make it easy. My friends and I are not here to buy the gladiators. I apologize, but we misled you."

"I'm sorry, what?" Beluchmel asked, having a difficult time understanding as the fear that had continued to grow within him had begun to make him feel sick, his desire to retch increasing.

"We're not here to purchase the gladiators," said Sirius. "Have no fear of that. No, instead we're here to take the gladiators."

"Take?" asked Beluchmel, his mind starting to shut down as his growing terror sent his body into an uncontrollable shivering. "The gladiators? You can't."

"We can and we will," interrupted Rafia. "We'll be taking all your gladiators."

It was then that the tall man who had stayed out of the conversation finally stepped forward to join his two companions. Beluchmel gasped as the person he took to be a guard dropped his hood. He knew that face. The scars. The flinty eyes that spoke only of a hardened ruthlessness. Never having expected to see again the figure now standing before him, the Master of the Colosseum turned a ghostly white.

"Enough of this," said the Volkun. "My friends weren't as clear as they should have been. We're not here to pay for the gladiators. We're here to free them. And you're going to help us. Get that through your thick skull."

Then, with his patience at an end, Bryen grabbed one of Beluchmel's fleshy arms, turned him toward the entrance to Declan's office, and pushed him through.

"We were handling it just fine," protested Sirius. "You just need to be a bit more patient."

"You were taking forever," said Bryen as he stepped into the dim light of the building, keeping Beluchmel in front of him. "If we'd stood out there any longer the soldiers on the walls would have gotten suspicious."

"I was just trying to get this Beluchmel to understand that …"

"Let it go, Sirius," said Rafia, who pushed past the Magus to follow Bryen. "The Protector is right. You were taking too long."

Sirius frowned in annoyance, then walked into the building.

"No respect for your elders," he grumbled. "No respect at all."

~

"QUITE AN ENTRANCE, LAD," said Declan, who sat calmly on the edge of his desk, two sawhorses supporting the broken door that had used to serve as the entrance to his office.

"It's good to see you again, Declan."

Bryen smiled, warming Declan's heart. The Master of the Gladiators had missed his fosterling more than he cared to admit to himself.

"I'm assuming that we need to deal with Beluchmel." Declan gestured to the large man Bryen had placed against the wall, sweat beading down his head and cheeks, his eyes large and terrified.

"We do," answered Bryen.

Hearing the lack of emotion in the Volkun's voice, Beluchmel's escalating fear almost sent him to the floor in a heap, his legs threatening to give out from under him. It wasn't long before he felt a trickle of warm liquid run down his leg, his bladder vacating.

"I've been wanting to do this for a long time," said Declan, the Master of the Gladiators pushing himself off his makeshift desk to stand in front of the terror-stricken Beluchmel. "Stealing money from the men and women who truly needed it, enriching himself at their expense, seeking the most dangerous creatures for the Pit so that he could appease a bloodthirsty crowd and monarch. Yes, I have been waiting for this chance for a very long time."

"Nothing too drawn out or bloody, I hope," said Bryen as if he were simply engaging in a normal conversation. "We don't have the time. It needs to be fast, and it needs to be quiet."

"I can do both with ease," said Declan, his predatory smile making Beluchmel feel faint, his eyes beginning to roll up in his head.

"Please, Declan, it was never my intention ..."

"To do anything for the gladiators," interrupted Bryen. "You always intended to use us for your own benefit, and you did. No matter how many were maimed. No matter how many died."

Rafia and Sirius watched the interaction between the two gladiators and the man who had made their lives so excruciatingly painful for so long with great interest. They had not expected that Declan and Bryen would consider taking such extreme measures, but neither felt that it was their place to intercede.

"Come along, Beluchmel," said Declan, who grabbed the large man by the arm and pulled him through a doorway in the back of his office, disappearing into the darkness. "It's time to end this."

They heard Beluchmel pleading with Declan, his words becoming no more than blubbering promises that he would change his ways, that he would make it right for all the gladiators, until those protestations were cut off by a slamming door. And then there was nothing but silence.

"Should we ..." Rafia began to ask, but the Magus closed her mouth when Bryen shook his head, his face stony and cold.

It wasn't long before Declan stepped back into the office with a big smile.

"You didn't kill him, did you?" asked Sirius. That possible result didn't really bother the Magus, he just hadn't taken the Master of the Gladiators to be so cold-blooded. Then again, regardless of what the man had done for Bryen, who could say what type of person he really was. Having to survive in the Colosseum for so many years obviously changed a man.

"He certainly deserves to die," responded Declan. "But no, I didn't. I locked him in the storeroom in back. No one will hear him, and he won't be able to escape. You thought I killed him?"

Sirius was about to respond, but when he saw how Declan stood poised for action, his expression suggesting that any insult could lead to a deadly encounter, the Magus did something that he had little practice in. He attempted to demonstrate some tact.

"It just seemed like the easiest thing to do."

Declan nodded knowingly, agreeing with Sirius. "You're probably right, but I prefer not to kill someone unless I have to. We can deal with him later. For now, he is not a problem."

"So this is the famed Declan?" Rafia stepped forward then, her eyes flashing with both amusement and curiosity regarding the barrel-chested, tree trunk-armed Master of the Gladiators.

"And you are?" asked Declan, his eyes hard, his smile at seeing Bryen now gone and replaced by a natural wariness. He could sense the strength in this woman, a power that he didn't quite understand.

"A great admirer," replied Rafia, her smile broadening. "Bryen has told me quite a bit about you."

"I don't know whether to be flattered or worried," replied Declan.

"Probably a little of both," murmured Bryen, who didn't bother to hide his grin.

"You're not helping," said Rafia, who shot the Protector a warning look.

"I'm not trying to help."

"Why do I put up with you?" asked Rafia, shaking her head in exasperation. "So smart, but sometimes too smart for your own good."

"I've said much the same," said Declan.

"I'm not surprised. You should be proud of Bryen. He has done incredibly well since leaving the Pit."

Declan nodded, pleased to hear the praise for the young man he viewed as his son. "That's kind of you to say."

"So as I had mentioned, Declan, I've heard much about you. Do you ever ..."

"Rafia, we don't have time for this," grumbled Sirius, frustrated and just a bit jealous.

"Too true," agreed Rafia. "Too true. There is much we must do tonight." She focused her sharp gaze back on the Master of the Gladiators, her initial inquisitiveness replaced by a seriousness in both tone and expression. "We'll talk again soon, Declan. We have so much to discuss."

Declan simply nodded as he continued to try to make sense of this whirlwind of a woman.

"You can handle things here?" Rafia directed her question to Bryen, who was struggling not to laugh at Declan's discomfiture. He had never seen his friend in such a state. Bryen even thought that Declan might be blushing, but he couldn't tell in the quickly fading light.

"I can. We'll take care of things here as we discussed."

"Then Sirius and I will be off," said Rafia, who grabbed Sirius' arm and pulled him back toward the door. "Bryen has taught me quite a lot since I've made his acquaintance, but sometimes I don't think that I have it all right. What's that saying that you have here? The one that you often use right before you enter the Pit for a combat?"

"I'll see you on the other side," answered Declan.

"Yes, that's the one," Rafia confirmed excitedly. "It is so rich with meaning." Having pushed Sirius back into the practice yard, Rafia gave Declan one more dazzling smile. "We have so much to discuss, Declan. I simply can't wait." She then nodded to him before turning to Bryen. "I'll see you on the other side."

She then walked out of the crumbling building, her gait suggesting that anyone getting in her way did so at his or her own peril.

"I'll see you on the other side." Declan stared after the woman, still not certain what to make of her. "Who were those two?"

"Two Magii who have agreed to help put my scheme into motion."

"How did you convince the two Magii to help?"

"It wasn't too difficult. I didn't really give them any choice. They want something from me. They have to help me first before I help them."

"What do you want from them?"

"While we're dealing with the Royal Guard, they're going to try to free the Duke and Lady Winborne and get them out of the city."

Declan nodded, thinking about all that he had just learned. "Was that wise? Trusting those two with such a heavy responsibility?"

"Probably not. But you work with what you have."

"You're so right, lad. So right." Declan then smiled and clapped him on the back. "Shall we get to work? The gladiators are waiting for you."

DECLAN STRODE PURPOSEFULLY through the administration building that housed his quarters, walking past the many storerooms that contained the food and the other supplies that the gladiators relied on. He smiled to himself when he went by the cellar in which he had stashed Beluchmel. The Master of the Colosseum deserved a worse punishment, in Declan's opinion. But this would do for now. All the fears and worries playing through the man's mind as he lay on the cold floor, tied up and gagged, would terrify him more than Declan ever could. Flesh usually healed faster and better than the mind.

"Do you have any ideas for opening the vaults?" asked Declan as they walked past one of the half dozen large, steel doors that held the weapons used by the gladiators.

Special keys were required to open the locked vaults and those were kept by the Royal Guard. At the beginning of each day, a troop of soldiers would work with Declan to determine what weapons would be needed by the gladiators, either for the Pit or for training. Those weapons would be counted by multiple soldiers, provided to the gladiators, and then counted by different soldiers again at the end of the day to ensure that all were returned before the weapons were locked away again for the night. It was just another of the protections put in place to ensure that the gladiators understood that escape was impossible.

"It shouldn't be a problem," replied Bryen, who strode next to Declan and held a sword in each hand. Bryen brought the two hilts together with a twist and a barely audible click to form his much preferred Spear of the Magii.

"How can you be so certain? Even if I attacked the Guard when they came to open the vaults, word would spread before we could touch a single weapon. I'm the only one allowed to be with them when they're pulling out what we need for the day."

Bryen heard the skepticism in Declan's voice. Rather than taking the time to explain what he could do, he decided that it would be easier to show his friend. When they came to the next vault, he stopped, Declan doing so as well, a frown creasing his brow. For just a second, Bryen stared at the rectangular steel door that stood in front of him. It rose from ceiling to floor and was wide enough to allow six men to enter shoulder to shoulder at the same time. Each door was a foot thick, and the hinges were on the inside. So there was no way to break through the two-ton entrance. It could only be opened with the keys. But even then, it wasn't just one lock that prevented access to the cache of weapons. It was three. One on each side and a third keyhole near the top that required three people to insert three uniquely designed skeleton keys into each lock and turn at the exact same time. Each lock controlled a steel deadbolt that was as thick as a man's forearm and slid more than a foot into the stone wall of the building.

A formidable vault. But one that Bryen was certain that he could crack. Closing his eyes, Bryen took hold of the Talent, then extended his senses into the door beginning with the lock to his left. In seconds he understood how the mechanism worked and knew what he had to do. Placing his hand close to the lock, a steady stream of the Talent shot through the keyhole. He didn't bother with the teeth or the other pieces of the lock. Instead, he cared only about the long metal bolt that extended into the wall.

"Bryen, what are you ..." Declan's words cut off in his throat when he saw the white glow emanating from the palm of Bryen's hand.

Ignoring Declan, Bryen turned his attention to the lock in the center of the door at the top, going through the same process as he did with the first, focusing a stream of the Talent on the bolt that shot up into the top of the stone frame, melting the metal, and then he did the same again with the keyhole to his right. Opening his eyes, he took in the steam billowing out of the three keyholes. He then grinned at his friend. With a flick of his wrist, Bryen used a tiny stream of the Talent to pull on the door, which swung open on its silent hinges to reveal the contents inside. The shelves in the back were covered with shields and mismatched pieces of body armor, bins to the left contained swords, falchions, and rapiers, and large metal rings affixed to the other wall held a variety of spears, halberds, and lances. Closest to the door was a table upon which several boxes sat that contained dozens of daggers of various shapes and sizes.

"How did you do that?" asked Declan, astonished at what Bryen had just accomplished.

"I used the Talent."

"I know you used the Talent," replied Declan with just a touch of irritation. "I might be a slave here, but I wasn't for quite a long time. When I was in the Royal Guard, I fought with Magii several times. You just did something I thought I'd never see again. I had no idea you had the capacity to do that. How did you learn to use the Talent?"

"It's a long story," said Bryen.

"Those two who came with you taught you?"

"Sirius and Rafia? Yes. They did." Feeling the press of time, Bryen turned away from the door and started walking down the hallway, this time Declan having to hurry to catch up, as Bryen headed for the barracks on the western side of the gladiators' compound where the mess hall was located. "There's a lot I need to tell you, Declan. It's only been a year, but with all that's happened it feels like a lifetime has passed. I promise. We can talk about it more later."

Declan accepted Bryen's offer with a grunt. Bryen wasn't sure if Declan was pleased or upset to learn that he could use the Talent. Many people in Caledonia were terrified of those few who could employ the natural power of the world, some of them even suggesting that it was unnatural, manipulating what shouldn't be manipulated. That, in part, helped to explain why many Magii tried to keep their abilities hidden. Why deal with the fear that Magii often engendered within the populace if it could be avoided?

But he didn't think Declan's practical mind worked that way. Declan probably viewed Bryen's skill in the Talent as a tool that could be used to their benefit. His irritation would come from the fact that he had just learned of Bryen's ability and was more surprised than anything else. It would just take some time for Declan to adjust his perspective. At least Bryen hoped that would prove to be the case.

"Where did you get the spear?" Declan asked, seeking to shift the topic of conversation.

Bryen smiled as he twirled the double-bladed spear slowly from one hand to the other as they continued to walk down the wide hallway, the exit to the barracks a lighter shadow that beckoned a few hundred yards down the corridor.

"I needed it apparently."

"You needed it?" asked Declan, not understanding. "What exactly does that mean?"

"I obtained the spear at the Aeyrie, the same place where I became a Magus," explained Bryen.

"You do know that this is a weapon touched by the Talent?" Declan asked. "Even I can sense that, and I have no skill in the Talent. The telltale sign is that the steel seems to pull in even the faintest light. It's always shining, even in a darkened passageway such as this one."

"I do," answered Bryen. "It's one of the reasons that I have the spear. I'm new to the Talent and Sirius thought that a way to help fine-tune my control would be to use a weapon such as this, the Spear of the Magii."

"Does it help you? From what I understand, you need to be careful. When I was younger, I fought with several new Magii. A few burned themselves out because they really didn't know what they were doing. You could easily kill yourself with the Talent if you make a mistake or draw in too much of the power of the natural world."

"It does help," said Bryen, who chose not to reveal the fact that the primary purpose of the Spear of the Magii was to help him maintain his control over the Dark Magic within him. And he had absolutely no desire to reveal that the Seventh Stone had decided to merge with him. Declan could handle a great deal, but Bryen thought it best to keep it to one shock at a time. "It gives me a good bit more control, which has proven useful since I'm new to all this. Sirius tells me that the spear was crafted by the Giants of the Rime."

"It's a beautiful weapon," said Declan. The Master of the Gladiators watched as the steel of the blades shimmered brightly even though there was barely any light in the long hallway but for a lone torch set in a steel sconce at the far end of the corridor. The grip in the center of the spear where the two blades came together was made of twisted steel wrapped in soft leather that prevented Bryen's hands from slipping even when covered by sweat or blood.

"What do the words mean?" asked Declan, pointing to the shaft of the spear along which runic lettering flickered in and out of the shadows.

"When the darkness surrounds, the light will prevail," translated Bryen.

"Sounds ominous. What does that mean?"

"I don't know," replied Bryen. "Maybe it has something to do with when the spear was made. Sirius said that it was during a time when the Magii needed weapons to fight an evil created by Dark Magic."

"Makes sense," said Declan. He smiled as they approached the doorway, the dim light of the evening beckoning, as they prepared to walk out into the practice yard before entering the western barracks. "It looks like it was made for your hands."

"It feels that way," agreed Bryen. "I don't know why, but it does."

"Are you sure you can handle that weapon?" asked a voice from just outside the barracks. "It's a much better quality than the one you used in the Pit. Sharper too, I expect. I wouldn't want you to cut yourself by mistake. Can we really trust you with a weapon such as that?"

"Better me than you," replied Bryen as he and Declan

stepped out of the building. "With your skinny legs, this spear probably would be wasted on you."

Rather than getting angry, Davin laughed. "Probably so." Davin then extended his hand and he and Bryen clasped arms. "The Volkun has returned."

"I have."

"Just couldn't bear to stay away from me, could you?"

"Actually he couldn't bear to stay away from me," said a tall, red-headed woman, her hair done in an intricate braid that ran down her back to just below her waist, who stepped up next to her brother.

"Lycia," Bryen said with a grin. "I've missed you."

Bryen's words brought a huge smile to Lycia's face. Stepping forward, she hugged Bryen with a strength that threatened to crush him. She didn't want to let go, but she realized that she had to when Declan cleared his throat. She stepped back reluctantly, but not before she gave Bryen a long kiss on the cheek.

"I've missed you too."

"So Declan said that you might be coming back," said Davin, who crossed his arms and leaned back against the wall of the building as if nothing had changed, despite the fact that his friend had been gone for more than a year. "Something about you wanting to free all of us and then remove King Beleron from the throne if we had the chance."

Bryen shrugged and then nodded as if it wasn't much of an ask. "Something like that."

It was Davin's turn to nod, during which he appeared to be contemplating the concept.

"Sounds like fun," he finally said. "Gives us something else to do besides bleed for the rich."

"I thought you might see it that way."

"I do," confirmed Davin. "You look different."

"It has been a year," responded Bryen, not sure what his friend could be referring to.

"No, not that. You look different, but I can't explain it." Davin shrugged again. "I mean, it's not like you were worth looking at to begin with, what with the scars, the dead eyes, and the menacing countenance. But not having seen you for a while, there's just something about you that's more ..."

"Distracting," finished Lycia. "There was always something about you that pulled the eye, but now ..." Unable to explain it, she pointed to the silver collar that circled his neck. "Where did you get that? I can't say that it's an improvement."

"One of the gifts you receive when you're required to serve as a Protector." Looking at his friends, Bryen could tell that all three had additional questions at the tips of their tongues, so he held up his hands. "I promise that I'll explain later. I'll just say for now that leaving the Pit didn't lead to my freedom. It was just another form of servitude."

LYCIA AND DAVIN slipped into the western barracks first, Lycia squeezing Bryen's forearm and giving him a slight nod and wink. He could hear the loud conversation rumbling out of the many broken windows and the several holes marring the ramshackle walls. Conditions certainly hadn't improved since he had left the stockade.

The noise reminded him of all the time that he had spent here, sharing stories with his few friends and discussing strategy with his peers. Many of those fighters were now gone, replaced by a never-ending stream of reluctant recruits. It was a hard life, a short life for most. These few hours during the day, when he and the other gladiators could relax if only for a short time, had served as a temporary refuge from the rigors of an existence that wore you down, both mentally and physically, until the white sand eventually took you.

"You ready, lad?" asked Declan.

The faraway look in Bryen's eyes told the Master of the Gladiators that Bryen's thoughts were elsewhere in that moment. Declan put a large hand on his shoulder, giving him an encouraging squeeze, knowing how difficult it was for him to return to a place holding so many memories, both good and bad. Declan corrected himself. Mostly bad. Declan also knew that though Bryen was skilled in many things, the lad tended to be quiet and didn't like talking in large groups. Although he had fought hundreds of times in front of thousands of people, he didn't like bringing attention to himself, at least not in situations such as this. Many of the gladiators enjoyed the opportunity to incite the crowd when they fought on the white sand, screaming and shouting, prancing around like they were on display. Bryen never did during a combat, allowing his actions to speak for him.

Bryen nodded after several heartbeats, using the trick that Declan had taught him to calm himself, pushing his nerves, his worries, his insecurities to the side.

"Yes. You know, I feel more nervous now than I ever did before a combat."

Declan chuckled, giving him one more squeeze on the shoulder and then a reassuring pat on the back.

"Finally, we've found one of the Volkun's few weaknesses. You'll be fine. Just speak from the heart."

With that Declan walked through the doorway and into the canteen. Taking a deep breath, and knowing that if he delayed any longer he'd only become more anxious, Bryen strode through the doorway after him.

Stopping just a few feet beyond the entrance, Bryen allowed the din to wash over him, bringing back a welcome familiarity and a slight smile to his lips. A few of the fighters kept their eyes on their food, quiet, stuck in their own heads. But many of the gladiators talked animatedly, discussing what they had done during their practice sessions that day, concentrating on what worked and what didn't, on what they could have done better, because those kinds of conversations correlated directly to their success during their combats. And they all wanted to be victorious, because failure on the white sand led to only one, all-too-final result.

Before Bryen could say anything, shouts of surprise began to rise over the loud chatter. Declan had told the gladiators that morning that they could expect Bryen to appear sometime in the next few days. A few still had ignored him, believing that the Master of the Gladiators was playing with them. Why would anyone in their right mind choose to return to the place where they had been a slave for much of their life? Where they had been forced to fight and bleed for the pleasure of others? It was too much for some of the gladiators to believe. If any of them had escaped the Pit as Bryen had, they never would have considered returning. They would have stayed as far away as possible. But Declan had spoken true.

"The Volkun!"

"The Wolf!"

"He really is back."

"Why would he come back? The boy's a fool."

And so it continued for several minutes, the conversations dying abruptly as more and more gladiators noticed the Volkun standing quietly at the front of the dining hall. When silence finally reigned, Bryen walked past the tables at the front, nodding a greeting to several of the gladiators, grasping a few hands, clasping a few shoulders, until he was standing in the middle of the room. He then drove the blade on the bottom end of his spear into the worn wooden floor with a loud thunk and leaned against his staff.

For just a moment, Bryen thought that his nervousness would get the better of him. But a quick smile from Lycia and a nod of her head pushed him past his fear.

"Several of you asked a good question. I escaped the Pit, so why would I ever come back here? Why would I ever return to this prison where the sentence for all, at some unknown point in the future, is death."

"Why did you?" asked a gladiator sitting at the back of the hall.

Bryen had no trouble picking out the fighter. Jenus was so broad that he had to turn slightly to the side to avoid scraping the frame of any doorway he walked through. He was built like a barrel, actually several barrels, and he used his size to great advantage in the Colosseum, absorbing blows and then responding with a viciousness and power that most other gladiators envied.

"Still impatient, Jenus?"

The large gladiator grinned, showing several broken teeth. "Of course. And you're still not much to look at. Some things don't change, especially here in the Pit."

Bryen laughed with many of the other gladiators at the barb, enjoying the camaraderie, something that he had missed until he had begun spending time with the Battersea Guard in the practice yard. It felt as if he had never truly left these men and women, though he had been gone for more than a year.

"You're right, Jenus. Some things never change, until we change them."

Bryen's smile evaporated, replaced by the hard, unnerving stare that many of these gladiators knew so well. His last comment silenced the murmurs and laughter that had started up again during the exchange. Just as he did when he fought in the Pit, when an innate sense told him when to attack, when to go for the kill, that same sense told him that now was the time to grab hold of his audience and not let go.

"Did I return because of the promise of money?" Bryen asked in a quiet voice that seized the attention of everyone in the room. "Did some lord offer me several bags of golds to fight just one more time on the white sand?" Bryen looked around the room, making sure that his eyes caught those of every gladiator before he continued. "No."

He smiled, which was returned by many of those listening to him. He hated speaking in this way. Loathed it. But surprisingly, he was good at it. Because he had seized the attention of these hardened fighters in seconds. Now he just had to capture their imaginations as well.

"Did I return because of an unrequited love? Was I forced to leave the Pit and the woman I loved, having no choice but to return once I gained my freedom, my heart demanding that I do so?"

For just a moment, Lycia felt a catch in her throat and her body flushing with an unexpected heat, her cheeks beginning to turn red, but then Asaia's words broke the spell and led to another round of laughter.

"I always knew that the Volkun would return for me."

Bryen smiled at that, but he didn't laugh, because his expression remained serious. Focused. Demanding. This was the countenance that so many of the gladiators were familiar with, the one that he wore before he entered the Pit.

"No, it was not because of love," he said softly. "Was it revenge?"

Bryen pulled the Spear of the Magii out of the floor and began to spin the weapon slowly in front of his body, the movement measured, constant, mesmerizing, the blades flashing brightly because of the light from the two fireplaces on each side of the long hall.

"I think we can agree that there are many people who deserve to pay for what they have done to us," said Bryen. "For what they do to us now. And believe me, I would love to be the one to sit in judgment and then carry out the sentence. To spill their blood on the white sand rather than ours. But no, I did not come back here for revenge, no matter how sweet the thought of it may be."

"Then why did you come back?"

This time the question came from Tehana, who clearly was snared in the spell that Bryen was weaving. She had arrived in the Colosseum around the same time that Davin and Lycia had. She was almost as fast as the brother and sister, and she was known for fighting with a shortened trident, though the spike in the center extended beyond the other two by at least a foot. Several of the other gladiators liked to joke about her weapon, suggesting that she fought with an oversized fork. But they never did so in her presence or anywhere that she could possibly overhear. Tehana had a very short temper and little patience for those who insulted her.

Bryen grinned. He had ensnared all the gladiators, catching their interest and reeling them in slowly, subtly. He knew it. He could feel it. They were with him now, whether they knew it or not. Rather than exhorting them to action, he had instead chosen to begin by telling them a story. And it had worked. Now they wanted to know how the story ended. They just hadn't realized that the conclusion of this saga would be for them to decide.

"I came back to the Pit because of seven words. I came back to you, for you."

Bryen's last comment set off an uproar among the gladiators, many of them shouting over one another, not understanding what Bryen meant. He allowed the clamor to continue for a bit longer before he finally raised the Spear of the Magii above his head, the metal gleaming in the light of the room, held tightly in his hands. A new hush fell quickly, and Bryen began to twirl the spear once again, the movement slow, constant, mesmerizing, drawing every eye to him.

"As you know, Declan has a lot of sayings ..." began Bryen.

"That he does," confirmed Asaia with a short laugh. Tall and thin, the dark-skinned Asaia had survived the Pit for more than a year because of her unique skill in using a barbed whip.

Few of her opponents knew how to defend against her attacks, and she never gave them the time to learn. She was older than most of the other gladiators, forced into the Colosseum with her short, dark hair well on its way to grey for a supposed crime that she never spoke of. "It's hard to keep track of them all."

That comment earned several laughs from the gladiators in the room, including Bryen.

"You're right about that, Asaia." Bryen chuckled a bit more as he saw the grimace that passed across Declan's face, a grumble escaping his lips that he assumed was a curse, because the Master of the Gladiators knew many of those as well. "He does have a lot of sayings. And I've heard them all. Many, many times. Let me explain."

Abruptly, Bryen stopped spinning the Spear of the Magii and slammed a blade back into the wooden floor, which startled several of the gladiators. But that's how he wanted them. On edge.

"When I was away, I never thought that I'd see the white sand again, because when I left the Pit, I simply exchanged one form of slavery for another. I was still required to fight, still required to die. I had no choice." He bit off the last few words harshly. "But then I was given the chance to actually be free, or whatever that actually means after spending ten years in the Colosseum. It was then that I discovered that once you step onto the white sand, you never really leave it."

Many of the gladiators nodded, understanding what the Volkun meant. They were unable to fathom the concept of being free again. Unable to believe that if you actually left the Pit, you could ever truly be free from the white sand, because the white sand never left you, even in death.

"When I was finally freed, Declan's words kept running through my mind. Seven words, as I said. The same seven words. Always the same seven words." Bryen shook his head with a knowing almost irritated grin. "I remember exactly when I heard those words for the first time. It was during my first combat on the white sand. I had been here no more than a few weeks, Declan teaching me all that he could, but he didn't expect me to live. I was too small. Too inexperienced. Too frightened. I was no more than a child fighting a monster of a man who had years of experience as a gladiator. I had never fought for my life before. Never killed anyone before. And then it didn't seem like I ever could."

Bryen's eyes swept across the room. He could see that his story resonated with them, many of these hardened fighters experiencing the same emotions as he did, having the same thoughts.

"When I walked out into the Pit, I could barely move, my legs feeling not my own. The first strike finally broke me from my terror. The other gladiator toyed with me, playing to the crowd. As the combat dragged on, I knew that it was no more than a show, the other gladiator simply having his fun before he killed me. I had dropped my sword because I couldn't use it effectively. It was too heavy for me, and I couldn't swing it fast enough. The gladiator laughed at me, and then he chased me around the Pit, every so often scoring me with the tip of his sword, and each time he did so, he elicited a roar of approval from the crowd. The gladiator relented, finally, having tired of his fun for a time, so he spent a few minutes inciting the crowd. While he did that, I realized that I had ended up by the gates where Declan always stood to watch the combats. He caught my eye, and he gave me the advice that has stuck with me to this day. That has brought me back to the Pit, back here to you."

"What were the words?" asked Dorlan, who, like many of the other gladiators, was sitting on the edge of his seat, completely enthralled by the Volkun.

"You must do what you must do," Bryen said softly, though the words carried easily through the silence so that the several hundred gladiators could hear them clearly. "You must do what you must do."

Bryen dropped his head for a moment, closing his eyes, his voice barely more than a whisper, forcing everyone in the room to lean in toward him so that they could hear. And they all wanted to hear.

"You must do what you must do. Seven simple words. Just words. But they saved my life then. For some reason, the paralyzing fear left me, replaced with a purpose, a fire, that I had never felt before. I pulled the dagger from my belt and in a matter of minutes I had survived my first combat. I couldn't fight that gladiator with a sword, but I could with a dagger. He was bigger than me. Stronger than me. But he wasn't faster than me. He wasn't smarter, because if he had been smart, he would have killed me at the start. I did what I had to do. He didn't. And those seven words stayed with me for the hundreds of combats that followed."

Bryen opened his eyes and lifted his head, catching the eyes of every single gladiator before he continued.

"You must do what you must do. Those words have tormented me. Those words started playing through my dreams when I became free. Every night. The same words. The same seven words played through my mind. You must do what you must do. And I knew why. I just didn't like it at first. I thought that if I was free, that I could ignore the words. That I could start a new life and forget the white sand. Forget you. But I couldn't. Supposedly I was free of the Pit, but as you all know, none of us can ever truly be free of the white sand."

Many of the gladiators nodded sagely, acknowledging what Bryen had said, Dorlan, Asaia, Tehana, and many others agreeing with him.

"You must do what you must do," Bryen said again. "When I realized that I could never truly be free, that there was only one way to truly be free, I knew what I had to do. Regardless of the consequences, whether I succeeded or failed, I had to at least try. I didn't have a choice. I had to come back, because finally I had discovered the truth, though I didn't like it. The only way to be free of the white sand was to come back to the white sand. Because we can never be free unless we choose to be, and to do that we must all decide if we have the courage and the desire to cast away our demons. No one can free us from the Pit. We can only free ourselves from the Pit, even if only for a minute, an hour, a day, a week."

"What are you suggesting?" asked Tehana. Her eyes sparkled in anticipation, as did the eyes of many of the gladiators in the room. Everything that the Volkun had said had resonated with her. She, like many of the others, had not only heard the Wolf's words, but she had felt them in her soul.

"I'm suggesting that we do what we must do. We are cursed by the white sand. We are haunted by the white sand. We are all condemned to the white sand. We will die. Eventually we will all color the white sand with the red of our blood. I came back here because I wanted to be free of the Pit, once and for all. And I realized while I was away that the only way to do that was to free myself. And if, in the end, I failed to free my body, at least I would know with certainty that I had freed my spirit."

"Death doesn't choose us," whispered Lycia, her words carrying to every gladiator across the hushed quiet that had settled within the room.

"We choose our death," completed Bryen.

Many of the other gladiators nodded their agreement, wanting to believe in the truth of those words.

"You must do what you must do," said Dorlan, nodding his large head, a sense of confidence building within him. For the first time in several years, the large man felt as if a weight had been lifted from his shoulders. "Only seven words as you said, Volkun. But powerful words. I assume that you have a plan."

Bryen gave the giant man a confident nod. He had spoken

from his heart, not knowing what he was going to say when he had walked into the barracks, uncertain of what the reaction would be. But now he was certain. Now he knew that these gladiators were with him.

"I do," he replied. "Let me take you through it, beyond what Declan has already shared with you, and I'll try to answer any questions you might have."

Bryen spent the next hour explaining what he had in mind, the gladiators listening intently. Several questions were raised, which Bryen answered, Declan often offering his expertise as well to sand down any rough points that gave them pause. There were several suggestions offered to improve the strategy Bryen was seeking to implement. Some were accepted, others were rejected for various reasons. But all the gladiators felt as if they had been heard, an uncommon experience for them, and they had reached the point where a decision needed to be made.

"It's for you to decide whether you want to participate," Bryen concluded. "You know the plan. All of it. The risks and the possible reward. The how. The when. The why. You also know the likely result. What say you?"

"And if we don't want to fight?" asked Tehana, though clearly she had already made up her mind and simply wanted to give Bryen a final chance to make his case.

"Then we die," Bryen said simply. "We die fighting on the white sand for the pleasure of others, our deaths decided by others, rather than fighting for ourselves. Fighting for our freedom."

"We all made our decisions as soon as the Volkun walked through the door," said Dorlan. "None of you will miss this chance. It's too good an opportunity. Do we die on the white sand, or do we die trying to gain our freedom? There is no choice to be made. As the Volkun said, you must do what you must do. We know what we must do."

"We do," confirmed Asaia, many other gladiators murmuring their agreement.

"Then let's get to it," said Dorlan. "When do we get started, Volkun?"

"Now."

A raucous cheer erupted among the gladiators, all of them leaping to their feet and shouting at the top of their lungs. Bryen raised his hands for silence. Once he finally gained it, he lifted the Spear of the Magii above his head and called out in a loud voice, "We will stand fast!"

The gladiators all knew the saying, having heard it repeated by Declan many times. Bryen's words were quickly drowned out as his friends and peers completed the adage for him.

"We will stand strong! We will stand free!"

A roar filled the hall once again, a submerged energy breaking free and sparking from one gladiator to the next as they remembered what they had been before they had been forced into the Colosseum. As they thought about what they wanted to be, if only for a minute, for an hour, for a day, for a week. They wanted to be free.

"Quite impressive," said Davin, clapping Bryen on the back. The red-haired gladiator was always smiling, but now his ever-present grin could only be described as predatory. "Now it's time to have some fun."

15

FORTUITOUS ENCOUNTER

The Captain of the Battersea Guard sat on his horse stiffly, back erect, as if he were on the parade ground. Despite being several weeks out of the Southern Marches and spending the last few days in a woodland, his uniform was spotless, his leather boots shined brightly, and his hair and mustache, the tips waxed and curled into points, were exactly as he preferred. Having served as a soldier for more than two decades, he understood that there were many things that you couldn't control in life. So he took particular pride in controlling those aspects of his life that he could, his appearance among them. But, in that very moment, as he stared out from the grove, he feared that he was about to lose control over what he already viewed as a precarious situation.

His companies remained hidden behind the reflective shield that the Magus Rafia had crafted before she, Sirius, and Bryen had traveled on toward Tintagel, the city on the far-off bluff more than a league to their north. The Guard had stayed here at the edge of the wood unseen for several days, waiting to embark on what could prove to be an incredible victory or a complete disaster. Unfortunately, Tarin feared that it could be the latter as he watched the large, long, twisting column of soldiers ride toward him across the grassland.

When he saw the mounted soldiers approach from several miles away, Tarin had considered moving his troops. But he had too many fighters with him and there was no way that he could adjust his position without being spotted, the magic set in place and not something that could move with them. So he had formed his companies into squares so that either they could fight among the trees if necessary or if he chose to have his troops emerge from the grove they easily could assume a battle formation on the plain that stretched out before them.

He heard the soldiers' horses around him whickering and stomping their hooves, the animals picking up on their riders' unease. The men and women of the Battersea Guard were ready for a fight if that's what it was to be that morning, but like most soldiers, they hated the waiting, the anticipation that played on their nerves as they sought to determine whether the advancing troops were friend or foe.

At first, Tarin worried that the Royal Guard approached, having finally awoken from their slumber and come out from the capital, as he had seen neither hide nor hare since the Battersea Guard had taken up residence in the wood. Then he smiled, finally getting a better look at the approaching army. Giving orders to his company commanders to prepare to march toward the city, Tarin nudged his horse from the wood, trotting out onto the grassland until he came to a stop in front of a small group that had broken off from the sinuous column, which was now turning to the northeast.

"Captain Tentillin, it's good to see you, but I didn't expect you to be here," said Noorsin Stelekel, the Duchess of Murcia. Her long chestnut hair swirled as gusts of wind played across the grassland, and her energized expression suggested that she was clearly enjoying this opportunity to be away from her Duchy and doing something that she viewed as both useful and necessary. "I thought that Lady Winborne ordered you to protect the Southern Marches."

"She did," replied Tarin, taking note of the two figures who had just rode up to join them. "You've been busy, Duchess Stelekel. I see that you've brought some friends with you."

Obviously, the Duchess of Murcia had not wasted her time upon returning to her province from the Southern Marches, recruiting several others to her cause. Cornelius Stennivere, the Duke of the Three Rivers, was an irascible, short-tempered fellow, but also fastidiously honest and trustworthy and a good friend to Kevan Winborne. Tall and bald, his one extravagance was a red beard that was so long that often he had to tuck it into his belt to keep it out of the way. This time, however, the Duke had braided it instead so that it wouldn't interfere if a fight ensued. Next to him was Wencel Roosarian. The Duke of Roo's Nest was a short man who appeared even smaller when riding his horse next to the imposing Duke of the Three Rivers. He had a short beard that just covered his chin to complement a bushy mustache with waxed tips that was so thick that it resembled the horns of the steers that were so common to his Duchy.

"Indeed I have, Captain. And I expect that a few more Dukes and Duchesses of the Kingdom are not too far behind us with their soldiers. Not enough to challenge the Royal Guard in a pitched battle, mind you, but if we do this right, we should be able to accomplish our purpose."

Tarin nodded his agreement. "How did you find us?"

Just then the soldiers of Battersea began to emerge from the grove onto the grassland, their battle squares shifting fluidly into a column that joined with the one that now streamed toward the north and the capital that beckoned.

"Quite a trick that," said Noorsin, motioning toward the wood. "Rafia's work?"

"Yes, it was. It proved quite useful, though I have to say I was somewhat surprised not to see a single patrol from the capital."

Noorsin nodded. "I thought as much. I sensed the Talent from several leagues away, and since the cause was on the way, it only seemed sensible to come here and check it out. I'm glad that I did. Adding your soldiers to ours will give the Royal Guard more of a headache. But Captain, you still haven't explained why you're here and not in the Southern Marches. Were you not supposed to guard the Duchy?"

"I was, Duchess Stelekel, you're correct," replied Tarin, a slight tinge of guilt leaking into his voice. He had an excellent reason for making the decision to come to Tintagel, but he still felt somewhat contrite about it. "But circumstances changed."

"How so?"

"Ghoules, Duchess Stelekel."

"Did you say Ghoules, Captain?" asked a scowling Duke Stennivere.

"The stories are true, then," said Duke Roosarian. "Duchess Stelekel told us of what happened on the coastal road, but I didn't want to believe it. It bodes ill for the Kingdom."

"I think we'd all like to hear about what's been happening in the Southern Marches since I returned to Murcia," said Duchess Stelekel.

At Noorsin's request, Tarin spent several minutes providing details on the Battle of the Horseshoe in the Southern Marches and the effort expended to remove the many Ghoule packs and Elders from the province.

"At the moment, the Southern Marches is clear of Ghoules, so I thought to ..." The Captain shrugged his shoulders, leaving the left unsaid.

"To storm the capital yourself and try to free Duke Winborne and Lady Aislinn."

"I assume that's why you are here as well, Duchess Stelekel."

"We are, indeed, Captain," said Duke Stennivere. "But I don't know how you thought that you could take the city with just the Battersea Guard. I have no doubt as to the prowess of your soldiers if you've been fighting Ghoules, but I fail to see how you planned to defeat the Royal Guard."

"That was never their intention, Cornelius," said Duke Roosarian, who tended to stay quiet and allow others to talk, hiding what was a razor-sharp mind. "There's something else at play here that the Captain has yet to reveal."

"Would you care to share, Captain?" asked Noorsin.

"Rafia and Sirius have gone to the Corinthian Palace in an attempt to free Duke Winborne and Lady Aislinn," began Tarin, knowing that what he was about to say next could come across as both desperate and crazy, "while the Protector seeks to pull King Beleron and as much of the Royal Guard as he can to the Colosseum by leading a gladiator revolt."

Noorsin, Cornelius, and Wencel stared at Tarin, astonished by what he had just revealed. Having spoken the words, Tarin shrugged his shoulders again, slightly uneasy as he thought about the scheme that he, Bryen, Sirius, and Rafia had put together. At the time, it had all made sense. But as he thought about it now a bit more deeply, he wondered if perhaps they had bitten off more than they could chew. Noorsin finally broke the stunned silence.

"So just so I understand, not only do we have Rafia Riverstone out of Haven for the first time in a decade, but she and Sirius will be breaking out Kevan and Aislinn from the Corinthian Palace. A challenge in and of itself. To complicate matters, our young friend, the Protector, will be seeking to topple the throne. Do I have it about right?"

"To clarify, Duchess Stelekel," offered Tarin, "taking down Marden likely would benefit us all, but our expectations of that were low to begin with. Bryen was simply seeking to free the gladiators and create as much chaos as he could in the city to aid their escape."

"So our young friend with a very dangerous set of skills is seeking to do what he does best, create problems for others."

"Yes, Duchess Stelekel, that is one of his stronger skills."

"So I've noticed."

"Of course, with the Protector running loose in Tintagel, that gives us an opportunity."

"Indeed it does," agreed Duchess Stelekel.

"What plan did you and this Protector come up with?" asked Duke Roosarian.

As the soldiers continued to ride by on their horses, the Battersea Guard having joined the column, Tarin explained the plan of attack.

"That was your strategy?" asked Duke Roosarian.

"It has its merits," countered Tarin sheepishly.

"That's not a plan, Captain, that's a fantasy."

"The Volkun can be quite persuasive, Duke Roosarian."

"The Volkun being the gladiator Duke Winborne bought to protect his daughter?" The Duke's distaste for that decision was clear in the tone of his voice.

"Yes, Duke Roosarian. One and the same."

"Well, I still say it's a fantasy. But I saw the Volkun take down Sharperson's Champion five, maybe six, years ago. If anyone can turn that fantasy into reality, it's him."

"So you anticipated sweeping in from the east, focusing on the Corinthian Palace first, and then once you accomplished your work there, moving down the promenade to the Colosseum if you could, and if not exiting through the same gate you entered," said Duke Stennivere.

"That's correct."

"If the Protector is successful in pulling the Royal Guard to him, then that makes our task much easier," Cornelius continued. "But it still will take time to swing our troops to the east.

What about getting through that gate? Marden won't leave that entrance undefended. If we don't get through quickly, we probably won't get through at all."

"I've already sought to address that."

"Why am I not surprised," said Noorsin. "You can tell us on the way, Captain. We need to get moving. We have seen no sign of the Royal Guard, but I have no doubt that we will be seen soon enough."

"How long can the Protector hold in the Colosseum?" asked Duke Roosarian as they all turned their horses toward the northeast. "I respect his ability to fight, but he is human after all."

"He will do everything that he can to make life difficult for Marden and the Royal Guard. But the reality is that he will have no more than a couple hundred gladiators fighting with him. If they must face the full brunt of the Royal Guard ..."

Tarin left the remainder of his thought unsaid, but they all understood what he was implying. Bravery was a virtue, but it could only take you so far when faced with overwhelming numbers.

"Then we need to move swiftly," said Duke Stennivere. "We need to at least give the Volkun and his gladiators a chance if for no other reason than the fact that it aids our enterprise as well."

"We do," agreed Noorsin. "The Protector deserves no less from us."

16

MAKING A BREAK

"I still can't believe that there are so few guards watching the stockade," said Bryen, as he turned his sharp eyes on Lycia. "So much has changed in just a year."

"It is kind of strange, isn't it? For so long the Crown's Royal Guard focused much of their effort on ensuring that we didn't try to escape, like that was even a possibility to begin with. Now, with everything that's going on in the city beyond the walls of the Colosseum, we're an afterthought. Except, of course, on those days when we're required to distract from the misery that's been foisted upon most of the populace."

"Yes, a sad result for many, but not unexpected when the Crown cares little for the people."

"Very true unfortunately."

"And something that we will use to our benefit. I'm beginning to think that this scheme might actually work."

"What do you mean might? You didn't think this was going to work from the very beginning?"

Lycia stood right next to Bryen, shoulder to shoulder, giving him a gentle push that set him off balance for a moment and elicited a small smile from them both. Bryen had been gone from the Pit for a year, but the teasing between them had begun again as if nothing had changed during that time. Bryen welcomed it. He was saddened by it as well, because some things had changed between them.

As they peered out from the doorway that led into Declan's office, the gladiators' compound was quiet. It tended to be like that at this time in the morning, the early hour still closer to night than day. Nothing stirred in the practice yard, only the shadows of the many obstacles and devices that Declan had conceived to train his gladiators broke up the darkness.

The few pinpricks of light came from the handful of torches that were placed randomly along the staggered walls abutting the compound. Bryen guessed that the torches actually would work to the advantage of the gladiators. If the guards stayed close to the dim light projected by the torches, and he had no doubt that they would, it would be just enough to ruin the soldiers' night vision. By the time the sentries realized what was happening, it would be too late.

From their vantage point, with the two barracks for the gladiators on each side, one to the west, the other to the east, Bryen and Lycia had a clear view of the only entrance that led into the compound at the far end of the stockade. The gates could only be opened from within a small gatehouse that was outside the compound, and it was a slow process, as several large winches pulled apart and closed the heavy steel barriers. There was no chance that the gladiators could storm those gates successfully, but that didn't mean they couldn't use the massive doors as a diversion for what Bryen really had in mind. That said, even with the reduced number of guards lining the walls, his gambit would still prove risky at best, suicidal at worst. Yet there was nothing for it.

Training yard for the gladiators it might be, the space functioned just as effectively as a prison. A ten-foot wall made of brick and mortar wrapped around the entire complex, and ten feet beyond that another wall rose up, this second barricade twenty feet in height. Ten feet beyond that barrier, a wall thirty feet in height towered over the other two. In between the walls barbed wire had been placed and large thorn bushes planted, their spikes several inches long, so that even if a gladiator succeeded in breaching the first wall, or even the second, they would be stuck between the two partitions, finding it too difficult to move safely, essentially becoming sitting ducks for the soldiers armed with crossbows who patrolled atop the walls.

Based on Bryen's experience in the compound, along each wall at fifty-foot intervals a guard stood looking down at the activities below. But that no longer seemed to be the case. Half as many soldiers as in the past manned the walls. So definitely an excellent opportunity, but not if they lost the element of surprise. That would be the primary factor in determining whether they lived or died.

True, the design for the stockade was ingenious. Yet even with the reduced number of guards, the chances of a successful escape attempt were slim at best, and that was being kind because of the last feature that ensured the security of the complex. The gladiators' compound was located at the back of the Colosseum. On its other three sides beyond the walls sat the permanent headquarters for the King's Royal Guard. So even if by some good fortune the gladiators made it to the top of the tallest wall, they had two choices and two choices only. The first was to try to climb down the wall. The second was to find some way to break through the two steel doors that were bolted on the other side that led down several flights of stairs to the ground. Regardless of the approach decided upon, it would leave any escapees stuck within the Royal Guards' compound. So even if the gladiators somehow found a way to escape from their small stockade, they still had to fight their way through the barracks that held Caledonia's largest army.

"He's just playing with you," said Davin with a grin and

raised eyebrows, who came up on Bryen's other side and punched his friend in the shoulder. "He didn't think this was going to work at all, but what has he got to lose? He's returned to the Colosseum and realized that he made a terrible mistake. He wants out, and this is the only way he can do it."

"You're not helping, Davin," said Bryen, now punching Davin in the shoulder to return the favor.

"You may have forgotten in your absence," said Lycia, Bryen detecting a hint of pique in her tone, "but Davin's rarely helpful. Actually, he's mostly annoying. You should know that."

"Are you children done?" asked Declan, the Master of the Gladiators having approached on silent feet so that he could have a look for himself to see if anything was going on beyond the gladiators' barracks. He nodded, apparently satisfied, when he was greeted with nothing but the scattered punctures of light in the darkness that appeared along the surrounding walls. "Time is wasting, and we have work to do."

"It's as you said, Declan," said Lycia, acknowledging the mild upbraiding. "There are barely any guards on the walls."

"Most have been pulled into the streets," he replied. "Marden is more worried about the riots than anything else. Even so that doesn't make our task any easier."

"No it doesn't," agreed Bryen. "If we're not fast enough, we're dead before we even begin."

"Then let's be fast, and let's get started," suggested Davin. He was ready to get going. He was never one who enjoyed waiting, the time leading up to his combats in the Pit often worse for him than the actual fight that followed.

"I need a handful of volunteers," said Bryen. "What we do next will be exceedingly dangerous."

"So you think we'll probably die?" asked Davin. "Perhaps even become heroes with the bards telling tales of our exploits for centuries to come?"

Bryen smiled, appreciating his friend's effort to reduce

some of the stress that they were all feeling. "It's a distinct possibility. It could lead to an epic for the ages."

Davin and Lycia looked at one another for a moment, then grinned and nodded. "We're in."

"Good," said Bryen. "Now find me a few more would-be warriors and we can make history."

THE GLADIATORS who Declan selected for Bryen's crew were lined up against the wall behind him, Lycia, and Davin. All wore the leather armor they used in the Pit, and they had all selected the weapons that they were most comfortable with in a fight. Bryen had also had them all strap to their backs one other tool that he had been looking for in the last weapons vault that he had broken into just an hour before. He had remembered the implements from when the Royal Guard had conducted an inventory of all the weapon caches. Declan had asked him to assist at the time, and he had for no other reason than it had given him something else to do for several days.

He had seen the tools in a dusty bin at the very back of the vault, most with rusty blades, but all still serviceable. When Bryen had come up with his escape plan, these weapons were critical to the effort, and thankfully, even though he hadn't been in the vault for several years, these tools still resided in the large bin at the very back of the strongroom, simply waiting for someone like him to put them to use.

The gladiators were quiet, still, and ready. This was no different from what they did two times a week now, walking out into the Pit to risk their lives. They were focused solely on what they needed to do next. And they were at peace with that. They knew the danger entailed. But they also valued the potential reward. So the hazard associated with their mission was worth it to them.

Even so, Bryen could sense the undercurrent of concern emanating from them. The few torches spanning the length of the walls would give the soldiers some light to work with, faint though it was, and any sound the gladiators made once they reached the walls would catch the attention of the guards even with what Declan was about to do. The gladiators all believed that they could achieve their task, but none were under the illusion that they could scale the walls without being noticed.

"Remember, we disable the Guards as fast as we can," said Bryen softly, his voice carrying to the gladiators who waited behind him. "If the soldiers resist or are slow to surrender, kill them. We need to get to the top of the third wall as quickly as possible. We don't stop for anything."

"Yes, but how are we to get to the wall before we're shot through with arrows?" asked Dorlan, the large gladiator standing right behind Lycia and Davin. "Even with what Declan is tasked to do, if just one of the guards atop the wall sees us, we're dead."

"Yes, Dorlan raises an excellent point. Not that we don't trust you, but how are we going to do this?" asked Lycia, giving Bryen a nudge. "You haven't told us everything, have you?"

"Do you trust me?" asked Bryen, giving Lycia the grin that reminded her of the many times that they had spent a few quiet hours together after their fights in the Pit.

Lycia looked at him, her own smile breaking out. "You told me never to trust anyone who asked me that question."

Bryen had to stifle a laugh. "I've been away for a year, and you still make things difficult for me by throwing my words right back at me. Will it always be that way?"

"Of course," she replied. "Just because we haven't been together doesn't mean things necessarily change."

Bryen nodded, that feeling of sadness seeping back into him. Several responses popped into his mind, almost all of which he decided to keep to himself. One issue at a time. And right now their focus needed to be on escaping the stockade.

"One thing that I learned when I left the Colosseum was that everything changes, it's just a question of how and when."

Not certain to what Bryen referred, but feeling a knot of worry form in her stomach, Lycia kept a smile on her face and decided to direct their conversation back to her friend's original question.

"Yes, I trust you," she offered. "I always have."

Bryen then gave her a wink. "Then trust me now. This will work."

He then turned to face the gladiators who waited patiently along the walls.

"Remember, we need to be fast. Declan and his group should capture the attention of most of the guards, but you can assume that once we go up the first wall our chances of being seen by the guards will increase. Dorlan, you clear the first wall with Cynthi, Rogin, and Kollea. Asaia, you have the second wall with Adriana, Ferus, and Stasia. I'll take the third wall with Lycia and Davin."

They all nodded, having gone over the plan multiple times. They knew what they needed to do, and they knew their individual responsibilities. Realizing that they were about to put in motion what some of the gladiators were calling the "Volkun's Vengeance," Dorlan pulled free the large scythe he had strapped to his back and held it in his right hand, coiling the long rope attached to it in his left. Cynthi, Rogin, and Kollea mimicked him, hefting the grapple a few times to be certain once again of the weight. None of them had had the chance to determine how difficult it would be to throw the blade over the top of the first wall, but they were confident that they could handle the task set before them and that the sharp teeth that ran down the scythe's steel would bite into the stone and give them the purchase that they needed to pull themselves up.

"I have no doubt that this can work, Volkun," said Cynthi, her crinkled brow revealing her concern. "But they'll see us before we get to the top."

"Will they?" Bryen asked mysteriously.

Suddenly, the gladiators with Bryen were shocked to discover that they could no longer see any of their compatriots standing with them. They had become invisible. Then Bryen released the Talent so that he could explain, the gladiators appearing once again to their peers.

"The solders will see what I want them to see, and they will not see you until it's too late. I will hold onto the illusion for as long as I can, and Declan's work will aid us in this respect. Be as quick as you can, be as quiet as you can, and all will go well. Yes?"

All the gladiators nodded, several of them with their eyes the size of saucers at having experienced what they could only assume was sorcery, and concocted by the Volkun no less, a handful licking their lips nervously.

"How did you do that?"

"Just a skill that I learned while I was away," replied Bryen.

"You certainly have been busy, haven't you," said Lycia. "Do you have any more of these skills that I should know about?"

"A few," he admitted, reluctant to offer any details. He didn't relish the conversation that he would need to have with his friends about his developing use of the Talent, assuming, of course, that they all survived the next few hours. "Some, like this one, have proven to be exceedingly useful."

"What other kinds of skills do you have?"

Bryen shrugged. "They tend to be more deadly than this one."

"Is that how you were able to open the weapon vaults?"

"Yes."

"Useful skills for certain," agreed Lycia. "When this is over you and I are going to have a talk. A long one."

"You and everyone else, I'm sure," he grumbled to himself. Then Bryen turned his attention back to the gladiators.

"Ready?"

They all nodded. Anxious, but excited as well. They all relished the chance to finally get back at those who had imprisoned them, who had forced them to fight and die.

Bryen gave Lycia one more smile, and then offered her one of Declan's favorite sayings: "Stand. Fight. Die."

Lycia corrected him. "I much prefer stand, fight, live."

"I like that one better, too," Bryen agreed. "Let's see if we can make that happen."

With a nod, Bryen stepped out from the barracks doorway into a strange silence of anticipation, all of the gladiators having made sure that their weapons didn't clank against any of the other metal on their armor as they followed Bryen into the darkness, half the group moving to the wall on their left, the remainder of the crew to the wall on their right.

The gladiators couldn't be seen, Bryen using the Talent to weave them into the darkness and hide them from any watching eyes from atop the wall. Now all they needed was the distraction that would give Bryen and his gladiators the few minutes that they needed to scale the first wall, and that task was in Declan's capable hands.

"LOOK ALIVE. It's almost time, and we only get one chance at this."

The gladiators lined up behind Declan stood quietly, nodding in response to his instructions. The Master of the Gladiators and twenty of his fighters had arrayed themselves along the walls inside the eastern barracks, which was the closest building to the main entrance of the compound, but still a bit more than fifty yards away from the rough-hewn steel gates.

As the minutes passed, the gladiators shuffled from one foot to the other, flexing their shoulders, stretching their backs, and cracking their necks. They also hefted every so often the equipment that they carried, but more out of nervous habit than concern. Declan didn't have enough of the large shields that had once been used by the centurions of old for all of the gladiators who were part of his team. There were plenty of bucklers, but those wouldn't prove very useful for accomplishing their assigned task.

Declan had wanted all of his fighters to have a rectangular steel scutum, the long shields concave in shape and covering almost every fighter except the very largest from head to toe. They were perfect for the assignment that the Volkun had given them, but only a dozen had been found in the weapons vaults that could still be used. So for the other half of Declan's squad they had gone into the dining hall and torn the tabletops from the legs, two gladiators partnering to carry one heavy wooden screen between them.

None of the gladiators had ever served as bait before, and for some it was a bit disconcerting to be placed in that position. But if it got them to their ultimate goal, they were happy to do whatever the Volkun needed.

"Remember, we make a break toward the gates like we're trying to force our way free," continued Declan. "Not at a run, but at the pace I showed you. We want to draw the attention of the soldiers on the walls. Stay under your shields. They'll figure it out eventually, so no heroics, clear? There's no way to open the gates from this side, so there's no point in trying."

All the gladiators nodded their comprehension. They had gone over the plan with the Master of the Gladiators several times, and as was his habit, Declan had ensured that there would be no misunderstandings.

Declan nodded in return, satisfied. "Then let's have some fun with this." That brought several rumbles of laughter from the gladiators with him, who bunched near the door, ready to begin what could be either a pivotal or disappointingly heartbreaking day.

The Master of the Gladiators trotted out of the barracks, his gladiators following, all of them brandishing their shields and yelling at the top of their lungs. At first, the soldiers atop the walls seemed more perplexed than anything else, unsure of what was happening. Declan was known for conducting some strange training exercises, often at the most unexpected times. So they hesitated now, staring down at the small group of gladiators as they moved out into the practice yard at a fast walk and headed toward the main gates.

The gladiators were a little surprised by the lack of response, but they stuck to their plan, moving at a slow but steady pace toward the entrance to the stockade. As they drew closer to the gates, Declan growled in irritation. He wasn't happy. The soldiers were watching them, but more with amusement than anything else, and that simply wouldn't do.

Pulling one of the three spears that he had strapped to his back, he hefted it in his left hand a few times, gaining a better sense of its weight, then threw it with all his strength toward a soldier outlined by a torch on the second wall. The missile sped through the air, no more than a shadowy streak in the dark. Declan cursed when he saw the result. Rather than striking the soldier, the spear instead slammed into the torch, knocking it from its sconce in a shower of sparks.

Following Declan's barked command, the gladiators crouched down, continuing at a steady pace toward the main gates, shields, both scuta and tabletops, raised above their heads. And just in time as Declan's attack woke the soldiers from their slumber, a few crossbow bolts beginning to shoot down from the walls toward the gladiators. It wasn't long before a steady stream of the deadly projectiles began slamming into the fighters' shields.

That was more like it, Declan thought, though he was still angry at himself for missing his target. He chalked it up to being out of practice, something that he expected that he could improve upon over the next several hours if events played out as he anticipated.

The gladiators continued their unwavering advance, the bolts from above raining down, yet they proved to be more of a nuisance than any real threat. The dozen soldiers atop the walls became frustrated when the tightly compressed formation, shields protecting the gladiators beneath, reached the gates. Despite loosing several dozen bolts, none of the missiles had struck home. But their perspective soon changed. The soldiers' accuracy kept the gladiators from doing nothing more than pounding weakly on the steel doors that led out from the stockade, none of the gladiators willing to step out from beneath the shell of steel and wood that protected them. What the soldiers viewed as the first attempted escape to be made in recent memory from the stockade continued apace, but caused little in the way of concern. The gladiators were going nowhere.

So if nothing else, despite their reduced numbers and the difficulty of firing at a moving target in the dark, the soldiers were pleased with themselves. Although the gladiators had managed to reach the gates, they would get no farther and had foolishly trapped themselves against the entrance. The soldiers had plenty of crossbow bolts to maintain a steady attack, and they were certain that word would spread quickly to the barracks. Once a company of the Royal Guard joined them along the walls, this ill-fated and desperate uprising would end before it even truly began.

At least that was what Declan thought was going through the minds of the soldiers, and if it was, that was fine with him. It would make the guards feel good about themselves. And with such a large target right below them, there was little chance that they would suspect another attack to come from where they least expected.

All Declan could do now was hunker down with his gladiators beneath their shields and hope that Bryen worked quickly. He and his fighters wouldn't last forever.

"Can we go yet?"

"No, not yet," replied Bryen, who peeked out from behind the doorframe, the darkness of the night still and silent as the gladiators waited beneath the covered porch. "Would you please stop asking? This is getting ridiculous."

"Shouldn't he have left the barracks by now?" asked Davin, bouncing on his toes, clearly anxious to begin what he viewed as an endeavor that would be fun while choosing to ignore the seriousness of the task they had been given. "I can't believe that it's taking him so long. He should have started by now."

"Relax, Davin," said Lycia, giving her brother a light punch on the shoulder. "Just because you hate waiting doesn't mean you need to take it out on the rest of us. You're making everyone else nervous. Stand still for once."

Davin looked behind him, taking in the gladiators lined up along the building. The men and women selected to try for the walls surrounding the stockade leaned against the stone, most with their heads bowed or eyes closed, seeking a few more moments of peace before they risked their lives once again, though this time for themselves and not for others, which made a world of difference and added a certain gravitas to their situation.

"I'm not bothering anyone," protested Davin.

"You're bothering me every time you open your mouth,"

countered Dorlan, who didn't bother to open his eyes when he responded.

"You say that every time, Dorlan. Every time!"

"Because it's true," Dorlan replied in a low rumble.

"Dorlan's just trying to get a rise out of you, Davin," said Lycia. "He does this to you before every combat. I can't believe he can bait you so easily."

"He does not ..."

But before Davin could continue, he caught the small smile that played across Dorlan's lips. For someone most took to be a large, dangerous man who rarely talked, the gladiator certainly had a unique talent for being a pain in the ass, at least in Davin's opinion.

"Get ready," ordered Bryen. "They're going."

The Volkun's words energized everyone waiting in the darkness, the gladiators pushing off the wall and checking their weapons and armor a final time, Davin finally having something to do with his bridled energy.

Bryen watched intently as Declan stepped out from the barracks on the western side of the stockade. For just a moment the Master of the Gladiators simply stood there, taking a deep breath as if he were testing the air before he went for a nighttime stroll. But that wasn't his purpose, because then at the top of his lungs he shouted, breaking the silence of the night and drawing the eyes of all the soldiers assigned to guard the compound.

"We are gladiators! We stand! We fight! We die!"

Then in a rush, the gladiators working with Declan pushed out of the barracks holding their scuta, the ones tasked with carrying the heavy tabletops lagging a few steps behind the others because of the weight of their makeshift shields. All the gladiators in the practice yard screamed loudly, making sure that the soldiers atop the walls had their full attention, before they formed into a tight rectangular formation. Once Declan was satisfied that all was in order, he began to lead his gladiators at a steady march toward the main gates, keeping the gaze of the soldiers on the walls away from the barracks and to the far side of the practice yard.

From the handful of faces that Bryen could see in the darkness, his gaze limited to those soldiers standing by the few torches lining the walls, it appeared that the guards were amused more than anything else by the actions of the gladiators. It took the soldiers quite a long time to realize that the gladiators, rather than conducting some strange training exercise devised by Declan, might actually be making a break for the gates and attempting to escape. And it required a spear thrown by Declan to do it. So finally, after several minutes had passed, the first crossbow bolt shot down, slamming into a scutum that Declan held at the front of the formation. That action jolted the other soldiers from their daze, the men along the walls immediately following the lead of the first, firing a steady stream of steel bolts down toward the gladiators.

Bryen waited a minute more, giving Declan and his crew the chance to get closer to the gates, before he nodded to himself, then turned back to the gladiators lined up behind him.

"They can't see you, but they will be able to hear you. And you will be able to see your comrades." Bryen didn't continue until every gladiator had met his eyes and nodded. "Stick to the plan. Move fast, but not too fast. Any awkward or strange movement will break the illusion. Stay quiet. That's the most important thing."

Then Bryen stepped out from beneath the porch and walked casually toward the northern wall, seemingly unconcerned about the soldiers now firing crossbow bolts toward Declan and his tightly grouped gladiators. For just a moment, the gladiators working with Bryen hesitated, still uncertain about whatever it was that the Volkun had done to make himself a part of the darkness. Then Davin broke the spell that had been woven around them by walking out after Bryen. Lycia came next and then Dorlan and the other gladiators, who broke into two teams, one following Bryen to the north, the other moving with Davin toward the south, both groups at a steady but unassuming walk.

The gladiators were nervous at first, walking gingerly from the barracks on silent feet, still uncomfortable because they were traipsing across the practice ground with no shields or other protection right under the noses of the soldiers above them, who continued to shoot bolt after bolt toward Declan and the gladiators by the gates. But it wasn't long before their concerns vanished. Whatever Bryen had done to them was working. They could see the soldiers, but the soldiers couldn't see them. That realization gave the gladiators an extra shot of confidence as they approached the stockade's walls.

At the same time, Dorlan at the northern wall and Cynthi at the southern wall threw the grapples with an economical underhanded motion over the top of the first parapet, the teeth biting into the stone. Both gladiators gave the ropes attached to the grapples a few hard tugs just to make sure they were set. Satisfied, they were the first to pull themselves up, the other gladiators following, the noise of the metal teeth biting into the stone and the few sounds of scrabbling hands and feet on the wall drowned out by all the noise that Declan and his band of gladiators were making in front of the main gates as they pounded on the steel.

Reaching the top of the first wall in seconds, Dorlan pulled his sword from the scabbard across his back and trotted down one side of the parapet. Kollea, who was right behind him as he climbed up the wall, took hold of her falchion and moved in the other direction along the walkway cut into the top of the wall, both intent on their assignment of clearing the balustrade of soldiers. They knew their assignment and they would do it rapidly and well.

Using the rope that Dorlan had left in place so that the gladiators following them could try for the second wall, Asaia and Ferus climbed up after Dorlan and Kollea. Seeing that the two were making good progress, Bryen glanced quickly toward the southern wall. Cynthi and Rogin were already moving down that far parapet with weapons drawn, the soldiers in their path still focused on Declan and his troop, completely unaware that two very determined and angry gladiators approached with drawn steel and no concerns whatsoever about using their weapons in a brutally efficient manner.

Adriana and Stasia, having joined Cynthi and Rogin atop the lower wall, were now swinging their scythes in gentle circles as they aimed for the top of the second wall. A harder throw because of the distance between the two walls. And while they did so, Davin was just now pulling himself up onto the first wall. From what Bryen could tell, all the gladiators were doing exactly as they had been instructed with an efficiency and speed that would have put most soldiers to shame. Of course, the gladiators certainly had a good incentive for staying on task. This would be their one and only chance to achieve something that they had never considered possible.

Just then, Bryen heard a few grunts of pain above him, followed by the beginnings of a scream that was smothered almost instantly by a loud thump. He looked just a few feet to the side, identifying the body that had just been thrown down from the first wall to the practice yard, the soldier stabbed in half a dozen places and mercifully breaking his neck when he hit the ground headfirst. Bryen glanced up to see Dorlan standing there, the large gladiator catching his eye and giving him a shrug that seemed to suggest that he didn't have any choice. Bryen nodded to Dorlan, trying to convey to the large man that he had done the right thing. He had no qualms about how the gladiators cleared the length of the wall so long as they completed their assignment quickly, quietly, and efficiently.

Lycia gave Bryen a little nudge with her elbow to get him out of the way. She then took hold of the rope and began to scramble up the first wall. He caught the hungry look in her eyes as she passed him, and he felt sorry for the soldiers who would have the misfortune of running into the Crimson Devil atop the wall. But he instantly stamped out that emotion. The soldiers above him would get what they deserved. Most had treated him and the other gladiators poorly, as no more than animals to be observed and derided. That would change today.

He then pulled himself up after Lycia. Asaia and Ferus had already flung their scythes across the gap between the two walls, the sharp teeth biting into the stone parapet of the second wall. Bryen smiled to himself. Everything was going to plan, and still the soldiers on the second and third walls had yet to realize that they were under attack, Dorlan and Kollea having already cleared the first wall. Glancing quickly to his rear, based on the movement that he saw, it appeared that much the same was occurring on the southern wall. Adriana and Stasia already had gained the top of the second wall, and Davin had just flung his scythe onto the parapet so that he could swing across the gap from the first to the second wall and then pull himself up.

Having reached the top of the first wall, Bryen pulled the scythe from the harness on his back and tested the weight with a few swings of the rope before he launched it across to the second wall, Lycia doing the same, Asaia and Ferus having already made their way across. It wasn't long before Bryen and Lycia joined them. There were only three soldiers on the second wall, and their attention remained on the screaming gladiators at the main gate who stayed hidden beneath their scuta and wooden tabletops. The soldiers had failed to harm the gladiators charging toward the main entrance to the stockade in any way, and they had yet to come up with a different strategy that might actually prove effective at stopping the gladiators' advance.

That lack of creativity cost them dearly as Asaia reached one of the soldiers who was attempting to pull back the string on his crossbow so that he could load a new steel bolt. The man didn't realize that he had been stabbed until he felt the sharp blade slide into his chest and out his back, his life draining along with his blood onto the stone balustrade from the two gruesome wounds he suffered in a single thrust. Grunting in pleasure, Asaia allowed the soldier to slide from her blade. She then shifted her focus to a soldier farther down the wall who still had no clue of the danger sneaking up behind him.

Satisfied that the second wall would be taken in short order, Bryen began to swing his rope with the scythe on the end after pulling it free from the balustrade, Lycia mimicking him. They released their hold at the same time, their scythes sailing through the air and catching on the parapet of the third wall, the scrape of metal on stone hidden by the noise coming from near the main gate. With a grin, Bryen nodded to Lycia and then stepped off the wall, allowing his momentum to carry him across the open space, soaring above the barbed wire and inches long thorns. He hit the far wall with his boots, bending his knees to lessen the impact, Lycia doing the same just a few feet away from him. They then pulled themselves up their ropes.

By now, despite Declan and his group continuing to put on their show in front of the gates, the soldiers on the third wall were beginning to realize that something was amiss. All of their compatriots on the lower walls were missing, and now that they knew to look for something out of the ordinary, the illusion that Bryen had crafted wore off.

For the first time, the soldiers on the third wall saw the shadows scrambling up the stone. Recognizing the immediate danger they faced, the guards no longer cared about what was happening in the practice yard and instead focused on Bryen, Lycia, and Davin as they pulled themselves to the top of the highest parapet. Several crossbow bolts slammed into the wall near the three gladiators, sparking on the stone. Bryen had no doubt that now that the soldiers could track their motion and had found the range, their next shots would find flesh rather than rock, which left them in a very difficult position.

As if one of the soldiers on the wall had read Bryen's mind, the grinning guard stood and pointed his newly loaded crossbow toward Bryen. Having few other options, and preferring to do something rather than waiting for something to happen, Bryen charged toward the soldier, sprinting across the top of the wall. Lycia screamed at him to get down, knowing that he wouldn't get far, but just when Bryen thought that he would feel the searing pain of a barbed bolt digging into his flesh, the soldier, now no more than thirty paces away from him and with a clean shot, screamed in agony, dropping his crossbow and attempting to clutch at a long length of wood that had sprouted from his back.

Bryen kept running, glancing down briefly to see Declan, standing by the main gate, give him a pleased nod, the Master of the Gladiators having found the range and cleared the way for Bryen, who with a quick swipe of his dagger across the wounded soldier's throat, put the man out of his misery. Lycia was right behind him, but there was little for her to do. Following Declan's lead, several other gladiators had targeted the soldiers on the third wall with their spears, and almost all of them had hit home, clearing the parapet of any remaining threat.

"We did it!" said Lycia, her excitement bringing a huge smile to her face.

She pulled Bryen into a hug that he returned, and he was

slightly disappointed when she let go so quickly. But there was still more they needed to accomplish, and time was short.

"We did. Now on to the next task."

Lycia nodded, then she headed toward the locked steel door at the very end of the parapet that led down to the barracks of the Royal Guard. If they failed to block the entrance and the second one atop the other wall, the King's soldiers could use them to retake the walls in force, something that Bryen wanted to prevent at all costs because that would end the rebellion before it even had a chance to take root.

THE THWACKS CAME at a frighteningly regular rhythm, the steady stream of crossbow bolts slamming into gladiators' scuta and tabletops thanks to the soldiers on the surrounding walls taking to their duty with an uncompromising, almost manic will. But that's really all that could be said for their efforts. The soldiers gave little thought to their actions. They gave little consideration to what they could possibly do to improve their chances of success. They just remained at their positions and fired steel bolts down at a mass of well-protected gladiators who refused to make themselves good targets.

Declan was fine with that failure in imagination, and he had expected it. He had served in the Royal Guard himself for more than ten years, and during his time the soldiers in the lower ranks rarely had demonstrated any initiative. They were trained to be more afraid of making a mistake than of taking a risk that might lead to a better path for accomplishing their mission. So Declan was happy to remain where he was, his gladiators protected against the dozens of crossbow bolts launched their way with competence and confidence, but with little effect.

Even so, he was getting a bit worried for Bryen and those

with him. Time was of the essence, and the longer it took the gladiators charged with scaling the walls to do so, the worse their chances of sweeping clean the parapets. But then he smiled, not having to look out from behind his scutum, understanding from the change in sound and rhythm that the skirmish was turning in the favor of the gladiators. The steady stream of bolts had lessened to half of what it had been at the start. In just a few minutes more even that became no more than a stray bolt or two. And then the barrage stopped.

Declan peeked out from behind his shield, several of the gladiators with him doing the same. He didn't see any soldiers on the first or second walls, the gladiators assigned with removing the guards from those balustrades having completed their work swiftly and thoroughly. The problem could be seen on the third wall, and it wasn't entirely unexpected.

Bryen had hoped that the illusion that he crafted would remain in place throughout the attack, allowing the gladiators to take all three walls before the soldiers realized what was going on, but he had warned that as soon as the soldiers comprehended that some of their comrades had fallen or disappeared from their posts, it would become much easier for those remaining on the walls to see through the deception that Bryen had woven around them.

Unfortunately, it appeared that Bryen had been right. The soldiers on the third wall had turned their attention away from the gladiators in the practice yard to Bryen, Lycia, and Davin, who had been forced to take what little cover was provided by the parapet as the soldiers shot their bolts toward these new attackers. But that negligible protection wouldn't last for long. As soon as the soldiers shifted their angle of attack, they could line up their crossbows with the defenseless gladiators and eliminate them at their leisure.

Grasping that something needed to be done, Declan reached for one of the two spears still strapped to his back.

Pulling it free, he took several long strides in the dirt of the practice yard and threw the weapon with all his might, the sleek steel streaking through the air. Because of the darkness of the early morning, Declan didn't see the weapon again until it appeared in the back of the soldier who had been moving to get a clear shot at Bryen.

Declan was about to target another soldier, but he realized that it was no longer necessary. Several other gladiators had followed Declan's lead, launching their spears at the few soldiers still standing atop the third wall. Much to the annoyance of the gladiators, they failed to strike down their targets, but they did enough to prevent the soldiers from firing toward the approaching gladiators. The soldiers had no choice but to stay crouched behind the wall or risk a spear in the belly.

In the end, it proved to be no choice at all, the soldiers falling to the vengeful Lycia and Davin who closed quickly with them and attacked with a barely contained ferocity. And then it was over, silence suddenly falling across the gladiators' compound. Many of the gladiators expected to see several companies of the Royal Guard come charging through the main gates or the doors located where the third wall connected to the Colosseum. But nothing happened. Nothing at all. Nothing but silence.

Declan took a moment to look around, and then he smiled. Normally the air in the practice yard smelled stale, offering the overwhelming taste of sweat and body odor. But now, for the first time in twenty years, the air smelled sweet.

"Well I'll be," he murmured to himself. "It actually worked. The lad did it."

At first, Declan had thought that Bryen's idea had a limited chance of success. The lad had even admitted as much. Now, the Master of the Gladiators wasn't so sure. The poor odds had improved somewhat because of the ease with which they had taken the walls, and perhaps with Bryen's surprising new abilities and the friends supposedly prepared to help them, their odds would improve even more. But he didn't want to get ahead of himself. There was still too much to do. He and his gladiators would still need to fight. And some of them, if not all, would die.

Declan waved to Bryen on the third wall, pride in his eyes. He was also proud of himself. He hadn't lost his skill with the spear. He just needed a couple throws to recapture the feel of the weapon since it had been years since he had hurled a spear at man or beast. But that was all the time that he was willing to give himself for self-congratulations or to celebrate their victory. This was only the first step in a much larger strategy. The sun would be up within the hour, and with it he and his gladiators would likely lose the element of surprise. So they needed to move fast if they were going to complete the next step, the most ambitious step, in time. If Bryen's plan was to have any chance of success, the gladiators needed to gain control of the Colosseum before the Royal Guard had any idea of what was going on.

"Jenus. Tehana."

The two gladiators appeared at his side in an instant.

"Tehana, you're responsible for the walls. Get your squad up there now just in case Bryen doesn't seal those doors in time. If any of the soldiers come through from the barracks, we need to keep them bottled up there rather than letting them get down here to the practice yard."

Tehana nodded and sprinted off, her scutum in one hand, her shortened trident in the other.

"Jenus, get the remaining gladiators to the gates leading into the Pit. Assuming Bryen succeeds in opening that passage, we need to be through in an instant. If we don't gain the Colosseum before the Royal Guard is roused, we're dead."

Jenus nodded, then ran off toward the barracks with a shocking speed for a man so large and wide. Declan was about to issue more orders, but he realized that he didn't need to. Gladiators already were running out with weapons in hand to find their places in the practice yard and prepare for their advance into the stadium, assuming that Bryen could open the way for them.

BRYEN HAD WAVED BACK to Declan from atop the third wall, a smile on his face, but his mind already was on what he had to do next. They had accomplished their first goal, but this was only the start. He was pleased that they'd gotten so far with no blood lost by the gladiators, but he understood with grim recognition that would come to an end soon. The real fight was about to begin.

Declan already had Jenus and Tehana moving on their next assignments. It was time he did so as well. He could come back to the main gates leading to the gladiators' stockade later, as Declan already had put several of the gladiators who had been part of his feint toward the gates to work with the goal of damaging the entryway so that the Royal Guard would not be able to come into the practice yard from that direction. But he knew that wouldn't be enough. Once they had the Colosseum, he could return to the practice yard and secure the gate in a way that would stop the Royal Guard from breaking through.

Bryen had no intention of holding the gladiators' stockade, only the Colosseum, but the Royal Guard didn't need to know that. If he shut the main entrance to the compound, the Royal Guard would be forced to waste soldiers and resources on a useless task. It would also give his gladiators a better chance in the larger fight, because it would mean fewer soldiers attacking the Colosseum.

Bryen continued along the wall, coming to the steel door that led down into the soldiers' barracks, the gladiators now scaling the walls and attempting to join him on the highest parapet.

"What are you going to do to seal it?" asked Lycia, who had trailed him along the balustrade.

"Something similar to what I did to the weapons' vaults, but just a little different."

"What do you ..."

The remainder of Lycia's words stuck in her throat as she watched a flow of scalding energy shoot from Bryen's palm. Her friend directed the stream along the frame of the door, the energy so hot that it melted the steel to the stone, creating a bond that would require the soldiers to knock down a large portion of the wall in order to get through.

Bryen then ran across to where Davin stood guarding the second steel door, his expression suggesting that he wouldn't mind if a soldier poked his head through the entryway by mistake, the Crimson Giant more than happy to chop it off. Lycia stayed with Bryen, a dozen questions popping into her mind. She watched in rapt fascination as Bryen did to the second door what he had done to the first, melting the steel to the stone to create an unbreakable bond.

Lycia knew that now wasn't the time, but she still couldn't help herself. The friend she had known had been full of nothing but surprises since he had returned from his yearlong absence, and he had only been back in the Colosseum for less than a day.

"You realize that we'll be talking about this, right?"

"What do you mean?" asked Bryen innocently.

"Whatever this is," Lycia said, not knowing how to clarify, "this energy that comes out of your hands. Your ability to hide people from the sight of others. I can only imagine what else you can do."

Bryen grinned. "Some of the other stuff I can do is pretty useful like I said."

"After what I've seen, I would expect as much," said Lycia, knowing that he was trying to distract her. "Regardless, we will be talking about this. Have no doubt of that."

"Of course," said Bryen. "Just not yet."

Bryen then reached for the scythe he had returned to the harness on his back after he had scaled the third wall, turning his gaze to the stone of the Colosseum. Because of the intricate design of the walls, there were plenty of places where the metal teeth of the grapple would catch.

"Where are you going?" asked Lycia as Bryen swung the scythe a few times with the rope and then released, the grapple soaring fifty feet into the air before it latched onto the arm of a statue of a gladiator that had been carved into the façade of the stadium.

"Up," he replied, as he tugged a few times on the rope to ensure that the metal teeth were secure, and then he began to climb. "I'll meet you at the gates."

17

OPENING THE WAY

The first fifty feet were the easiest for Bryen. Once he was certain that the serrated teeth of the scythe had sunk into the statue's arm, and that the arm wouldn't break off when he added his weight to the rope, it was a straightforward and fast climb. But once he reached the ledge that held the statue, his ascent became more difficult. He left the scythe where it was as it would no longer help him.

The decoration on the exterior of the Colosseum continued from there to the top in the form of friezes that depicted the history of Caledonia, but in a much more muted fashion in that there were no good places where he could affix the long blade of his grapple. He would need to focus on the nooks and crannies instead, and that meant the need for more patience and caution, two characteristics that he had little of at the moment. Time was pressing. He could feel it weighing down on him. He needed to get to the gates leading to and from the Pit as soon as possible.

So he pulled the two daggers from the sheaths on his thighs and began to drive the sharp blades into the crumbling stone, creating crevices that he used to pull himself up. It was a difficult climb with the blades, his feet often needing to find barely seen ledges or fissures to give him better balance and a needed boost. As he climbed slowly up the outside wall of the Colosseum, foot by foot, he was thankful to Declan once again for forcing him to do something like this as part of his preparations for his combats in the Pit. So he did have some experience with the undertaking.

Every few minutes, Bryen stopped, finding chinks in the stone façade where he could grab hold with one hand while working out the tired muscles in the other, his feet safely lodged in a cleft in the white stone. It was arduous work, but he was making good progress up the several hundred feet he needed to scale.

Through it all, Lycia watched Bryen with bated breath, terrified that one slip or a poorly placed blade or a weakened ledge or worn down stone would send him tumbling to his death. But Bryen seemed to be doing well, climbing at a steady rate. Then her heart slid into her throat as the blade in Bryen's right hand slipped free as a large slab of stone crumbled when he drove the steel into a crevice, leaving Bryen hanging by just a single blade more than a hundred feet in the air from the outside of the Colosseum, his feet jolted loose as well by the unexpected motion. And there was nothing that she could do to help him.

Bryen didn't panic, which allowed her to breathe again. As Lycia watched from the highest wall surrounding the gladiators' compound, she added this decision to climb the exterior of the Colosseum to the list of items that she planned to talk to him about. It seemed like he was doing his best to send her to an early grave as the number of topics that required discussion grew longer and longer.

When the stone fragmented and the blade in his right hand slipped free from the wall, Bryen wondered briefly if he could save himself with the Talent if he fell. He had learned a great deal from Sirius and Rafia, but nothing that immediately came to mind offered a solution to keep him from smashing into the stone several hundred feet below him. But he didn't lose his head, something else that he could thank Declan for, and that's likely what saved him as the knife in his left hand stayed safely embedded within the stone. Taking a deep breath to settle himself, he looked carefully at the frieze and found other cracks in the stone where he could set his feet and improve his balance. Then he drove the blade in his right hand back into the stone.

A momentary crisis averted. But he needed to be more careful. The higher up he went the weaker the stone appeared to be. So he slowed down, locking away his impatience, taking his time, caution now taking precedence over speed. He began to climb again, doing his best to make sure that the weathered stone he selected for his daggers and his footholds was strong enough to hold him. It wasn't long before he could see the top of the stadium just a few feet above his head.

Sheathing one dagger so that he could get a hand on the top ledge, and then doing the same with the other blade once he had gripped the overhang, he pulled himself on top of the wall. Laying across the stone for a moment to catch his breath, he looked down. Lycia stared back at him, an angry glare marring her beautiful features. He could understand why she might be upset.

As he examined how far he had come, he had to admit that it was definitely a more dangerous climb than he had anticipated, and perhaps if he had given it some more thought, he wouldn't have attempted it. But he had had little choice. This was the only way to get from the gladiators' stockade into the Colosseum without having to sneak through the barracks of the Royal Guard, so in his opinion the climb had been worth the risk.

Bryen gave Lycia a big grin and a wave, knowing that it

would irritate her all the more, before sliding over the stone into the last row of benches in the Colosseum. He took a few minutes to rub out the pain from his hands, the climb with the daggers not an easy chore with his fingers cramping regularly. Never having been in the top stand before, he took a moment to look around. Imagining the thousands of people who would normally fill the wooden benches, it certainly offered a different perspective now that all was quiet, though he couldn't say that it was a better one. The Colosseum still exercised a grip on him that burdened his soul every time he entered the massive arena.

Knowing that time was tight, he began to make his way down the aisle. He pulled his double swords from the scabbards on his back, placing the hilts against one another. With a twist they clicked together, the Spear of the Magii once again in his hands. A surge of warmth shot through him in that moment, and the weariness of the last few hours that had set within his bones was washed away. He felt energized. Focused. Ready. And expectant, because he understood that the next few hours would determine not only his own fate, but also those of the several hundred gladiators who now depended on him, who now fought with him and because of him.

Finally at the stadium's mezzanine, which was the level that was just above the Pit, Bryen turned to his right and entered the corridor that took him to the broad hallway that circled the Colosseum. He had been expecting soldiers to be stationed throughout the arena. Strangely, there was no one about. The silence was almost eerie, but he took that to be a good sign. People made noise. If there weren't any soldiers here, and apparently there weren't, Marden likely having assigned them to other duties because of the unrest within the city, then he was more than happy to turn that miscalculation to his advantage.

The uprising was progressing better than Bryen could have

anticipated. The question now was how much longer his luck would hold. When he turned the corner and entered the hallway that led to the staircase that would take him down to the Pit, he smiled broadly. It seemed that his luck was going to stay with him just a little bit longer.

Bryen recognized the young lord who strode toward him, wearing clothes the cost of which could feed a dozen families for an entire year. His red hair was longer now, though still spiky, and the acne on his cheeks was still there, as was the arrogant twist of his thin lips. By the look of him, this young lord reveled in his privilege and power, and he had picked the absolute worst possible time to wander the Colosseum on his own.

"You, boy," called Talus Sharperson, Duke of Sharston, motioning toward Bryen. After visiting with Marden Beleron and having a great deal of fun the night before -- the revelry going well into the early morning -- he had come to the Colosseum without bothering to sleep, wanting to watch the gladiators train so that he could identify the best prospects to focus on for Saturday. Because of his desire to emulate the King of Caledonia and his less than savory inclinations, Talus' debts had been increasing in recent years. He had raised the taxes on his people to an almost backbreaking level as a result, so his options were limited now in that respect. But rather than seek to reduce his expenses, change his ways, or perhaps find some other method to pay what he owed, and because he viewed himself as a shrewd judge of character and a fighter's martial abilities, he thought to address his financial troubles by betting on the combats. To do that, he needed to see the gladiators for himself. "Where is Beluchmel? I have business scheduled with the Master of the Colosseum but he is nowhere to be found. Fetch him for ..."

The arrogant Duke of Sharston stopped in his tracks, staring at the man at the other end of the hallway. There was something about him that was familiar. His hair and beard were white, prematurely so. He wore the leather armor so common to the gladiators of the Colosseum. He also held a double-bladed spear in his hands. It didn't take long for Talus to recognize who stood before him, as this was the man who haunted his dreams.

"You!" exclaimed Talus. It was because of this gladiator that he was in the predicament that he was in now. He had made a huge amount of money based on the success of his Champion, Stil Sheldgard, giving Talus the means to pursue the lifestyle he believed that he so richly deserved. But when the Champion lost in the Pit to this man, to this charlatan known as the Volkun, it had all come crashing down. "You cost me everything when you murdered my Champion!"

"I didn't murder him," Bryen replied, shaking his head in amusement. Even after all this time, some people never changed. "I killed him. There's a big difference between the two."

"Your words mean nothing!" shouted Talus. "Stil should never have died! You murdered him. That's the only way to explain what happened. Stil couldn't die in a combat. It was impossible!"

Bryen sighed, having little patience for this fool. "And yet he did. Your fighter lost. That's how it goes on the white sand."

"You should have died that day, not him. No one should have been able to kill my Champion."

"And why is that?" Bryen knew that time was short, that he needed to move on to the next step in his larger strategy, but this popinjay had piqued his interest. He had always wondered about how the monstrous Champion of the West had survived for so long during their combat despite the numerous wounds he had inflicted upon the mountain of a man.

"Do you know how much money I spent to adapt him to the rigors of the duel?" demanded Talus, who saw no harm in revealing the truth. It didn't matter now. Seeing the Volkun again brought all the bad memories crashing back. He couldn't buy this slave. He needed to kill him, and he promised himself that he would kill the Wolf before the hour was out and finally rid himself of the man who continued to torture him even after six long, difficult years had passed.

"I can't imagine," prodded Bryen, wanting the details.

"No, you can't, can you," agreed Talus, seeming to think that because the Volkun was a gladiator, he wasn't intelligent enough to understand what he was about to explain, but he would try to do so anyway. "The King's Advisor was more than happy to work with me so long as I paid him what he wanted. Using the Talent, he enhanced the Champion in many ways that made him more than human. Greater strength. Greater stamina. Greater aggressiveness. Not impervious to steel, but certainly more resistant to it. And the ability to heal quickly. A slash that would take another man's leg was no more than a slice across his skin that would mend itself in a day or less. He was the ultimate fighter. An unstoppable fighter. And I brought him to the Pit not only to beat you, but also to show Corinthus Beleron what could be done if we enhanced the soldiers of the Royal Guard in much the same way. They would have been unbeatable. And I would have made a fortune. But you stole that from me when you murdered Stil. You stole my future!"

It was exactly as Declan had suspected. Bryen remembered that combat with a vividness that was rare because of his many fights on the white sand, most of his combats simply running together and becoming a blur of blood, pain, and sweat. But not this one. Not the duel against Stil Sheldgard, the Champion of Sharston. Handpicked by Duke Talus Sharperson, in seven years the huge combatant had never been defeated, vanquishing both man and beast with equal ease with barely a scratch on him. Until he had come up against the Volkun.

Bryen remembered watching Stil glance quickly at the royal

box and catching Tetric's intense stare during the fight. That was when Bryen had first suspected that he had been right, that something else had been at play during the combat that had favored the Champion. But that's as far as Bryen had gotten in his thinking, more concerned with killing the man than confirming why he differed so greatly from all the other fighters he had faced on the white sand.

Bryen shook his head with a mixture of disappointment and disgust as he cleared his mind of the memory. The things that he had been required to do had sickened him, yet he had no choice but to do them. Kill or be killed. The mantra of the gladiator. And so true. Of course, now he was in a different position. Now he could possibly end the gladiatorial games for good. Now he could free his friends and peers. And he could gain his revenge on the Duke of Sharston, who had sought to have him become no more than another prize killed by his enhanced Champion, Bryen being no more than fresh meat to be served to the King of Caledonia and the bloodthirsty crowd.

As he turned his focus back toward Talus Sharperson, that blazing fury that had helped Bryen to survive that combat surged through him now, begging to be released. He doubted that the Duke standing before him would offer him a challenge comparable to that presented by the now dead Champion of the West, but there was only one way to find out.

"And yet despite all that you did to turn the combat in your favor, your Champion died anyway," said Bryen, shaking his head in mock sympathy. "What a pity."

"Yes, he died. He died because of you and whatever trickery you used to defeat him."

Talus was so used to his position of power, so used to other people bowing down to him and telling him what he wanted to hear rather than what he needed to hear, that he didn't listen to the tiny voice in the back of his head that tried to warn him that what he planned to do next could have very deadly, final consequences. He had never had to listen to that voice, so why begin doing so now? Besides, he was an excellent judge of fighters, and he had judged the Volkun those six years before, finding him lacking and lucky, a street fighter at best. So now Talus would take this opportunity to put the Volkun in his place, to demonstrate what it was like to fight a real warrior such as himself, before he put the gladiator in the ground.

The Duke's face twisted into a snarl. "And now I shall finally have my revenge. You will pay with your life for what you have done to me."

Talus began to pull his sword from the scabbard at his hip and walk toward the Volkun, who continued to stand calmly in the hallway, apparently unconcerned by the approaching Duke. Rather, he seemed to be more amused than anything else with just a hint of anticipation showing behind his normally cold eyes.

"You know, it wasn't the Talent that Tetric used on your Champion."

Bryen's comment stopped Talus short. "What do you mean that it wasn't the Talent? It had to be."

"No, Talus. I knew you were a fool, but clearly I misjudged you." Bryen's insult struck home, the Duke's face turning red with rage. "Apparently, you are more of a fool than either of us thought possible." Bryen finally moved, having stood stock still since the beginning of what was becoming a tedious conversation. "What Tetric did to your Champion wasn't natural. He didn't use the Talent for that. He used Dark Magic. Just as there is a big difference between murder and killing on the white sand, there is a huge distinction between the Talent and Dark Magic."

For just a moment, Talus didn't know what to say, his anger dissolving as he considered how Tetric may have swindled him. Could this gladiator actually be right? Did Tetric betray him by using Dark Magic on his Champion? Was that perhaps why Stil had died? Not because of this oversold Volkun but because of something that Tetric had done?

It was a very disturbing proposition. But at this point, did it really matter? He would kill the Volkun first since he had been the one to behead his esteemed Champion, and then he would decide whether he wanted to deal with Tetric. There was something about the King's Advisor that frightened him, so perhaps there was some truth to the gladiator's words. And if so, perhaps better to leave that alone and exact his vengeance on the one primarily responsible for Stil's murder.

"It doesn't matter now," replied Talus. "Whether it was the Talent or Dark Magic is no longer relevant. You should never have been able to break through my Champion's defenses, yet you did. You cheated him, and you cheated me. And you will pay for that treachery. Now."

"So tell me, Talus," Bryen said, using just his first name again and enjoying how not providing the respect that the Duke of Sharston demanded bothered him, "are you shielded with the Dark Magic that Tetric used on your Champion? Are you as much of a coward as Sheldgard was, not having the courage to fight on the white sand just like any other combatant? Do you need special protection just like your Champion did because you doubt your skills and abilities?"

"I never needed Tetric's help," hissed Talus, Bryen's insults biting deeply. "And I don't need Tetric's help now. I don't need anyone's help to kill you, the famed and fraudulent Volkun. Just think what people will say when I kill you. You are nothing more than a pretender, and when I take your head and show it to the people, they will know it just as well as I do."

"I'm here now," prompted Bryen, his expression becoming wolfish. "Are you done talking? Or are you afraid? Too worried that you will soil yourself by fighting a lowly gladiator?"

Enraged by Bryen's comments, Talus charged forward. He swung viciously for Bryen's neck in an overhead cut, but Talus missed by several feet, Bryen having stepped to the side, the Duke's momentum taking him well past his opponent. Talus tried again, swinging wildly with a backhanded slash aimed for Bryen's hip, but again the gladiator wasn't there when the steel sliced through the air where Bryen had been. And finally a third time, as Talus went through a long series of various attacks, cuts, jabs, slices, and slashes, yet through it all Bryen simply dodged out of the way. Perhaps most impressively, he never gave ground. Rather, he just sidestepped or twisted his body out of the way, always staying close to the Duke, allowing Talus to learn through his actions that he was not the fighter that he thought himself to be, and that the Volkun was every bit the warrior that he had shown himself to be when fighting on the white sand.

Finally Talus stepped back and stared with a burning hatred in his eyes at Bryen, who smiled at him pleasantly. The Duke of Sharston realized with a sickening shame that this gladiator didn't view him as a threat. The Volkun hadn't felt the need to raise his steel to defend himself a single time despite every attack that he had attempted.

"Fight me, slave!" screamed Talus, his growing humiliation sending unfamiliar and unwanted feelings of embarrassment and emasculation through him. The Volkun would pay for what he was doing to him now. He would not live to regret the mistake of not taking him seriously. "Fight me!"

"Is that what you really want, Talus?"

"That's why I'm here now, you coward!" screamed Talus. "I am your better, and you will understand that. You will understand that when I slide my sword through your chest and you bleed out on the stone of the Colosseum."

"Brave words, Talus," said Bryen, simply nodding his head as if he needed to consider what the Duke had just told him. "Very brave words. But there's something that you will never understand."

"Really," scoffed Talus. "What's that?"

"That a person's value isn't found in their blood, but rather in their heart. In the end, it doesn't matter who you are. It only matters what you do."

Before Talus could respond, Bryen brought one of the blades on his spear down with stunning speed, slicing across the Duke's hip. Continuing with the motion, he pivoted on his back foot and brought the steel of the second blade across the lord's gut. Talus screamed in agony with each wound, almost dropping his sword, never having felt such pain before as he reached for his midsection, a long slice of red having appeared as blood trickled down his legs. But it wasn't over. Not yet.

Square once again to Talus, Bryen pushed on the indentation in the haft of the Spear of the Magii, grasping the hilts of the two swords that formed the weapon. In a single motion that was too fast for Talus to see, Bryen slashed with his swords, cutting through the Duke's neck. For just a moment, Talus stood there, his pain forgotten, his mind trying to comprehend what had just occurred. Then his body collapsed to the white stone to Bryen's right and his head hit the floor to his left, rolling a few feet before coming to a stop against the wall, Talus' lips still moving and his eyes pleading, as if the Duke of Sharston still had not yet realized that he was dead.

Bryen didn't even bother to look at what was left of his opponent. It had been a fortuitous meeting for Bryen, though not so for the now deceased Duke of Sharston. But he shouldn't have allowed himself to be distracted. He had wasted more time than he should have during this combat. He needed to move. Declan and the others were waiting for him.

18

WALKING THE HALLS

Having left the remains of the Duke of Sharston in the main corridor, Bryen strode through the hallways of the Colosseum toward the small gatehouse that held the mechanism that controlled the portal separating the Pit from the gladiators' compound. The Spear of the Magii twirled slowly from his right hand to his left and then back again more out of habit than anything else. Every shadow, every doorway, every alcove could hide a soldier of the Royal Guard with sword in hand. Yet none appeared.

Every few seconds Bryen paused and listened, trying to pick out any sound that would suggest that he had been discovered. He had assumed that if Talus' shouts didn't bring any soldiers running that the loud clash of steel on steel echoing down the hallways would have captured the attention of any of the soldiers stationed in or near the stadium. But still nothing. All was quiet. All was still. It felt as if he had the entire Colosseum to himself, and perhaps he did. Maybe that was what had set his nerves on edge. Not walking into what he had expected to walk into.

For a few minutes, he worried that perhaps it was all a trap.

That a company of soldiers had hidden themselves within the Colosseum, the men of the Royal Guard simply waiting for all the gladiators to enter the stadium from the compound before they closed the net. Then the Royal Guard could eliminate them all in one fell swoop. But then he realized that he was being foolish. He was overthinking it. It was exactly as Declan had suggested that it would be. Marden had pulled most of the soldiers normally assigned to guard the Colosseum to the Palace, his fear over the increasingly violent unrest within the city forcing him into another bad decision and demonstrating that his primary concern was maintaining his own safety rather than seeking to help his people.

With Bryen now walking freely through the Colosseum and the gladiators having taken control of the stockade, clearly Marden's choice had been a huge mistake. A mistake to be used to the gladiators' advantage. A mistake that could come back to bite the good King Beleron at the least opportune time. Or so Bryen hoped.

"Give me a moment," Bryen whispered as he reached the gates behind which the gladiators had massed. "This won't take long."

None of the fighters said a word, understanding the importance of silence and having faith that Bryen would open the path shortly. How could they not after he had scaled the outside of the Colosseum? But several were beginning to show their nerves. They were becoming anxious. Not at the thought of soon fighting the Royal Guard. That possibility didn't bother them in the least. In fact, they welcomed it. Many of the soldiers who had drawn the duty of guarding the stockade had insulted and belittled the gladiators at every opportunity. Getting through these gates would give the gladiators the chance to gain some comeuppance.

No, they were beginning to show their nerves because they had never expected that they would get even this far, that they would have the chance to charge into the Colosseum unopposed. And it was an opportunity that they didn't want to lose just because a soldier came wandering by at the worst possible moment.

As his gladiators waited impatiently within the portal, Bryen took a moment to examine the lock on the door to the small gatehouse that housed the gears for opening the gates. The contraption was nothing more than a single, heavy steel bolt. Child's play thanks to the trick that Sirius had taught him and that already had proven so effective when opening the weapon caches.

Taking hold of the Talent, he concentrated a tiny stream into the lock, the energy melting the steel. Bryen was done in a matter of seconds. Then, he slammed the door in with one good kick, the wood smashing against the far wall of the gatehouse. He didn't do it for show, but rather just to make sure that if there was anyone hiding in the small room, the action would either startle the individual or the swinging door would knock him off balance, reducing the threat that Bryen would face upon entering. But, again, nothing. The gatehouse was empty. And despite the noise that he had made, silence continued to reign within the Colosseum.

Still wary of his good fortune, Bryen moved quickly to the two levers at the far end of the small room. Pushing both up, the grating sounds were music to his ears. The steel gates slowly began to open.

By the time that he had exited the gatehouse, gladiators had already started to stream through the opening. Asaia, Dorlan, Kollea, Jenus, and Tehana were the first to sprint through with their squads of ten gladiators each. Each team already knew their assignments, having been charged with seizing and defending one of the twelve gates ringing the Colosseum with the goal of keeping out the Royal Guard for as long as possible. And, if the Guard attempted to force their way past them, each team of gladiators was to exact as high a cost as possible with the hope that a staunch defense would make the soldiers rethink the feasibility of their efforts.

Five more squads ran into the Pit next, scrambling up the walls and then down the tunnels that were like the spokes of a wheel, leading to the corridor that circled the stadium. First was Caellia, who was almost as broad as Dorlan and just as dangerous, though she tended to smile more, often most brightly when her steel was sliding into her enemy's flesh. Chesin was right behind her. One of the oldest gladiators currently in the Pit, he was respected by the fighters in his team not only for his fierceness, but also because of his intelligence. He was not one to rush into a fight, but once he engaged, he always did so with a plan that so far had kept him alive on the white sand, and they hoped that his approach would keep them alive as well when they faced the soldiers of the Royal Guard.

Majdi came next. A large man with a big laugh, he was difficult to anger, but you did so at your own peril, because once his rage took hold, he could barely be controlled. It was better just to stay out of the way when he needed to release his fury. Nkia was right next to him. The two had formed a bond of sorts during their time in the Pit. The dark-skinned woman never spoke, which suited Majdi just fine because he rarely stopped talking. Her tongue had been cut out when she was a child, so she allowed her ever-present jambiyas, the traditional curved daggers of her homeland, to do her talking for her. Then finally Renata led her gladiators into the Pit and up and over the wall. She appeared to be a kindly grandmother until you took in the hard glint of her eyes, which demonstrated a complete lack of compassion, as well as her skill with the morning stars that she favored as a weapon, the spiked metal affixed to the end of her two long clubs deadly in her quick and sure hands.

Lycia and Davin led the last two squads, Davin offering

Bryen a large grin when he passed, Lycia smiling brightly and giving him a light tap on the shoulder. Bryen had assigned his two friends the two gates that served as the main entrance to the Colosseum, which opened up onto the plaza that extended on a straight line all the way to the Corinthian Palace. He expected the hardest fighting to take place there, and he wanted the Crimson Giant and the Crimson Devil to be in the thick of the action. Their skill and composure would buttress the gladiators' confidence and perhaps even make the soldiers there hesitate before they attacked.

Declan walked calmly through the gates after all the teams had dispersed throughout the Colosseum. He set another squad of gladiators to guard the long tunnel that led to the white sand of the Pit. Then he entered the gatehouse and pulled down the levers so that the steel gates swung back into place. The gladiators then started wrapping the gates with the heavy steel chains they had found in one of the weapon vaults to make it just a little bit more difficult for the Royal Guard when they tried to retake this entrance to the Colosseum, because they had no doubt that the soldiers loyal to King Beleron would attack. It was only a matter of time.

And it was time that Bryen felt was slipping by too quickly as he stalked like a caged beast down the long tunnel, the rising sun beginning to burn away the shadows in the Pit. He climbed to the top of the wall, pulled himself over, and then headed down the corridor that he had followed to the gates and the gladiators' compound just a few minutes before. The gladiators' success at taking the Colosseum was based entirely on speed. They needed to be fast, because as soon as the Royal Guard discovered what was happening, all the advantages that the gladiators currently benefited from would disappear.

When he was fighting in the Pit, or when he was taking on the Ghoules on the coastal road in the Southern Marches or in the Deep Wood, Bryen had never felt so tense as he did now.

Then, he had been just a fighter. His responsibilities were more limited. He had to focus solely on himself. He was not used to the added weight of being responsible for so many others. If the gladiators proved victorious, then that was their success to be savored. But if any of the squads failed to take their assigned gate, that failure would fall on him, and it would mean that the entire endeavor would collapse before it really even got started. He couldn't say that he enjoyed having this additional burden on his shoulders, but he understood that it was necessary, and he would not allow it to keep him from doing his very best for the men and women who had put their lives in his hands.

Declan caught up to Bryen right when he turned onto the main concourse, both wanting to check on the progress of all the squads and assist if there was a need. Having spent ten years with Bryen and having seen him grow from a terrified child into a confident and deadly young man, Declan felt that at times he knew Bryen better than Bryen knew himself. And as he walked next to the Volkun, the Master of the Gladiators had a good feel for what was going through Bryen's mind.

"You've done all that you can, lad. You need to leave it be for now. It's in the hands of your fighters now. Worrying about what might happen won't help."

"It doesn't feel like I've done all that I should," replied Bryen. "I feel like I've missed something. Something important."

"No, it never does feel that way, does it?" asked Declan with a sympathetic smile. "One of the perils of leadership, lad. The doubt is always there, at least in the minds of those who care about the men and women fighting for them. Don't let anyone tell you otherwise. It'll never go away, it never should, but you'll get used to it."

"You're assuming we'll survive this uprising. That I'll have another chance to lead at some point in the future."

"I don't assume," said Declan with supreme confidence. "I

know. This is just the beginning of a day that will shatter the Kingdom and likely take down a dynasty."

"How can you be so certain? The odds are not in our favor. And there are too many variables that are beyond our control to guarantee our success."

"It's a good plan, lad," said Declan. "I believe it will work. So do the gladiators. Right now, that's all that matters."

"But as you've said so many times, the best plans always change when the fight begins."

"I have said that," Declan grumbled with a laugh, pleased that Bryen had been listening. "And I'm right. But we've worked through almost every possible scenario that we could face as a result of our initial strategy. We've done all that we can to prepare for those many possible eventualities. That's the best that we can do. If we allow our minds to focus on what could happen, we'll freeze. We need to focus on what is happening. We can do something about that."

"I know you're right, Declan," sighed Bryen. "I'm still worried though."

"That I can understand, but remember one thing, lad. There is one advantage that Marden and the soldiers of the Royal Guard don't have that could prove decisive."

"What's that?"

"The soldiers are fighting for a King who doesn't care about them. And they know it. Our gladiators are fighting for each other, for their freedom, and those are two very powerful incentives."

"That's a good point, and I don't disagree with you," said Bryen, feeling somewhat heartened not only upon hearing steel gates slamming off to their side as the gladiators gained control of the entranceways to the stadium, but also because of Declan's comment. "At least that's one advantage the Guard can't take from us."

"Too true, lad. And there's one other advantage that we have going for us."

"What would that be?"

"You, lad. Asaia, Dorlan, Nkia, Lycia, Davin ... all of us know that we're here, now, walking freely through the Colosseum, because of you. Live or die, we have this opportunity because of you. All of us appreciate that you came back to do this, to lead us. It gives you a power the King could never have."

"And that would be?" asked Bryen, who was trying to get used to the fact that the normally taciturn and curmudgeonly Declan was now trying to encourage him. He certainly appreciated it, but it seemed distinctly out of character for his friend and made him wonder if the Master of the Gladiators believed his own words of just a few minutes past.

"Trust, lad. The gladiators trust you. And that can be a very powerful edge for us, along with one other advantage."

"You keep listing more advantages, Declan," Bryen said with a smile. "It's very out of character for you. What would this one be?"

"We have the Volkun fighting in the Pit once again. We have the Volkun fighting to free the gladiators. That's a story that will capture the minds and hearts of the people. We can use that as well."

"How are the people of Tintagel even going to know what's going on here?" asked Bryen, looking at Declan with a questioning eye. Encouraging and cunning? These were two traits that Bryen had never before seen in the Master of the Gladiators.

"I may have started spreading the word right before all this began, sending out some of the kids who work in the Colosseum to start some rumors that I'm sure will spread just as quickly as the sun's rays spread through the city. Who knows what could come from them?"

"Who knows?" laughed Bryen. "You really have a devious mind, you know that, Declan?"

"I do," agreed Declan unrepentantly. "Thank you for the compliment." Declan motioned to the body slumped in the hallway and the head that had rolled up against the far wall. "Your work?"

Bryen nodded, not bothering to look. His mind was well beyond the very short combat with the now deceased Duke of Sharston.

"Is that the same fool from that duel so many years ago? The Duke who brought the Champion here that you bested?"

"One and the same."

Declan shook his head in disgust. "Did he finally get his wish? The combat that he wanted?"

"He did. Though it didn't go well for him."

"Obviously." Declan shrugged. "He was a fool then, he was a fool now. Some things don't change. He got what he deserved."

Bryen nodded. He didn't feel any satisfaction in killing the Duke. It was just something that he had needed to do. The Duke was no more than an obstacle to remove so that he could get on to his more important task.

"It's too quiet," said Bryen. "I don't like it."

"It is," replied Declan. "You think it's a trap."

"That possibility had crossed my mind. Several times, in fact."

"Mine too."

"But you're not worried."

"No. It's quiet because it's quiet. If there was a problem, we would have found it already. Or rather it would have found us."

"Probably so," agreed Bryen, his eyes scanning every shadow, every doorway and possible hiding place, just to be certain as he walked through the corridors.

"Let it go, lad. A gift has fallen from above. Take it. Use it."

"Always words of wisdom," said Bryen with a smile. "And as you said, some things never change, even in the midst of an uprising."

"You have to value the constancy of life when you can," offered Declan.

"I couldn't agree more. I just don't like not knowing what I don't know."

"Where did you get that saying?" asked Declan. "It has a nice ring to it."

"A Magus who I've had to spend more time with than I'd like. It's one his favorite sayings."

"Sounds like he's a smart man."

"He is. But he's also irritating. He likes to keep secrets."

"As do we all. Let it go for now. He has his secrets, and you might not like it, but that doesn't mean there isn't any value in what you can learn from him. I get the sense that you already are, and not just his favorite sayings."

"You're right about that."

"We'll talk more about that later. For now ..."

"For now, let's bring down the Crown."

DAVIN strode down the corridor much as he did when fighting in the Pit, his steps suggesting an economy and dexterity in his movement that appeared to be almost unnatural for a person of his size. His team of gladiators trotted with him as they moved swiftly toward the eastern side of the Colosseum, a few of his fighters already having broken off from the larger group to check the upper floors and ensure that they were clear of anyone who shouldn't be there, such as a soldier or two who might have decided to take a nap during the night in one of the many nooks hidden within the stadium only to wake up in the middle of a rebellion.

Just as fast as the gladiators left Davin, they returned, usually just nodding their heads to confirm that there was nothing that they needed to worry about. At least not yet.

Sorin had just visited the suites on this side of the Colosseum set aside for nobles, while Tellea had come back from a quick scouting mission to the main entrance, her predatory smile suggesting that for now all was clear. Oriol and Anna likely would return soon. Davin had charged them with ripping free as many wooden benches in the stadium as they could so that they could be affixed to the gates to provide additional protection to the gladiators defending the entrances.

Revolutionaries, Davin corrected silently. They were all revolutionaries now. He had never thought that such would ever be the case, that this opportunity would ever present itself. But it had. Because of the Volkun. Strange events seemed to circle his friend like a soothsayer surrounded by the spirits of the dead. And Davin was more than willing to go along for the ride. The Volkun and the otherworldly power that he seemed to exercise had never steered him wrong before, and he didn't think that it would now.

Davin nodded with approval as Oriol and Anna trotted out of a hallway carrying between them more than a dozen several-inch-thick, ten-foot lengths of wood. They handed them to two of the other gladiators with Davin and then headed back the way that they had come to continue their scavenging. These would do nicely. Davin wanted to keep the soldiers who would eventually attack them guessing about what they faced on the other side of the gates, and the thick wooden benches not only would make it more difficult for the Royal Guard to break through, but they also would limit what the soldiers could see. And that would give him and his gladiators -- revolutionaries, he corrected himself -- a slight advantage at least for a time. And that's all that he was looking for.

As Bryen had noted, they didn't need to win a battle or a

combat. They needed to achieve a grand victory. That meant that they needed to play for time. The longer that they could hold within the Colosseum, the better the odds of a positive outcome, assuming, of course, that all the other pieces of the plan came together as they envisioned. More hope than reality, perhaps, but he would take what he could get.

Having reached his assigned position, Davin smiled. All was quiet, just as Tellea had said. Nothing moved out on the plaza but for a few stray pieces of paper caught by the wind.

The gladiators with him immediately closed and locked the gates and then began to loop the heavy steel links of the chains that they had discovered in one of the weapon caches through the thick bars. Davin nodded with satisfaction. He had no doubt that the soldiers forced to attack here would find this gate to be a tough nut to crack.

Davin then spit out a stream of additional orders, the gladiators responding to his commands quickly, not needing to think, only needing to do. They knew what was required. They had gone through their assignments and what was expected of them multiple times with Declan just as they did when discussing tactics with him before a combat. They would carry out the Master of the Gladiators' instructions exactly as he required.

If they failed against the Royal Guard, so be it. They failed. It wasn't like their lives as gladiators offered them anything more than certain death. But they would do all that they could to ensure that didn't happen. Because right now they were free.

The Volkun had given them an opportunity that they had never expected would come their way. They would not risk it by not doing all that they possibly could to ensure their success. Many of the gladiators felt more alive than they had in years. And they would make the most of it. If necessary, they would repay with their lives the trust that the Wolf was showing in them by giving them this chance, because that was the only thing of value that they had to give.

As his gladiators finished running the chains through the gate and then began to affix the benches, using long nails hammered into the wood that they then curled around the bars, making sure that the sharp ends stuck outward to add just one more challenge for any attacking Guards, Davin caught sight of something that he hadn't anticipated, especially with the sun just beginning to rise in the sky. A dozen or so men, all dressed in assorted finery, meandered across the plaza toward him. As they drew closer, their animated conversations came to an end, quizzical expressions dawning on their faces.

"You can help me, young man," demanded the portly fellow who stepped up close to the gate and took on the role of leader of the sundry group. "Direct me to the Pit. Is it not through these gates? We need to examine the gladiators scheduled to fight this coming Saturday so that we know how best to wager on them. We're also thinking of buying a few."

How the paunchy man, his obvious bulk hidden behind a very large and very expensive wool cloak, spoke of the gladiators, as if they were specimens rather than human beings, was not lost on Davin and the gladiators working at the gate, though none of them stopped what they were doing.

"We were told to come here at this time as the training would begin shortly," piped up a smaller man with a reedy voice who had pushed his way to the front of the group, then just as quickly he retreated behind a few of the taller men after receiving a nasty glare from the man who had first approached Davin.

"Sorry, my friends," Davin replied with a huge smile and a wicked glint in his eyes. "But the Colosseum is closed."

"Closed?" asked the obviously well-off lord who put his nose up against the gates to get a better view of the work being done even as the gladiators continued to bend the sharp nails around the bars in order to attach the benches from the stadium. "For how long? We have business that can't wait."

"Permanently, my friend," replied Davin, his grin growing even broader. "The Colosseum is under new management."

"But that can't be possible," scoffed the fat fellow plaintively, at first thinking that the very tall, red-haired man on the other side of the steel bars was playing with him. "I'm scheduled to meet with Beluchmel, the Master of Colosseum."

"Aren't you the Crimson Giant?" asked the small man who had found the courage to push his way back to the front of the group.

This time the portly lord didn't bother to put his colleague in his place, instead staring at Davin as if he was seeing him for the first time because he was beginning to suspect that the mousy man might be right. And if so, why was the Crimson Giant here rather than in the Pit or the stockade?

"Beluchmel is indisposed, having been removed from his position," said Davin. "And yes, I am the Crimson Giant."

Davin didn't offer confirmation of who he was with pride, but rather resignation. Much like Bryen and his sister and so many of the other gladiators, he had never enjoyed his time fighting on the white sand and all that went with it. For the crowd, it was a chance for them to escape, to live vicariously through the actions of a select few, to watch the ultimate battle take place before them without having to face any of the consequences themselves. But for Davin and his peers, it was a time of pain, sweat, fear, and death, whether theirs or their opponents. And the names bequeathed to them by the crowd simply served as reminders of that.

"What are you doing here rather than in the stockade?" demanded the smaller man, his voice no better than a shrill squeak.

Davin simply ignored him and addressed his comments to the large fellow who had taken a few steps back from the steel bars, beginning to understand the severity of the situation that he and his associates had walked into unwittingly. If one of the most famed gladiators in all of Tintagel was here at the entrance to the Colosseum, barricading the gates, he and his peers had a great deal more to worry about than making sure they wagered correctly on the combats.

"I'm sorry, my friend," explained Davin. "But Beluchmel's only reliable characteristic is his grasping nature and his desire to put an extra coin in his purse whenever the opportunity presents itself. As a result, Beluchmel is no longer in a position to assist those seeking to profit from the deaths of my friends, my fellow gladiators."

"But that's simply not possible," said the smaller man, who still didn't seem to pick up on the shifting mood of the encounter as his compatriots had, many of whom had begun to walk back from the gates slowly as if they were seeking to escape a wild animal with the hope that they wouldn't be noticed until they reached a place of safety. "The King won't permit it!"

Davin laughed then, as did the gladiators who were with him. But his fighters never stopped working. They all knew that time was passing faster than they would like and that the Royal Guard would soon learn about what was going on right next door to their barracks.

"Anything is possible, little man," said Davin. "If the King wishes to take issue with what's going on in the Colosseum, I suggest that he come down here himself. Please tell him that the Volkun is here. Waiting for him. Waiting for the duel that was denied him years ago."

Hearing that the most feared gladiator in Tintagel in the last ten years had returned to the Colosseum made several of the men standing across from Davin jump with fear. Davin couldn't stop the smirk that broke out on his face, and he didn't want to. Bryen had been right. Names did hold power. And Davin had lost patience with this group of fools.

"Now I suggest that you leave while you still can. Find some other form of entertainment to pursue. And if you should happen to run into the good King Beleron, please tell him that the Volkun and his Company of Blood await his presence. I have no doubt that royal blood spilled in the Pit will still turn the white sand red."

Lycia swept around the northern side of the Colosseum toward the rising sun as if she owned the massive stadium, much like she did when she fought on the white sand. One of the first things that Bryen had taught her before she entered the Pit for the first time was that demonstrating confidence, even when you weren't feeling confident, was essential to your success. She had taken that advice to heart and tried to do that now. She knew how to fight. Now she needed to learn how to lead. Or at least pretend that she knew how.

As they moved toward the gate that Declan had assigned them, the gladiators who made up her team broke off at regular intervals to explore the hallways and alcoves that appeared along the way. After ensuring that no one else was about, they quickly returned. Derin, a grizzled fighter who lacked most of his teeth after begging on the streets for several years, had seen that the Crimson Giant had set some of his gladiators the task of ripping up the benches in the stadium to aid their efforts at keeping the Guard from breaking through their gate.

When Derin had informed her of his discovery, Lycia had been impressed. It was a surprisingly good idea for her brother, who was known less for his calculated thinking and more for his impulsive decision making. She had adopted the practice as well, sending Derin and one other gladiator to tear out benches for their own use. She assumed that the Royal Guard would break through their defenses eventually, if only because of their much greater numbers, but as Bryen had noted while briefing the gladiators, keeping the Caledonian soldiers out of the Colosseum, though certainly important, wasn't realistic.

What would prove essential to their endeavor was whether they could prevent the Royal Guard from retaking the Colosseum for an extended period of time. Lycia would do all that she could to help Bryen in that regard, understanding that the success of the Volkun's overall plan depended on her and the other gladiators' ability to delay the Royal Guard. And if, by chance, the King of Caledonia felt the need to show his face at the Colosseum because his soldiers were struggling to recapture what they had lost, then all the better. That was simply another step in the Volkun's larger strategy.

"Is this enough, Lycia? Or should we go back for another batch?"

"Well done, Derin." The wiry gladiator had appeared out of a corridor on her left, Attilia accompanying him as they both carried more than a dozen large benches between them. Yes, these would do nicely, she thought. Nicely, indeed. She could not only affix these to the bars, but also have her fighters fashion them into larger shields to be used when the inevitable breakthrough occurred. "Let's get these to the gate, and then you and Attilia can make one more trip into the stadium. We should have all that we need after that."

Derin nodded and fell in with the group. Lycia could sense the energy that infused Derin, Attilia, and the other gladiators with her. An energy that she, herself, was feeling. That she was relishing. It was good to be heading into combat for herself rather than for the desires of the crowd, and for the first time in quite a while she was excited and looking forward to the fight to come.

Life in the Colosseum was rigorous and highly structured,

all thanks to Declan, who treated his gladiators like soldiers, using his own experiences in the Royal Guard before his enslavement as a way to instill discipline and camaraderie among people with little hope of surviving their time in the arena. He believed that constant training and preparation would aid the men and women condemned to the Pit in their efforts to stay alive. And he was right. It did. Without his efforts the number of fighters getting dragged from the white sand each week would have exceeded the number of forced recruits that appeared at the gates to the gladiators' compound every month.

When Lycia had first arrived in the Pit, she had accepted Declan's demands without complaint, easily adopting the regimen and routine that organized a gladiator's life. It had become a part of her, and now she couldn't imagine any other way to live, particularly after the chaos and uncertainty that she and her brother had experienced while living in the slums of Tintagel before being swept up by the City Watch and sold into the Colosseum.

But during the past year the life that had become so important to her, that had reshaped her into the Crimson Devil, one of the best and most feared fighters in the Pit, had become monotonous and soul-draining. It was as if her existence had lost all its color and spice. She knew that this could happen when fighting in the Colosseum. Declan had warned her that it would happen, in fact. He warned all the gladiators that eventually the Woe would take them, a malaise or lassitude that would settle over each gladiator. It was just a matter of when.

Declan had suggested that it was often when the gladiator realized that their fate was set, that there was nothing that they could do to change it, and that they were on a path that would lead to only one definitive end. When the Woe fell upon gladiators, their time in the Pit would be reduced to days or just a few weeks at the most, as a lethargy set in that would slow their thinking and movement and greatly enhance their chances of being dragged across the white sand. Because they didn't care anymore. Whether they lived or died no longer mattered. They just wanted to leave the Pit, and there was only one way to accomplish that.

Her brother had noticed it coming upon Lycia first. He tended to take life less seriously than she did, so it wasn't surprising that he didn't seem to be affected by their difficult circumstances as much as she was. But when he had broached the topic with her, his concern obvious, he had suggested that he didn't think the Woe falling upon her had anything to do with their inevitable fate. Rather, he argued that her languor and listlessness resulted because someone important to her had been taken from her.

Davin wasn't the most self-aware person that she knew, but that didn't mean that he wasn't right from time to time. She had become desensitized to the combats in the Pit. She didn't enjoy them, instead viewing them as something that she simply needed to survive. But they didn't bother her, at least she didn't think that they did. What bothered her was that she had lost Bryen. She hated when her brother was right, but took solace in the fact that he rarely was.

She had thought that she would never see Bryen again when he had been taken from the Pit. But here he was. He had returned. To her. To them. And because of that she felt energized, the Woe dissipating as soon as she saw Bryen standing in the gladiators' barracks. Even so, Bryen reappearing also confused her.

Bryen had returned to the Colosseum for multiple reasons. In addition to seeking to free the gladiators, he was leading a rebellion against the Crown in part to save the Duke and the daughter who had enslaved him as a Protector. She was having a hard time making sense of that. Why did he feel indebted to them? Or was there something else to it? Did it have something to do with the girl that he had been charged with protecting? The girl who clearly had been trained by Bryen and had dueled Davin in the Pit.

Lycia hadn't had the courage to ask Bryen about it before all this began. There simply wasn't time with all that the gladiators needed to do to prepare for this moment. But she promised herself that she would when this was over, assuming, of course, that they were all still alive.

Her thoughts were stuck on those questions when she emerged in front of the gate she had been charged with defending. She almost ran into Derin before she noticed that he and her other gladiators had stopped. Derin and Attilia had placed the benches taken from the stadium on the stone floor and pulled their short swords, the other gladiators already having their weapons in hand. It was quiet and still, but she could detect the underlying energy circulating within her fighters. The cause for that rush stood right in front of her, no more than a few dozen paces away.

A score of soldiers had appeared on the other side of the open gate, their expressions and movement uncertain, worried. They were clearly just as surprised to see the gladiators as the gladiators were to see them.

Bad luck for them, Lycia thought. Why these soldiers were here now she couldn't say. Any change in the guards usually didn't occur until later in the morning. She would have preferred to close the gate before these members of the Royal Guard had appeared, but it really didn't matter to her. The bloodshed was bound to start sooner rather than later, so why not now with these unfortunate fools.

Without Lycia having to say a word, the gladiators with her spread out, putting some space between themselves. She knew what they were doing. They wanted some room to maneuver so that they didn't have to worry about their compatriots getting in their way. But they also had shifted ever so slightly in response to how the soldiers across from them were standing. The gladiators were picking their targets for their wrath.

"What's the meaning of this?" demanded the Sergeant who reluctantly stepped in front of his men, his loud voice unable to hide his fear at coming across men and women who should have been imprisoned within the stockade.

Lycia stared at the Sergeant with a grin that resembled a cat examining a bird just before it pounced. She then pulled the matching swords from the scabbards across her back, the sharpened steel catching the early morning rays.

"I suggest you leave," she said in a deadly quiet voice. "This is the only chance that I will give you. You have no place here. The Colosseum belongs to us now."

The Sergeant took an involuntary step backward, his fear almost getting the better of him. But he stopped himself, realizing what could happen if he gave in to the dread rising within him. He had a squad of the King's Finest at his back. He needed to maintain control of this situation. But the Sergeant never realized that he never had control to begin with, and that lack of comprehension was going to cost him and his men dearly. Control actually belonged to the red-haired young woman who stared at him as if he were her next meal.

"You are gladiators," said the Sergeant. "No more than slaves. Return to your compound this instant or you shall face the wrath of the Royal Guard."

"Well done," Lycia replied, bringing her two swords together lightly to mimic clapping, the sound of steel raking against steel sending a shiver of fear through many of the soldiers who realized that they had walked into circumstances that they had no wish to be a part of and, worse, they had no good way to escape. "You figured it out. But you're wrong in one respect. We're not slaves. Not anymore."

Derin, Attilia, and the other gladiators then stalked forward, their hands gripping their weapons loosely, their eyes locked on the prey that they had selected. In just a few steps, the fighters from the Pit were at a sprint, charging silently at the terrified soldiers. The Sergeant and a few of his men stumbled backward in shock, a handful of the soldiers struggling to pull their weapons from their sheaths, recognizing too late that the second that they had just lost would cost them their lives as the clash began.

The only screams came from the soldiers, the gladiators fighting quietly. Intent on their tasks. The primary sounds heard in that section of the Colosseum were the scrape of blade across blade or the squelch as a sword, dagger, or spear bit through leather armor then into flesh.

Lycia was the first gladiator to engage the soldiers, killing the Sergeant with a well-placed cut across his throat, then she pushed farther into the melee, her twin swords slashing and slicing with deadly efficiency, her gladiators right behind her.

In less than two minutes more than half of the soldiers had fallen, never to rise again, and those few who tried to defend themselves as the odds shifted in the favor of the gladiators were torn between continuing to fight and running. The surviving soldiers discerned that though they had outnumbered the gladiators at the start, numbers didn't matter here and now. They could not match their opponents in their controlled savagery and skill.

Lycia had no sympathy for these members of the Royal Guard. These soldiers should have been more decisive, but they hadn't been. They had hesitated. Now they were paying the price, and Lycia and her gladiators were more than happy to expel these soldiers permanently from the Colosseum. As Declan liked to say so often, gladiators were expected to stand, fight, and die. Today they would stand and fight, but it would be the soldiers of the Royal Guard who would be doing the dying.

19

———————

CONTEMPLATING TREASON

The sun had broken through the misty clouds for the first time in days, yet the open-aired practice ground in Tintagel Palace was strangely quiet for midday. Usually much of the Royal Guard would be in training by now under the watchful eye of the Blademaster, but not today. Although the soldiers who regularly attended had come as they usually did, there was little interest in sparring. Instead, they had broken off into small groups, talking among themselves, many having pulled out whetstones to sharpen their blades. There was a feeling of anticipation in the air. They could all sense it, which put several on edge, their nerves threatening to get the better of them. Thus the hushed conversations and the attempts to release their nervous energy. The soldiers understood that something was coming. Something big. Something important But they weren't certain what it would be or when.

Perhaps in part it was because Aislinn Winborne had joined them later than usual. As a rule, she was there for training first thing in the morning, most of the residents of the Palace still asleep, the only sounds carrying down the long, covered hallways emanating from the kitchen as the cooks heated the ovens to make fresh loaves of bread.

But this morning Aislinn had eschewed her normal routine, staying in her rooms, having gotten little sleep the night before. Every time she closed her eyes images of Marden pawing her or Tetric using the collar around her father's neck to torture him played behind her closed eyes. They had reached the point that her father had warned her that they would. Marden had lost patience. He was no longer willing to play the game. Their time had run out.

She had wracked her brains in the early morning hours for some way to avoid the trap that the King and his Advisor had set for her and her father. It turned out to be wasted effort. No new ideas had come to mind. No new possibilities of escape. Not with that cursed collar around her father's neck, and still she had no idea how to remove it. It had become an exercise in futility, her anger first replaced by frustration and then by despair.

She considered trying to visit her father that morning, but doubted that Marden would allow it. Not after last night. And for quite some time she felt ashamed, because the thought of actually leaving her chamber had terrified her. She was worried that Marden or Tetric would be waiting for her just outside the doors to enforce his latest decree. Then as the sun broke through the clouds to light up much of her suite, she remembered who she was. Regardless of what fate held for her, she was the Lady of the Southern Marches. She was a Magus. And she would act as such. She would not be cowed by bullies. So with that thought circling in her mind, she took several deep breaths and pulled open her doors.

When she looked out from her chamber, Aislinn hesitated for a moment in surprise. She had expected the regular two guards standing to each side of the door, or perhaps even Tetric with a few more soldiers waiting to take her to Marden. Instead, a dozen soldiers stood on each side of the entrance, lined up not against the wall, but facing outward in a battle formation, as if they expected trouble to come from farther down the hallway that led away from her rooms. She recognized the men guarding her. All of them had trained with her on the practice ground. All of them were loyal to the Blademaster. Grinning slightly, she decided to start her day as she would any other, walking to the practice yard with the soldiers marching along with her in tight order.

"I must apologize again for King Beleron's behavior, Lady Winborne," said Jurgen Klines, ashamed by what he had witnessed the evening before. "I have known the King since he was a child. He has faults, yes, just like all of us. But I still cannot believe that he treated you in such a way. It was appalling and inexcusable."

Upon returning the Lady Winborne safely to her suite after her confrontation with Marden and Tetric, the Blademaster strengthened the guard around her and gave the soldiers very explicit orders that no one was to be permitted entry into the Lady's rooms, not even the King. She was not to walk the halls of the Palace without a full squad around her at all times. And if Tetric or Marden approached her, he was to be informed at once. He would come in force.

The Blademaster was still coming to grips with what he had seen upon entering King Beleron's chamber. He was embarrassed that he hadn't been able to stop the assault on both the Lady and her father. He was embarrassed that he could do no more than get her and her father out of Marden's room before anything worse occurred. He was embarrassed that he hadn't responded more forcefully, pulling his blade and inflicting some pain on that miserable Advisor, who seemed to have preyed upon Marden's weaknesses as soon as he had arrived in

Tintagel in a way that had helped to create the man who now sat on Caledonia's throne. A man clearly lacking in basic human decency.

What had happened last night was not the action of a monarch who deserved respect or trust. How could you put your faith in the decisions your King made when all the decisions the King made were designed to enhance his own standing or his own pleasure or his own wealth?

Jurgen believed that the purpose of a monarch was to rule, to make difficult decisions for the betterment of all. He also believed that before you could rule a Kingdom effectively, you needed to demonstrate that you could rule yourself first. And, clearly, Marden Beleron had been found lacking in that regard. Time and time again.

"There is nothing to apologize for, Captain Klines," replied Aislinn, patting his arm to support her words. "You weren't there until the end. You didn't know what was going on. You can't hold yourself responsible for what occurred. Only King Beleron can be held responsible."

Aislinn had not expected that her appearance at the practice yard would lead to a continuing apology from the Blademaster. Much to her surprise, it appeared that she had managed the situation better than he had.

"That may be, but it should never have come to this," continued Klines. "You should never have been placed in such egregious circumstances. I should have done something to prevent it."

"Captain Klines, this must stop," said Aislinn in the powerful voice of the Lady of the Southern Marches. She appreciated the Blademaster's remorse, but that did little to aid her with respect to her current dilemma. She needed to focus on what she was going to do next, not on what had happened, even though her emotions were still raw and her options were limited if not nonexistent altogether. "I appreciate your disgust at the machinations of the King and his Advisor, but we must move on. And remember, you rescued me and my father. So take some solace in that. I cannot thank you enough for putting an end to it."

"You are being far too kind, Lady Winborne," replied Jurgen contritely. "I did far too little."

"You did enough," said Aislinn, "and for that I thank you."

The Blademaster nodded, accepting the comment reluctantly, finally letting the matter drop. He then glanced around the practice yard to get a sense of who was with him, though he had little intention of putting these soldiers through their paces today. Today felt different. Change was in the air. He sensed that a storm was coming. But what this storm might be, whether for good or ill, he couldn't foretell. He could only be ready for whatever might come.

The soldiers gathered in the yard appeared to be sensing much the same as their Blademaster. Looking at all the faces, Jurgen verified that these were the same men who had been training in the early morning with the Lady Winborne. The Blademaster had not called these soldiers here. They had come of their own volition. The Blademaster hadn't told them what had happened to the Lady of the Southern Marches in the King's chamber, but word had spread, nonetheless.

These were not happy soldiers. They were primed for action, because to them it wasn't the Lady of the Southern Marches who the King had assaulted, but rather one of their own. A fellow fighter who had shared the dirt of the ring, sweated with them, sparred with them, bled with them, learned with them, and treated them with the courtesy and respect of a peer. These soldiers were ready to fight, and not for their King. Having confirmed his suspicions, Jurgen turned his attention back to the young lady he had grown to like and respect.

"What are your plans, Lady Winborne?"

"To do what must be done, Captain Klines. I will stay here. I have few other choices."

"There are always choices other than the most obvious, Lady Winborne. The city is becoming more restless. If it continues, and I expect that it will, perhaps it's an opportunity."

"Are you suggesting that I leave, Captain Klines?"

"Of course I am, Lady Winborne. I'm certain that any of the soldiers with us would be honored to guide you safely from Tintagel and then back to the Southern Marches where you would be in a better position to protect yourself and your Duchy."

"You know I can't do that, Captain Klines."

"Your father doesn't want you here either, Lady Winborne. I know your father. He is many things, but he is not a fool. I have no doubt that he has already told you that he wants you away from here, even if he can't follow."

"That may be so," Aislinn admitted reluctantly. "But that doesn't mean that he's right."

"You should listen to him. He is right, Lady Winborne. At least in this. You need to get away from here while you still can. You and your Duchy are more important than your father is. He sees it. Why can't you?"

"I can't leave him here," she said in a soft voice.

"You can't stay here. Your father knew his fate as soon as he arrived in Tintagel. He accepted it. You do not have to accept your fate. You can still do something about it."

"Blademaster, I won't dispute the truth of your argument. And you do make a good one. But I'm not leaving. I'm not leaving without my father. There is nothing that you can say that will change my mind."

"Blast it, child!" Jurgen said in exasperation, his anger, so rarely seen, rising to the surface. "You remind me of my daughter."

"Your daughter?"

"Yes, my daughter," Jurgen sighed. "She was strong-willed, just like you. Sure of herself. Confident. No matter the risk, she believed that she could work her way through any problem, any challenge, and come out unscathed. In the end that proved to be her downfall."

"Was?"

"Yes, she died several years ago," he said sorrowfully. "She was murdered."

"I'm sorry, Captain Klines. I didn't know."

"There's nothing to be sorry for. I rarely speak of her. But the more time I spend with you, the more I think of her. You two are very much alike. I don't want you to share the same or a worse fate."

Aislinn smiled warmly, touched by his concern. "You have nothing to fear in that regard, Captain."

"How can you be so sure, Lady Winborne?"

"Because I have you, Blademaster. You and your soldiers."

"We may not be able to protect you for long, Lady Winborne."

"You don't need to, Blademaster. You need only do so for a time."

It was then that a very broad soldier hustled into the practice yard, catching the attention of the other soldiers, all of them staring intently as he approached the Blademaster and the Lady of the Southern Marches.

"You're late, Benin. You should have been here an hour ago."

"My apologies, Blademaster," offered Benin, saluting the Captain and nodding to Lady Winborne respectfully. "I was in the Guards' compound but had to take my time before leaving. There was a great deal more activity than I expected."

"How so, Benin?" asked the Blademaster.

"More soldiers were coming into the barracks, all of them pulled in from other assignments. The rumors are flying.

Supposedly Killen Sourban will be taking the Guard into the streets in greater force."

"What's the excuse?" asked Aislinn. "The streets are already filled with soldiers. There have already been several incidents in just the last few days that could have set off another riot."

"True, Lady Winborne, but that doesn't seem to matter. From the snippets I was able to pick up, almost the entire Royal Guard will be moving into Tintagel to ensure that the current unrest doesn't shift from words to action."

"But that's a fool's task," countered Aislinn. "By bringing more soldiers in, Sourban is simply adding tinder to the flames. It will only be a matter of time before a spark is struck."

"I agree, Lady Winborne," Benin said with a nod, acknowledging the wisdom of her words.

"It's to be expected," said the Blademaster. "The leadership of the Guard has demonstrated a distinct lack of creativity for quite some time."

"There's more, Blademaster."

"With what you've already shared, Benin, what more could there be?"

"It's just a rumor circulating in the streets, Blademaster. It might not be worth your time with everything else that is going on."

"Out with it, Benin. You wouldn't have mentioned it if you didn't think it was worth hearing."

"The School of Gladiators, Blademaster," said Benin, though he seemed uncertain in the information that he was providing. "Rumors are spreading in the streets that the gladiators have taken the Colosseum and are preparing to escape."

"Are you certain of that?" asked the Blademaster. "That seems a bit farfetched."

"I agree, Blademaster. But there are also rumors that there are those who have entered the city to help them. These rumors also suggest that the reason the bulk of the Royal

Guard has been called into the city isn't because of unrest among the people, but rather because of these rumors regarding the gladiators."

"But that's preposterous," argued the Blademaster. "The Guards are stationed just on the other side of the Colosseum from the gladiators with specific entrances for forcing their way into the stockade if necessary. Declan would never ..."

Aislinn cut off the Blademaster, having listened with growing interest to what the young soldier had to say.

"Who supposedly has entered the city to aid the gladiators?"

"The Volkun, my Lady Winborne. The Wolf has returned, or so the rumors say."

"How certain are you of this?" asked the Blademaster, understanding the magnitude of the information if it was accurate. Lady Winborne had been correct that only a little tinder was needed to set off a potentially uncontrollable fire, and news of the Volkun, a favorite of the crowd, having come back to Tintagel to aid his peers would certainly serve that purpose.

"Nothing has been confirmed, Blademaster. As I said, it's just a whisper. But the word on the street is that the Volkun means to free his compatriots and then storm the Palace."

Hearing these rumors of the Wolf having returned to Tintagel sent a sliver of hope through Aislinn. Multiple thoughts played through her mind at once, so she had to take a moment to gather herself. Was this an opportunity that she could use to her advantage? Could Bryen actually have come back? Would he do that for her? Or if he had come back, was he here for a different reason entirely?

"I find that last hard to believe, Benin. These are only rumors. We do not act based solely on rumors. We act on good information."

"Of course, Blademaster," replied Benin. "I was only

reporting what I had heard. I didn't have the opportunity to explore these rumors any further."

"He's here," interrupted Aislinn, her voice filled with a confidence that she had thought had been quashed the moment she had stepped within the walls of the Corinthian Palace.

"Who's here?" asked the Blademaster.

"Bryen," began Aislinn, but then she quickly realized that neither the Blademaster nor Benin would know who that was. "The Volkun. He's in Tintagel. I can sense him."

"You can sense him?" asked the Blademaster incredulously.

Rather than offer a long explanation, she kept it short, knowing that time was of the essence.

"When my father put the Protector's collar on the Wolf, it created a connection between us. Even though I learned how to weaken that connection, it's still there. When I think of him, think of the Wolf, I can feel where he is."

"And he's in Tintagel this very moment?" asked the Blademaster, choosing not to challenge what Lady Winborne had said. He didn't know much about the collars worn by Protectors, but there was no good reason to doubt her.

"He is," Aislinn confirmed with a nod.

"Where exactly?"

"He's in the Colosseum," she said, but then corrected herself to provide a bit more precision. "In the gladiators' stockade."

"How could he have gotten into the stockade?" wondered Benin. "It's as difficult to get in there as it is to get out."

Jurgen Klines ignored the question, even though he knew that Benin's comment was spot on. He had sensed that today would bring significant change. This news appeared to confirm it. And it could be only the start. If the Volkun was with the gladiators and the Royal Guard was being called in, the riots of the last few weeks would be nothing compared to the eruption that he would expect to occur in the streets. Lady Winborne had said that she had no other options. Perhaps this was one that she could use to her benefit. But to make it work, he needed to confirm a few things first.

"Benin, take two men into the city as citizens, not soldiers. Do you understand why?"

"Yes, Blademaster."

"Good. You'll still need to stay sharp in order to complete the assignment I'm giving you. See what you can discover at the School of the Gladiators. Once you do, find me immediately. I likely won't be here. If the Volkun is back in the city and has found his way to the gladiators, then we will need to move quickly. Is that clear?"

"Yes, Blademaster. It should take no more than a few hours."

"Good," nodded Jurgen. "Also, get a feel for the city as you head toward the Colosseum. See if you can confirm where the Guards coming into Tintagel are being sent. That information is absolutely essential. We need to know that before we can do anything else."

"Understood, Blademaster."

"If you're not back by late afternoon, then I will assume the worst. Now go."

Benin nodded and then trotted out of the practice yard, calling to two soldiers along the way who picked up their gear and followed after him.

Jurgen then turned his sharp gaze toward the Lady Winborne. "You understand the danger we face if we go forward with this." There was no need to explain what he was talking about.

"I do," she replied, her eyes displaying a new resolve.

So like his daughter, he thought. If only the two could have met. He had no doubt that they would have been friends.

"Everyone dies, not everyone dies with honor," he

murmured, echoing a saying that his good friend had taught him many years before.

"I've heard that before," said Aislinn.

"No doubt you have, having spent so much time with the Volkun. Now it's time to move."

The Blademaster was about to bring together his Sergeants so that he could issue a set of commands when a contingent of the Royal Guard rushed into the practice yard, blocking the exit. The soldiers who had congregated with the Blademaster watched with interest as Timmons, a very large Sergeant with little imagination who long ago had tied his future to that of the Captain of the Guard stepped from among his men.

"Jurgen Klines!" said Timmons in a shout that was completely unnecessary in the enclosed space. "You are under arrest!"

"On whose order," asked the Blademaster calmly.

"By the order of the King," the Sergeant replied with a smug grin, believing that the matter was closed now that he had informed the Blademaster on whose authority he acted. No one, not even the Blademaster, would have the temerity to oppose the King.

"And the charge?"

"Treason!" shouted Timmons, his grin extending into a broad smile. He had never liked the Blademaster, and this opportunity to put him in his place -- permanently -- was one to be savored.

"Treason?" asked Jurgen, his mind already working its way through the maze. It didn't take him long to find the exit. Killen had found the excuse that he had been searching for after all these years, and he was making use of it. Jurgen shook his head with a sly smile. A pity that it would come back to bite the Captain of the Guard in the ass. "What treason might that be?"

"I do not need to answer your questions, Blademaster,"

scoffed Timmons. "You will be the one to answer the questions put to you."

"Yes, yes, I understand that you're enjoying this Sergeant. But think carefully, would you? You have created a situation where you have no good exit strategy. Your lack of ingenuity could be the death of you and your men."

Timmons struggled to control his temper, his dislike for the Blademaster intensifying. In part because the Blademaster was a better fighter than he was, but even more so because he felt like the Captain always looked down upon him. But rather than giving rein to his temper, he decided to try one more time in an effort to avoid bloodshed.

"You will come, one way or the other, Blademaster. Of your own volition or in chains. The choice is yours."

"The choice is mine, you say?" challenged the Blademaster. "Then so be it. I choose not to go. You may leave, Timmons, and take your men with you. This will be your only warning."

"My only warning?" asked Timmons, a laugh bursting out of his huge frame.

"Yes, your only warning. Choose wisely. You will not like the result if you don't."

"Enough of this!" shouted the Sergeant, motioning to his men. "Take him. If he resists, kill him!"

The soldiers who had accompanied Timmons pushed forward, all of them beginning to pull their swords from the scabbards on their hips. They didn't make it far. In an instant, they were surrounded by a wall of steel, the soldiers in the practice yard having formed two circles. A small one around the Blademaster and the Lady Winborne. A larger one around Timmons and his soldiers.

With just a nod from the Blademaster, Timmons' soldiers, recognizing how drastically circumstances had turned against them, released their grip on the hilts of their swords, allowing them to slide back into their sheaths. Watching this all play out so quickly at first shocked Timmons, and then it enraged him. He reached for his own sword, thinking that he could be faster than his men and simply bull his way through the soldiers to his front and get to his target. But he stopped short when he felt the steel tip wedged against his throat.

"That would be a big mistake, lad," said the Blademaster. "Let it go. There's nothing you can do here but get yourself and your men killed. No one wants that."

For a moment it appeared as if the Sergeant was going to disagree with the Blademaster, but then he grumbled a few curses under his breath and nodded reluctantly, releasing his grip on the hilt of his sword.

"Where should we take them, Blademaster?" asked one of the soldiers.

"Put them in the storehouse just beyond the practice yard, Jeffers. They won't be able to break through the door once you lock them in. No bloodshed if you can avoid it. But if any of them tries to escape, do whatever you need to do to make sure they don't."

The Blademaster had spoken so that all could hear, and his soldiers moved quickly to obey. Klines understood that a great deal of blood was about to be spilled. But it didn't need to start quite yet.

As Captain Klines defused what could have been an incendiary situation, Aislinn turned her thoughts to what she needed to do next. She needed to get to Bryen. But first she needed to find her father and do what she could to ensure that he remained safe.

It wasn't long before the Blademaster stalked through the seemingly endless halls of the Corinthian Palace, the Lady Winborne right beside him, the number of soldiers joining their ranks increasing by the minute. As he issued a stream of commands to his Sergeants, Klines realized that in almost the blink of an eye, he had committed treason, a conclusion that his soldiers had likely reached as well, and they seemed unfazed by it. But he understood that he had committed treason well before now, his allegiance having already shifted to the young woman striding so determinedly next to him.

A momentous day, indeed. And it was only getting started.

20

ALL GOOD

The silence was disconcerting to a very large extent, if only because it was so uncommon, so jarring in a space where noise, whether laughter or screams, curses or jeers, cries of terror or shrieks of distress, were so customary. The routine voices and sounds were gone, replaced by a stillness that Bryen was certain wouldn't last for much longer. But he would enjoy the peace nonetheless for however long it remained.

The Volkun walked along the lowest concourse of the Colosseum, which circled the stadium and gave him a view of the open promenade several hundred paces wide that separated the massive arena from the rest of the city. On most days stalls and small markets appeared in the plaza, and though the number of merchants and customers had dwindled in recent weeks because of the unrest in the capital, there were always a few industrious, entrepreneurial, or desperate vendors who set up shop there selling whatever might be available at that moment.

But not today. Not a sound emanated in the immediate vicinity of the Colosseum, and not a soul stirred. A hushed anticipation had fallen over this section of Tintagel that seemed to suggest that either great or terrible events would occur this day, perhaps both, in fact, and that your perspective on what occurred would depend on how those events played out in the next few hours. Either in your favor or against.

Every once in a while, Bryen heard shouts echoing down the streets and alleys just a few blocks away, which were then replaced by a dull rumble of what he took to be the voices of thousands of people who had come together but had yet to make an appearance. He could even see a few streams of wispy smoke drifting into the air farther down the boulevard that led toward the Corinthian Palace.

He had not been in the city long enough to get a feel for the rhythm of life in Tintagel, but he had a feeling that the riots of the last few weeks were about to start again, perhaps at an unprecedented level. He hoped that the actions that the gladiators had taken in the last few hours would serve as the spark that would set the whole city ablaze. Or maybe the gladiators were simply a smaller part of a larger drama preparing to be played out in the streets. Bryen really didn't care. He only cared about what he needed to do next so that his plan continued to move forward, and any additional unrest in Tintagel certainly wouldn't hurt in that respect.

He had started his circuit of the main corridor twenty minutes before, checking each of the twelve entrances that led from the plaza into the Colosseum, and he was now returning to where he had begun his loop. He was impressed but not surprised. His gladiators had worked efficiently and effectively, following the strategy that he and Declan had laid out the night before with a practiced ease.

Bryen had used the Talent to fuse the doors opening to the barracks of the Royal Guard that were set in the highest wall that overlooked the gladiators' compound with the stone in which they had been placed. If the Guard attempted to break through those two doors to get at the gladiators from behind, they would simply be wasting their time and effort, which was fine with Bryen. And if by chance the Guard somehow penetrated the wall near the doors, or tried to climb the walls, Bryen had left waiting for them several nasty surprises that he had learned from Rafia that would impede their progress further.

So Bryen wasn't worried about those doors that connected to the barracks of the Royal Guard or the walls. No, his main concern remained the Colosseum entrances. Each gate swung out from the stadium, but the gladiators had locked the thick bars of steel into the stone of the plaza and the top frame of the entrance, as well as the gates themselves, a team of gladiators standing guard at each one. They had then linked thick steel chains through the bars of each gate to harden their defense. And thanks to the ingenuity of several of the gladiators, benches torn from the arena had been attached to the bars with long nails protruding from the wood and pointing out toward the plaza and their expected attackers. Bryen's gladiators certainly had made good use of the tools and resources that they had available, something that the Royal Guard probably wouldn't appreciate when they attacked.

Bryen smiled every time he walked by a gate, nodding with pleasure. He stopped at each one to speak with his fighters. He knew that they understood their task. He just wanted to get a sense of their mood, and to a man and woman, they were confident, excited, and ready. Exactly as he had hoped.

Many of the gladiators nodded to him, even bowed to him slightly, which he found a bit disconcerting. A sign of respect, Bryen knew, and one that he appreciated, because he had done his best to make certain that all of the gladiators understood the likely path they would be following if they agreed to his plan. He didn't try to hide the truth or coat it with sugar. He told them bluntly that this rebellion likely would fail if all the other pieces didn't come together as he hoped, that they would die on the white sand just as was expected of them as gladiators, but in this instance, they would have the chance to die for something that they believed in rather than for the whims and fancies of someone else.

All of the gladiators were willing to make that sacrifice. They understood the risk, and they were willing to take it. And Bryen had realized that they had come to this decision not just because of who he was, not just because of the fact that he was the Volkun, a gladiator just like them, but because of what he was giving them. That sent a surge of pride through him that he had never experienced before. He had avoided getting too close to most of these fighters when he was in the Pit because he didn't want to deal with the pain and loss when they were dragged from the white sand. But now, he craved that closeness as he felt a strange and unexpected responsibility for them. A camaraderie that he hadn't felt before except with a select few.

When the Royal Guard attacked -- and Bryen was certain that they would, as he assumed that the delay in their response to the gladiators' revolt resulted from the King's desire to gather as many soldiers as he could so that he could make a grand entrance into the plaza fronting the Colosseum and perhaps terrify the gladiators into submission -- Marden Beleron and his soldiers were going to have a very hard time of it. His gladiators, several with military experience just like Declan, had made the Colosseum into their very own fortress. No matter what the King or Sourban tried, many of the Caledonian soldiers were going to die. And every death would give the gladiators that much more time to complete their mission.

Even so, Bryen was realistic. He only had a few hundred gladiators holding the Colosseum, and to defend effectively the fortification that they had created required at least ten times as many fighters. The twelve large gates ringing the Colosseum opened well past thirty feet wide, which meant that once a gate fell, ten soldiers standing abreast of one another could march through. With only a dozen fighters at each entrance, eventually the Royal Guard would gain a breakthrough that he and his gladiators would struggle to close. All of his gladiators were excellent fighters, Declan had seen to that. They were all dangerous fighters, and Bryen would put any of the men and women fighting for him up against any soldier in the Royal Guard.

But Sourban would bring the full might of the Royal Guard to bear, likely several thousand soldiers attacking at once. With that kind of advantage in manpower, it was only a matter of time. That was all right with Bryen. This entire exercise was designed to drag out the fight and gain time. His gladiators would hold for as long as they could. Eventually their lack of numbers would catch up to them. And then he and Declan would shift the strategy to adjust to the gladiators' circumstances, although through it all they would be guided by the overarching goal of not only killing the soldiers of the Royal Guard, but also killing their will to fight.

With such an approach, hopefully his gladiators would be able to last long enough to give Rafia and Sirius the time that they needed to free Duke Winborne and Aislinn, and perhaps even long enough for Tarin and the Battersea Guard to appear. But as these worries played through his thoughts for the thousandth time that morning, one of the many sayings that Bryen had picked up in recent years crossed his mind. In this instance, it was one of Sirius': "Hoping doesn't make it real."

The Magus was right, and Bryen wasn't a fool, nor were any of his gladiators. He knew what was at stake. He knew the odds that he faced. He knew the likely result. And he had made sure before all this began that his gladiators knew it all as well, so that when they chose to engage in this insurrection, their decision was based on reality rather than fantasy.

It wasn't long before Bryen reached the Colosseum's two main gates and what he viewed as the weakest point in his defenses. Each gate was twice as wide as the other entrances with no more than thirty feet separating the two from one another. That meant twenty soldiers standing abreast of one another could march through each gate and from there not only overwhelm the gladiators stationed here, but also push down the main concourse and attack the gladiators holding the other gates from behind.

This was where Declan and Bryen expected the Royal Guard would make their initial charge, the Captain of the Royal Guard likely assuming that if the Caledonian soldiers forced their way through here, the rebellion would end within hours of it beginning. And that's why Davin and Lycia, along with their squads that they had handpicked, had been assigned here. If anyone could hold the Guard at the most vulnerable point in their defenses, it would be them.

"All good?" asked Bryen.

"All good," both Davin and Lycia replied in unison.

"For now," Davin couldn't resist offering. "Ask me again later. I might have a different response."

"For now," Bryen agreed with a smile.

Davin fought with a deadly efficiency on the white sand, but off it he demonstrated a loquaciousness that irritated his sister to no end and Bryen often struggled to follow.

Bryen stared out from between the bars where there were a few openings between the long wooden planks the gladiators had attached. He saw that there was some activity beginning at the far edge of the plaza. A few soldiers were peeking out from behind the corners of the alleys and streets that led into the mall, trying to get a sense of what might be going on in the Colosseum. Good luck with that, he thought. He doubted that they'd be able to see much with the benches blocking their view.

Bryen even identified a few arrows that had been loosed from the streets on the far side of the public square toward the Colosseum that had shattered against the stadium's façade and lay broken on the cobbled stone, hopefully not a metaphor for how the day would end for Bryen and his gladiators.

Probably just gauging range, he assumed, but who could say? Perhaps a few enterprising soldiers were seeking to make a lucky shot. Either way, the gladiators didn't appear to be concerned. They were ready for whatever might come. The big show hadn't begun yet, though it would start soon.

"What's this Company of Blood I keep hearing about?" asked Bryen, turning his attention back to Davin. "I understand you had something to do with it."

"What Company of Blood?" asked Lycia, not yet having heard the term.

"I thought it sounded good," replied Davin sheepishly. "It seemed appropriate."

"Davin took it upon himself to name us the Company of Blood when he expelled some nobles from the plaza earlier this morning," explained Bryen. "Apparently the gladiators liked the moniker so much that they've been spreading the word from gate to gate. The Blood Company holds the Colosseum."

"But why that name?" asked Lycia. It was just like her brother, always impulsive, spouting whatever was in his head rather than giving it some thought first.

"It just came to me," replied Davin with a shrug. "I thought that something that sounded scary would be best. The Company of Blood seemed to fit the bill."

"Scary, huh? That was the best that you could do?"

"The other gladiators liked it," protested Davin. "So why not? It's got a nice ring to it."

Before the discussion between brother and sister denigrated to the level of an argument, which it likely would based on past experience, Bryen intervened.

"What's done is done. If the other gladiators like the name, then so be it. We are now the Blood Company."

Davin seemed inordinately pleased with that announcement. Before Lycia could offer another dig at her brother, and Bryen could tell that she was about to with the flash in her eyes and the twist of her lips, he sought to shift the conversation.

"How was it in the Pit while I was gone?"

Davin was about to answer, but Lycia stopped him short with a look, worried that her brother was going to reveal her struggles with the Woe after Bryen had been taken from the white sand.

"It got worse," Lycia said.

"How so?" asked Bryen.

"Combats twice a week," replied Davin. "No time to rest or recover appropriately. Little time to train between bouts."

"More dangerous beasts," continued Lycia. "Instead of one starved tiger you'd fight three. Instead of fighting two murderers from the prison you'd be matched against four."

"More gladiators were dying than should have," confirmed Davin. "And through no fault of their own."

"All for the pleasure of the King," said Bryen sadly.

Lycia nodded. "For the pleasure of the King and for the pleasure of the crowd. It was no more than an attempt at distraction. To give people a few hours to forget the misery of their own existence."

Bryen stared at Lycia for several long seconds, catching on one of the last words that she had used. Distraction. It was certainly appropriate in that moment for a variety of reasons, not the least of which the uprising that they had begun. But Bryen sensed that there was something more personal about it as well. He could see it in her eyes, as she had never been very good at hiding her feelings. Lycia wasn't revealing everything that had happened. He'd have to talk with her about it later, if they had the chance.

"What about you?" asked Davin. "What happened when you were taken from the Pit?"

"It was just another form of slavery," Bryen replied with a shrug and a grimace. "I was made a Protector for the Lady of the Southern Marches."

Lycia looked at Bryen closely. She had expected some anger in his voice, perhaps even hate at the fate that he had been given, but she couldn't detect it. Instead, his tone was more one of resignation or acceptance than anything else, and that surprised and worried her.

"What did that entail?" asked Davin.

"A Protector is required to defend their charge from all danger whether they want to or not," Bryen answered quietly. "You have no choice. You're compelled to do it."

"How so?"

"You're bound to your charge through the collar," answered Bryen, motioning to the silver torque around his neck. "Once locked in place, the Protector's collar can never be removed. There's a magic that runs through it. That magic links you to your charge and requires you to put your life at risk. You are bound to your charge. You can feel where your charge is, you can feel their emotions, you can sense what they're thinking. And the collar won't allow you to be more than a few hundred feet away from your charge. If your charge is in danger, you fight, no matter the odds, no matter the threat."

"You can't fight the magic?" asked Lycia.

"No, you can't. I tried."

"What happens if you're not as close to your charge as you're supposed to be?" asked Davin.

"Pain," Bryen answered simply, not really desiring to share the most intimate details regarding what had happened. "Crippling pain until you're back within range of your charge."

Davin grimaced in distaste, horrified that his friend had to go through such an experience.

"How is it that you're here now?" asked Lycia. "The Lady of

the Southern Marches is in the Corinthian Palace, which is a mile or more away. Isn't that too far?"

"It would have been," said Bryen. "But before Aislinn came to Tintagel, she freed me from the restrictions of the collar, at least as best as she could. She eliminated the requirement that I remain close to her as well as the compulsion to protect her at all costs, but despite her best efforts she couldn't remove the collar itself."

"Aislinn?" asked Lycia, her voice sharper than she intended because of the hint of jealousy that shot through her.

"The Lady of the Southern Marches," offered Bryen with a look that suggested that he didn't know why Lycia was upset, his response causing Davin to grin, who for once was reading the situation much better than his friend was.

"I know Aislinn Winborne is the Lady of the Southern Marches," said Lycia, her voice becoming louder. "We've met her. Davin dueled her on the white sand. If she enslaved you, why do you call her Aislinn?"

For a moment, Bryen stood there, his eyes growing big, uncertain of what to say next. He hadn't expected such a response from Lycia, and why she was acting this way he didn't know, although Davin clearly did. Unfortunately for Bryen, Davin wasn't offering any assistance, choosing to remain silent with that stupid grin on his face, waiting to see how things would play out between his friend and his sister.

"We became ..." Bryen started, in an effort to explain, but Lycia quickly cut him off.

"Don't you dare tell me you became friends," she said. "Not after she and her father enslaved you."

"She didn't enslave me. Her father was the one who ..."

"It doesn't matter if she had a direct role or not. She is just as complicit in your servitude as her father was," argued Lycia.

"I wasn't going to say that. I was going to say ..."

"Remember, the apple never falls very far from the tree. The Lady of the Southern Marches is no better than ..."

"Lycia, are you done?" asked Bryen, his voice gaining some heat. "I appreciate your anger for what I had to deal with, but I can't really tell you about it unless you allow me to do so."

"Sorry," grumbled Lycia, about to say more until she noticed with some embarrassment that some of the gladiators by the two gates were now looking at them, curious as to the raised voices. "You're right. I just still feel ..."

"Protective of me," completed Bryen with a small smile. "I understand, and I appreciate your concern."

Lycia nodded, not wanting to dig any deeper into the feelings that she was currently experiencing as she wasn't certain how to navigate them.

"As I was saying," Bryen continued, "Lady Winborne and I seemed to reach an agreement of sorts. I didn't want to be her Protector. She didn't want me to be her Protector. But neither of us had any choice so we had to make the best of it."

"Is that why you're here?" asked Davin, demonstrating a surprising acuity for reading the larger situation. "To free her from Marden's grip?"

"In part," replied Bryen. "Strangely I do feel a debt to her for freeing me from most of the demands of the collar." He held up his hand before Lycia could offer a caustic comment that was on the tip of her tongue and that he was certain wouldn't prove helpful to the conversation. "But I'm also here for you and for me. Even when Aislinn freed me from the collar, I didn't feel free. As I explained last night, I still feel as if I'm fighting on the white sand. I'll always feel that way. Unless I can free myself, free all of you, I'll never be free of the white sand."

Davin nodded, satisfied with his friend's response, because just like all the other gladiators, he knew exactly what Bryen meant.

"You trained her quite well," Davin said. "She more than

held her own during our duel. And then she put the King in his place, making a fool of him in the Pit."

"I'm not surprised," said Bryen with a grin. "She reminds me of someone."

"Who?" asked Lycia. She was still attempting to control her temper, but she couldn't resist asking the question.

"You," Bryen said with another smile. "Tough. Determined. Brave. Never gives up."

Bryen's words defused the anger surging within Lycia in an instant, even bringing a slight smile to her lips. She reached out with her right hand and touched the silver encircling Bryen's neck. It was cool to the touch, but she thought that she felt a tiny jolt of energy running through it. She then allowed her fingers to run above the metal and touch the scar on Bryen's neck and cheek before she finally removed her hand, her fingers lingering a bit longer than she originally intended. At the same time, she looked up into Bryen's eyes. For just an instant Lycia thought that she saw a spark of white, but then she questioned her initial belief, thinking now that it was most likely just a reflection of the light as the sun introduced itself in the plaza.

Although she may have been wrong about the white flash, she was certain in her feeling that Bryen had changed in many ways since he had been sold a year before. He had always been quiet. Always stoic. He rarely revealed anything and didn't share much about himself. And somehow, he had made himself harder and tougher during the last twelve months than she had thought possible. Harder than the stone used to construct the Colosseum. But strangely, she sensed that there was a fracture somewhere in that stone now, a tiny crack, although Lycia didn't believe that it was a weakness.

Rather, she believed that that crack in his armor somehow had made Bryen stronger. More whole. More complete. Although he still might view himself as a gladiator, in her mind he was no longer just a gladiator. He was something more. Something more dangerous. Something more powerful. She didn't know what could have caused the change within him, whether it was an event or a person or something else. But she didn't view how Bryen had changed since he had been gone as a bad thing. It was just a bit disorienting for her.

Lycia knew the Bryen from before he was taken to the Southern Marches. She needed to learn more about the man that he had become, because she was absolutely certain that he was not sharing with her and Davin everything that had happened since he'd been gone. She couldn't delve into it now, but she would get him to talk. She promised herself that. She could do it when they used to spend time together in the gladiators' barracks, and she would figure out a way to do it now. Assuming, of course, that they both survived the attack to come.

"So after we defeat the Royal Guard, free the Duke and Lady Winborne, and then topple the throne of Caledonia, what do you plan to do next?" asked Davin, clearly uncomfortable with the direction the conversation had taken and seeking to change its course before it became even worse for him.

Bryen nodded his thanks for what Davin had done, then took a few seconds before responding. "I want a fresh start. I want to go where no one will know me. Where I can be what I want to be."

"And where would that be?" asked Davin with a laugh. "Because after today the entire Kingdom will know our names far and wide."

Her brother's assumption that they would succeed brought a smile to Lycia's pixielike face. Bryen couldn't help but smile as well, Davin's grin and confidence infectious.

"I was thinking the Territories," said Bryen. Many of the gladiators had talked of their dreams to go to the Territories, to leave Caledonia. They knew in their hearts that based on their circumstances it was an impossible wish. But the desire to visit the land far to the west on the other side of the Burnt Ocean had remained for most of them. It had only been the last few years that adventurers, prospectors, and others had begun to leave Caledonia for that far continent, and it held an almost mythical hold upon them. A place where they could be free from their past.

Lycia laughed at Bryen's response, gripping his forearm affectionately. "Dreams are all well and good, but I expect we'll all be dead fairly soon, despite what my brother seems to believe. So all I want is for my blood to cover the white sand."

"Blood on the sand," said Davin, nodding to Lycia in respect.

"Blood on the sand," repeated Bryen, his voice quiet as he fought to control the emotion that threatened to burst from him.

Lycia was right. Dreams were all well and good, but the reality of their situation suggested only one conclusion. Bryen had offered the gladiators an opportunity that none wanted to lose. An opportunity to die on their own terms. He hoped that their deaths would mean something in the end.

21

A SHOW FOR MARDEN

"That's the advice you would offer me, Captain?" Marden stared at Sourban with undisguised contempt. "A revolt is underway in my Kingdom, in my city, and that's what you want me to do?"

The Captain of the Royal Guard had rushed into Marden's private quarters with the sun barely in the sky, Tetric following right behind. The only reason Marden hadn't exploded into a rage at having his sleep disturbed was that he hadn't been sleeping. He had started his entertainment late the night before and had found no good reason to go to bed, deciding instead to continue on with his activities into the morning. The only twinge of irritation he had felt was when Sourban had ordered the two women passed out in his bed to leave. When the servants had proven unresponsive, Sourban had instructed the two Guards at the King's door to carry them out. Marden was a touch piqued at that, as he had enjoyed a great deal of fun with them the night before, at least he thought that he had, the poppy root laced in the wine blurring his memories.

That mild annoyance dissipated swiftly when Sourban explained that the gladiators had revolted during the night, killing the soldiers assigned to guard the stockade and then secretly gaining control of the Colosseum before the Royal Guard stationed in the barracks right next door got wind of the scheme. Having learned just an hour before of what had happened from a gaggle of upset, terrified lesser lords who arrived at the Palace gates believing that the rebels were pursuing them all the way down the promenade, Sourban had sent several companies of soldiers from the Palace to surround the Colosseum, directing them to stay in the streets encircling the arena and out of the plaza, his focus on keeping the gladiators in place and not allowing them to attempt their escape from the city.

Yet the gladiators' decision to fortify the Colosseum bothered Sourban. The actions of these men and women, who he thought would be desperate to get away, made him think that there was more going on than just an attempted breakout. Rather than seeking to bolt once they had taken the Colosseum, the gladiators had instead settled into place and didn't appear to be in a rush to leave. Why not just slink into the city and hide before anyone was the wiser? Some of them would get out of the capital eventually.

Perhaps the appearance of his soldiers so quickly at the border of the plaza had spooked the gladiators, forcing them to rethink their plans. And now their delay had cost them any chance of leaving Tintagel and trying their luck in the countryside. With word of their uprising spreading through the city faster than a windswept inferno, the gladiators had no choice now but to hold the Colosseum for as long as they could, understanding that if they made for the streets his soldiers would cut them down with ease once Sourban brought his greater numbers to bear.

"You would leave them there?" asked Marden incredulously, his shock coming out more like a shriek. "You would allow them to stay in my Colosseum?"

"Only for a time, my King," Sourban replied, realizing that he had walked into dangerous territory, made even more treacherous by Marden's bloodshot eyes and his twitching cheek. The Captain of the Royal Guard was certain that the King was still feeling the effects of the poppy root he had taken the night before, and that meant his decisions would be more erratic than usual if he wasn't careful in how he approached the next few minutes. "Ignore them for a few days. Show the residents of the capital that the gladiators have no meaning. Their revolt doesn't even rise to a level where you need to even pay attention, my King."

"How could you even think that ..."

Sourban cut off his monarch, understanding the risk that he was taking, seeing the rage that appeared in Marden's inflamed eyes, but doing so anyway because he feared the consequences of his King moving too quickly.

"I am not suggesting that we leave the gladiators there, my King. Never that. We will crush them." Sourban's ice-cold blue eyes bore into Marden, trying to win him to his cause. "I am simply suggesting that we wait a few days. The Royal Guard is spread thinly throughout the city and in the surrounding countryside. From what I've been able to piece together the gladiators have done an excellent job of fortifying the Colosseum. The doors that would allow us to enter the gladiators' stockade have been welded shut. It will take days to open them, so we have no easy way to get at them from behind."

"But you want me to ..." Marden could barely get the words out, unable to comprehend what Sourban was suggesting. He couldn't appear weak. He refused to appear weak. And he feared that the strategy his Captain had proposed did just that.

"We'll need to attack through the gates, my King," continued Sourban, "but to do that, and to ensure our success, I need to marshal our forces. That will take a few days. By then, the gladiators will be on edge, waiting for us to come, each hour that they have to wait playing upon their fears. That and the fact that they only have a few days of food stocks means the longer we wait to attack, the greater the chance that the gladiators will be tired and hungry and less able to defend themselves well."

"I will not demonstrate weakness," said Marden in a dangerously quiet voice, the twitch in his cheek getting worse as his temper threatened to break free. The poppy root, in most people, tended to serve as a slight sedative and provided a feeling of euphoria. But in some, extreme agitation was a distinct possibility, even violent behavior, when provoked. In Marden's case, he had to make a visible effort to get his rising fury under control. "Is that what you're suggesting, Killen? Are you suggesting that I'm weak?"

"No, my King!" replied Sourban forcefully, realizing that he had gone well past dangerous territory and that his neck wasn't too far from the noose in that moment. "I am simply suggesting that we wait a few days. We show the city that the gladiators are unimportant. During that time, we gather the bulk of the Royal Guard and then attack in force. If we can't open the doors connecting the barracks to the Colosseum, it doesn't matter. We attack all twelve gates at once. We'll crush the gladiators when we choose to. We control the timing of the attack. We dictate the timing of the gladiators' demise. They are slaves, my King. Despite their insurrection, we can still make them to be seen as answering to us."

"You just made a key point, Killen," said Marden, his anger now at just a low simmer rather than a full boil as he listened through the haze of the poppy root to his Captain's argument. "The gladiators are slaves, nothing more."

"Yes, my King," agreed Sourban.

"Yet you seem impressed by these slaves, Killen," said Marden with just a touch of scorn and intrigue in his voice. "Perhaps even impressed by their efforts. By their initiative."

Sourban ignored the insinuation, understanding the risk of heading down that road.

"I am not impressed, my King. I am trying to be realistic. I have watched them in their combats. But more important, I have watched them in training. They know how to fight. The Master of the Gladiators has seen to that."

"And they fight as well as my soldiers?" scoffed Marden. "Do you truly believe that? A gladiator can stand against a soldier of the Royal Guard?"

Sourban took a moment before responding, knowing that speaking the truth now would be a mistake. "No, my King. A gladiator cannot stand against one of your soldiers." But he couldn't stop himself from qualifying his statement just a bit. "Not for any length of time."

"So you're not frightened of this Volkun having returned to the Colosseum to lead this rebellion?" questioned Marden. "During his time in the Pit he was considered the deadliest fighter to walk the white sand in the last few decades."

Sourban bristled at the insult offered to him by his liege. "No, my King. If the Volkun truly was foolish enough to return here, he is still no more than a gladiator. He is not a soldier. I will kill him just as easily as I would kill any of the other rebels."

"Bold words," said Marden, "assuming, of course, that you believe what you are saying."

"True words," countered Sourban. "Besides, rumors of the Volkun are solely that. Rumors. No one has seen the Wolf enter Tintagel in the last few days. And no one has seen him since the gladiators took the Colosseum."

"Difficult to see when the gladiators have succeeded in boarding over the gates," chuckled Tetric, finally deciding to enter the conversation, allowing the brunt of the King's anger to fall on Sourban first so that he wouldn't have to waste much time making his argument on how Marden should proceed. "Tell us, Captain, what is going on in the streets?"

"The people are restless, my King." Sourban made it a point to address his comments to Marden, choosing not to engage directly with the King's Advisor. The man with eyes blacker than the night made him distinctly uncomfortable. Sourban was confident that he could kill anything alive with his steel. He was not so certain about Tetric, and that was a realization that chilled him to his very core. "The sun is just a few hours in the sky but already the Royal Guard is out in force to manage five large crowds in the squares leading from the Corinthian Palace to the Colosseum." Sourban tried one more time to make the argument that he had offered at the beginning of this conversation. "That's in large part why I'm suggesting that we let the gladiators stew for a while. The gladiators are not a threat to us, but if those crowds become violent -- and our experiences of the last few weeks suggest that's a distinct possibility -- then those mobs will be a threat to the Crown. If I need to pull soldiers to storm the Colosseum, who knows what could happen in the city with the rabble running free. We would be taking a huge risk, my King, leaving the people without a sure sign of your power in the form of the Royal Guard."

"I must say, Captain, that I disagree with most of your argument," said Tetric, earning an angry glare from Sourban that the former Magus ignored. "Except for one part."

"And what would that be, Advisor?" asked Sourban, his hand caressing the hilt of his sword as if he were actually thinking of drawing the steel from its scabbard if he didn't like what Tetric had to say.

"You mentioned the need to display a sure sign of the King's power," replied Tetric calmly, the threat being made by the Captain having no impact upon him. "In that, and that alone, I completely agree."

"What did you have in mind, Tetric?" asked Marden, his

eyes clearing a bit as his eagerness at what he thought his Advisor was going to suggest energized him and helped to burn off the poppy root that was still flowing through his body.

"I believe the gladiators have given us an excellent opportunity, King Beleron. The fools will allow us to kill two birds with one stone."

"How so, Tetric?" asked Marden. His voice was quiet, collected, but his eyes had begun to blaze with an almost manic energy that had nothing to do with the drug that he enjoyed so frequently.

"Although I appreciate everything that our esteemed Captain has said, I believe he is looking at this uprising in the wrong way. This is not a threat, my King. This is the chance that we have been waiting for."

"My King, I must protest. We need to …"

Marden raised his hand, not bothering to turn toward Sourban, his attention focused solely on his Advisor. "You had your chance, Captain. Allow Tetric to finish his thought. I do hope, Tetric, that your approach doesn't involve my allowing the gladiators to maintain control of one of the most recognized buildings in my capital."

"It does not, King Beleron," Tetric confirmed.

"Good. Please explain what you have in mind."

"It is really quite simple, King Beleron. We have the strongest army in Caledonia. We use the Royal Guard to quash the gladiators' rebellion. How many gladiators are there, Captain? One hundred? Two hundred at most?"

"Two hundred," replied Sourban sullenly.

"Two hundred gladiators," repeated Tetric. "Two hundred gladiators against what, five or six thousand soldiers all told that we could take from the Corinthian Palace and then add to our ranks as we make our way down the boulevard that leads to the Colosseum?"

"Yes, around six thousand," Sourban replied reluctantly.

"I believe, King Beleron, that six thousand soldiers of the Royal Guard are more than a match for the two hundred gladiators who have dared to challenge your authority. My idea is really quite basic, and I'm certain that the Captain will understand after I explain it but one time."

A burst of rage shot through Sourban at Tetric's insult, his face turning bright red. But he chose to keep his peace, understanding that anything he said now would be a waste of his breath. Tetric had already won. He had captured the King's imagination.

"No one can stand against the Royal Guard. No Duchy, and certainly not two hundred gladiators pulled from the dregs of society. Thieves. Murderers. Beggars. We leave the Corinthian Palace with all the troops that we can muster and we parade down the promenade to the Colosseum, our grand and courageous King in the lead. Along the way, we integrate the soldiers assigned to manage the crowds. We then surround the Colosseum, issue our ultimatum, and then storm the gates when they refuse. It will all be over in a matter of hours."

"And what of the crowds that could so easily become mobs?" asked Sourban, unable to contain himself. "The multitude will significantly outnumber my soldiers."

"Yes, but the commoners are not soldiers," replied Tetric, the scorn in his voice forcing Sourban to fight to control his fury at being outmaneuvered so easily. "And they are not properly armed. They are shop owners and merchants, the poor and the destitute, who simply need to be reminded of their place in this Kingdom. Once they see the ease with which the Royal Guard eliminates the gladiators, their minds will grasp immediately how the soldiers of Caledonia could easily be turned on them. These crowds that so frequently become riotous mobs will stop in an instant. We will have peace in Tintagel once again and, most importantly, no one will think to challenge your rule, King Beleron."

"And what if it doesn't work that way?" asked Sourban. "What if the people are emboldened instead by the actions of these gladiators?"

For the first time Tetric turned his hypnotic eyes to the Captain, his expression revealing his disdain for the veteran soldier and hopefully concealing the glee that he felt at the prospect of sowing even more confusion in the capital.

"Then we make an example of them," replied Tetric. "If slaughtering the gladiators isn't enough, slaughtering a few thousand rioters should do the trick."

"Quite a simple strategy just as you said," said Marden with a nod, seemingly unconcerned by the possible loss of life. "And direct. I like it."

"I thought you might, King Beleron. I've always found that simple is often best. This gladiator uprising is the best thing that could have happened. This gives you an opportunity to exercise your power. The actions of the Royal Guard will demonstrate your ability as the King, and it will bring the people back to you. A strong hand in distressing and fearful times such as these is needed and appreciated. Perhaps most important, it will remind the people that any attempted rebellion will be put down quickly and viciously."

Marden nodded his head in appreciation at Tetric's suggested course of action, his smile growing as he allowed the proposal to percolate in his mind.

"How long before you can have the soldiers stationed here at the Palace ready to march toward the Colosseum, Killen?"

"Within the hour, my King," the Captain replied, a touch of nausea settling in his stomach. Tetric had won, and Sourban worried now that the consequences of his failure to sway the King could be more severe than any of them suspected.

"Do it," Marden ordered, which earned a victorious smile from his Advisor. "All of the Royal Guard is to march to the Colosseum. As soon as we leave the Palace, I want riders sent ahead so that the soldiers along the way will be prepared to join us. The sooner we get to the Colosseum and put down this insurrection in the harshest possible manner the better."

"My King, we can't leave the Palace undefended," protested Sourban.

"Fine," agreed Marden with some frustration, his eyes focused on the glory that he believed that he could achieve through the strategy proffered by Tetric while ignoring the associated risk. "I'm sure a skeleton guard can be left behind. I expect to see you both at the gates to the Palace in one hour. We march for the Colosseum. Death to any who defy me!"

22

TAKING THE GATE

"This doesn't bode well, Sergeant. Not well at all."

Sergeant Aristes, commander of the Royal Guard company assigned the task of guarding Tintagel's eastern gate, normally didn't spend much time listening to Corel. His Corporal was a good soldier. He did what he was told, what was expected of him, when he was expected to do it. He was an excellent fighter. Stayed out of trouble for the most part unless he drank too much, and that happened infrequently. Aristes' only complaint regarding Corel was that he tended to always see the worst in every situation and having spent so much time with Corel over the years, that characteristic had begun to irritate Aristes. Life was hard enough without having to see nothing but doom and gloom on the horizon.

Yet this time Aristes actually agreed with his Corporal. "You might be right," he replied in a murmur.

Smoke over the city had become a regular occurrence in recent weeks, and Aristes had come to dread it, as did many of his fellow soldiers. Smoke meant that a riot was brewing. Another riot. And the increasing frequency with which these riots were occurring worried Aristes. Just a few months ago, such a display by the common people would have been unheard of, but no more. Now, one or two times a week rampaging mobs would work their way through the city until the Royal Guard regained control of the situation and choked off the chaos.

In the beginning, the people involved in the unrest tended to disperse peacefully as soon as they saw the large formation of Royal Guard approaching. But the last few times the appearance of the Caledonian soldiers hadn't had the desired effect, inciting rather than cowing the protesters.

Aristes enjoyed his service in the Royal Guard, having dedicated the last twenty years of his life to the Caledonian Army and rising through the ranks because of his experience and expertise. Until this past year.

The soldiers had felt the pinch just as much as the people living in and around Tintagel. Lack of supplies. Lack of fresh food. Lack of basic services such as clean water and sanitation. All of this leading to more people living in the streets, more people searching for food, more people desperate to feed their families, all of them looking for someone to blame.

What better target for their anger than the Royal Guard? During the last few weeks the mob had turned against the soldiers of Caledonia, as they were the most visible reminder of Marden Beleron's rule. They never saw the King. But they saw his soldiers on every street corner and in every square. Three times Aristes and the men with him had fought the mob, pushing them back, stopping them from attacking the Corinthian Palace. But his heart hadn't been in it because he sympathized with the protestors.

For the first time since he had joined the Royal Guard, he had received assignments that he thought had been wrong. Instead of protecting the people from external threats, the Guard was ordered to disperse the people of Tintagel through whatever means proved necessary. If the Caledonian citizens refused to disband, they were to be treated as insurrectionists.

He didn't have the stomach to fight people who were hungry, who were scared, who had been ignored by the Crown. He had done his duty, as had his fellow soldiers, but most had done so reluctantly. They had joined the Royal Guard to protect Caledonia. They had not committed their lives to the army so that they could fight their own people.

Because of the extreme measures put forward by Captain Sourban, a broiling discontent was spreading quickly throughout the Royal Guard. There were always a few soldiers who took a unique pleasure in exercising their authority and harming others simply because they could. But most were like Aristes and wanted to conduct themselves with honor and uphold the traditions of the Guard. Unfortunately, Aristes would be the first to admit that it was very difficult to remain loyal to the Crown when the Crown failed to demonstrate loyalty to the people it was sworn to aid and protect.

Aristes pushed the increasingly dark thoughts that had been bothering him for the last few weeks to the side as he glimpsed several more plumes of smoke rising above the crowded homes and buildings of Tintagel.

"It looks like those fires are coming from the squares near the main boulevard," said Corel. "Maybe even from the plaza surrounding the Colosseum."

Aristes nodded. "That was my guess as well."

"Any word, Sergeant, on what might be happening?" asked Corel. "The men have been feasting on a stew of rumors. Any truth you can add to the pot?"

Aristes looked behind him when Corel gestured in that direction, his soldiers at their posts exactly as they should be, but he could tell that they were nervous. It was obvious in their eyes and their postures. His men also spent more time looking in toward the city rather than out through the gate to see if anything like a merchant caravan might be coming their way, which of course made sense with what was occurring in Tintagel and the fact that traders had been few and far between on the roads recently.

All morning his soldiers had been asking the same questions of one another that Aristes had been asking of himself. What was happening? Just more riots? Or was it something else? Something more coordinated? Because for some reason today felt different than all the other days. Today Aristes had the feeling that something momentous was going to happen, but he didn't know why he thought that, what it could be, or what it could mean.

"I would if I could," Aristes responded. "When several of our squads were ordered elsewhere earlier this morning Captain Sourban didn't offer much in the way of detail. He just mumbled something about moving toward the Colosseum with as strong a force as possible at all speed."

Corel nodded, a thoughtful expression crossing his sharp features. "Then maybe it's true."

"Maybe what's true?" asked Aristes, not understanding to what Corel could be referring.

"One of the soldiers I ran into in the barracks this morning said that the gladiators had stormed the Colosseum," replied Corel. "Not a drop of blood was spilled, at least with respect to the gladiators."

"I find that hard to believe," scoffed Aristes. "They live in the shadow of our barracks."

"I won't argue with you, Sergeant. I'm simply repeating what I heard. At first, I didn't believe it. But then I caught another rumor that suggested the first could be true."

"What was that, Corel?"

"The Volkun has returned, Sergeant. The rumor is that the Volkun is leading the gladiators' revolt. That they already have control over the Colosseum and now no one knows what they'll do. Not with the Wolf stalking the white sand again."

Aristes was about to laugh off what Corel had just said, but then he took a moment to think about it. Could there be some truth to it? The smoke darkening the early morning sky appeared to be centered around the Colosseum. The Volkun had been the deadliest fighter in the Pit for a decade and was probably one of the greatest ever. Not only because of his ability to fight, but because he roused the crowd and pulled them to his side with a powerful charisma rarely seen on the white sand. The Sergeant had watched several of his combats, marveling at his speed and tenacity. In his mind, the gladiator was aptly named. He certainly fought like a wolf. If the gladiators were going to risk an uprising, it made sense that the Volkun would be in the middle of it, though why he would ever return here once he had escaped the Pit he didn't know.

And, of course, he had lost most of his soldiers this morning, pulled away to combat some unknown disturbance. A fact that was beginning to bother Aristes more and more as he heard the rumblings of a large crowd emanating from the surrounding streets and the smoke from the fires began to drift into the small square that fronted the eastern gate, decreasing his visibility to the point where the few people moving across the space had become no more than shadows.

"Corel, how many squads do we have left?"

The soldier standing next to Aristes had grown increasingly uncomfortable as well as the acrid haze continued to drift in from the streets and the alleys.

"Just the one, Sergeant," he replied, coughing a few times to clear his throat of the increasingly irritating smoke. "And just a handful of men remain in the gatehouse."

Aristes nodded. He had already known the answer to his question, but he had been hoping that Corel would give him a better one. All the veteran soldier had done was intensify

Aristes' nervousness. He could feel it in his bones. Something was going to happen today, something important, something unexpected. He had gotten these feelings a few times in the past, and they had always been right. Unfortunately so. And that worried him even more. Because he wasn't sure that he wanted to be here at the eastern gate when whatever was going to happen actually did.

JERAD STOOD at the corner of a street in Tintagel, staying hidden behind a large building that he thought might have once been a tavern but was now shuttered. His position gave him an excellent view of the square and just beyond that the eastern gate. The large portcullis was raised this smoky morning to allow what few travelers might want to enter or exit the capital to do so, but he knew how quickly that steel barrier could come crashing down. He had slipped into the city under the guise of a peripatetic craftsman the day before and had learned upon arriving that there were several soldiers who exercised control over the mechanism tucked safely away in the modest gatehouse that was built into the wall. They could release the catch and seal the passage in the blink of an eye.

Two squads of the Battersea Guard had also entered Tintagel in disguise, and during the night they had congregated here with him as well as along several of the other streets that fed the square he was staring out upon at that moment. He, like all his soldiers, wore heavy, dark cloaks that hid their leather armor and the weapons that they carried.

Yesterday, when he had put his plan into motion, Jerad had worried that some of his soldiers would be found out by the Royal Guard and that the ruse would be up before it even began. But the Sergeant of the Battersea Guard soon discovered that he had nothing to fear. The Royal Guards spent most of their time focused on what was going on in the city, more interested in the large groups of people that were roaming the streets and occasionally coming near a gate rather than in any of the handful of travelers foolish enough to enter such a restless and potentially dangerous situation.

As he had worked his way through the capital during the night, grabbing just a few hours of sleep before making his way to the eastern gate, he had listened to all the talk and felt the tension surging through the streets. In his estimation, this city was about to explode, the unrest simmering for the last few weeks threatening to boil over. The whispers that he had heard, the large crowds gathering in the squares and facing off against the Royal Guard, suggested as much.

He knew to be false much of what he had heard. But the rumors were catching like wildfire and what he knew to be true seemed to be what was driving the people out of their homes this morning and adding to the instability within the city.

The talk centered around the gladiators and how they had revolted and taken control of the Colosseum. There was also talk that had spread like wildfire that the Volkun had returned to lead the uprising and had challenged the King to a duel. He wasn't sure if that last bit was true, but that was a combat he would enjoy watching. He had little doubt as to the outcome.

"You and the others ready, Dani?" asked Jerad.

"Always ready for you, Sergeant," replied the soldier who stood next to Jerad, her back against the wall and her shoulder touching his.

Her words sent a welcome shot of warmth into Jerad on what was a chilly morning. They also threatened to distract him from the task at hand.

"You know, Corporal, I feel like you're always playing with me. That with just a word or a look, you think that you can make me feel uncomfortable."

"That's not true, Sergeant," replied Dani with a knowing

smile that increased the size of her dimples and made it even harder for Jerad to take his eyes from her. "If I decide to ever play with you, you'll know that I'm playing with you, and you'll feel very comfortable."

Jerad stared into the Corporal's blue eyes, captured by the sparkle and the hint of something more to come. He had memorized every detail about her, from her long blond hair that was usually tied in a braid to her bowlegged walk because of all the time that she spent in the saddle, to her strong and lithe shape and her slightly curved eyes that were always so focused and intent.

He had started to adjust his days so that he could spend more time with her, understanding that he was playing with fire. They both knew that their banter was completely inappropriate given their ranks. They had a job to do, and the job always came first. But at times like these it was nice to feel something different. They were careful about crossing any lines. Still, there appeared to be a mutual attraction that neither wanted to ignore.

Dani had earned her rank because of her actions in combat. During the Battle of the Horseshoe, she had demonstrated a bravery and skill that was both a pleasure and frightening to watch. She had also saved Jerad's life. Yet despite her promotion and her additional responsibilities, she continued to find assignments that allowed her to work with Jerad. Inevitably she also found ways to needle Jerad. At first, he had thought that she had done it because she could. Then he realized that there was more to it than just that.

Jerad tried not to chuckle at Dani's words, but he couldn't help himself. How could one person have such an obvious, unsettling, and exciting effect upon him?

"I'll keep that in mind," Jerad said, his eyes once more peeking around the corner of the building to get a glimpse of the eastern gate and the few soldiers stationed there to defend the entrance. "Be ready. You know what to do."

He was about to step out into the square to begin the charade when Jerad felt a strong hand on his arm, holding him in place.

"Be careful," said Dani, her large and revealing eyes suggesting that her interest in his well-being was based on more than just their professional relationship. "I'll be right here behind you if you need me."

Jerad smiled again, this time giving her a quick nod and a raised eyebrow. "I'd much prefer that you were in front of me."

With that, he stepped out from the street and sprinted across the stone, a smile still on his lips as he remembered the touch of surprise that had passed across Dani's beautiful face, her eyes laughing at his quip.

As he bore down on the soldiers on the other side of the square, Jerad shifted his focus to the task at hand. The rumors that were flying through the streets meant that Bryen had succeeded in getting into the Colosseum and freeing the gladiators, at least for now. He had worried that his friend wouldn't get that far, that the task might be too much even for him. But he realized that his fears had been misplaced.

If Bryen was at the Colosseum, then Sirius and Rafia would be near the Corinthian Palace, and Captain Tentillin would be approaching the city right now on the eastern road. So he and the soldiers with him needed to get to work. They needed to take the gate before the portcullis came down, which would prevent the Battersea Guard from entering the city. He was heartened by the fact that there were fewer soldiers to deal with at this time of the morning, guessing that many of the men he had seen the day before had been pulled toward the crowds or the Colosseum, but he still faced a difficult challenge.

As he drew closer to the soldiers at the gate, he could see only shapes until he was but a few feet away, the smoky mist making it difficult to see and breathe, which only increased the men's edginess. Jerad grinned again, then wiped it off his face, instantly shifting into the role that he needed to play. The smoke and all that was going on in the city would work in his favor if he managed the next few minutes well.

"Sergeant! Sergeant!" Jerad yelled at the top of his lungs as he skidded to a stop in front of the soldier he took to be in charge of the squad positioned at the gate, hands on his knees and his head bent over to suggest that he had been running for quite a long time through the streets of the city. He was about to learn if all the work that he and his soldiers had done to prepare for this moment had paid off.

Jerad had shed his cloak along the way. With the smoke, his leather armor didn't look any different from the armor worn by the soldiers standing in front of him, several of whom had left their posts to gather around him because of their growing unease and thirst for information. If you looked closely enough, you could see the faint tinge of blue to Jerad's leather armor and the Duke of the Southern Marches' sigil, the three-masted ship skimming across the waves, on the breast. But the soldiers were concerned about more pressing matters at the moment, in particular the increasing number of shapes that appeared to be running through the smoke-filled square.

"What is it, man?" growled Aristes, as he waited impatiently for the soldier to catch his breath. His earlier fears seemed to be coming true as he felt an icy cold course through his blood.

"They're coming!" Jerad shouted, making sure that every soldier at the gate heard what he had to say.

"Who is coming, soldier?"

"Them!" replied Jerad, allowing a touch of fear to seep into his voice as he pointed into the smoke and in the general direction of the Colosseum. "The people! The mob! They're rioting, and they're coming this way!"

"Why would they be coming this way?" asked Aristes, somewhat perplexed by this new, unconfirmed information.

"I don't know," answered Jerad, the fear pouring from his voice having an obvious effect on the soldiers around him, all of whom were now shuffling from one foot to the other and gripping the hafts of their spears nervously. "We were in the square, keeping the mob at bay. And then everything fell apart. People flooded into the plaza from every direction. We were outnumbered. And the mob didn't want anything but us. Two of my friends were taken down in seconds. One was torn apart, limb by limb. I couldn't watch it. And I couldn't help him. I couldn't help him! I tried, but I couldn't help him."

"It's all right, lad," said Aristes, placing a comforting hand on Jerad's shoulder. He had worried that this might happen. He had seen for himself how the crowd could turn into a blood-thirsty rabble in an instant. So he had no reason to doubt this obviously distraught soldier's story. "It's all right. Where is the mob now?"

"They're close, Sergeant. Very close. I lost most of my squad holding them back, Sergeant. We tried. We tried. But there were too many." Jerad's voice quivered when he said the last, his obvious fear beginning to infect the soldiers around him.

With a perfect sense of timing Dani and several more of Jerad's soldiers sprinted out of the smoke to stand in front of Aristes and his men. With a quick command from Dani, they turned as one and faced out into the square, forming into a defensive shell in anticipation of the mob bursting momentarily into the square. In response, several of the soldiers with Aristes immediately did the same, joining in the defensive line that had taken shape in front of the eastern gate.

"Where is the mob, lad? How close?" Aristes assumed that the soldiers who had just appeared were part of the shaken soldier's command.

"They're right behind me, Sergeant," said Jerad. "Dani, how far now?"

"No more than two blocks," she replied, not turning around, keeping her eyes focused on the swirling figures in the smoke that had made the early morning seem more like dusk, the shapes flitting through the murk actually members of the Battersea Guard.

That was enough to convince Aristes that his greatest fear was about to come true and that he needed to take action.

"Corel!" shouted Aristes, though there was no need to do so, as the soldier was standing right next to him.

"Yes, Sergeant."

"Get the soldiers out of the gatehouse and have them join us here. We're going to need them against the mob."

"Yes, Sergeant," Corel replied, who trotted toward the gatehouse, not realizing that Dani and several other soldiers who had just run out of the smoke followed after him.

"Everyone else, into the line!" directed Aristes, the soldiers under his command who had not already done so moving quickly to obey his command. The Sergeant was pleased that his men responded so fast, but he knew that he had too few with him. There was no way that they could hold back the mob when it appeared in the square. They could only hope to defend themselves.

It wasn't long before Corel reappeared with a handful of soldiers who formed into ranks within the defensive line. Looking toward the gatehouse, Jerad saw Dani standing in the doorway with a grin, then she nodded.

At that, Jerad pushed himself to his full height, then smiled. Aristes stared at him in surprise, the fear that he had seen in the man's features suddenly gone.

"Sergeant, I must apologize, but this was necessary. We had no desire for any unnecessary bloodshed."

"What do you mean?" demanded Aristes, not understanding what this soldier standing before him meant.

"For the Marches!" Jerad called out in a loud voice.

In an instant, the soldiers of the Battersea Guard who had mixed themselves among the Royal Guard turned their weapons on the men of the Caledonian Army, Jerad whipping out his sword and placing the cold steel against Aristes' throat.

"What is this?" asked Aristes in a whisper, afraid to speak louder with the cold blade pressed against his jugular.

"A rebellion, Sergeant," replied Jerad, "aided by the Volkun and the soldiers of the Southern Marches. We have no quarrel with you or your soldiers, only with the King. Do you understand?"

Aristes nodded, clearly having no choice but to do so as he watched the soldiers from the Southern Marches disarm his own and march them toward the closed tavern at the corner of the square.

"If you need anything, Sergeant, my name is Jerad. I am the Sergeant of the Battersea Guard. You will go with your men. They and you will on your honor stay in that building until given permission to leave, and you will not attempt to escape."

"And if we do?" asked Aristes, his normal fire still burning, though at a very low simmer at the moment as he realized that he was in a deadly and untenable situation.

"Then you and all your men will die, Sergeant. And I think that would truly be a waste, don't you?"

Aristes thought about that for only a few seconds before nodding. "On my honor."

"Good," said Jerad. "I'm glad we see things from the same perspective."

With that, one of Jerad's soldiers came over to lead Aristes to his men. An even broader smile broke out on Jerad's usually grinning countenance. His plan had actually worked and none of his soldiers had been hurt. Of course, this was just the easy part. The hard part was about to begin.

"The gatehouse is ours, Sergeant," said Dani, the tall soldier coming to stand next to him as he stared out through the gate at the road that twisted away from Caledonia to the east.

"Excellent work, Dani," said Jerad. "Please send two soldiers beyond the gate and down the road about a league. The sooner they find Captain Tentillin and the Battersea Guard, the sooner we can move on to the next part of the plan."

"Right away, Sergeant," replied Dani, who motioned to two soldiers who spent a few minutes listening to what she had to say before trotting through the gateway. She then returned to Jerad's side.

"Quite an impressive display in the square, Sergeant."

"Thank you, Dani."

"I didn't know you could act. Any other hidden skills that I should know about?"

Dani's suggestive glance once again sent Jerad's mind down an unsettling but pleasing path, and for a moment he didn't know how to reply.

"Nothing that really comes to mind," he replied sheepishly.

"That's too bad," said Dani, "what with the gatehouse being empty."

23

TO THE RESCUE

"What are we waiting for?" demanded Rafia, her patience, never good to begin with, eroding. She and Sirius had been huddled at the corner of the alley that opened onto the plaza that encircled the Corinthian Palace for more than an hour.

The constant construction at the Palace had required the regular extension of the outer curtain, fifty feet in height at its lowest point and dotted with a variety of mismatched towers along the parapet, until it stretched for more than a half mile from east to west and half that length from north to south. Rafia always marveled at the mishmash of buildings within that reflected the different styles that were popular when they were built, all connected by cloistered walkways, the roofs made of slate tiles, the columns carved with intricate designs to display the history of Caledonia, and in between the buildings and covered paths colorful gardens sprouted that contained examples of the flora from the entire Kingdom. Rafia had always enjoyed walking those gardens, but at the moment thanks to her companion's hesitancy and lack of urgency she doubted that she ever would again.

"Would you please just be patient," hissed Sirius, his patience with his partner now wearing thin as well. "Just a few minutes more and we should be in the clear."

"We're running out of time, Sirius. We need to move."

"Just a few minutes more," grated Sirius, making clear that his last comment had not been a request.

Rafia huffed a protest, but didn't offer anything further, keeping her eyes on the plaza to her front and the commotion occurring there.

They had selected this alley because it gave them a good view of both the southern wall and the main entrance on the western side of the fortress. So they watched with great interest when the Royal Guard began marching out from the Palace gates and then down the promenade that led directly to the Colosseum. Rafia wasn't surprised that the Protector had succeeded in taking the arena, requiring the Crown to respond quickly and decisively. She had expected no less from him. There was a quiet confidence and drive within Bryen that she had seen in few others.

As Marden and his troops passed, it became clear to Rafia that there was little in the way of adoration among the people for their young monarch. Instead of the cheers for Marden that she had seen so many of his predecessors receive, he rode his war charger out onto the boulevard, an honor guard of a hundred soldiers surrounding him, to the sound of silence and even a few jeers. That certainly caught the attention of the King, but there was no way to determine who might have insulted him as the crowd watching the demonstration grew in size and then began to track the soldiers down the promenade.

Rafia could sense a sullenness among the people observing, their discontent shifting to anger as the King passed in his battle armor. And she could tell that though Marden put on a brave face, continuing to smile, even wave a few times at the surly crowd, his reception by the citizens of Tintagel was affecting him poorly. She could read it in his posture, his stiff back, and how he was holding too tightly to his horse's reins, forcing the large animal to prance along the cobblestones. She smiled as Marden left her sight, moving farther down the street. Tetric followed a few hundred yards behind him, allowing the King to receive the adulation, or rather displeasure, of his people on his own.

If this was how Marden was reacting to the frosty reception given to him by his own people, she had a good idea as to how he would respond when he reached the Colosseum and came face to face with the Volkun. If Bryen was smart about it, and she was certain that he would be, he could use Marden's barely restrained emotions against him. And she had no doubt that he would after all the time that he had spent fighting on the white sand. The Volkun knew how to rile someone up when necessary, and it wouldn't take much effort on his part with respect to the King.

As the last of the soldiers made their way out from under the gate, Rafia reached for Sirius' arm to get his attention. Not receiving a response from him, she grabbed more tightly, eliciting a grunt that quickly became a curse when her hold on him strengthened. She realized that he was focused not on the Palace, but rather a small inn a block from the plaza and at the far end of the street.

"Sirius, the Guard is gone. Now's our chance."

She had assumed that to enter the Palace they would disguise themselves with the Talent and simply walk in, as going over the wall, even with so few soldiers about, didn't appeal to her. But before she could step out onto the square, Sirius grabbed hold of her shoulder.

"We're going to try to avoid using the Talent as much as we can," he said.

"But why would we ..." Rafia began, but then she understood. Even as Tetric moved away from them toward the Colosseum, there was a chance that he could sense their use of the Talent. And, of course, there was also the possibility that he had set traps throughout the grounds that would alert him if anyone used the natural magic of the world within the Corinthian Palace. She wouldn't be surprised if he had done so to keep Aislinn and her Talent caged.

"If we can't use the Talent to any great extent, then did you have something else in mind?" she asked.

"Come with me."

Sirius then turned on his heel and walked quickly down the street, away from the Palace and toward the small inn.

"We're going the wrong way, Sirius," protested Rafia.

"Patience, please, Rafia. Have no fear."

Sirius continued down the street, then pushed the door open to the sleepy inn, holding it for Rafia so that she could step through. The empty reception desk was off to the left, the bar and tavern to the right. It was no different than she suspected was the case in the many other inns and taverns in the city. Quiet. No more than one or two people there with most everyone else staying in their homes or joining the crowds in the streets.

Rafia followed Sirius toward the back, keeping her eyes open for any surprises, but sensing nothing amiss about the inn.

"What can I get for you?" asked the massive man behind the bar, his large belly resting on the brightly shining wood counter that had places for twelve stools that were currently unoccupied.

"Not what, but who," replied Sirius. He didn't recognize the man behind the counter, but that wasn't surprising. He hadn't been here for several years. "I'm looking for Celia."

The barkeep stared at Sirius for a time, trying to judge his intentions, but finding the task difficult. The old man standing in front of him appeared to be nothing more than that. An old man, and raggedly dressed to boot. Although there was something about him that made the barkeep slightly uneasy. The bartender ignored the warning, instead curious as to why this old man with the wild hair wanted to see his boss.

"You want to see Celia?"

"I wouldn't have asked otherwise," replied Sirius, his voice as dry as the dust in a sealed tomb.

The barkeep took a step back from where he had been standing because of that voice, also catching a dangerous flash in the old man's eyes in response to his question.

"It's all right, Brunson. I know him."

Rafia watched as a woman walked out from the door behind the bar, her eyes never leaving Sirius'. She could see in the mirror that ran the length of the wall that Sirius was smiling as well, and for some reason that irked her.

"I know him quite well, in fact," Celia continued. "We had so much fun together the last time, Sirius, that I thought that you would have visited sooner."

She placed her hands on the bar, pushed herself up, leaned over the smooth wood, and gave Sirius a kiss on the cheek, though her lips seemed to linger a lot longer than necessary in Rafia's opinion.

"I'm sorry, Celia, but I've been busy," Sirius replied, his blush obvious after feeling Celia's lips on his skin, though he certainly didn't seem to mind the display of affection.

"You're always busy, Sirius. That was the problem. Never here long enough to settle down because you always had business elsewhere."

"One of the downsides of my profession," Sirius replied.

"Yes, so you've said many times." Celia laughed softly, the sound rich and throaty and conjuring up for Sirius some memories that he knew probably were best left in the past, but still played across his mind despite his best efforts to keep them locked away. "You know, the entire time we were together, you never once mentioned what your profession was."

"A little bit of this," answered Sirius. "A little bit of that."

"Sirius, we need to get going," cut in Rafia. "We have somewhere we need to be."

Rafia tried to exercise what restraint that she could, but as the conversation continued between Sirius and the owner of the inn who had so easily enthralled him, her agitation was rising to the surface.

"And who might this be, Sirius?" asked Celia, turning to Rafia. Celia's eyes locked with Rafia's, both women sizing each other up with neither willing to look away first.

"A colleague," answered Sirius. Beneath the bar he reached for Rafia's forearm and squeezed, giving her a signal that she should stay quiet.

"A colleague, you say," nodded Celia, who leaned against the bar, her forearms on the wood. Sirius had a difficult time keeping his eyes off of Celia's very prominent features, and it took a kick to his shin by Rafia for him to raise his eyes back to Celia's.

"Yes, a colleague," replied Sirius. "We have pressing business, and I was hoping that we could make an unannounced entrance."

Celia stared at Sirius shrewdly. After more than a minute she finally nodded.

"I do owe you for that last favor," Celia said. "But after this, we're square. If you want anything from me in the future, you're going to have to work for it." The innkeeper said the last with a raised eyebrow, wanting to make sure that Sirius understood her meaning.

"Agreed," replied Sirius.

"Good," said Celia, pleased that she could pay off her debt and set the stage for another meeting with Sirius. The old man was exceedingly unreliable in terms of when he appeared in

Tintagel, but whenever he did, she always had a great deal of fun and picked up a few favors from him along the way that always proved useful. "Come along."

Celia lifted the top of the bar at the far end so that Sirius and Rafia could follow her through the door that led into the room behind the tavern. Once there, they walked down a long, narrow hallway, and then through a doorway that required them to step carefully down a narrow flight of rickety steps.

"Was this another of your conquests?" Rafia whispered with some heat.

"She was not a conquest," Sirius protested. "Besides, when I was with Celia, we weren't together."

"Regardless, it seemed that you were never lacking in female companionship," Rafia noted.

"That's not fair, Rafia. And if I remember correctly, we agreed that spending some time apart would be a good thing. That we didn't want to have a traditional relationship."

"Then why did you ask me to marry you?" demanded Rafia.

"Could we discuss this later?" hissed Sirius as they entered the storage room beneath the inn. "Now is not the time."

"There's never a good time, is there, Sirius?"

Sirius chose not to reply to Rafia's last barb, understanding that anything he said now wouldn't help matters. Instead, he focused his attention on the end of the long room where Celia pulled on a drawstring concealed within the wall that caused a hidden door to turn inward on silent hinges, revealing a dry, dark passageway.

"You're certain the way is clear?" asked Sirius. "I haven't gone this way for several years."

Celia nodded with a knowing smile. "Used it just the other week."

"For what?" asked Rafia.

"Business," Celia replied cryptically, following Sirius' lead and obviously not feeling the need to offer any more than that.

"The door will close automatically behind you. If you're caught, I don't know you. And I don't know how you got into my storeroom."

With that, Celia walked up the creaky steps, not giving Sirius and Rafia a second glance. Although she did offer a final comment when she reached the top of the landing.

"And next time you're in town, Sirius, make sure you come by for a longer visit. We need to catch up."

Rafia rolled her eyes at Sirius, then she turned her thoughts to the mission set before them.

"Are you certain about this, Sirius?"

"Trust me, Rafia."

"I trusted you in the past and it didn't work out for either of us."

Sirius grumbled rather than replying, knowing that offering anything additional would only feed the animosity between them. Instead, he reached for the Talent to light his way, just a tiny amount that would only be detectable if you were within a few dozen feet, and began walking down the musty tunnel that led beneath the plaza toward the Corinthian Palace.

"Are you certain that we're in the right place?" asked Rafia.

"I'm certain," confirmed Sirius. "She's here. And if her father isn't, she'll know where he is."

Rafia nodded, accepting Sirius' answer. He had been right so far, so there was no reason not to believe him now, though putting her faith in him irritated her just a bit. She knew there was likely nothing to her annoyance with him other than their long history together. Their quarrel had occurred a decade ago, and she realized that it was time to let go of what she had been holding onto for so long. It hadn't helped her, only eating away at her emotions.

They had come out of the tunnel in a storage room beneath the southern wall of the Corinthian Palace. Using a small, barely noticeable stream of the Talent, Sirius had burned through the metal to unlock the door, and they had found themselves in the warren of hallways servants used to move from one end of the keep to the other without being seen or noticed. They had worried that the corridors would be full of the men and women responsible for keeping the Palace running, but apparently with Marden and most of the Royal Guard having left because of the gladiator uprising much of the day's normal activity had come to a standstill.

As Sirius and Rafia moved through the underground hallways, each time a servant appeared usually they were able to slip into a vacant storeroom without being noticed. And the handful of times they couldn't, they used just a touch of the Talent to blend into their surroundings, a task made easier because of the poor lighting along the shadowy and dark corridors. So with relative ease they had reached the eastern side of the Palace, then made their way up several flights of stairs to the third and highest floor.

Even here, the hallways were quiet. No servants were about, and the few soldiers wandering the corridors and paths bordering the gardens were easily avoided. It had taken them less than twenty minutes to reach the ornate double doors they now stood in front of, and both Sirius and Rafia hoped that based on the ease of their intrusion, they could use the same way they had entered the Palace to exit just as quickly.

"Can you sense her?" asked Rafia.

"I can," replied Sirius. He was certain that they had found her rooms and that she was inside. There was no doubt in his mind.

He touched the handle to the door and pressed down gently. Locked. A slight difficulty, and one that could be solved easily. Using a small stream of the Talent just as he did to exit the storeroom, Sirius burned through the metal of the mechanism in seconds. With a gentle push, the doors swung open without making a sound.

Sirius' confident smile at having gotten them so far without being discovered twisted into a scowl when he and Rafia walked into the antechamber of Aislinn's suite. Several dozen soldiers of the Royal Guard stood in front of them in two lines, their weapons drawn, their serious expressions suggesting that they weren't amused by the appearance of these two intruders.

"Were you expecting this reception?" asked Rafia. She reached for the Talent, sensing that Sirius had done so as well, more concerned by the soldiers standing before them than the threat of Tetric learning of their presence through their use of the natural power of the world.

"No, I wasn't," he admitted reluctantly. "Something of a surprise."

"Well, we seem to be facing a bit of a predicament," said Rafia, her eyes never leaving the soldiers.

Strangely, not a word had been uttered by the soldiers. Silence reigned in the chamber, neither side apparently wanting to be the first to move. So it was left to someone else to take the next step.

"Move forward please," said a quiet but strong voice behind Sirius and Rafia. Sirius felt the touch of steel in the small of his back, Rafia catching the glint of the light off the metal out of the corner of her eye. "Know that I can kill you both before either of you can do anything to me or my soldiers with the power you control. Do we understand each other?"

Both Sirius and Rafia nodded, and then because of a slight nudge against Sirius by the man with the blade, they both walked farther into the room. A handful of soldiers followed, several remaining outside the chamber when the doors were pulled closed quietly.

The man with the blade then moved away from Sirius and

Rafia to stand before them. His long, grey hair was pulled back tightly and held in place at the nape of his neck with a black leather string, his impeccably groomed mustache and beard highlighting the sharp planes of his face.

"Hello, Blademaster," said Sirius quietly, offering his captor a slight nod of respect and greetings. "It's been quite some time."

"Magus," replied Jurgen Klines. "What are you doing here? There are other, safer, more appropriate ways to enter the Palace."

"I'm here for my apprentice. I doubt that the King would appreciate that."

"Your apprentice?" For just a moment, the Blademaster appeared to be confused. But it didn't take him long to figure it out. Although Lady Winborne had been prohibited from using the Talent here in the Corinthian Palace, he had heard the stories of her exploits while fighting the Elder Ghoule on the coastal road in the Southern Marches.

"May I ask why you're here?" Rafia stared at Klines with a raptorial glare.

For the first time in many years, the Blademaster felt a slight tremor of unease upon facing off with this very intimidating woman. Better to stay on her good side, if he could. But that would all depend on the next few minutes.

"We protect and serve the Vedra," replied the Blademaster.

The Vedra? Sirius hadn't heard that term in centuries. It meant the *witch* in the old tongue.

"The Lady Winborne is the Vedra?" asked Rafia.

"She is, indeed, Magus," replied the Blademaster.

"A shift in allegiances, Blademaster?" asked Sirius. "I find that hard to believe with you."

Klines stared at Sirius for a moment, a host of different emotions surging within him as he considered how to respond, none of those emotions actually showing on his face.

"I serve the Crown, Magus. The one who sits on the throne currently does not serve the Crown."

"That I can understand," said Sirius.

"Sirius! What are you doing here?"

Aislinn Winborne walked between the soldiers, the men at arms nodding their heads respectfully as they stepped out of her way.

"My friend and I," said Sirius, motioning toward Rafia, "are here to get you out of the city."

"That might be easier said than done," said Kevan Winborne, who came to stand next to his daughter.

Sirius took one look at the Duke of the Southern Marches and he could tell that something was off with him. Normally full of energy and drive, he appeared tired and wan. It could be the result of his captivity here in the Palace, but Sirius thought that there was more to it than that. It was as if he had been beaten or flogged but it had been done in such a way as to leave no marks.

Rafia nudged Sirius in the side, and then nodded toward Kevan, gesturing with her hand. Then Sirius saw the collar, and he began to understand. The black torque appeared to draw in all the surrounding light, radiating a malevolence that the human eye couldn't see, but was clearly visible to someone trained in the Talent.

"May I?" asked Rafia, motioning toward the black metal.

Kevan nodded his approval, and Rafia stepped forward. She ran her fingers just above the collar, not yet willing to touch the steel.

"It's much like a Protector's collar, is it not?" she asked.

"It is," Kevan replied. "I am restricted in my movements and actions as a result. I am only permitted a certain distance from the Palace."

"And if you go too far, then what? Pain?"

Kevan nodded. "Pain."

Now it was Rafia's turn to nod. "Ironic."

"Indeed," replied Kevan, who smiled flatly. "I won't dispute you in that regard. A bit of my own medicine, you could say."

"You're taking it better than I would expect someone of your stature would," said Rafia.

"Not at the beginning. Not when it was first placed around my neck." Kevan admitted it reluctantly but honestly, a humbleness in his eyes that Sirius had never seen before. "But after a time it seemed a fair penance for what I did."

"Maybe," replied Rafia. "Maybe not. A good lesson if nothing else. Tetric's work?"

"Yes."

After sliding her hand through the air just above the collar for several seconds more, she finally touched the roughly shaped blackened metal. She only kept her fingers there on the links for a heartbeat, the Dark Magic in the steel pushing back at her use of the Talent, but in that moment, she learned everything that she needed to know.

"This is a problem," Rafia said. "A very serious problem."

"How is this different from a Protector's collar," asked Sirius.

"It's not in many respects," answered Rafia. "It is very similar, but at the same time it's much worse."

"How could it be worse?" asked Aislinn, her concern for her father obvious in her voice.

"We can't take your father out of the city," explained Rafia. "Bryen was bonded to you through the Protector's collar. With this monstrous creation, your father is bonded to Tetric."

"Yes, but how is that ..." Before Aislinn could get her entire question out, Rafia cut her off.

"It is much the same, but the problem is that Tetric used Dark Magic to create this collar. And that Dark Magic has begun to seep into your father. It is poisoning him, slowly but surely."

That last left both Aislinn and her father in shock, Kevan's face turning whiter than it already was. Kevan reached for the collar as he often did, sometimes a dozen or more times a day. He gave a sharp tug to the metal, knowing that his attempt to break the torque wouldn't work, but he needed to try to do something to change his fate, no matter how useless that action might be.

Rafia looked at Sirius, a questioning gaze. "Did you know about this?"

"I suspected the last time that we talked in Battersea that Tetric had turned down that path. But I wasn't certain."

"Why would he do it?" Rafia knew it was a foolish question before all the words had left her mouth.

"Why wouldn't he? He was expelled from the Order of the Magii because he craved power and was willing to do things that had been forbidden for millennia. He should never have passed the Test. I should never have allowed him to pass the Test."

"That failure is something for you to manage on your own, Sirius," interrupted Rafia. "We don't have time for remorse now. We need to focus on how we're going to deal with this collar. And then after that the Dark Magic."

"You're right," Sirius admitted. "He has made his choice."

"If he's using Dark Magic now," said Rafia, her mind already moving toward an inevitable, terrifying conclusion, "then that means ..."

"Yes," Sirius replied with a disappointed shake of his head. "Tetric is allied to the Ghoule Overlord. This answers many of the questions that have bothered me since the Ghoules began appearing in greater numbers in Caledonia."

That realization got the attention of everyone in the room, even the Blademaster, who had been listening intently, unsettled by the claim that the King's Advisor was working against the Crown. It didn't surprise him, though, and just as it did for

Sirius, it answered several of his own questions about Tetric's behavior in Tintagel.

"Yes, we are all a bit unsettled by the discovery that Tetric is in league with the Ghoule Overlord," said Aislinn in a sharp voice that cut through the murmurs of conversation that had erupted within the antechamber. "But there is nothing that we can do now. We must focus on the collar and help my father."

"You're right, Lady Winborne," said the Blademaster. "We must consider our next steps carefully. And we cannot stay here. We must move."

Aislinn nodded sagely, then turned her sharp gaze toward Sirius, already having a plan in mind.

"I know Bryen is close. What is he planning on doing?"

24

SPREADING LIKE WILDFIRE

"I think this tells us what we need to know," said Eltin. He stood on the side of the avenue watching a long column of the Royal Guard march past. He was beginning to worry. More and more people were filling the streets, and their mood wasn't good. Sharper. On edge. Just a step away from violence. "Don't you think?"

"Definitely confirmation," agreed Rory.

They observed the procession carefully, but at the same time their eyes tracked any movement around them. People were becoming more and more desperate. These rapidly forming crowds were an excellent opportunity to get your purse cut or even a knife in the ribs if a hungry thief didn't find the spare change he or she was looking for quickly.

"I still would have liked to see him. Just to make sure that what we're hearing is accurate."

Benin shook his head in irritation. He and the two soldiers who he had selected for this mission had left their leather armor and uniforms at the Corinthian Palace, donning the garb of commoners to make their way surreptitiously through the city to the Colosseum. The Blademaster had wanted a better sense of what was going on in the streets, and the only way to do that was to go where the action was.

They had gotten as close as they could, peering out from one of the streets that led out onto the plaza upon which the arena had been built, but they had seen little more than several companies of soldiers scurrying about in the nearby alleys and streets, none making any real effort to attack the gladiators who had taken the Colosseum. The gladiators had done a very effective job of covering the barred gates so that any soldiers assaulting the stadium wouldn't know what was happening within or what they would face once they entered.

"Isn't this enough?" asked Rory, gesturing to the company of men trudging by.

Eltin nodded his head in agreement. "I don't think the King would empty the Palace of the Royal Guard unless he had cause to do so. He doesn't like leaving the Palace as it is. There must be some truth to the rumors. Why else would he risk himself?"

Benin spent a few more minutes watching several companies of soldiers pass them by, recognizing many of the men making their way down Tintagel's promenade toward the Colosseum. The King had led the procession, though he likely wasn't receiving the welcome that he had expected or wanted from the people. Benin had almost laughed when he saw King Beleron's scowl when he rode by surrounded by his personal guard and the only sounds that came from the crowd were a few brave boos and hisses.

It made sense. Benin served in the Palace, but his family lived in the city. He was doing what he could to help them, but like so many other families, they were struggling to find the basic necessities of life. Few had seen a good cut of meat in over a year. The soldiers of the Royal Guard were still enjoying that privilege, even when many of the butchers in the city had been forced to close their shops because their supply had dried up.

Fruits and vegetables were still coming into the capital, but at a trickle of what should be expected for this time in the season compared to just a year ago, which meant prices higher than many people could afford.

Still, the people had adapted as best as they could, even with the increased taxes imposed upon them by the Crown. But when there was no more grain for bread, and Benin had no doubt that they would reach that point soon because he had heard from the soldiers stationed at the granaries that the massive silos were barely a quarter full, then the riots of the last few weeks would seem like nothing but minor disturbances compared to what would come next.

The people were angry now and becoming more despairing by the day. So he doubted that King Beleron would leave his Palace without good cause, and certainly not to parade through the city when seeing the reality of his people's existence would chip away at the fantasy in which he lived.

"You're both right," agreed Benin.

Then a surge of energy shot through the crowd as several loud voices rose above the din created by so many people being packed together so tightly.

"The Volkun! The Volkun is here!"

"The Volkun has returned!"

"The gladiators fight with the Volkun!"

"The Volkun has challenged the King to a combat!"

"Victory to the Volkun!"

"Freedom for the gladiators!"

Benin didn't know who was spouting such rumors as he could see little more than the milling bodies around him now that the Royal Guard was gone, but he didn't need to in order to know what would happen next. Much of the crowd already had begun to move west down the promenade, more and more people joining the mix from the squares that lined the boulevard. As the multitude moved as one, Benin sensed a change in the crowd as it began to stream toward the Colosseum. Not just anger and desperation, but also interest. Curiosity. Even a faint touch of hope. They wanted to find out if the rumors were true. They wanted to know if the Volkun had returned. They wanted to know if the King had the courage to accept the Volkun's challenge.

"Come on," said Benin to Eltin and Rory as he began shouldering his way through the throng. "We need to get back to the Palace. The Blademaster needs to know what's going on."

25

ALWAYS HUNGRY

The screams echoed off the surrounding mountains, the terror and pain almost palpable. Nibli had heard it many times before, and each time he did it never failed to send a quiver of excitement through him.

The Elder watched dispassionately as his Ghoules dragged the women and children from their burning cottages, the men already having been slaughtered after their brave but doomed defense of their village. Bad luck for them. They weren't soldiers, or at least if they had been it had been a long time since they had fought a foe as dangerous as his Ghoules.

Nibli cared nothing for these humans supporting themselves off the rugged land near the Winter Pass and the Breakwater Plateau. They had made a mistake. They had chosen the wrong place to live. They were nothing more than a nuisance that needed to be cleared.

The Ghoule Legions had last come this way a thousand years before. Most of the Caledonians had forgotten about the deadly creatures from the Lost Land who had been forced behind the Weir. Most had never considered the possibility that the Ghoules would return, that they were not just a myth, but were real. The humans would pay for that failure. They would pay for their lassitude, for their forgetting the past, for their desire to see the world as they wanted to, rather than as it really was.

A towering Ghoule sprinted up to Nibli and skidded to a stop, his clawed feet digging into the rocky soil. The Ghoule offered a nod of respect before letting loose a string of grunts and hisses that were unintelligible to the humans cowering nearby. Nibli didn't feel the need to interrupt while the Ghoule provided his update. He simply listened, his eyes never leaving the humans who huddled together in fear.

All was going forward as Nibli had designed. The Ghoule Overlord had been sending packs through the Weir for the last several years, searching for an artifact essential to the destruction of the magical barrier that kept the humans safe. The Ghoules had failed to find it, despite their traveling across most of Caledonia. Until now. The Overlord finally knew where the artifact was hidden, so it was only a matter of time before he took it and moved forward with his plans. To aid his efforts the Overlord had charged Nibli with taking as many Legions as he could through the Weir.

Crossing the magical barrier was fraught with danger and this time was no exception. A good number of Ghoules, including Elders, perished as they were caught within the magical barricade. Even so, the Overlord believed the price paid in Ghoule lives was worth it. Nibli couldn't disagree with him.

The loss of life was necessary with the Ghoules so close to achieving their goal. Why else would the Ghoule Overlord have risked coming into Caledonia himself while leaving his Legions north of the Winter Pass and in the surrounding mountains?

It could mean only one thing. The time to set loose the Legions was approaching, and when that happened all the humans of this land would experience what these poor souls in this isolated village were slowly beginning to understand. The Ghoules were not a myth. They were real. A stronger race. More powerful. More skilled as fighters. And the humans were no more than food. A resource to be used, no better than the animals these humans fed upon themselves. Fodder for his Ghoules.

Satisfied with the scout's report, Nibli issued a short, sharp stream of orders that the Ghoule immediately sprinted off to deliver. Nibli would do as he had been instructed. He would use his Legion to prepare the way for the Legions to come. Ghoule packs were not enough to complete the task set for them. Several Legions were now required as the humans, at least in the Southern Marches, had demonstrated a unique ability to fight the Ghoules and not only survive, but also prove victorious. Nibli had never thought it possible, but he had seen it with his own eyes.

More Ghoules were needed both to make up for the ones lost in the Southern Marches and because of the unexpected opportunity that the Ghoule Overlord had discovered in the Caledonian capital. The human King faced a challenge to his rule. In consequence, all human eyes were looking toward Tintagel rather than the Weir. What better time for the Ghoules to cross into the Kingdom than in the midst of such chaos?

Nibli had directed the scout to find the various Ghoule packs located in the surrounding hills and order them to take up defensive positions and chokepoints that led back toward the Winter Pass and the Shattered Peaks. More Ghoule Legions would be coming through in the next few weeks, and he wanted to make sure that his Ghoules couldn't be dislodged if the humans discovered that their land had been invaded for the first time in a thousand years.

Pleased that his Ghoules were making good progress, the humans unaware of what was occurring at the southern edge of the Winter Pass, Nibli pulled free his bone knife from the sheath on his hip. He had earned the blade years before, killing a human soldier on patrol in the Shattered Peaks, then eating his remains while carving the knife from the bone of the unlucky fellow's femur.

It had been a long last few days, his Ghoules having pushed their way through the Weir and then rushed down the Winter Pass to reach the lower hills as quickly as they could. And now he was hungry.

He walked slowly toward the humans yet to be carved up who had huddled together into a single mass, desperate for help, but knowing in their hearts that they were on their own. There was no one to help them.

As Nibli reached for a woman's arm and pulled her loose from the other humans, her screams falling on deaf ears as she tried to claw her way back into the group but failed to break free from Nibli's grip, he saw in her eyes the subtle shift that he had seen so many times before when raiding the human lands. The terror always changed to resignation when the humans realized that there was no escape. That their lives were no longer theirs. That their deaths were certain. It was a moment to be savored.

Nibli would eat quickly. There was another village just a few leagues to the west. He wanted to move in that direction when the sun set. His Ghoules would slaughter the humans living in that village while they slept. The timing would be good. The humans in this village were not enough to feed all the Ghoules with him, and his Ghoules would be even hungrier then. Of course, they were always hungry.

26

THE BATTLE BEGINS

When Declan had served in the Royal Guard, there were times when he was exceedingly bored, the mantra being hurry up and wait. But when there was action, whether dealing with brigands in the Dark Forest or clearing pirates from the western coast and the Burnt Ocean, he had felt more alive than he ever had before. It wasn't the fighting and the killing that often resulted from his service in the Guard. He viewed that as a necessary evil of his chosen profession. He did it well, but he didn't take any pleasure in it.

No, it was the adrenaline, the risk, the excitement of knowing that his next decision could be his last. And that was what he was sensing now, that spark of energy that he never thought that he would experience again, as he strode purposefully through the corridors of the Colosseum, checking on the teams of gladiators assigned to defend each of the twelve gates that allowed entrance into the arena, but also thinking about where he would position the small reserve of gladiators that he wanted to create so that they could have the greatest impact in the coming fight.

"So, Declan, what did you have in mind?" asked Bryen.

The scarred gladiator, the Spear of the Magii held gently in his left hand, the haft leaning against his shoulder, had walked with the Master of the Gladiators for the last hour, allowing Declan to do what he did best. Ensure that the gladiators, the men and women who had taken to the name the Company of Blood with a great deal of pleasure and pride, were prepared to fight, while Bryen offered a few words of encouragement here and there, finding it slightly strange and extremely uncomfortable that so many of his peers now looked upon him with such deference.

"What do you mean me, lad?" asked Declan. "You're the one who started this. The gladiators joined this uprising because of the Volkun, not because of me."

"Yes, and that's what I needed to do," said Bryen with a smile. The gladiators had taken the Colosseum with such efficiency, it had even surprised them when they had locked and then blocked all the gates in just a matter of hours after making sure the arena was clear of any soldiers or others they didn't want there. Their success was due in large part to Declan, who had worked closely with Bryen to refine and improve upon his plan. "Now it's your turn. Now you need to buy us time. We need to hold the Colosseum for as long as we can until Marden has no choice but to come for us."

"And I ask again, why me? This is your rebellion. From what some of the gladiators have been saying, they've been hearing a great deal of commotion in the streets around us. Even some howls that sounded very much like those we used to hear in the Colosseum during your combats."

"That may be," replied Bryen. "But you're the man with ten-plus years in the Royal Guard before they drummed you out because of a lord who couldn't fight his way out of a cloth sack. You've been in situations such as this before. You know what needs to be done because you know what to expect from the

Royal Guard when they attack. Who else but you to lead the defense?"

"Bryen, I haven't been a soldier for twenty years."

"Why does that matter? You've likely forgotten more about being a soldier than any of us here in the Colosseum could ever know. Think of it as an opportunity to give back to those who treated you poorly."

Bryen continued to walk beside Declan, glancing through one of the few openings in the main gates guarded by Davin, Lycia, and their teams that still offered a glimpse, restricted though it might be, of what was going on in the plaza. Bryen was pleased to see that at the moment nothing was happening, but it wouldn't stay that way for much longer.

He could hear the rumbling cadence of the Royal Guard making its way toward the Colosseum. It was just a matter of time before the soldiers arrived, and that was fine with him. That's what he wanted. If the Guard didn't come, then their initial efforts to capture the Colosseum would have been meaningless. Besides, he was looking forward to giving the King a bloody nose at the very least, and if he had a chance to slide his dagger between his ribs, he wouldn't hesitate to do so.

"You know that I'm right, Declan. No one else can do it but you. So the job is yours."

Declan grumbled in response, yet secretly he was pleased not so much by the opportunity but by the fact that Bryen and the other gladiators trusted him in this role.

"No matter what we do, son, we can't hold the Colosseum. We're too few. The Guard are too many."

"I didn't say that we needed to hold the Colosseum. I said that we needed to hold it for as long as we could. Big difference."

"You're making a distinction without a difference."

"I'm making a distinction that is critical to what we're trying to do."

"Fine. Fine." Declan thought for a moment. "Find me these gladiators and send them to me. I'll be here at the main gates." Declan then quickly named six fighters in the cadence of a man who had spent a great deal of time on the parade ground. "These gladiators were all Sergeants in the army. They'll follow orders, and they'll get the gladiators assigned to them to follow orders as well."

Bryen headed off with a grin to complete his assignment, having just concluded what he viewed as the most important task that he would manage that morning. Placing Declan in his new position. Bryen could serve as the rallying cry, as the leader of the Company of Blood. But every leader needed a good general to help him, and Bryen had no doubt that Declan would play his new role to perfection.

"TODORI!"

One of Sourban's Sergeants nudged his horse forward so that he was now riding side by side with his commander.

"Yes, Captain!"

The Captain of the Royal Guard tried to not roll his eyes while he fought to keep the smile that wanted to break free from his twisting lips. Todori didn't have the sharpest mind, but that wasn't why he had achieved his high rank in the Guard. He was brave, almost stupidly so. He did as he was told, following his instructions to the letter. He never caused any trouble. And he demonstrated a passion that was often contagious with the soldiers he commanded.

"Every other company to the right then left," ordered Sourban. "The Colosseum is to be surrounded. I want one company prepared to advance on each gate so that we can attack immediately."

"Yes, Captain!" responded Todori with a shout and a crisp

salute. The Sergeant pulled sharply on his reins to turn his mount, then commanded several soldiers behind him to come with him so that he could begin directing into position the companies fast approaching the plaza.

Sourban had rode at the head of the Royal Guard, the King with him for a time, as the soldiers made their way down the boulevard, the rising sun at their backs. With the six thousand soldiers behind him, the large column stretched from the entrance to the plaza circling the Colosseum all the way back to the Corinthian Palace. As he sat on his horse at the edge of the square opposite the two main gates of the arena, the companies of the Guard coming toward him from behind curled off to the north and south as directed by Sergeant Todori and his subordinates.

His troops moved as ordered with a measured and practiced step as they took their positions around the Colosseum. Even better, he saw that the soldiers who had emerged from the barracks on the far side of the Colosseum had already completed their assigned task, blocking off the streets that led to the Colosseum but for the main boulevard now filled by the soldiers of the Royal Guard. He hoped that such a display of strength would intimidate the gladiators, and he nodded to himself in satisfaction, quite pleased with and taking a good deal of credit for the discipline demonstrated by his troops. The encirclement of the gladiators' bastion demonstrated a coordination and competence that was second to none. To his eyes, it looked almost mechanical in its precision. Exactly how he liked it.

But then a strange and unwanted sense of unease began to seep into him, replacing the satisfaction that he had bathed in for just a moment. In just as coordinated a fashion as his soldiers, the people of Tintagel who had been following his troops down the boulevard orchestrated their own movement with a precision that he found surprising and distinctly unsettling.

The massive flood of onlookers broke off into smaller streams when they reached the square, working their way through the alleys and the streets, until they came to a stop at the boundary of the plaza, forming a deep cordon around his soldiers. The people weren't stepping onto the plaza where his soldiers were continuing to form into ranks. Rather, the Caledonians, once they filled in the paths leading to the square, stood there quietly, their eyes focused on the mall filling with soldiers, many people even entering the buildings that fronted the plaza and peeking out from the windows so that they would have a good view of the action to come.

Sourban hadn't expected that, and he didn't know what to make of it. Nor was he certain what to do. He had thought that once the Royal Guard had formed into its squares for battle, the people would disperse, wary of getting caught up in the fight. But he had been mistaken. Obviously, the Caledonian citizens viewed the spectacle of rousting the gladiators from the Colosseum as something akin to watching those slaves engage in combats on the white sand. They didn't see the upcoming battle as a fight so much as they viewed it as entertainment.

There was nothing to be done about it, of course, as there was no cause to disperse the crowd, especially since King Beleron wanted all to see him exercise his authority in retaking the Colosseum, so Sourban tried to ignore the thousands of people taking their places behind his troops.

His companies of soldiers continued to file around him as he stared at the two main gates of the Colosseum, no movement visible on any level of the arena. Sourban understood that he was in a precarious position, both dangerous and potentially advantageous. On the one hand, if the Royal Guard failed to take the Colosseum, his King would blame him. On the other hand, if the Royal Guard did as commanded, slaughtering the gladiators and quickly expelling them from the Colosseum as the King demanded, then that would provide Sourban with the opportunity that he had been waiting on for quite some time.

Success this morning would give him a chance to demonstrate his abilities not only as a soldier, but also as a strategist, and perhaps as a result he could gain a bit more favor and influence in the King's eyes than he had now. The Advisor had succeeded in clouding Marden's perspective with ease, Tetric needing only to whisper into the King's ear for a few seconds to gain whatever he desired while Sourban found his attempts to do the same much more difficult and taxing. Defeating the gladiators was a key first step in expanding his power within the halls of the Corinthian Palace. So he needed to make an example of these slaves. And that required putting his plan in place with absolute rigor.

The bright sunlight of the morning shining off the white stone of the plaza forced Sourban to shade his eyes with a hand on his brow. The strategy he had outlined to his Sergeants played through his mind as he watched his soldiers get into position, still waiting for any sign from the gladiators as to how they were preparing to defend themselves, but the rebels gave nothing away, not a sound coming from the Colosseum.

Yes, what he planned to do next entailed some risk, but he wasn't worried. All was exactly as his scouts had described it to him. The gates to the Colosseum were locked, chained, and boarded up. It would do the gladiators little good. Perhaps some in the crowd would view the efforts of these slaves as valiant, maybe even heroic, but it was a wasted effort, a suicidal act on their part, because the King had already told Sourban that there were to be no survivors.

That order likely resulted from the fact that Marden's premature victory parade had been anything but, the procession not what the King had anticipated or wanted as he rode his prancing horse down the thoroughfare, his white leather armor demonstrating a stark contrast not only to the black leather armor worn by his soldiers, but also to the dirt and grime that covered the people watching the slow progression. White in this fracturing city was a symbol of privilege, of success, of what most people could no longer achieve. Survival was now their only concern, and survival wasn't a world of sharp color, but rather one of drab grey, black, and dried blood.

In consequence, the people simply stared at the King with blank expressions or looks of discontent, some even glaring at him and shouting harsh words or making rude gestures. That had affected Marden. Badly. He had never expected such a poor welcome. So much so that Marden had decided to shift his position in the column to the middle, preferring the protection offered to him by being surrounded by companies of soldiers rather than just his personal guard and ordering Sourban to take the lead.

Sourban closed his eyes and shook his head in aggravation, seeking to clear his thoughts. He couldn't be bothered by his King's fears or the people's anger right now. He had a job to do. The people crowding the streets wanted to watch a drama. There was nothing better to take their minds from their own current problems than the Royal Guard slaughtering the gladiators. And there couldn't be more than a couple hundred gladiators in the arena. Why the slaves hadn't made a run for it as soon as they got loose from their stockade he didn't know. But he would make every last one of the fools pay for that very poor decision. There was no way that so few could defend effectively such a large structure.

The Colosseum was a massive edifice, and that alone would work against the gladiators. Once his soldiers forced their way through one of the twelve gates, the Royal Guard would overrun the rebels rapidly. He'd already had soldiers try the steel doors that opened onto the walls surrounding the gladiators' stockade, but somehow the rebels had succeeded in sealing them shut. How they accomplished that he had no idea, but it wouldn't matter in the end. He didn't want to waste his effort on trying to break through there. They were chokepoints. Even if his soldiers were able to reopen the doors, it would take just a few gladiators on each door to hold their places on the wall for quite some time. And assuming that those entrances would be watched, there would be no good way for his soldiers to climb the walls of the stockade undetected. If they tried, they'd simply be giving the advantage to the defenders, his soldiers nothing more than flies to be swatted from the wall.

Initially, Sourban had considered breaking into the gladiators' stockade and then making for the gate that led into the Pit, coming at the rebels from the rear. But again, in his mind, it was just another chokepoint. His soldiers should be able to force their way into the compound with little trouble, but the entrance into the Pit at the far end of the stockade was the narrowest of all the gates, only a few feet across, and once through there they would have to traverse a long tunnel before actually reaching the white sand of the Pit. So another path to be avoided, at least for the time being.

Choosing to ignore those two options because of the ease with which the gladiators could bog down his soldiers' assault, his strategy turned in a different direction. Sourban had assumed that the gladiators would be guarding all the gates, since they likely would expect the Royal Guard to attack all the gates at once. If Sourban was correct, if the gladiators had distributed their forces evenly around the Colosseum, that meant that the already few defenders would be spread even thinner, and they would be unable to bring any real strength to bear where it might be most needed.

So Sourban decided that he would start by attacking the two main gates. His soldiers could push through quickly, and then he could send additional companies forward to flood the Colosseum with his soldiers and end this uprising just as quickly as it had begun. There was no reason to be sly or crafty. He had never been known for that. But he was known for being direct and often heavy handed. He had an overwhelming number of soldiers to use against a few hundred gladiators. He would put that advantage into play right from the start at what he believed was the gladiators' weakest point in their defense.

But he also desired to put on a good show, and by that he meant a vicious, blood-filled exercise in efficient killing. Sourban viewed this insurrection as a way to strengthen the position of the Royal Guard in the city. If the Guard could force their way into the Colosseum quickly and put the rebel gladiators to the sword within the hour, it would send a strong and potentially terrifying message to the thousands of people finding places to watch what was about to happen, many of them responsible for the unrest and riots tearing through Tintagel on a much too regular basis. Straightforward and early success against the gladiators would make his soldiers' work easier if the people understood just how efficiently and effectively the Royal Guard, when given the chance to use the full might of their arms, could stamp out unrest and eliminate those foolish enough to challenge the Crown.

"Rodren! Furkal!"

The Sergeants of the two companies facing the main gates of the Colosseum trotted up to the Captain, saluting and coming to attention. Sourban had made sure that these two companies would lead the assault, the Sergeants and the soldiers beholden to him.

"Break through the gates," Sourban ordered.

Without a word, the two Sergeants saluted, then trotted back to their companies, ordering their soldiers to move forward, their twenty by twenty squares advancing in unison.

Sourban gave another satisfied nod as his soldiers marched confidently toward the two primary entrances to the Colosseum. The end to this rebellion had just begun.

THE MASTER of the Gladiators stood on the second level of the Colosseum, just above the main gates, hidden behind the huge statues that depicted some of the early monarchs of the Beleron dynasty. He couldn't remember the names of the mostly men and one woman sculpted and placed there to remind the people of Caledonia of their early heritage, but he could say with absolute certainty that likely all of them were more competent in managing the affairs of the Kingdom than their ancestor, the current ruler, Marden Beleron. None had ever faced what Marden needed to deal with now. Rebellion.

Several sharp commands by the Sergeants leading the two companies lined up directly across from the main gates drew Declan's attention back to what was occurring in the square outside the stadium. He had watched with interest as the soldiers of the Royal Guard marched into the plaza, moving with an exactness that most would be impressed by as they alternated to the north and south and then formed up into their company squares once they reached their assigned positions.

But he had learned through hard-won experience that there was a big difference between maneuvering on a parade ground such as the plaza and shifting formation and advancing against a determined and skilled enemy. So he'd keep close his opinion of the Royal Guard until the King's soldiers had a chance to match swords and spears against the men and women of the Blood Company.

"You guessed right, Declan," said Bryen, who peeked out from behind a statue next to the one Declan was using for concealment. "Even down to where they would try to break through first."

"It was fairly obvious, lad," replied Declan. It wasn't how he would have attacked the gladiators if he had been the Captain of the Royal Guard, but that didn't matter. To get a sense of how events might play out, he just needed to think like Killen Sourban, and that wasn't very difficult to do. Sourban wasn't known for his creativity. But he was known for his ambition and his desire to make a statement, and for the last that would require creating the circumstances for putting on a good show for the King. "I figured that Sourban would want the sun at their backs, thinking that his soldiers could use it to their advantage. But it's still early in the morning so it will have little effect. The sun playing off the white tiles of the square with that gleam probably will cause more problems for the Guard than for us. We'll be fighting in shadow the entire time. When the soldiers approach the gates, they'll be coming from sun to shade because of the Colosseum's arched stone balconies that overhang the plaza. It will take some time for their eyes to adjust."

"Why not just attack all the gates at once?" asked Bryen. "They certainly have the manpower for it."

"You know as well as I do, lad."

Bryen smiled. Some things never changed. In the Colosseum when Declan was training Bryen how to fight or teaching him mathematics, geography, or some other subject that he thought a boy his age needed to learn, he rarely gave an answer to Bryen's questions, expecting him to find the answer for himself.

"Marden."

"Correct, lad," said Declan with a satisfied nod. "Care to explain?"

"Politics and a play for power, nothing more," answered Bryen. "Sourban is certain of his success against us. Marden wants a victory that will offer a lesson to the people and cement his hold on the throne. So Sourban means to give it to him. Having the Royal Guard attack all the gates at once defeats that purpose. Too much will be going on. There will be too many distractions. The attention of the people watching will be pulled in too many directions. But here on just the eastern side of the Colosseum, all eyes will be focused on the two main gates. Once the Guard force their way through, Marden will follow. He'll have the victory that he wants as well as the image of him walking over the dead bodies of the rebels, and Sourban will have given it to him."

"There you go, lad," said Declan, a small smile breaking out, pleased that Bryen had read the situation so quickly and so well. "If we play our cards right, we can use that arrogance against them."

"Doesn't look like we'll have to wait any longer," said Bryen. "Here we go."

Two Sergeants had just left Sourban and sprinted toward their companies, screaming orders at their soldiers to advance.

"Let's get down to where the fun is going to be," suggested Declan.

Both he and Bryen left their places among the statues and took the steps leading down to the main gates two at a time. Davin, Lycia, and their squads were already ready for the attack. Spears to the front, short swords just behind to offer support if needed.

An almost eerie silence had descended within the Colosseum, the gladiators standing at their positions calmly, many revealing confident grins as Bryen and Declan walked among them. The threat of the Royal Guard attacking was no different than what they had to deal with when they entered the Pit for a combat. And despite the overwhelming odds that the gladiators faced, Bryen and Declan sensed something perhaps not unexpected, but certainly new.

The nervous energy that was often surging through the gladiators before they fought for their lives in the Colosseum was nowhere to be found. It had been replaced with a different kind of charge, though one that was just as invigorating, if not more so. It was not hope, because that would be asking too much in the current moment -- the overwhelming numbers of the Royal Guard could not be ignored -- and perhaps even would be dangerous as it would cloud their focus on what needed to be done. Rather, it was a sense of purpose. A sense that they were involved in something bigger than themselves. Something that they could be proud of, regardless of how it all ended.

Yes, just as in the Pit they would be fighting for their lives. But in just minutes they would be fighting against the Royal Guard. They would be fighting for a cause. For some, it was a feeling that they had never encountered before. For others, it was a feeling that they had lost and thought that they would never experience again. But all felt an unfamiliar thrill, an exhilaration, because they knew that they were not fighting on their own anymore. They were fighting with their brothers and sisters. They were fighting as a company. And since they had no expectation of winning, they had nothing to lose.

Yet, surprisingly, there was a touch of fear as well. Not that the Guard would defeat them -- they weren't fools, they expected that to happen, it was just a question of when -- but that they would let down their comrades. And that was something that they refused to permit. If they were to die this day, they would die with honor. They would die fighting with their fellow gladiators. They would die fighting with and for the Volkun.

Declan could sense what was running through the minds of the gladiators as they prepared mentally for the battle. It pleased him. It also increased the chances that the strategy that he and Bryen had agreed to had a good chance of working, at least against this preliminary assault by the Royal Guard.

Once Declan had determined the approach that he believed Sourban would take for storming the Colosseum, he had left two gladiators at every gate to provide a warning if the attack by the Royal Guard expanded beyond the two main gates. The gladiators could move quickly throughout the Colosseum, their internal lines of maneuver shorter and faster than what the soldiers of the Royal Guard had to deal with, so he had formed the gladiators pulled from the other gates into six additional teams.

Three of those squads were now positioned at the gates the Royal Guard was about to attack, right behind Davin and Lycia's gladiators. Three squads were positioned more toward the center of the Colosseum and closer to the Pit. Those three teams held in reserve could move quickly to aid those fighting at the gates or to another gate if the Guard shifted their strategy on the fly, though knowing Sourban that was unlikely. He wasn't known for his quick or innovative thinking.

For now, these extra squads would provide a defense in depth. Although Declan knew that the Guard would change their strategy eventually, he wanted to take advantage of the opportunity the Captain of the Guard was giving to him right now because of his desire to please the King. If Declan did this right, the Royal Guard would get more than a black eye during their initial engagement with the Company of Blood.

If the gladiators were able to push back the attack, it might place a seed of doubt in the minds of some of the soldiers. Perhaps just a kernel and no more than that, but the longer the gladiators were able to hold their ground, the more opportunity there would be for that seed to grow and spread. As the battle progressed, the gladiators would benefit from that doubt.

"We shouldn't have any problem holding back this attack," declared Declan, loud enough for all the gladiators to hear, which led to several more smiles. He then spoke more quietly so that only Bryen could hear. "However, once we throw back the Royal Guard, Sourban will shift his approach and attack all the gates at once. That's when we'll be in trouble."

"And I assume you have some thoughts about what we can do to defend against that eventuality."

"I do."

"Let's hear them," said Bryen. "I'd like to prepare for that scenario now rather than when we're fighting for our lives."

"Always looking ahead," chuckled Declan.

"When you're fighting in the Pit, there's nowhere else to look but ahead. The past is too bloody and the present is too depressing."

"So it is, lad. So it is."

"You taught me well, Declan."

"Perhaps too well," grumbled Declan. "Come on, lad. Let's get these fighters ready. We're going to make the King regret his decision to leave the safety of his Palace and take a step into the real world. We're going to show that bastard and his Captain what it really means to challenge desperate and dangerous gladiators."

"Stand, fight, die," offered Bryen with a grim smile.

"You really did pay attention to what I said, didn't you?"

"You really didn't give me much choice," answered Bryen with a short laugh.

"I guess I didn't," Declan nodded. "As you said, lad. Stand, fight, die. That's who we are. That's what we do."

"You understand what I expect, Captain?" asked Marden Beleron, the King of Caledonia having pulled on the reins of his resplendent, armored warhorse so that he came to a stop next to Killen Sourban, his personal guard of one hundred soldiers forming up around the both of them.

"You made it eminently clear, my King," replied Sourban. He wasn't worried. The odds were in his favor. The only thing that he was nervous about was how long it might take for his soldiers to penetrate the gates. The longer the gladiators held the entrances, the more irritated Marden likely would become, which would only make Sourban's job that much more difficult. The King was not known for his patience in military endeavors, or much of anything else for that matter. "I have no doubt that the battle to come will go exactly to plan. Have no fear of that, my King."

"You seem quite confident, Sourban. I hope your confidence is justified."

"More than justified, my King," replied the Captain. "We begin now. The companies advance."

Marden turned his gaze away from his Captain back toward the square, watching as the two companies of the Royal Guard tasked with forcing their way through the main gates marched across the plaza at a fast walk, shields in one hand, long spears in the other, short swords on their hips.

Nothing happened until the advancing soldiers were halfway across the square. Then a handful of arrows shot down from the balconies built into the outside of the Colosseum's higher levels. And then another flight. And then one more. For a moment, Sourban was worried. If the gladiators had a stronger force, those steel-tipped missiles would prove more dangerous to his soldiers and perhaps even stop their advance. But the gladiators couldn't devote many of their number to serving as archers, having to focus most of their attention on protecting the gates.

So Sourban's fears quickly evaporated. A dozen of his soldiers fell during the barrage, but the remainder raised their shields in time to defend themselves. His troops would simply need to deal with this additional irritant, breaking through the gates still their primary objective. And the loss of life, taking into account the forces that Sourban had at his disposal, certainly was acceptable if not negligible.

"Very impressive, Captain," said the King, feeling a bit better about his current circumstances now that he had arrived in front of the Colosseum.

Marden was still smarting from how his people had reacted to his appearing in the streets of Tintagel. He had expected adoration, perhaps even some displays of warmth and undying devotion, and if not that because of the current troubles that his people suffered through, at least respect. He was their King. They were nothing but commoners. They served him after all. The people were expected to demonstrate respect for authority, for his authority, at all times. And to not do so brought the risk of punishment, but it seemed that they had forgotten that.

Had he not treated them well? Had he not done what he could to improve their lives? Had he not told them with his regular proclamations that they were always in his thoughts? What he needed from them? What he expected of them?

Yet as soon as he had left the Corinthian Palace, he had seen nothing to suggest that they had been paying attention. Apparently, the people refused to listen to him, did not hear, or did not care about what he said. On some of the faces lining the boulevard he had seen what he could only assume was contempt. He had been shocked at first, and then that shock had transformed into anger. He had experienced an over-whelming desire to show these commoners what it meant to be a King. What it meant to go against the Crown. What it meant to disrespect his authority.

But the gladiators needed to be dealt with first. Once he cleared the Colosseum of these rebels, once he saw the white sand of the Pit completely covered in their blood, he would remind these ungrateful peasants who had insulted him that he was their King, a ruler deserving of their reverence. There was a price to be paid for not understanding the pressure that he was under, for not understanding the challenges that he faced in keeping the city and the Kingdom safe and prosperous, for not understanding and not caring about the sacrifices that he made for them on a daily basis. He would show them the cost of dissent, the cost of not believing in him, and at the same time eliminate the possibility of any threat to his rule for a long time to come.

"Thank you, my King. The Guard is well trained. They know what is expected of them. They will do their duty."

Marden nodded distractedly, observing those soldiers unlucky to be caught unaware or too slow to raise their shields collapse with long shafts of wood sprouting from their bodies.

"Just as you know what I expect of you," said the King. "And losing a symbol of my power, even for a short time, to these slaves is not something that I expected my Guard and my Captain ever would allow. Will this take long?"

Sourban looked at Marden, not sure of how to respond because of the King's irritation and placement of blame. So he tried caution and a bit of hedging.

"I would think that it won't take long, my King. But you never know what can happen during a battle. Those archers are just one example of how circumstance can change suddenly."

"Those archers are just an annoyance, Sourban," replied Marden, the testiness in his voice making his Captain nervous. "Against the Royal Guard they are no more than gnats." Marden's forced composure, designed to demonstrate his strength in the face of battle, disintegrated into a harsh glare. "You're not answering my question, Sourban." The King's eyes blazed fiercely, Marden clearly lacking patience for Sourban's attempt to deflect. "Will this take long?"

Catching the dangerous glint in the King's eyes, the Captain cleared his throat, knowing that there was only one way that he could respond and still keep his head, at least for now. "No, my King. It shouldn't take long at all."

But then his heart dropped into his stomach as the shouts and screams began to echo across the plaza, much earlier than he had expected, and from his troops rather than from the gladiators.

He pulled his eyes away from Marden's and looked toward

the Colosseum towering above them. That trickle of arrows shooting down from the higher levels of the arena had become a steady stream, the defenders obviously having added more archers to the task now that they knew that the primary attack was focused on the eastern side of the Colosseum.

In response, the Sergeants leading the two companies called for a faster advance at a hard march, but still the archers on the protruding balconies skewered the charging soldiers, concentrating their attack on the first few ranks. As more and more of the Guard fell to the ground, dark red blood beginning to stain the white tile of the square, the charge actually turned more into a walk as the soldiers were forced to slow their pace, stepping over their fallen comrades and closing up the spaces in their squares so that they could link their shields above their heads and protect against the accelerating onslaught.

THE SCREAMS of pain and anguish, mixed with curses of disgust and grunts of effort and dismay, echoed beneath the covered main gates to the Colosseum and bounced back into the plaza for all to hear. Yet the din of battle but for the scrape of steel against the bars that prevented the King's soldiers from entering the arena emanated only from the soldiers of the Royal Guard.

The gladiators led by Davin and Lycia and charged with defending the main gates fought fiercely, but they did so silently. Another lesson learned from the Master of the Gladiators. Why waste your wind shouting or screaming when you could put it to better use, like drawing in deep, measured breaths so that you could better maintain your focus on the task at hand? Better to kill than be killed, after all.

At the beginning of their assault, the soldiers thought that they would have a fairly easy time of it. They had been told how few in number the rebels were, and they assumed that once they worked free the chains from the bars, it wouldn't be long before they smashed the large gates inward. But they had been dissuaded of that belief rather quickly and jarringly by the unwavering gladiators.

For the soldiers ordered to pierce the gladiators' defenses, it was like trying to kill a vicious, unyielding porcupine. The gladiators thrust long spears through the strategically placed gaps between the bars and the benches attached to the gates, then pulled the lances back just as quickly as they were propelled forward. Then spears shot through the gaps between the boards in different spots along the gates. It was a never-ending danger for the soldiers, lances launching forward and then retracting, a constant flow of activity. There was no rhyme or reason to it, at least none that the attackers could discern, and that made their job all the more difficult.

Although the attackers couldn't figure it out, the gladiators did have a rhythm to their work. They thrust at the sides of the company of soldiers to push the men into a larger mass near the middle of the gates. The defending gladiators would strike there next, hoping to catch a few attackers with a spear because the press of their comrades would prevent the soldiers from moving out of the way. As a result, there was little that the soldiers could do but suffer the consequences of their failure to discern the gladiator's strategy.

Even worse, these two companies of the Royal Guard were now stuck in place. They couldn't move close enough to the gates to attempt to remove the thick chains wrapped around the bars because of the constant spear thrusts, and they couldn't move back because they wanted to stay beneath the protection provided by the balconies overhanging the plaza to avoid the archers waiting above them.

The archers situated on those balconies, despite their limited numbers at the beginning of the skirmish, had done excellent work, slowing the Guard's charge so that they couldn't rush the gates as they had desired. The archers were so successful, in fact, that Declan had decided to add more gladiators to their ranks, increasing the stream of arrows slamming into the soldiers to a steady, deadly flow.

So now the soldiers charged with breaking into the Colosseum were instead bunched in front of the gates. They didn't have the strength in numbers to force their way past the defending gladiators and they dreaded retreating, not so much because the King was watching, but because of their fear of showing themselves to the archers who had demonstrated such lethal accuracy when they had crossed the plaza the first time.

"What's your next step, Captain?" The King's impatience at the stalled assault was rapidly turning into anger. He could see just as well as everyone else that this initial attack was not going to plan.

The crowd behind them strangely remained silent, but the King could sense the undercurrent building within the people watching the fight. Their disaffection and dissatisfaction with the Crown, with him, seemed to naturally sway their allegiance toward the gladiators, and the exceedingly competent defense demonstrated by those same gladiators appeared to be strengthening the connection between these rebel upstarts and the citizens of Caledonia. That was something that Marden had not anticipated and simply could not tolerate.

"We'll wait just a bit longer, my King," replied Sourban, his gaze never leaving the fight in front of them. "Have faith in the ability of your soldiers. They will get the job done."

"Faith isn't what's needed now, Captain," said Marden, motioning to the people standing at the perimeter of the square. Still quiet, still in place, observing intently, observing him as well and making him distinctly uncomfortable. "What we need now is victory. An unforgettable demonstration of strength that terrifies the mob behind me and makes them understand their place in my world."

"Of course, my King. Do not fear. We will destroy these rebels in short order. I promise you."

Sourban cursed silently to himself. He hoped only a few more minutes would be needed, but if he believed that he would only be kidding himself. He would give his attacking troops just a little bit more time to try to complete their assigned task, but he expected that soon he would need to shift to a different strategy to achieve his objective.

He saw no way that the companies assigned to breaking into the Colosseum could be successful, the gladiators' defense proving too strong. The main gates were holding, the chains linked through the bars helping to keep the thick metal barriers locked in place. And it didn't appear that the gladiators were working too hard to keep it that way.

With the benches affixed to the gates, even if the Guard could avoid the spears shooting through the gaps, the defenders had nullified easily his soldiers' strength in numbers. The members of the Royal Guard didn't have time to try to slide their spears through the gaps, and they had no reason to draw their short swords because they had no use for them in their current circumstances. Although the gladiators weren't necessarily killing his soldiers, at least not now that his troops had become wise to their tactics, they were certainly making it extremely difficult for them to do anything more than focus on their own defense.

Sourban had to give the gladiators credit. They had a plan and they were executing it well.

He was certain that this defensive strategy was the work of Declan, putting his knowledge as a former soldier in the Royal Guard to good use. When his forces finally got into the Colosseum -- and they would, of that he had no doubt -- Sourban promised himself that he would be the one to kill the Master of the Gladiators. And he was going to enjoy doing it. He was going to take his time and make it hurt to pay back that irascible disgraced soldier for all the grief that he was causing him now.

~

"THAT'S ANOTHER ONE," said Davin, his voice calm and controlled as he stood behind the gladiators who formed his team and were defending one of the two main gates that led into the Colosseum with immaculate skill. "Seventeen now."

"You're still behind by three," replied Lycia, his sister only thirty feet away, standing behind her gladiators who were charged with defending the other main gate. "Make that four. No, five. Excellent strike, Johanna. Well done!"

Davin grumbled in anger. He didn't like losing, especially to his sister. After they had finished preparing to defend the main gates, they had made a wager on the number of soldiers each of their squads would eliminate from the fight. At the moment, his sister was enjoying better luck than he was.

Declan's plan had worked to perfection so far, the archers on the higher levels of the Colosseum an added touch that had proven more effective than expected, while also making the defense of the main gates a much easier task. But even with that early and unanticipated success, the gladiators led by Davin and Lycia had not lost their focus. Instead, they had fought with an almost soulless precision that the soldiers of the Royal Guard had no chance of defeating.

"Eighteen," called Davin as he saw a spear thrust by Lucresia take a soldier in the shoulder close to his heart. Whether or not the man died, he was definitely out of the fight, and that was all that mattered. "Nineteen." Lucresia had waited for another soldier to try to pull the wounded one out of the way and had taken advantage of the opening given to her, spearing him in the upper thigh. By the looks of things, blood spurting into the air, she had severed an artery.

"Still three behind, brother," said Lycia. Then she saw Atticus slide the tip of his spear into a soldier's groin. The man had thought to protect himself with his shield, but he had held it too high, giving the wiry gladiator the chance to thrust his steel with a painful precision. "Make that four."

"Are you sure you're counting correctly?" Davin called to his sister. "Math was never your strong suit."

"Feel free to come take a look," Lycia replied. "Just be careful about getting stuck in the eye if you decide to count for yourself. You never know when one of these soldiers is going to get lucky."

"No thanks. I guess I have no choice but to take your word for it."

"Then stop complaining," suggested Lycia.

"I am not complaining," complained Davin. "I am simply trying to clarify a concern that I have."

"Now you're whining," stated Lycia, knowing that she was working her way under her brother's skin, which was one of her favorite pastimes.

Davin's usual smile evaporated. Why did he allow his sister to do this to him so often? She took great pleasure in irritating him and had, in fact, mastered the skill. Yet he still allowed her to provoke him.

His rising anger quickly disappeared, his smile returning. "Twenty two! Twenty three!" A quick succession of strikes from his gladiators had hit home, the soldiers in front of the gate unable to move out of the way in time when the pattern of spear thrusts through the bars had changed. "Well done! It looks like we've got a real contest again."

THE CAPTAIN of the Guard closed his eyes in frustration. The King had said nothing during the last few minutes, but he hadn't needed to for Sourban to understand how displeased he was. Sourban could feel the irritation roiling through Marden Beleron and rolling off onto him, all because the fight had continued for several more minutes and still no progress had been made.

The two companies of soldiers were still stuck in front of the gate. They had given no sign that they would be able to do anything more than what they were doing now, and they were reluctant to move back and charge forward again with the archers stationed above them keenly waiting for another chance to fire down into their ranks. His soldiers were stuck, and there was no easy way for them to disengage without putting themselves at even greater risk.

"Should we send another company, Captain?" growled the King, his scowl at the current situation making clear his opinion of Sourban's tactics. He had never thought that his Royal Guard could be brought to a standstill so quickly and easily.

"A good thought, my King," replied Sourban solicitously. "But there is no room. If we add a company or two now, it will only create confusion and make their task more difficult. And it will give the archers a larger target."

"Even so, Captain, I find it hard to believe that your supposedly well-trained soldiers have failed to enter the Colosseum. There are only two hundred fighters opposing us. That number cannot be denied. Yes, the gladiators are good fighters. But most of them are not soldiers. The Royal Guard should have already retaken the Colosseum and crushed the insurgents. The fact that they haven't is giving hope not only to the slaves fighting against us, but also to the people watching their efforts. This is not supposed to be a lesson in hope. It is supposed to be a lesson in power. This was not how this spectacle was designed to play out."

Sourban had no good response for his King, so he kept his mouth shut. Admitting to himself that his first attempt at removing the gladiators had failed, though it pained him to do so, he was about to send runners to the Sergeants leading those two companies stuck against the gates with instructions to pull back their troops so that he could issue new orders.

He needed to adjust his strategy. But that lump in his belly, initially formed out of unease and concern, was rapidly turning into nausea thanks to his increasing fear. Because the gladiators had changed their strategy first, and when he realized what they were doing he knew that there was nothing that he could do to counter it fast enough.

WHEN BRYEN HAD PROPOSED a change to their scheme, at first Declan had balked. Not with regard to the suggested adjustment -- he thought that it was an excellent idea -- but rather at who would be involved.

The Master of the Gladiators had argued vociferously with Bryen. Yes, several teams of gladiators could be used for the purpose that Bryen had suggested, but Declan didn't want Bryen directly involved. He couldn't join them on the assignment. It was too dangerous. Too risky. The gladiators could do it. The gladiators would. They were primed for it. They were ready. They were looking forward to it. But Bryen himself couldn't do it.

Declan continued to refuse to allow Bryen's participation. The gladiators needed him. He was the leader of the revolt, a symbol of the gladiators' efforts, of what they were fighting for, and it was his name that the people had been shouting in the streets when news of the uprising had spread throughout the city.

Bryen had allowed Declan to continue with his many arguments until he had lost his momentum. Then Bryen had smiled and patted Declan on the shoulder, telling him that he appreciated his concern. He understood from experience that the best way to win an argument with Declan was to agree with him, and he did just that when he offered his counterargument.

"Declan, you're right. But that's why I need to do this. That's why I need to be a part of this. If I'm a symbol of this rebellion, then I need to be seen as that symbol. I can't hide in the Colosseum waiting for the Royal Guard to break through. I need to fight for our freedom in the plaza. The gladiators need to see me in the middle of the battle. More importantly, the people watching from the streets need to see me. That's the only way we can win this."

Declan had stared at Bryen for more than a minute, his face betraying a range of emotions from disbelief to anger to understanding to resignation, before he had nodded his head grudgingly.

"Dammit, lad, you know that you drive me crazy?" he grumbled. "I hate it when you use my own logic against me. If you ever have children, I hope that they pay you back in spades."

Bryen smiled at remembering the exchange, but that smile instantly shifted to a fierce concentration. He needed to focus on the risk that he and the other gladiators with him were about to take. They would have one chance and once chance only to do this. They needed to make it count.

Both he and Declan were certain that the Royal Guard would not be attacking any of the other gates, at least not yet. Not while two companies were still engaged at the two main gates. They also knew that Davin and Lycia could more than hold their own, not needing the three teams of gladiators Declan had held in reserve to assist them if needed. It was also quite obvious that the large number of soldiers in the plaza hindered the ability of the Royal Guard to maneuver quickly, so Declan had moved the extra squads of gladiators, placing three teams each at the two gates closest to the two main gates.

Because of the circular concourse, Bryen could see Declan at the far end, standing at the gate, his gladiators lined up in front of him. There and at the entrance at which Bryen now stood, the gladiators had removed the chains and unlocked one gate without the soldiers noticing.

Raising his spear above his head, he saw Declan nod.

"Ready?" asked Bryen.

The three teams of gladiators waiting with him, less than twenty fighters all told, murmured their affirmative replies. They were crouched down, balanced on their toes, ready for action.

Bryen could feel the energy flowing within them. They were finally getting into the battle. And if circumstances worked out as they hoped, they were about to have a crushing impact on their adversaries.

Pleased, Bryen slashed down with his spear. At the prearranged signal, the gladiators in front of Bryen pulled open the unlocked gate and sprinted out silently into the plaza, Bryen following them after he had confirmed that the gladiators under Declan's command were doing the same on the far side of the concourse.

It really wasn't fair, Bryen thought, as he quickly caught up to the other gladiators who had fanned out into a long line. But then again, fighting fairly had little to do with winning a battle. If you wanted to win, you had to use everything at your disposal that could prove useful. And the fact that Lycia and Davin's squads had captured the full attention of the two companies of Royal Guard sent to force their way into the Colosseum certainly qualified as something useful and to be used.

Before the soldiers struggling in front of the main gates knew what was happening, Bryen and his three teams, and Declan and his three teams on the other side, slammed into the unsuspecting soldiers and cut far into their ranks. The gladiators fought with a brutal efficiency, using short swords and long daggers to stab and slice their way deep into the two companies of Royal Guard.

They were so efficient, in fact, that Bryen, slashing and twisting his double-bladed spear in a deadly arc that resembled a blurred figure eight, almost met Declan in the middle of the two formations, the Master of the Gladiators demonstrating the skill and expertise that had kept him alive for so long on the white sand and that he had been instilling in the men and women forced into the Pit for more than a decade.

Bryen and Declan had agreed that the purpose of this surprise attack was to make a point, not to attempt to destroy two companies of soldiers. The reason for that was quite simple. The soldiers were too many and the gladiators were too few. They couldn't risk getting drawn into a pitched battle with so many other soldiers in the Plaza watching and waiting to get into the conflict. So they would fight for two minutes only, each gladiator counting to one hundred and twenty in his or her head. Despite the speed with which the seconds slipped away, that was still plenty of time for the gladiators to demonstrate their martial prowess and shatter the will of the two companies, leaving them in complete disarray and spent as fighting units.

"Time!" shouted Declan.

Hearing the Master of the Gladiators' commanding voice, the gladiators disengaged and sprinted back through the gates, not a single one wounded, their surprise complete and the soldiers failing to mount an effective defense. But rather than following his compatriots back through the gates, Bryen did as he and Declan had discussed.

He was a symbol. A symbol who needed to be seen. So

instead Bryen walked slowly toward the King until he was almost in the middle of the plaza. Marden Beleron appeared to be mesmerized by the audacity of his opponent, Sourban and the soldiers arrayed around him too stunned by the success of the gladiators' attack to do anything but observe what was to happen next.

"We are gladiators, but we are no longer slaves," said Bryen in a strong voice that carried throughout the huge square. "We are the Blood Company. We will stand fast! We will stand strong! And we will stand free!"

As he stated his opposition to the Crown, Bryen lifted his double-bladed spear above his head, the morning sunlight shining brightly on the sharp steel. For a moment, there was nothing but silence. Then a huge roar erupted from the crowd ringing the plaza that shocked the King and the Royal Guard.

With shouts for the Volkun trailing him, Bryen walked calmly from the plaza, twirling his weapon from one hand to the next, seemingly unconcerned by the soldiers all around him. He then waved to the crowd with the Spear of the Magii, which elicited an even louder hue and cry, before he stepped calmly back through the gate, the steel barrier slamming shut emphatically.

27

DOING WHAT'S RIGHT

"**B**ryen is trying to achieve multiple objectives all with one roll of the dice," said Sirius. "He and the gladiators currently hold the Colosseum. Marden has already left the Palace with most of the Royal Guard, unable to resist the temptation to make himself appear the hero. Besides, it's another distraction for a hostile and restive citizenry. So Marden views the gladiators' actions in an even more positive light. He perceives the uprising as a gift and he hasn't considered yet how any failure on his part to address this unrest could have a larger impact on his ability to rule."

"That's not unexpected," said Jurgen Klines. The Blademaster had stationed the two dozen soldiers he had secreted in the Lady Winborne's suite out in the hallway, a formidable force if any were foolish enough to try to enter her chambers without an invitation. He had also sent runners throughout the Corinthian Palace to all the other soldiers stationed there who were loyal to him and the Crown and not to Killen Sourban. It would take time to bring his troops together because of the size of the Palace and the need for discretion. But once word got out, Klines would have several hundred soldiers providing protection to Lady Winborne and her father. "King Beleron is a cunning ruler, almost dangerously so, but he's still young and callow. He doesn't always see what he should see because he only sees what he wants to see."

"A fascinating assessment. One you came up with on your own?" asked Rafia, who stood on the balcony looking out onto the garden several hundred feet below. The riotous colors of the thousands of blossoming flowers and trees were beginning to give her a headache if she stared at them for too long, so she turned her attention back to the Blademaster.

"No, actually it isn't," he replied, his honesty always front and center. "A friend shared his thoughts with me. I thought his appraisal was right on the mark."

"Which friend would that be?" asked Rafia, her interest clearly piqued.

"Declan, the Master of the Gladiators. If you spend any time with him, several of his many adages unavoidably will rub off onto you."

"Interesting," replied Rafia, not surprised at hearing Declan's name. A trainer of killers and a philosopher when the need demanded it. An interesting man, indeed.

"That's one piece," said Kevan, having ignored the conversation between the Blademaster and the Magus, his interest focused solely on how to get his daughter out of the city and back to the safety of the Southern Marches. "And it certainly will distract Marden. But that won't be enough to accomplish our primary task. What other pieces are you putting into play?"

"Captain Tentillin will be bringing the Battersea Guard to the eastern gate of the city," answered Sirius, having looked at Rafia with a jaundiced eye because of her continuing interest in Declan, a man she had just met. Why she was so intrigued by him just because he spouted a few witty aphorisms -- although he did have to admit that they tended to be right on point -- was lost on him.

Sirius had to make a real effort to shift his thoughts away from the Master of the Gladiators and back to what he took to be more important matters. "If all goes well, the soldiers of the Southern Marches will enter the city and establish a foothold at the eastern gate and provide us with a route out. Once secure, Captain Tentillin will lead a large contingent of the Battersea Guard toward the Colosseum with the goal of catching the King from behind."

"What if Tarin can't make it very far into the city?" asked Kevan.

The Duke of the Southern Marches very much believed in the abilities and intelligence of the Captain of his Guard, but he had his doubts about how far his troops could push into Tintagel. Not because of their lack of prowess, but rather because of the danger of fighting in unknown streets and the size of their opposition. Even if his soldiers breached the gate, the troops loyal to Marden outnumbered the Battersea Guard by at least four to one and still could bring those numbers to bear even when faced with the additional challenge of rebellious gladiators taking over the Colosseum.

"Then he makes some noise at the gate and stays there," answered Rafia.

"And what if by some good fortune Tarin succeeds in reaching the Colosseum? The Royal Guard still outstrips him. I don't want my Guard decimated on my account. Their primary mission should be protecting Aislinn and getting her back home."

"Captain Tentillin is well aware of that," replied Rafia. "He's clearly quite competent. I experienced that firsthand during the Battle of the Horseshoe. He will not make a rash decision, and we have several contingencies in place so that we can adjust based on the circumstances that he and the Battersea Guard face here in the capital. Furthermore, he understands that his primary objective is to get Aislinn to safety. That's what he intends to do. Thus his desire to make some noise and distract those opposed to us and ...”

“Thereby give us a chance to escape,” completed Sirius. “Despite its simplicity, it really is a quite elegant plan.”

“You call that a simple plan?” asked Aislinn, still annoyed at how current events were playing out.

“Simple in its design,” corrected Rafia. “Not necessarily in its execution.”

“Assuming all of this plays out as we hope, what of the gladiators once we’re gone?” asked Aislinn.

“Assuming that we can connect with the Battersea Guard, if there’s a chance to help them escape, we’ll do what we can,” replied Rafia, but those words sounded hollow to her as soon as she spoke them.

“And if the Battersea Guard can’t make it past the gate into the city or can’t move toward the Colosseum once they reach the Palace?”

Aislinn was quite confident that Tarin could breach the gate. He was not lacking in guile when the situation called for it. But she was also realistic. Even if the Captain had brought the entire Battersea Guard with him, and she doubted that he had as he would never leave the Southern Marches undefended, they would only make it so far before getting bogged down in the city, and that was something that Tarin would not permit. He would do everything in his power to avoid getting trapped in the capital. Because of his close interaction with Bryen, Tarin was beginning to demonstrate some flexibility in his thinking and his approach. But he was not about to risk his primary mission on behalf of the gladiators, so she already knew the answer to her question before she asked it. She just wanted confirmation. She wanted to hear it with her own ears.

Sirius shook his head in resignation. “Then the gladiators are on their own against the King and the Royal Guard.”

“Bryen agreed to this? I know he takes risks that others

wouldn't, but this is suicidal. He has virtually no chance of escaping."

Aislinn tried to keep the emotion rising within her from her voice, but she failed miserably. Why would her Protector do this? She had freed him. She had given him a chance to start a new life. Yes, the collar still encircled his neck, but it was no more than an artifact now. A reminder of a difficult experience, and with time his memories of her and the Southern Marches would fade. She didn't want to be the cause of his death. She didn't want him to waste his life on a fool's quest.

"He did," Rafia answered quietly, having some sense of the many emotions roiling through the Lady of the Southern Marches. "He was the one who suggested it."

"But why would he do this?" Aislinn asked again. "Why would the gladiators? They are risking themselves for me, for my father, despite the fact that their brave efforts will be for naught. Let's be completely realistic with our assessments now. The chance of Tarin making it any farther from the eastern gate than the Corinthian Palace is slim at best. Bryen has to know that. The gladiators have to know that. They have to know that if the Battersea Guard doesn't reach them, they've signed their own death warrants."

"'We are gladiators' was what Bryen told me when I asked him that exact same question," Sirius said. "'We stand. We fight. We die. That's who we are. That's what we do. And we do it well.'"

"Another of Declan's sayings," Rafia explained, Bryen having given her a brief lesson in some of his favorite maxims that he had learned from the Master of the Gladiators. "I really do hope that I can speak with this man."

"Now is not the time," Sirius whispered fiercely. "We have bigger issues to deal with."

"What does that even mean?" demanded Aislinn, ignoring the old Magus. "We die well? I cannot believe that Bryen is such a fool that he would sacrifice himself in this way. If he was here, standing in front of me right now, I would tell him ... I would tell him ... I would tell him ..." But what would she tell him? Why was he doing this? Her thoughts were in such a jumble that she was having a difficult time thinking clearly.

Sirius tried to offer a better explanation as to what might be going through the Protector's mind.

"I asked Bryen much the same as you ask me now," said her instructor in the Talent. "He took a moment before replying, and I remember the look that he gave me when he finally did. It was a sad look, a look of someone still tortured by the memories of a life that had been filled with blood and pain. He told me that once you fought on the white sand, you can never escape the white sand. He said that the only way to be free of the white sand was to free yourself from the white sand. No one could do it for you."

"But that is no more than ..." Aislinn stopped herself, remembering some of the conversations that she had engaged in with her Protector. Although she didn't like it, she was beginning to understand Bryen's twisted logic. As all the pieces fit into place for her, her understanding growing, a cold lump of fear settled in her stomach. "Even if that means your death. Freeing yourself from the white sand even if that means your death."

"A brave lad," said the Blademaster, having listened to the discussion intently. He had heard much from Lady Winborne about her Protector during their time training together, and he had enjoyed the privilege of watching the Volkun fight in the Pit. He rarely attended the gladiatorial games, having little interest in the gory spectacle, but he had heard a great deal about this unconventional, deadly fighter, and he had been just as impressed by the young man's composure and maturity as by his martial skills. He fought because he had to, not because he wanted to. "And a young man to be respected."

Sirius nodded his agreement before locking eyes with Aislinn. "Yes, even if it means your death. The gladiators want to live. Bryen made that very clear to me. But he noted that he was unique in that gladiators never escaped the Colosseum except in death. He is the one exception, and it eats at him. He feels as if he left his friends and his comrades, his family, behind. He wants to be there. He wants to do what he can for them, because he needs to do it for himself. He understands the risks. He understands the various scenarios and how they all likely play out. The gladiators know all this as well. So they don't want to die, but they are not afraid to die. They just want to have a ..."

"Choice," interrupted Aislinn, nodding as full understanding finally dawned upon her. "They want to have a choice."

She remembered having this dialogue with Bryen before. The issue of choice, of having the ability to decide your own fate. That she could understand. For Bryen it had always been about choice. That's what had bothered him the most about becoming a Protector. He had never had a choice. He had been forced to it, not asked. And after a decade of being forced to fight in the Pit, he had grown tired of being told what he had to do. He simply wanted to have a choice. He wanted the other gladiators to have a choice as well. And now they did.

"Yes, choice," said Sirius wistfully. "They wanted a choice in whether they would live or die. If they lived, then all the better. But if they were to die, they wanted to die on their own terms rather than on someone else's."

"A brave young man indeed," whispered Kevan, his decision to make the lad his daughter's Protector weighing on him even more heavily now. He had done what he believed was needed to protect his daughter, but he had never considered Bryen to be anything more than a solution to a problem. He had failed to see him as a person. He had been such a fool. Such an arrogant, selfish fool. And now the lad was about to make the ultimate sacrifice despite all that had been forced upon him. "With many brave friends and comrades."

"I think we can all agree with that," said Rafia respectfully.

"Aislinn, as soon as Tarin reaches the eastern gate, you need to go there. I'm sure that the Blademaster and his soldiers can get you to him safely."

Kevan watched as his daughter's gaze shot toward him. He understood what she wanted and that she viewed his constant demand that she return to the Southern Marches as a betrayal. But he needed to continue to push her as well. He needed her to go. He couldn't, not with the cursed collar around his neck. So he would take his chances here. But she was the future of the Southern Marches, and if his Duchy was to have any future, she needed to be there.

"We can't do this to him," protested Aislinn. "We can't leave him here to die."

"We're not doing anything to him," said Kevan gently, his eyes sad but his expression unwavering. He had never expected that she would form such a strong connection with her Protector, but she had, so he understood his daughter's reluctance. On the one hand he found that somewhat disconcerting. On the other hand, he was impressed by her conviction and her desire to stand by someone who had stood by her. That boded well for her future as the Duchess of the Southern Marches, assuming, of course, she actually left Tintagel now and returned to the province so that she could help build that future. "He is doing this for us. Why he would after what I did to him, I don't know, but I would ask that we accept his gift."

"He's not doing it for you, father," replied Aislinn quietly, beginning to really comprehend the significance of this gift offered to her by her Protector. "He's doing it for me."

"Oh my," said Rafia, now seeing it for herself, realizing what

Bryen's decision to put himself at risk really meant. "I knew there was a reason I liked that young man so much."

"We need to go, Aislinn," said Sirius. "We don't have time to wait. We need to connect with the Battersea Guard, whether in the city or beyond the walls. We need to go now."

"Please, Aislinn," her father said with a hopeful voice. "Please go with Sirius and the Blademaster. I must remain here, but you don't have to. You should not remain here. There are bigger challenges that you must face. Your Protector understands that. That's why he's doing this."

"We can't leave him," said Aislinn in a barely audible tone. She had tried to convince herself that she didn't have a stronger connection to Bryen beyond the collar, but she had only been fooling herself. There was a stronger connection. Stronger than steel. And though he was willing to sacrifice himself for her, she refused to allow him to do it. If he was to fight the King and the Royal Guard, then she would fight with him.

"He's doing this for you!" shouted Sirius. "If the Battersea Guard can reach the gladiators, they will. If they can't, then it won't be for lack of effort. You know Tarin. You know he likes the lad even if he does his best not to show it. Please, Aislinn. Please don't make your Protector's sacrifice something that has no meaning. As your father said, he's giving you a gift that should be valued."

"I know that," she replied boldly. Her voice was no longer soft, no longer sad, but forceful. Bryen would do as he thought best, and so would she.

"Then why hesitate. We need to ..."

"My father is helpless with that collar around his neck. I will not leave him. My mind has not changed."

"But there is nothing that you can do for me," protested Kevan. "Aislinn, you must ..."

"Nevertheless, that is not the only reason that I cannot leave."

The Blademaster looked at the Lady of the Southern Marches with appraising eyes. He had spent a great deal of time with the young lady on the practice ground and had watched how she had interacted with the soldiers who trained with her. Like his daughter, she was made of steel. Not easily swayed, though she would shift with the wind if there was good cause to do so. And if there was not good cause, she would remain firm in her beliefs. Once she made up her mind, there was no moving her.

"Honor," murmured the Blademaster, not thinking that anyone had heard him, but Lady Winborne had.

"Yes, Captain Klines, exactly that," confirmed Aislinn with a delicate smile. "Bryen shared many of the sayings that he had learned from the Master of the Gladiators. One of those sayings continues to run through my mind right now, and I cannot in good conscience ignore it."

"What is it?" asked Rafia.

"You must do what you believe is right, because no one else will."

Rafia nodded, her agreement with that statement clear, as did the Blademaster. Even her father acknowledged the logic that one sentence held.

Yet Sirius still shook his head in irritation. "Stubborn, willful child ..."

The old Magus was about to offer another argument in just one more attempt to sway Aislinn, but Rafia cut him off before he could.

"Enough of this," said Rafia. "These arguments are a waste of time and energy."

"Rafia, what are you ..."

"Sirius, now is not the time." She understood just as Aislinn did what Bryen's decision truly meant, even if Kevan and Sirius had missed it. There was no point in arguing with Aislinn. She would not be moved. Not if she was listening to the wisdom of a man likely to be dead in just a few hours. Not if she was listening to her heart.

The Blademaster stepped forward then, his eyes as sharp as his features, his posture suggesting that the time for words had come to an end. Now it was time for steel.

"The Lady of the Southern Marches has spoken. What would you have of us, Lady Winborne?"

Aislinn nodded to Rafia and then Captain Klines in silent thanks, Sirius and Kevan somewhat stunned by the quick turn of events and the role that the young woman who at times they still viewed as a young girl had assumed. Klines stood expectantly in front of Lady Winborne, clearly pleased by the fire shown by the young lady from the east.

"Where is the Volkun?" Aislinn asked in a strong voice, a voice of steel, a voice designed to lead.

"Where he believes he needs to be."

"Then we make for the Pit," said Aislinn. "We will not allow the gladiators to sacrifice themselves. We will fight with them, no matter the cost."

Sirius was about to protest again, but Rafia elbowed him in the ribs, eliciting a gasp of air and preventing him from getting any words out.

"Seems like the best course," Rafia whispered to the old Magus. "The only way to free Kevan from the collar is to kill Tetric. And we both want a chance at that. Free the Duke and we can likely get Aislinn out of the city."

Sirius nodded, unable to disagree with her logic. "Then it needs to be done," he grumbled, though he understood just how difficult a task they had just set for themselves. He should have been irritated that Aislinn had ignored his advice, that she had stood against him. But secretly he was pleased. Her strength of will had simply demonstrated how his young charge had grown in the last few years into a competent young woman. "We need to find Tetric, and we need to kill him."

"I have no doubt that Tetric is with the King," said the Blademaster. "Find the King, you find Tetric. And my guess is that the King will be near the ..."

"Colosseum," finished Aislinn. "He'll want to play to the crowd. He'll try to use the gladiators' uprising to strengthen his own position. If he crushes the gladiators, he'll think that he can put in the minds of the people the knowledge that the Royal Guard can be set against them as well. It might put a stop to the unrest and riots."

"It might," agreed Rafia. "But even with the huge advantage in soldiers Marden enjoys, he underestimates your Protector. And he does so at his peril."

"Agreed," said Sirius. With the arguments now over, he was fully on board with what was to come next, even if Aislinn's father continued to have his doubts as shown by his glum expression. "If the King isn't careful, the Volkun will make him pay a high price for allowing his arrogance to take the place of his intelligence."

"Marden is never careful," offered Kevan. "He is willful and impulsive, two qualities that I'm sure Aislinn's Protector will use against him."

"Lady Winborne," said the Blademaster, nodding respectfully toward her with a satisfied glint in his eye. If events worked as he hoped they would, while the Volkun earned a chance to kill the King, Klines hoped that he'd have a chance to settle a long-held debt with the Captain of the Royal Guard. "Your orders?"

"We make for the Colosseum, Blademaster. With all possible speed."

28

A GRAND ENTRANCE

Declan and Bryen worked their way rapidly around the Colosseum, moving from one squad of gladiators to the next. The Blood Company was now fully engaged in battle, every gladiator fighting with an iron will as they sought to prevent the Royal Guard from piercing their defenses. All the gates continued to be watched by two gladiators, and the six extra teams of fighters that Declan had formed had been repositioned to defend the additional gates that Sourban had chosen to attack.

The gladiators were employing the same strategies that they had when the Royal Guard first assaulted the two front gates, using the steel bars and the benches affixed to them to their advantage by making the work of the attacking Caledonians as difficult as possible. The men and women of the Pit ramming their spears through the gaps continued to be a major problem for the Royal Guard, many a combatant wounded or killed because a sudden thrust of steel caught them by surprise or they failed to get out of the way because of the crush of soldiers around them. But it was more of a challenge now for the gladiators to hold their ground. The Royal Guard pressed the gladiators hard, beginning to bring their greater numbers to bear.

Unfortunately for the Blood Company, the Royal Guard also was beginning to figure out how to address the deadly threat that the gladiators presented. At a few gates the soldiers had been able to push their way right up to the bars despite heavy losses. The front rank held their scuta made of curved steel against the gates to prevent the gladiators' spears from striking them, several soldiers often needing to hold one scutum in place because of the power with which the gladiators thrust their spears through the gaps. But that was enough to give their compatriots a chance to saw through the chains that were helping to hold the gates in place. It was dangerous and slow work. Still, the soldiers were making progress. Repeated strikes by the gladiators often pierced the shields, killing one or two soldiers each time. But that didn't stop the soldiers from continuing their efforts as men from the ranks behind stepped over their fallen comrades to take their place and raise new shields against the gates.

That's when Declan realized that the tide of battle was about to shift, and not in his favor. The additional fighters Declan had ordered into the battle had done well, they were performing a critical service, but he knew that his latest move only delayed the inevitable. The gladiators were fighting on borrowed time now. When that time ran out, the end would come, in part because Declan's primary antagonist had given up his desire to put on a show for the King and now approached the fight for the Colosseum as the battle that it truly was.

Learning from the mistake that he had made at the beginning of the fight, Sourban had ordered his troops to attack six gates at once, none of those points of access next to each other. This new strategy returned the advantage to the Royal Guard, the gladiators struggling to hold their own against the more than twelve hundred soldiers attacking all at one time across their fortified arena.

Blood dripped from both blades of the Spear of the Magii, Bryen having jumped into the fiercest fighting as he made his circuit around the Colosseum. In fact, he had just stopped at the main gates for a few minutes, helping Davin and Lycia release some of the pressure being applied there, the Royal Guard having pushed hard to force their way through but still having failed to penetrate the gladiators' defenses. At least this time.

"As bad as we thought?" asked Declan, Bryen rejoining him after having assisted his friends.

"Probably a bit worse," replied Bryen, who had suggested that he and Declan leave the balcony above the main gates and walk the Colosseum's primary concourse so that they could get a better sense of the larger picture. "We'll hold for as long as we can, but several of the gates are under extreme pressure. Even with the reinforcements that you sent, half the gates under attack are now being held by half the number that we started with. It's only a matter of time."

"We've got excellent fighters," said Declan. "But only so much can be expected of them. Any one of them is a better warrior than a soldier of the Royal Guard, but individual combats mean nothing now. Not in this mad scramble. Sourban changed his strategy, and I hate to admit it, but it's working."

"Then we need to change our strategy as well," said Bryen. "Stay one step ahead of him if we can."

"Indeed we do, lad," agreed Declan. "Indeed we do."

Just then Torfinn sprinted up to Declan, a well-used short sword in hand, several bloody slashes marring his forearms and one thigh.

"The gate on the northern side is about to fall," he gasped out, the heavy fighting taking its toll on his endurance. "They got their shields up against the gates and they just sawed through the chains. We're too few to keep them from pulling the chain from the bars. Once they do that, they will have the momentum that they need. They'll finally be in the Colosseum."

"I expected as much," grumbled Declan. "If one gate falls then we have no choice but to fall back. If the Guard get onto the concourse before we can clear out, we're done for. They'll sweep us up just like the dust on the floor."

But Bryen wasn't there to hear Declan, the Volkun having sprinted in the direction Torfinn had just come from as soon as he heard the bad but not unexpected news. It didn't take him long to get to the gladiators' weakest point in their current defense, and he realized that in the time that it had taken Torfinn to make his report, the situation had gone from bad to worse.

Not only had the soldiers sawed off the chain and removed several of the steel links threaded through the gate, but they had also broken one of the locks in the ceiling that held the gate in place on the left side. The steel bars were beginning to bend backward under the pressure from the mass of soldiers pushing against the barrier, and only a couple fighters remained alive to stop them, though Bryen could tell that neither gladiator had long to live after glancing at their grievous injuries and realizing with a painful regret that he had no time to heal them.

Understanding that he needed to give Declan time to put the next step of their plan into motion, Bryen rushed into the fighting, his double-bladed spear a blur as he stabbed three soldiers in the chest before any of the attackers realized that a new foe had joined the skirmish. For several minutes Bryen held the gate on his own, the two gladiators who so bravely had tried to continue fighting sadly succumbing to their wounds, but he knew that the sands of time were passing him by.

The initial shock of seeing this new devil opposing them having worn off, the soldiers, desperate to break through, locked their shields once again and pushed against the broken gate, the metal screeching as it was bent even more out of shape, creating an opening that allowed two soldiers at a time to slip through. The first pair didn't get far.

Bryen spun and glided as if he were fighting on the white sand of the Pit, the blades of his spear slicing across one soldier's throat, the man slumping to the ground as his life pumped out onto the white stone. He then stabbed backward to catch the dying soldier's companion in his gut with the other blade on his spear, the man thinking to take advantage of the distraction provided by his partner to stab Bryen in the back and failing to realize that the Protector had expected just such an attack.

The second pair through the gate fought more intelligently. Staying together, they tried to force Bryen back so that more space would open up in front of the gates to allow more of their compatriots to push their way into the Colosseum. Bryen refused to allow it. He held his ground, the Spear of the Magii a blur of steel in front of him as he kept the two soldiers in place.

One of the soldiers feinted to his left, thinking that this gladiator would go for his ploy, which then would allow his fellow soldier to come at their adversary from his undefended side. Bryen didn't fall for it. Instead, he ignored the feint and drove the blade of his spear into the other soldier's groin before the man could advance on him. The soldier fell to the tile with a screech of pain, the remainder of his life now counted in only minutes. His comrade stood frozen in place for just a second, shocked by two things. The speed with which this gladiator had attacked his friend and the fact that he hadn't fallen for the trick.

Then it all came together for the soldier in a terrible way as he finally recognized the double-bladed spear. He fought the

Volkun. The deadliest fighter in the Colosseum's recent history. Before that knowledge could send a shiver of fear through his body, the soldier grunted in pain as the Volkun slid his blade into his chest. The man's body became numb in seconds. He wanted to say something. To scream in terror. To shout in agony. But no sound would come out of his throat, the Volkun having driven his spear right into his lungs, his breath leaking from the horrible wound. The light left the soldier's eyes before he slid off the steel and came to rest against the broken gate.

Having eliminated the first soldiers through the breach, Bryen turned to his right, sensing the movement there. He realized much to his regret that he was going to be too slow. The four soldiers that he had killed had done their job, even though they would never know it. More of the Royal Guard had followed their comrades through as they engaged him, and one of those soldiers was about to drive his sword into Bryen's back.

Before Bryen felt the cold steel slice into his flesh, he heard a grunt of surprise. Continuing his turn, Bryen saw that Declan was there, having thrust his blade through the soldier's armpit and into his heart. And then for several minutes he could do nothing but focus on the fight in front of him, he and Declan the last two obstacles to the hundreds of soldiers trying to force their way through the gap between the broken gates.

For a time there was only movement, instinct taking the place of thought, as the two gladiators cut down more than a dozen soldiers, covering their weapons and themselves in blood and gore until they appeared to be avenging spirits risen from the dead. And though the Guard continued to try to push into the Colosseum through the broken gate, the many bodies of their comrades who had died in the breach had now become an obstruction that hindered their efforts.

So with a great deal of reluctance, the Sergeant commanding the company ordered his soldiers to pull back. They would regroup, and then they would attack again. Once they increased the size of the gap in the gates, these two gladiators, despite their obvious prowess and bravery, would have no chance to hold back the onslaught the Royal Guard would unleash upon them.

"Come on, lad," said Declan, breathing heavily after the long and hard fight, Bryen seeming to have been barely affected, which irritated the older man to no end. "We won't be able to stop their next attack. It's time to adjust our strategy as we had agreed."

Bryen didn't bother to reply, simply following the Master of the Gladiators as they moved toward the center of the Colosseum. It had been a hard and bloody fight to hold the breach, but he knew in his heart that it wouldn't compare to the fight that would come next.

"THIS IS THE MOMENT, SOURBAN," the King proclaimed. "This is my moment! This is the moment I ride to glory!"

Sourban finally had the breakthrough that he had been waiting for. He had received word that one of the companies attacking on the northern side of the arena had breached the gates. The resistance had been fierce, but beyond that he really couldn't be sure what exactly was going on there.

Some garbled reports suggested that only two gladiators had filled the gap and forced his troops back outside the stadium, the Sergeant leading that company choosing to reform his soldiers before advancing again into the Colosseum. Other reports offered a grander tale of his soldiers taking on the remainder of the gladiators still alive in the stadium, the fight bloody and raw, his soldiers after killing almost all the rebels only disengaging reluctantly so that they could broaden the breach between the gates to get more of their comrades onto the main concourse.

He didn't know the truth, not having had a chance to explore the far side of the Colosseum, but he didn't really care at this point. All that mattered was that his soldiers had cracked the rebels' defenses at one gate, and they had come close to doing so on a few others. That confirmed that his strategy was working. He was wearing down the gladiators, weakening them, and when he attacked a third time, the rebels wouldn't be able to stand against the charge of the Royal Guard. His soldiers simply would crush the gladiators beneath their feet. But first he needed to deal with a possibly more dangerous challenge, the issue requiring a delicate touch to ensure that he kept his head … literally.

As soon as news of the breach reached Sourban, King Beleron began to prepare himself to ride with his personal guard in the final assault on the Colosseum. Not wanting to put his monarch at risk, but even more so understanding that any participation by the King in the attack could derail his carefully laid plans, the King's visions of glory and grandeur getting in the way of needing to exterminate the vermin populating the greatest symbol of Caledonia's might, Sourban had struggled to keep the King from joining the larger attack. Every argument that Sourban offered, King Beleron either ignored or deflected with ease. And it wasn't long before Sourban realized that he was about to lose the struggle.

"I am a better fighter than any of the men here," declared the King. "I appreciate your desire to keep me safe, but your concern is unnecessary, Captain. Should I not be at the head of my troops? Should I not show my soldiers and the people watching the type of King who rules them? A King of action. A King of power and strength. A King to be feared."

That was, in fact, Sourban's greatest concern. He wasn't certain that he wanted King Beleron to display his martial prowess, fearing that any slip, any mistake, any demonstration of a lack of ability, would only feed the fire in the thousands of people watching the battle take place in the plaza. Finally, after several minutes of gentle cajoling, and the suggestion that once his soldiers forced their way through the main gates he could charge through on his destrier with his personal guard streaming behind him, giving the people watching the show that they deserved, Sourban's argument appeared to hit home with the King. Even so, Marden hesitated, waffling on the utility of Sourban's suggestion.

Then Tetric fortuitously appeared at the King's side, having finally made his way down the boulevard from the Corinthian Palace. And it was in that moment that the continuing argument with the King shifted in Sourban's favor. For once, Sourban actually was glad that the King's Advisor was there. It only took a few whispered words from Tetric to gain the King's agreement with Sourban's proposal. Sourban wasn't happy that Tetric had succeeded where he had failed. But he was happy that he no longer had to worry about the King getting in the way of what should be Sourban's crowning achievement. Exterminating the gladiators.

Still, Sourban failed to eliminate the whisper of doubt that had worked its way into the base of his spine and was now slowly but steadily working its way up his back. The citizens of Tintagel didn't seem to be impressed with the Royal Guard or their King, and somehow even less so with the King's Advisor, Tetric's appearance apparently serving as the lever that helped to transition the observing crowd into something potentially more worrisome. Clearly, the citizens of Tintagel were not pleased with how events were playing out, as their allegiance appeared to favor the gladiators.

The silence that had turned to unsettled rumbling and anger had shifted to something else now. It was subtle, but after months of dealing on an almost weekly basis with crowds that transformed into riotous mobs in a flash, he picked up on it instantly. That distillation of anger had begun to percolate, spreading swiftly among the people packed into the streets and watching from the buildings. The hushed conversations had shifted from quiet interest to angry whispers that were growing in volume and intensity. The question was, would that anger mutate into action?

Wanting to ensure that his final attack on the Colosseum went off without any unforeseen challenges or surprises, Sourban had ordered several companies of the Guard to turn toward the people watching from the streets. Just to be safe and, if nothing else, to give the Caledonians pause before any of the firebrands in the crowd attempted to incite their fellow citizens into action.

He was used to the unrest becoming something more dangerous, but he couldn't afford any mistakes with the King here with him. The only way to eliminate this additional potential threat was to deal with the gladiators swiftly and remorselessly, giving those foolish enough to think that they could take on his Royal Guard pause.

And that was something that he was about to do. Attacking six gates rather than two had proven much more successful. Sourban was going to end the fight now by ordering the Royal Guard to attack all twelve gates at once. Perhaps that's the strategy he should have adopted at the start, but it was of no relevance now. He was certain that half the gladiators who had started the fight were dead by now. With their dwindling resources stretched so thinly, there was no chance that the rebels would be able to defend against this final foray.

The King now safely behind him, Tetric at Marden's side, his personal guard surrounding him, Sourban returned his focus to the plaza. The remains of the initial attack on the main gates were still visible. Dead men lay on the white tile, gear lost in the fight littering the stone, weapons having slipped from dying hands, the boards affixed to the gates chipped and broken in dozens of different places, some of the steel bars bent almost to the point of breaking.

Yes, now was the time. Now was the time to end a rebellion that had been doomed from the very start. Now was the time to make the gladiators pay for what they had done.

With a quick slash of his sword through the air, Sourban's command was relayed to the companies surrounding the Colosseum, the soldiers moving forward as one. First at a walk, then at a trot. When they were only a hundred feet away from their targets, the Royal Guard shifted into what was almost a sprint before they slammed into the gates, the clatter of steel shields on steel gates resounding throughout the square.

In only a few minutes, the two main gates crashed down and several companies of soldiers charged through, screaming in rage for their friends and comrades who had already been lost in the battle, searching for those responsible so that they could exact their vengeance.

A broad smile broke out on Sourban's usually cold face. Everything was going according to plan now, and he assumed that much the same was occurring at all the other gates, his soldiers streaming into the Colosseum to slaughter the gladiators, as the King had already given the order that no prisoners were to be taken. This was a battle, true, but perhaps more important for the Crown, it was a mass execution.

Sourban's smile slipped a bit when the Sergeant responsible for the attack on the main gates stepped back out into the plaza and then sprinted toward him.

"What's the matter, Kennie?" asked Sourban, trying to determine why his Master Sergeant had such a strange expression on his face when he came to a stop in front of him and saluted.

"There's no one there, Captain."

"What do you mean there's no one there? There has to be someone there. The gladiators were there just minutes ago."

"Yes, Captain," replied Kennie, a large man with more grey in his short hair than black. His years in the Royal Guard had not been kind to him. The hard work and too regular fighting had left him with bad knees, a bad back, and a neck that he could barely turn to either side when he woke up in the morning. "You're correct. But there are no gladiators there now. Several of the other Sergeants are reporting the same. They faced no resistance when taking the gates."

For a moment, Sourban looked strangely at Kennie, his mind trying to catch up to what he had just been told. Why would the gladiators leave the gates undefended after fighting so ferociously during the first two attacks? And where could the gladiators have gone?

A warning bell went off in the back of the Captain of the Royal Guard's head, a sound that he listened to whenever it occurred because it had never been wrong. Something wasn't right. He was beginning to sense a danger that he couldn't understand or explain. Why was Declan inviting his soldiers into the Colosseum?

TRYING to defend the entire Colosseum from the attack of the Royal Guard had been a fool's errand from the start. But the gladiators had accepted that. They understood that their efforts were simply an attempt to buy time. That was fine with them, and they understood that their time had run out as soon as the first gate had been breached and the Royal Guard had pulled back so that they could assault all twelve gates at once.

Following the strategy that had been worked out the night before, Declan had pulled his gladiators back from the gates and into the eastern quarter of the Colosseum. The gladiators already had blocked all the entrances that led toward this quarter of the stadium. Or rather Bryen had, despite how tiring the work was, using the Talent to bring down tons of stone, destroying the entrances and corridors so that the Royal Guard could not attack the gladiators from any direction but this one. A funnel of death, as Davin had described it, and it seemed appropriate to have the white sand of the Pit at their backs.

The Master of the Gladiators had wanted to narrow the fight, and he had done so in a way that the Royal Guard would not have suspected possible. The Caledonian soldiers had no choice but to fight the gladiators in this one large tunnel. There was no other way to get at them. The gladiators had negated much of the advantage the Royal Guard enjoyed because of their overwhelming numbers. Now the gladiators could engage in a more evenly matched fight as only so many soldiers could enter the tunnel at one time.

The Royal Guard still had the upper hand. Slowly, the gladiators would be whittled down in number until the Caledonian soldiers overran them, but it would take them time to do so. And as all the gladiators knew, time was the key. Time was the one variable that might give them what they truly wanted, although they all refused to get their hopes up, knowing that hopes and dreams never equated to reality.

It was at the entrance to the Pit that Declan, Bryen, Davin, and Lycia met as they prepared to defend against Sourban's next attack. The four of them had agreed that Sourban's primary goal was to kill them all. He was not a nuanced individual. If he needed to hammer in a nail, he preferred to use a sledgehammer for the task. But Bryen believed that Marden wanted something more than just a fast victory. He believed that the King wanted a chance to claim his victory. He expected that the King dreamed of striding on to the white sand, the prospect of walking over dead gladiators to get there too much of a temptation for him to resist. But that remained to be seen.

To draw out the battle for as long as possible, Declan had arranged the gladiators into a version of the testudo of ancient times. Shield bearers stood shoulder to shoulder to the front protecting those wielding spears right behind them. Next came fighters with swords and arrayed behind them a line of gladiators with bows. It was a good defensive strategy. But it was not one designed to achieve victory, because the gladiators understood that victory likely couldn't be gained on this day. Still, that didn't bother them. Finally, they had been given a choice, and they aimed to make the most of the choice that they had made.

"When do you think they'll come?" asked Davin with his ready smile.

"Soon," replied Declan. "It'll take them a little while to figure out what's going on. And then when the King hears about what's been done to slow down his retaking the Colosseum, Sourban will have to deal with that tantrum before he can shift his troops to engage with us here."

"That tantrum might work to our advantage," suggested Bryen.

"Do you really think Marden would be so foolish as to fight against us?" asked Lycia. "He has no cause to do so. He'd be taking a risk that he doesn't need to take. He'll be able to tout his victory whether he bloodies his sword or not."

"True," replied Davin. "But remember when we met him in the practice yard?"

"It was hard to forget," grumbled Lycia. "Vain. Arrogant. Spoiled."

"Just like most kings," offered Declan.

"Yes, I won't disagree with you," said Davin. "But there was something else there. A weakness that he was trying to hide."

"Doubt," Bryen said softly.

"That's it exactly," Davin said, nodding his head in agreement. "He doubted himself and everything he did that day seemed to be designed to eliminate the doubt that plagued him."

"He doesn't feel as if he deserves to be king," said Lycia, impressed by her brother's very intuitive perspective.

"He doesn't deserve to be king," said Declan. "But you're right, and Davin is right. Doubt tortures him, and the only way to remove the doubt, to confirm in his own mind that he is who he thinks he is ..."

"Is to be who he thinks he needs to be rather than who he really is," finished Davin.

"Well said, lad," said Declan. "Couldn't have said it better myself."

"You think because of the King's doubt we can play him. We can get him here."

"I hope so, Lycia. It would be a fitting way to end this," confirmed Bryen. "What do you think, Declan? If we do this right, can we get what we want?"

Declan looked at Bryen, his usual scowl turning into a brief smile.

"We can," he said. "I believe that we can. But it's going to take some work."

"What do you want?" asked Lycia.

"To kill the King," Bryen replied simply, his eyes blazing maliciously.

Sourban cursed silently, his frustration increasing by the minute. His soldiers had been engaged with the gladiators for more than an hour with little progress having been made, and he had just received word that the King was growing impatient. How was that different from any other time that the King wanted something done? The King was always impatient. Sourban didn't need this additional aggravation now. Besides, no one could have guessed that the gladiators would have prepared their final defense so effectively. How did they even do it in the space of just a few hours? That's what he wanted to know.

Leading the attack himself, thinking that slaughtering a hundred or so gladiators once his troops entered the Colosseum wouldn't be much of a challenge, Sourban hadn't been prepared for what he had discovered. Somehow the gladiators had brought down the stonework at all the other entrances but this one, effectively sealing off the other hallways and eliminating the advantage the Royal Guard enjoyed by preventing them from surrounding the rebel gladiators.

Sourban had shifted his forces as best as he could in response, but he could only bring so many troops to bear against the gladiators while they made good use of the confines of this, the only tunnel not filled by tons of collapsed stone. He and his soldiers had succeeded in pushing the gladiators back toward the Pit, but by no more than a few dozen feet. The gladiators' formation remained strong and unbroken, and he was certain that the gladiators had spilled more of his soldiers' blood than his soldiers had theirs. The trail of dead bodies behind him, almost all of them his men, certainly testified to that disconcerting reality.

Growling in frustration, Sourban stepped back and issued a command, his soldiers responding as quickly as they could, many finding it difficult to disengage from their adversaries and gaining serious wounds or losing their lives in their attempts to do so. After several minutes, the Royal Guard finally retreated far enough within the tunnel to put a dozen feet between them and the rebels. Sourban shook his head in irritation. His soldiers seemed tired, worn out, as if they had been fighting all day even though it had only been a few hours. The gladiators appeared confident, certain in themselves and their comrades, energized, as if the last few hours of combat were no more than a practice session with the main event still to come.

"Where is the Master of the Gladiators?" called out Sourban.

The gladiators simply stared at him in response, their eyes hard, their bodies poised to jump back into the fight. A few more minutes passed before Declan pushed his way between his gladiators to stand before the Captain of the Guard.

"Your gladiators do you credit," said Sourban, staring at his opponent with hate-filled eyes. This battle would have been over by now if not for the incessant training that the Master of the Gladiators gave to his charges.

"They do themselves credit," Declan responded in a soft voice, though his words traveled throughout the tunnel and gave his gladiators an extra boost of energy, their posture becoming straighter, their eyes shining more brightly.

"As you say," Sourban said.

"What do you want, Captain? It's not to heap praise on my fighters."

"No, you're right about that. I wish to make you an offer."

"What offer would that be?"

"If your gladiators return to their barracks this very second, there will be no repercussions. They will be permitted to fight in the Pit once again. They will be allowed to live until such time as they fall on the white sand."

"I'm supposed to believe this?" asked Declan, who failed to keep his disbelief from his voice.

"On the word of King Beleron."

For a moment a tense silence settled within the tunnel, then Declan could hold back his laughter no longer, many of the gladiators joining him. It took almost a full minute for Declan to return to himself, and during that time Sourban's face turned a bright shade of red, his embarrassment plain.

"If it was on the word of his father, I'd believe you," said Declan. "Corinthus Beleron may have ended up under the thrall of that sniveling advisor of his, but he was a man of his word. His son, however, does not demonstrate the same integrity as his father did."

"Are you impugning the honor of the King?" demanded Sourban.

"I am," Declan replied with a smile. "Sorry, but I'd be a fool to trust him."

"You'll die if you don't," said Sourban through gritted teeth.

"I'll die if I do. Besides, I like my chances fighting against you. You're just as much of a fool as your master is. And now a liar as well, because we all know that your only objective is to kill us all. So instead of acting the coward by trying to escape this fight, come at us, Captain. We're ready for you. We're ready to make you bleed."

As Declan's words washed over him, Sourban's vision blurred, his eyes seeing the world through a red film as his uncontrollable fury threatened to consume him. Screaming in rage, Sourban charged forward, his soldiers following him. Declan met Sourban there, refusing to step back, steel clashing with steel, then the crush of soldiers joining the fight pushed them away from each other.

Declan used that opportunity to slip behind the front line of his gladiators so that his fighters with their long spears could do their deadly work. Getting Sourban angry was what Declan had wanted to do, and it hadn't taken much to make that happen. He hoped that the Captain of the Guard would allow his anger to rule his thinking, because that increased the chances of Sourban making a bad decision. And when the Captain of the Royal Guard did, Declan would be ready to make use of it.

For several minutes the battle raged, and then one of the gladiators in the front line fell, a lucky slash of steel cutting across the top of his shield to take him in the neck. The gladiator with the spear standing behind him couldn't pick up the shield fast enough, and when he finally did, a cold-eyed soldier stood above him. With a curse, the soldier drove his blade through the gladiator's eye, and then several more soldiers rushed forward, hoping to exploit the small crack that had finally opened in the gladiators' line.

Before the soldiers could take another step, Bryen was there, Davin and Lycia right next to him. Bryen had separated his spear into its composite twin blades so that he could fight more effectively in the tight space, his steel slicing into the soldiers who had tried to fill the gap, paying the price for their temerity with their lives. Davin and Lycia continued cutting and slicing until the gladiators in the back of the formation advanced to pick up the dropped spear and shield and reform the line.

But Bryen didn't stop there. He sensed a chance to regain the ground that they had lost, and he meant to take it. Raising the sword in his right hand above his head while he defended himself with the sword in his left hand, deflecting a slash from a soldier on his left and then lunging forward to drive his blade through the man's gut, his yell echoed down the covered corridor.

"We stand fast! We stand strong! We stand free!"

A roar of approval rose up from the gladiators around him, and then as one they surged forward, driving deeply into the soldiers' ranks, the world around Bryen, Davin, and Lycia turning red with blood, sweat, pain, and death.

29

INTO THE CAPITAL

"Sergeant!"

Dani trotted up from the gate to where Jerad stood at the edge of the small square that connected to the main street that led directly toward the Corinthian Palace. He was staring as far down the avenue as he could, looking for any movement. Any hint of what might come their way next.

There was nothing. Nothing at all. But there did seem to be a touch of concern in his Corporal's voice, which worried him. All the city's focus seemed to be directed toward what was happening at the Colosseum. And though he and his soldiers couldn't see what was going on more than a mile down the road, every once in a while, they could pick up the faint sounds of a battle on the wind.

All had gone well since he and the other members of the Battersea Guard had infiltrated the city and captured the eastern gate by subterfuge. A few soldiers of the Royal Guard had wandered into the square since then, and they had been taken into custody quickly, sent to join their comrades in the deserted tavern that had been put to use as a temporary stockade.

Almost too well, in Jerad's opinion. Having served under Tarin for more than five years, although he had maintained his cheery disposition and ever-present smile during that time, he had adopted several of his commander's tendencies, such as looking at the world with a more jaundiced eye. So in situations such as this, he expected the worst and hoped for the best. Although his troops had achieved their objective with great success, he worried about whether the other shoe was about to drop as they could not defend for long what they had taken if a much larger force appeared.

"Yes, Dani, what do you have for me?"

A huge smile curled his Corporal's lips when she heard Jerad's question.

"More than you can likely handle, Sergeant," she replied, never missing a chance to joke with Jerad and ease the tension of the moment.

When Dani had joined the Battersea Guard a few years before, she had thrown herself into her choice with a determined abandon. She had wanted to escape the world that she had inhabited before and the complications that had caused her so much grief. So becoming a soldier was the perfect choice. The required discipline helped her gain control of her life, and she learned new skills and took on tasks she never thought that she could accomplish that helped her rebuild the confidence in herself that she had almost lost.

Yet her Sergeant, with his curly hair and uneven grin, somehow had the ability to distract her. What's worse, he didn't even know it. So she made an effort to distract him whenever she could. It had started as a game for her. But now, she wasn't certain that it was a game. She wondered if perhaps it had become something more.

"We'll just have to see about that, Dani," replied Jerad, unwilling to give in to his Corporal's teasing. "I do enjoy a challenge, though, when the time is right."

"You're going to want to take a look at this, Sergeant," Dani finally replied, for a long moment the always sharp-witted soldier at a loss for words, Jerad having parried her verbal lunge deftly, leaving matters innocuous and vague but also suggestive.

Dani then turned toward the gate, Jerad following her. He heard what approached before he saw as he stepped under the portcullis and out into the highway. A long column of soldiers rode their horses along the twisting, beaten down road, making Jerad think of a very large snake. His smile at the arrival of his comrades grew even larger as he realized that the approaching column was bigger than it should be, and that could mean only one thing. Captain Tentillin had found some friends along the way.

The Battersea Guard rode at the front of the winding column and continued straight under the gate and into the city, moving onto the main avenue that would take them directly to the Palace. Behind them several other banners representing the other Duchies that had joined their cause flapped in the wind. He was not surprised to see Murcia with them, the ancient symbols for health and knowledge starkly visible on a white banner. But farther behind came the deep blue banner of Wencel Roosarian, Duke of Roo's Nest, the famous white cliffs of the west sewn in a silver thread flashing in the sunlight, followed by the sketch of a forge appearing on the red cloth signifying that the soldiers of Cornelius Stennivere, Duke of the Three Rivers, brought up the rear.

"Well done, Sergeant," said Captain Tentillin, pulling his horse from the front of the column so that he could speak with Jerad as his soldiers moved into the city. "I congratulate you for your excellent work."

"Thank you, Captain, but all credit to the Corporal and all the others," replied Jerad. "They performed above expectations."

Dani stood a bit straighter at the compliment, appreciating that her Sergeant would acknowledge the work of her and her fellow soldiers.

The conversation at the entrance to Tintagel soon expanded as Noorsin, Wencel, and Cornelius left the column and joined them.

"Where do we stand, Sergeant?" asked Noorsin, her tone all business.

"Some sporadic fighting in the streets by the gate," reported Jerad. "But we put a stop to that immediately. Only a few soldiers opposed us, so I doubt that anyone knows what's happening here, or at least they won't for some time."

The soldiers continued to stream through the gate. Many maintained their course toward the Palace, but not all as smaller columns of mounted soldiers began to break off from the larger so that they could wind their way through the city. Clearly, with the larger number of soldiers at their disposal, the original plan had changed somewhat. If the reports that Jerad had received on the strength of the Royal Guard within Tintagel were accurate, then the troops entering the city now would be more than a match.

That knowledge brought a spark to his eyes. When this plan was first put into action, he had thought that his friend had little chance of surviving the scheme. But now, he wasn't so sure. Now there might be a chance. It all depended on whether they could get to the Colosseum in time and play a role in the proceedings. Pushing that thought to the side, the Sergeant continued with his update on what had happened within the capital of Caledonia since capturing the eastern gate.

"I've been getting regular reports from the scouts in the city," said Jerad. "By all accounts, the Royal Guard has surrounded the Colosseum."

"As we expected," nodded Tarin.

"Yes, but there are two other developments you need to be

aware of," continued Jerad. "First, it appears that the King has left the Palace with the Royal Guard. Based on when I received this information, I expect that he's at the Colosseum now with most of the soldiers stationed within the city."

"He's looking to make a show of it," said Duchess Stelekel. "He wants to be center stage."

"Yes, it seems that Bryen is getting what he wanted," said Jerad. "I just hope that he can survive it."

"Have no fears about that, Captain," Noorsin replied confidently, trying to offer some comfort. "If anyone can, it is the Protector. Any word on Duke Winborne and Lady Aislinn?"

"Nothing, Duchess Stelekel."

"Which suggests that they remain in the Palace," offered Duke Roosarian.

"Agreed," said Duke Stennivere.

"And the other development?" asked Tarin.

"There is a large crowd building around the outskirts of the Colosseum. They've encircled the soldiers."

"Violent?" asked Cornelius, having heard of the deadly riots that were sweeping through the capital on a much too regular basis.

"Not that I've heard," replied Jerad.

"Any idea as to their intentions?" asked Wencel.

"No, Duke Roosarian. But from the reports that the scouts are providing, they are not supporters of the King."

"How can you tell?" asked Cornelius.

"They are chanting for the Volkun, Duke Stennivere. Many are howling like a wolf, the sound drifting through the surrounding streets."

The Duchess and the Dukes looked at one another meaningfully, pleased with this new information. If they moved quickly, they might have a chance to set their trap before the King realized the danger that he faced.

"Then let's get a move on, Sergeant," said Tarin. "The

Protector can be extremely irritating, but he's grown on me since I first met him. I'd hate to see him die just yet."

After their quick conversation at the eastern gate, Noorsin, Wencel, Cornelius, and Tarin pushed ahead with Jerad toward the Palace, the massive structure now no more than a quarter mile away. If all went according to plan, they wouldn't need to breach the gates to gain entrance, having some other options in mind.

Their thoughts were on that next step, mulling those choices to be considered, so it took them some time to realize just how eerily silent the streets were. The city, at least this section of it, appeared to be abandoned. As the soldiers of the allied Duchies rode their horses through the neighborhoods, only a few people could be seen moving about, and they did so quickly. No one wanted to get caught up with the very long line of soldiers heading for Marden Beleron's seat of power.

Right where the street opened into a large plaza, which provided a better view of the monstrosity that served as the ruling center of Caledonia, a large group of soldiers stood at attention in a square formation. Clearly, these men were a company of the Royal Guard, the first they had come across, but as the column of mounted soldiers approached, they made no move for their weapons, instead waiting patiently.

As Noorsin entered the square, Cornelius, Wencel, Tarin, and Jerad right behind her, she raised her hand, giving the command for the column of soldiers to come to a halt, which they did with a practiced precision.

"Soldier, your purpose here?" she asked in her most commanding tone.

"Waiting for you, Duchess Stelekel," responded the man standing in front of the formation. "I am Sergeant Benin,

Duchess. If you would permit me, I can take you to the individuals you are seeking."

"They are in the Palace?" asked Wencel.

"No, Duke Roosarian. But they are near. The Duke and the Lady Winborne are under the protection of the Blademaster."

That information was a surprise, but a welcome one at that. They all knew Captain Jurgen Klines. A man of honor and one to be respected.

"Where is the King, Sergeant?" asked Cornelius.

"He and the Advisor have gone to the Colosseum, Duke Stennivere. Because of that, the Blademaster has taken the liberty of assuming control of the Palace. But I doubt that he is still there."

"Why do you say that?" asked Tarin.

"Because the Lady Winborne has a strong will. She has been most insistent that they make for the Colosseum at all possible speed. I expect that the Captain has acceded to her request and that they are on their way there now."

"That sounds about right," said Tarin, grumbling under his breath, though Noorsin smiled, having heard and agreed with the comment.

"Why should we trust you?" asked Duke Stennivere, always wary, particularly with the good fortune just gifted to them. He had not expected that they would get this far so easily.

"The Blademaster thought that you might be concerned," said Benin. "He guarantees your safety." The Sergeant then pulled a sword from the scabbard on his hip. "He offers his blade as collateral."

"That's good enough for me," said Noorsin, watching as the sunlight flashed off the steel that the Duchess of Murcia had seen before. The etchings in the metal confirmed that it was, indeed, the weapon of Caledonia's Blademaster.

With that, Benin issued a quick command and the square of soldiers turned on their heels and began to march at a fast clip for the main gate of the Corinthian Palace, the Duchess and Dukes following.

"We are also here for the gladiators," said Noorsin, leaning down from her saddle so that Sergeant Benin could hear what she was saying.

"To fight them?" he asked, his tone suggesting that he did not approve that course of action.

"No, Sergeant," replied Duke Stennivere. "To fight with them. I have heard a great deal about this Volkun. I'd like to see him for myself."

Benin smiled, the open gates of the Palace appearing before them. "Then follow me, my Lords and Lady. For the real show has already begun."

30

PUSHING WITH WORDS

Marden had waited in the plaza for more than two hours, his personal guard with him, a half dozen companies of soldiers there as well, although their attention remained focused primarily on the crowd that had inched closer to the white stone of the square. The citizens of Caledonia were becoming much louder and unruly as the Royal Guard made their final attack on the gladiators defending the Colosseum, which began to worry the soldiers charged with protecting the King.

An impetuous and testy person to begin with, Marden began to fear that the people watching behind him would think less of him if he didn't engage in the fight, so finding it difficult to contain his mounting anxiety and not able to wait any longer, he had dismounted from his horse and stomped into the Colosseum, his personal guard trailing him. Finding Sourban proved quite easy since the gladiators had molded the battlefield so effectively in their favor, the Royal Guard only able to attack them from one direction.

The battle had raged for several hours after that, consuming much of the day, the sun now beginning to fall in the sky. Yet still Sourban and his troops had made little progress, unable to crack the strong defense offered by the gladiators. Marden's troops were still stuck fighting in the tunnel, losing a dozen or more soldiers for every foot that they gained.

"Enough, Sourban," said Marden, having lost patience with his Captain's leadership. He had allowed Sourban to implement the strategy that he had suggested, yet it had gotten them very little other than more casualties among the ranks of his soldiers than it should have.

"But my King," protested Sourban. "We are close. We cut at their edges, and soon the rebels won't be able to hold the tunnel. Their numbers will be too few."

"That was your mistake, Sourban," countered Marden. "Your desire to cut at the extremities. We should have gone for the throat right from the beginning."

"My King, please, allow my men to ..."

"Enough, Sourban. Recall them. I wish to speak with our adversaries."

Sighing with displeasure, but having no good reason to disobey his monarch, Sourban issued the command to his Sergeants, who then ordered the soldiers of the Royal Guard fighting in the tunnel to pull back, a duty that took several minutes to complete. The Captain then stepped reluctantly out of the way so that Marden could walk forward. Several soldiers who made up his personal guard remained around him, ready to raise their long shields in case any archers in the back of the gladiators' formation decided to take a shot at him.

Yes, Marden had lost his patience, but he also viewed this as another opportunity to demonstrate his competence, to show that he was in charge. He stopped when he was only twenty feet away from the front row of gladiators, many bloodied, battered, and bruised, yet the men and women of the Colosseum stood there proudly, their expressions suggesting that they had little respect for the man standing before them.

"This foolishness stops now," declared the King of Caledonia. "I demand that you surrender this instant. You have no way to win this fight. Throw down your arms and rather than having you butchered as you deserve, I will allow you to live out the remainder of your miserable existences on the white sand of the Pit."

"We decline your gracious offer," replied Bryen derisively, the Volkun stepping forward from the front rank of gladiators, his well-known double-bladed spear gripped in his hands. "We have no reason to trust you, and we have no desire to make your task any easier. We are here to fight. Are you, Marden Beleron, King of Caledonia, here to fight? Or are you here to talk?"

"You!" exclaimed Marden, recognizing the tall figure standing before him, having come face to face with this gladiator two times in the past and remembering that he had been linked to his betrothed through a Protector's collar, ostensibly to protect her from him. Marden had heard whispers of the Volkun coming from the crowd as he made his way to the Colosseum, but he hadn't expected those rumors to be true.

"Me," Bryen replied simply, his gaze hard and unyielding.

"So the Wolf has returned to his lair," laughed Marden, enjoying what he viewed as the irony of it all. This gladiator had escaped the Pit, yet for some reason he had come back. A desire to die, most likely. Marden would be more than willing to assist in helping this fool achieve that objective. "The last I saw of you, you were a slave."

"But no longer."

"Yes, well, we can fix that," suggested Marden. "Once this is over, if you actually survive, you're going to wish that you were dead rather than a slave." The King shook his head as if he were trying to figure something out. "You know, I still don't understand why you're doing this. You were free, yet you couldn't stay away. Why is that?"

It was then that Lycia stepped next to Bryen on one side, Davin on the other. Recognition blossomed in Marden's mind. He remembered these two. They had been training when he had visited the stockade to learn more about the gladiator that the Duke of the Southern Marches had purchased. The Crimson Devil and the Crimson Giant if he recalled correctly. And now he understood.

"Are you certain you won't consider my offer?" asked Marden. "If not for you, then for your friends." Marden smiled lasciviously at Lycia. "Such a beautiful woman and a fighter to boot. There's no reason for her to die, or any of your friends for that matter. Think hard. I will not give you this chance again."

"Thank you, but no. I know what your word is truly worth, Marden."

The insult bit deeply for the King, the truth of it hitting too closely to the mark. But he knew that losing his temper now wouldn't prove helpful to his efforts.

"I remember meeting you for the first time the night before your combat against the Champion of Sharston," said Marden, trying a different tack. "The Volkun brought to the Palace by my father so that he could be put on display. I wasn't impressed then, you know."

"Neither was I," replied Bryen, the sharpness of his comment causing Marden to curl his lip in annoyance, though the King was able to master the temptation within him that demanded that he punish the commoner who had insulted him once again.

"It was quite a combat," continued Marden, once again in control of himself, if just barely. "I actually lost a good bit of money on you. No one expected you to survive against the undefeated Stil Sheldgard, yet here you are."

"Here I am," answered Bryen. "Perhaps you should have considered that before you sent the Royal Guard against us.

You lost the last time you bet against me. Why risk betting against me now? You'll likely get the same result."

Marden actually laughed at Bryen's comment. "Confident. I like that. I'm sure that quality served you well in the Pit. You made a fool of that muscle-bound Champion. I'll give you that. You made a fool of Duke Sharperson as well." For just a moment, Marden's brow scrunched up as he recalled something that hadn't been top of mind that day. "Talus was coming down here today. Any chance you ran into him?"

"Fancy you should mention that," replied Bryen. "In fact, I did run into him."

"Are you holding him hostage?" wondered Marden. "Because if you are, he's of little value to me. You really have no good way out of this disaster you've created for yourselves other than through my good graces."

"I thought as much," responded Bryen, his already cold eyes somehow becoming even frostier. "When I last saw your friend in the Pit, he challenged me to a combat. He accused me of cheating."

"He did, didn't he. He was a fool."

"He was. Because when I saw him earlier this morning, he challenged me again. I must say, if nothing else he is consistent. Brave as well, since he actually had the courage to match blades with me."

"What happened to him?"

"I killed him." Bryen stepped forward then so that he was no more than two quick steps from driving his spear into Marden's chest, the soldiers standing with the King raising their shields just a little bit higher as their worry increased. But Bryen held his ground as he watched Marden process what he had just told him.

"If I remember correctly, Marden," continued Bryen, "right after that combat against the Champion, when you entered the Pit, you argued with your father for a chance to fight me. You seemed quite confident that you could defeat me. But he wouldn't allow it. King Beleron was worried about his little boy. He didn't believe you had the skill to take me on."

Marden's face turned bright red, his rage coming to the surface. But his fury was evenly divided now between his father, who had humiliated him by not allowing him to fight, and this slave who had just insulted him for a third time in so many minutes.

"But now your father isn't here," prodded Bryen, doing his best to infuriate Marden and hoping that his effort would lead to the desired result. "Now you have a chance to fight me. There is no one here who can protect you from me now. No one to tell you what to do. If you have the courage. Talus Sharperson did. Do you, Marden? Do you have his courage?"

"You are a slave. You are ..."

"Tell me, Marden," said Bryen, cutting off the King. "Do you have the courage to fight me now? Do you have the courage to risk death? Or do you prefer to sit in your box looking down upon the white sand, watching others bleed, watching others die, too frightened to demonstrate your prowess in the Pit? Too frightened to show your people that you are no better than a slave to your fear? Too frightened to reveal that you are actually just a coward?"

A red haze fell across Marden's vision, his fury knowing no bounds. This slave dared to challenge him. Him! The King of Caledonia! He could feel his blood boiling, his rage clearing his mind, hardening his purpose. He wanted to fight this slave. He needed to fight the Volkun. He needed to prove something to his people, to himself. He needed to win.

Then he heard a soft voice whisper into his ear, calming him, diminishing the anger that threatened to explode within him to a more manageable level. Tetric. Marden struggled to regain control over himself, but a few more quiet words, gentle suggestions, from his Advisor played through his mind, quelling the fury within him and allowing him to make a calmer, better decision, because Marden had realized something when dealing with the Volkun. The Wolf was the key. He was the linchpin in the gladiators' defense.

"You can have your freedom right now if you step away from the other gladiators and leave them to their fates," offered Marden, his calculating gaze once more on Bryen. "The Volkun can live. And Tetric tells me that he can remove that collar from your neck, just as he offered to do so before. So not only can you live, but you can be free. Truly free."

Bryen smiled, his scorn barely contained. "You can't give me my freedom. I have earned my freedom already. That's why I'm here. I choose freely to fight now. I choose freely to oppose you. Because it's not freedom that drives me. It never has been. It's choice. I choose to be here. I choose to fight with my friends. I choose to fight you."

"You're a fool, you and all the others," declared Marden. "You have no chance against my Royal Guard. Your deaths are certain."

"We'll see," replied Bryen. "If you want us, come and get us."

"When this is over," began Marden, "I will have you drawn and quartered. I will ..."

"Enough words, Marden," cut in Bryen, wanting to give the King one more push before the clash began again. "Go back to hiding behind your soldiers. Go back to your Advisor so that he can protect you. Cowards don't belong in the Pit."

With a final look of contempt, Bryen turned on his heel, Davin and Lycia following him, leaving the King of Caledonia standing there alone, feeling naked and inept under the scornful gazes of the gladiators who had fought his vaunted Royal Guard to a standstill.

31

BLOOD IN THE TUNNEL

When Marden ordered his soldiers forward once again, Declan sought to energize his gladiators, his appeal galvanizing them to even greater efforts: "You are gladiators. You stand. You fight. You die. That's who you are. That's what you do. Do it well!"

The fighters from the Pit had heard those words before, just as they had heard almost all of Declan's sayings so often during their time in the Colosseum. But they took what he said to heart. They used his exhortation because they needed it. They needed anything that would help them to continue their resistance, because the fighting was growing graver by the minute. Although the Guard suffered mightily in their efforts to penetrate the gladiators' line, the rebels were few to begin with, and every time one of the gladiators fell dead or wounded, their circumstances became more dire, the odds of the Guard overrunning them increasing.

Whenever a gap appeared in the gladiators' formation, Davin, Lycia, and Bryen rushed forward, stepping into the breach, giving their comrades the time that they needed to close the hole. All sense of time disappeared. The only hint of the passing day was the lengthening shadows kissing the western entrance to the tunnel. For the gladiators, there was only motion and instinct, screams of rage and shouts of pain, fears and hopes battling within their mind, all coming together in a never-ending dance in which they taunted death, doing all that they could to hold back the Royal Guard's advance, but knowing as well that eventually death would find them. It was inevitable.

All they were doing now was fighting for time. Just a little bit longer with every jab of a spear or slash of a sword. Just a little bit longer with every thrust of a dagger or release of an arrow.

They were at peace with the fact that they would die for the Volkun -- they could think of no better end -- and they promised themselves that they would not disappoint him. They would give every last ounce of strength, every last drop of blood, because they chose to do so.

Yet despite the gladiators' efforts, Bryen could sense it now, the realization beginning to set in that their lethal resistance was coming to an end. As their numbers dwindled, they gave up precious space in the tunnel. Once they were pushed back toward the Pit and into the lower levels of the Colosseum, they would be done for. The soldiers would be able to attack from multiple sides and simply overwhelm them.

Bryen wasn't ready to allow that to happen. Not yet. And as he watched Asaia, a woman he had known for several years, a woman who he had helped to train, take a sword thrust to the shoulder, forcing her to step back from the line, a cold fury began to burn within Bryen, an anger that he had rarely felt while fighting on the white sand.

Then, he had maintained his composure just as Declan had taught him, staying calm regardless of whatever danger he might face, using his composure to his advantage. But now, he couldn't do that. Now, he had to give in to his fury. To give in to the emotion that he had repressed for so long. He needed to harness it. He needed to give the men and women fighting with him one more chance to show that although they may have been made slaves, in their hearts they were free.

"We will stand fast!" shouted Bryen, just as he had earlier in the day, his words echoing down the stone tunnel and drifting out into the square for all to hear. "We will stand strong! We will stand free!"

Bryen then charged forward, stepping beyond the line, becoming a whirlwind of steel, his spear spinning through the air, the double blades on each end dripping with dark red blood as he forced his way in among the attacking soldiers. For several seconds he was alone, cut off from his friends, a terrifying figure bringing death to all those foolish enough to challenge him. But then Declan was there, his sword singing through the air with every slash, broadening the space that Bryen had created for himself. Davin and Lycia joined them, the twins covered in blood, very little of it their own, the Crimson Giant and the Crimson Devil staying true to the names bestowed upon them by the crowd.

That's when Bryen sensed it, a subtle shift in the Royal Guard fighting in the shaft. An uncomfortable feeling of indecision rippled through the soldiers, and then seemingly as one they took a step back, followed by another. As the column of soldiers began to retreat slowly but steadily, Dorlan joined Bryen, followed by the wounded Asaia, and Kollea, and then all the gladiators stepped forward as one. With an inexorable will, their wall of steel pushed the soldiers back, step by step, the gladiators stepping over the dead littering the floor, until they had almost forced the soldiers of the Royal Guard completely out of the tunnel, the fading light in the east beckoning to them, calling to them. The men and women of the Pit would not be denied. Step by step, they scraped their way toward the tunnel entrance.

"Stop this, Sourban!" demanded a livid Marden. "Stop this!" The King of Caledonia had been standing behind the soldiers fighting in the tunnel and now he'd been forced back out onto the main concourse of the Colosseum to fall once again under the gaze of the swelling crowd. "My soldiers must not retreat! They must advance! They must always advance!"

The Captain of the Royal Guard ignored his King, believing that Marden didn't understand the normal flow of battle. But a small part of him, the part that often offered useful warnings of approaching danger, agreed with the King. It should not be this difficult for his soldiers to defeat the gladiators. His troops should have crushed the rebels by now, yet to those who were watching at the far end of the plaza, it appeared that the gladiators were winning the day.

Even through the clamor of battle, even as he continued to push forward, his friends and fellow gladiators fighting by his side, Bryen heard the King demanding that his Captain counterattack and drive the gladiators back. But that wasn't going to happen. Not in this moment. As he drove the sharp steel of the Spear of the Magii into the chest of a soldier who overextended on a sword thrust, the unfortunate man leaving himself exposed, and then whipped his weapon back around so that the other blade sliced through the neck of the soldier who had stepped forward to take his fallen comrade's place, losing his head for his diligence, Bryen realized that the gladiators had won this skirmish. But he also knew that in the end it wouldn't be enough.

His gladiators had given everything that they had to force back the Royal Guard. They would not be able to do so again. They were almost spent, physically and mentally. They were down to no more than a hundred fighters now, the other half having fought and died. The next time the Royal Guard attacked, the gladiators would be slaughtered and their short-lived rebellion would be swept into the annals of history.

32

THE DUEL

"What do you think, Declan?"

Bryen stood a few feet in front of the other gladiators, talking quietly with his friend and mentor. Both were tired, blood dripping down their arms and legs. Some of it their own, most of it belonging to the soldiers they'd been fighting since before the sun had risen. The Royal Guard stood in the concourse, the gladiators having regained control of the tunnel. But though they had proven successful in retaking the space that they had lost, they knew what was going to happen next. The Caledonian soldiers would charge once again, Sourban already massing his troops, and this time the Guard would likely shatter the gladiators' defense through the sheer force of their greater numbers.

"I think we've put up a good fight."

"Agreed," said Bryen. "But ..."

Declan sighed. "But you know as well as I do, lad. It's a numbers' game now. We're running out of fighters, and that means that we're running out of time."

"I'm sorry, Declan," said Bryen, his eyes becoming watery. "I thought this would work, that help would arrive. I didn't want to bring us to this point."

Declan looked at Bryen with a warm smile, then grasped his shoulder affectionately. "You didn't bring this on us. You said it yourself when you confronted Marden. It comes down to choice. Just as you chose to be with us here today, we chose to be here with you. This was our choice. Don't try to take it away from us."

Bryen nodded sheepishly, not realizing what he was doing and regretting it. "Sorry, Declan, that wasn't my intention."

"I know that, lad. I know." Declan looked across the space separating the gladiators from the soldiers. The men and women of the Pit had fought like demons, but only so much could be expected of them when they were so heavily outnumbered. He appreciated that Bryen was looking for some way to save his gladiators, but their current course wasn't it. For a moment, he wondered if another path might give them a chance of escaping their doom. It was slim at best, more like nonexistent in fact, but why not give it a shot? They had nothing to lose. "We can never win this fight with steel, no matter how much more skilled we are in arms. But perhaps we can win this another way."

"What do you mean, Declan?"

"Words, lad. Perhaps we can get what we want with words." Declan stepped in close to the young man he viewed as a son. "Your words with Marden were just as cutting as your blade. They wounded the King deeply. Marden is a cunning, devious backstabber who knows how to use his power, but he is also insecure and unsure of himself, and you were hitting him where it hurt. Maybe if you try again, and you use the right words, you might get the chance to actually cut that arrogant bastard with your blade and give your friends a little more time to do what they need to do."

Bryen grinned maliciously. There was no harm in trying

again. Besides, even if it didn't work, his efforts would buy his gladiators just a few more minutes to prepare for the final battle, which was really all that they could hope for now.

"Are you still afraid of a slave?" called out Bryen, his words reverberating in the tunnel as he stepped closer to the massing soldiers, the King standing next to Sourban at the back of the company. "Are you frightened by a lowly gladiator, Marden? Still too scared to cross blades with me?"

Marden stalked toward Bryen, stopping when he stood with the front rank of his soldiers.

"You will address me with respect!" demanded Marden. "I am your King!"

"Respect is earned, not given," replied Bryen in a soft voice that still traveled throughout the tunnel and into the plaza so that all could hear. "Tell me, Marden. Why should I respect you? We are exactly where we were just a few hours ago and nothing has changed within this tunnel. You have achieved nothing but the deaths of a good number of your soldiers. Men who didn't deserve to die. And while your soldiers have died, you have hidden behind them. Watching the fight. Not fighting yourself. Allowing them to bleed for you."

Bryen saw that his words caught the attention not only of his gladiators, but also the soldiers forming back into ranks. Several of the Royal Guard who had fought the gladiators for most of the day had expressions that suggested that they agreed with the leader of the rebels. Their King, supposedly a fearless master of the blade, had not risked himself, only their blood having been spilled. That realization sent an unexpected, unsettling murmur of discontent through the soldiers that was not lost on the King.

"You are a gladiator," replied Marden, his voice a hiss as his anger began to build once again. "I am a King. I am a general. Therefore, I must lead. I don't have time to waste fighting you and the scum of the Pit."

"You are a coward!" Bryen said harshly, his words striking Marden like a slap to the face. "The best leaders lead from the front. They do not hide behind their troops. They fight with them."

Another murmur of dissent rumbled through the assembling soldiers, the Volkun's words having their intended effect. None of the soldiers could disagree with what the blood-soaked gladiator had said, because he was only speaking the truth.

"How dare you!" Marden's face turned red with rage, Sourban worrying that his King was about to throw an apoplectic fit. "You are not worth my time, slave. I don't waste my time fighting the dregs of Caledonian society. I don't ..."

"And yet your soldiers are forced to do what you are afraid to do yourself," cut in Bryen. "You are afraid to bloody your sword. You are afraid to fight us. You are afraid to fight me."

"I am not afraid!" protested Marden shrilly, but his words were lost in the grumbles beginning to rumble through the soldiers just outside the tunnel.

"And what of your people, Marden? You have quite a crowd just beyond the plaza. Are you afraid of them?"

"I am not afraid of my people."

"Are you afraid that your people think more of the Volkun than they do their King? That they think more of a gladiator than the inept ruler of their land?"

"My people love me!"

"Then why disappoint them? Why not give them the spectacle that they really want?"

"You are beneath me gladiator. I do not fight slaves!"

"I am a free man, a slave no more," Bryen replied, nodding as he took in the King as if for the first time, weighing him, measuring him, and with a disappointed shake of his head finding him wanting. The gesture only aggravated Marden all the more. "I can see it in your eyes, Marden. You are afraid of me. Even more, you are afraid that your father was right. You are afraid that you are not man enough to kill me."

"I am not afraid of you! You are no more than a bug to be crushed beneath my boot."

Sourban tried to intercede then, to stop Marden from moving down a dangerous path, as he could sense how this altercation was turning, the Volkun deftly working his way beneath the King's skin.

"Please, my King. Do not allow this gladiator to sway you. He is seeking to manipulate you." But Sourban's warning was lost on Marden, who had been entrapped by Bryen's web of words.

"You are afraid of me," continued Bryen with a soft chuckle, overriding what Marden was about to say. "Come now, Marden. Have you lost your spine now that you sit on the throne? When I fought the Champion of Sharston and killed him, you challenged me. You wanted to fight me. But your father wouldn't permit it, and you allowed him to do that to you. It made you look the coward. But I know you, Marden. I know you still want to fight me. Then again, perhaps that's all it is. A dream, since you're too much of a coward to challenge me."

"I had to obey my father. I had no choice!"

Bryen realized then that he had the King, that he had hooked Marden with his lure, so he tried to entangle him with just one more loop of his trap. "Your father isn't with us anymore. He's not here to protect you. You can't hide behind him. If you don't have the courage to fight me, Marden, then everyone here will know that it was you who chose not to step onto the white sand. Everyone will know that you truly are the coward that I know you are. There is no one to hide behind now, Marden. There is no way to prevent your people from seeing the coward that you are."

Bryen understood that he had pushed as far as he could. Now all he could do was to hope and to give Marden a little time as a series of conflicting emotions played across the King's face, Marden so infuriated that for a moment he could not speak. And that's when Bryen offered his final barb.

"Once you challenged me to a combat, Marden. Yet you weren't allowed to fight me. Your father knew the truth. He knew what would happen to you if you fought me on the white sand."

"I would have killed you!" screamed Marden, his building rage bursting forth. "I would have spilled your blood and laughed while I was doing it."

"Then prove it," said Bryen in a very soft voice. "I challenge you, our brave King of Caledonia, to a combat in the Pit. Do you have the courage to accept? Or will you continue to hide behind your soldiers?"

THE SOLDIERS loyal to the Blademaster walked through the tunnel, blades drawn, the Lady of the Southern Marches and her father walking in their midst, two Magii striding right behind them. With such an escort, Jurgen Klines had little to fear as they strode by the dead, most of them soldiers of the Royal Guard, their bodies pushed up against the side of the entrance.

They had arrived at the plaza just minutes after King Beleron had declared a truce with the gladiators, having accepted the Volkun's challenge to duel on the white sand. As part of the agreement, only one company of the Royal Guard was permitted in the Colosseum, the others required to stand at attention in the square. The gladiators had formed a ring around the top of the Pit so that they could look down on the white sand, honoring the young man who would be fighting for them. The hardened warriors stood there stoically, not saying a word, still as the stone statues carved into the exterior of the Colosseum.

The Blademaster directed the Lady Winborne and her father to the front row, placing his soldiers around them, wanting to ensure their protection. Then he watched with some amazement as the people of Tintagel began streaming through the only open tunnel into the Colosseum, filling the rows of seats above them, climbing over tons of rubble to get to the other sections of the stadium that had been blocked off from the inside.

As part of his agreement with the Volkun, in addition to granting the gladiators their freedom if Bryen won, the King had to permit the citizens of Tintagel to watch the fight. Marden had balked at the first, only acceding when he realized his refusal to do so would demonstrate a lack of faith in his own abilities, and he happily accepted the second, because he wanted as many people as possible watching when he killed the Volkun. Word would spread quickly through the capital, strengthening his rule.

"Quite impressive," said Rafia as she scanned the destruction of the eleven other tunnels that led into the stadium and forced the incoming spectators to make various detours around the ruins to find open seats, many of the benches in the lower rows missing.

"Quite impressive indeed," said Sirius, a hint of pride in his voice. The only way the other tunnels and corridors could have been blocked so thoroughly and so quickly without taking down the entire Colosseum was through the careful application of the Talent. The old Magus felt a touch of pride, his and Rafia's lessons obviously benefiting Bryen. The young man was learning the precision that they had been seeking to teach him.

"Why not just use the Talent during the fight in the tunnel?" asked Rafia. "Or to kill the King for that matter?"

She was the type of person who was always looking for the

most direct solution to every problem. As Sirius liked to describe it, Rafia preferred to use a hammer, whether she needed to hit a nail or a person. It got the job done, though the consequences weren't always what you wanted.

"The lad isn't trying to just kill the King," replied Sirius. "He needs to handle the situation with greater delicacy. He's trying to start a rebellion. Fighting as a Magus, he can't do that. But fighting as the Volkun, a gladiator of the people, he can."

Rafia nodded, reluctantly agreeing with Sirius' logic. She much preferred a swift, decisive approach. "Makes sense. Although I doubt that I could exercise as much control as Bryen has so far."

"You and me both," agreed Sirius.

"The Duke and his daughter should be safe," said the Blademaster, who came to stand next to them and broke into their conversation once his soldiers were positioned exactly as he desired.

"Of that I have no doubt, Captain Klines," said Rafia. "The men with us as well as the five hundred in the square serve as quite the deterrent."

"And the thousand more you've hidden among the crowd lining the plaza should be useful as well if a quick escape is needed," agreed Sirius.

"Yes, but I still wish Lady Winborne had left the city as you requested," said Klines. "It would have eliminated a great deal of the risk."

"I can't disagree with you, Blademaster," said Sirius. "During the years that I've served her, I've learned many things about the Lady of the Southern Marches. First and foremost is the fact that she can be more stubborn than a mule."

"It didn't take me long to discover that as well," agreed Klines.

"Are you calling me a mule, Sirius?" asked Aislinn, who had

lifted her gaze from the white sand to stare at the old Magus with a hard glare.

"No, Aislinn," answered Rafia. "He said that you were like a mule."

"Is there much difference in that?" Aislinn challenged.

Rafia smiled. "I guess that would depend on your perspective."

Not wanting to get sidetracked by a circular conversation with two Magii, Aislinn grumbled her disagreement and then turned her attention back to the Pit, desperate to catch a glimpse of Bryen. Her anxiety was rolling off her in waves, something that the Blademaster noticed.

"Do not fear, Lady Winborne," consoled the Blademaster, sensing her worry. "The only one who should be afraid is the King."

"Is there any way to stop this?" asked Kevan. His greatest fear was that Tetric would somehow convince Marden to not go through with the combat. Having watched the Protector in the training circle multiple times, he believed that he knew the outcome of the combat before it even began.

But Aislinn wasn't as confident as her father. In part because of her concern for Bryen, but also because of something that he had explained to her many times in the practice yard. Each combat was different, and anything could happen. A slip. A fall. The sun blinding you at the worst possible moment. A lucky strike. You can only control so much in a combat, and there was no certainty other than the fact that someone would die. But it wasn't always the combatant that you expected. And the thought of Tetric allowing the duel to actually take place worried her. She understood the power that he controlled, the dark power that frightened her. He would not have allowed the duel to move forward unless he had something to gain ... or some way to ensure the outcome was the one that he wanted.

"There isn't," she replied. "It would make Marden appear

weak, and he certainly doesn't want that. This is the only way that this could end."

Rafia nodded. "Agreed. And there is only one way this will end."

"Which means we need to be ready," said the Blademaster.

"Why?" asked Aislinn. "There are no guarantees that Bryen will win."

"Maybe not, Lady Winborne," replied the Blademaster. "I am not a betting man, but were I to put a wager on this combat, then I would put it on the Volkun. When your Protector kills the King, we don't know what's going to happen, and that bothers me a great deal."

MARDEN BELERON, King of Caledonia, strode into the Pit with a cocky grin and a saunter that suggested that he owned the world. Perhaps in his own mind he did. His leather armor, dyed white so that he was always visible no matter where he was in a combat, flashed every time it caught the fading sunlight.

"I am your King!" shouted Marden as he walked around Bryen in a wide circle.

The Volkun stood calmly on the white sand, Spear of the Magii in his hands, bloodied and battered, his black leather armor scarred in a dozen places to match the wounds on his arms and legs. He watched Marden with a hint of amusement. Apparently, the King believed that this combat was just another part of the show. Bryen would do his best to dissuade him of that perspective.

"I am your King!" Marden called again, raising his hands above his head, his right holding a two-handed broadsword that had been passed down from the first Beleron to rule Caledonia. "Cheer for your King, citizens of Caledonia! Cheer for the King who will kill the Volkun!"

Marden's shouts echoed throughout the Colosseum, yet he didn't receive the reaction that he craved. Instead of the cheers, instead of the screams of adoration and joy, much like his pilgrimage from the Corinthian Palace to the arena, the fifty thousand people who had pushed their way into the stadium greeted his proclamations with absolute silence. The stillness and quiet of the crowd threatened to unnerve Marden. The hard stares of the people he could pick out in the first few rows made him think that these citizens of Caledonia were not spectators, but rather a jury, and he was the person on trial, not the traitorous Volkun. These commoners would weigh his guilt and announce their sentence at the conclusion of the combat.

"If you're done acting the fool, perhaps we could get started," proposed Bryen, who had remained where he was, a sardonic rise of his eyebrow indicating that he was less than impressed with Marden's antics. The watching crowd appeared to agree with him, as a loud chuckle rippled through the spectators, Bryen's words traveling to the highest reaches of the stadium.

Marden's cocky grin twisted into a sneer as he came to a stop no more than ten feet away from the Volkun.

"You have disrespected me for the last time," said the King, charging toward Bryen, his heavy sword pulled back behind his right shoulder, Marden trying for a killing blow right from the start of the duel.

But rather than Marden's steel cutting halfway through the Volkun, the King stumbled, his momentum carrying him farther across the sand than he wanted when Bryen sidestepped out of the way, the long blade slashing harmlessly into the white sand.

"If that's the best that you can do, Marden, this is going to be a very quick fight," suggested Bryen, who had circled back around the King and now stood behind him after avoiding his initial strike.

"You seek to make me look the fool?" challenged Marden, his voice a raspy hiss that revealed his rising anger. "I won't permit it!"

The King then launched into a series of slashes and cuts, Marden often swinging wildly as the weight of the blade that he rarely used threw him off balance. He had thought that with a weapon such as this, he need only land one strike to cut the Volkun in two. But that strategy was proving more difficult than he had anticipated. The Volkun was fast he admitted grudgingly. Faster than he had remembered.

"I need not," replied Bryen. "You seem to be making a fool of yourself all on your own." His words brought another bout of laughter from the crowd.

Bryen continued to dance away from his overconfident opponent, Marden unable to catch up to him as he glided across the white sand. And through it all, silence reigned in the Colosseum, the spectators watching with interest, but choosing not to engage as they would if this were a duel that was a part of the gladiatorial games. For several minutes more, Marden attacked the Volkun. Most of the time, Bryen simply stepped out of the way, easily avoiding his adversary's attacks. In a few instances, Bryen parried a blow with the haft of his spear, just to remind Marden that he was still there.

As the combat continued, Bryen watched a weariness seep into the King, his shoulders beginning to slump a bit, his movements becoming a bit slower. It was what he had expected. Marden was a good fighter. He had benefited from excellent training. But he had never fought in the Pit before. And he had never been taught how to fight by the Master of the Gladiators.

After several more minutes of ineffective attacks, Marden finally stopped, resting his sword on his shoulder as he stared across the sand at the Volkun. Bryen saw that there was a touch of reluctant understanding appearing behind Marden's eyes. A touch of resignation mixed with miscalculation and fear. The

King was beginning to recognize that he may have bit off more than he could chew.

"Why sacrifice yourself for a people who enslaved you?" asked Marden. "Why give yourself to those who only want to see your blood? Who want to see your death? Is it not better to live? To be free? Tetric can help you. You need only ask. You need only ask your King for your freedom and you can live the life that you've always wanted."

Whether the King was trying to buy some additional time to rest or he was seeking some way to end the combat without his own blood covering the white sand, Bryen didn't know and he didn't care, but he decided to humor Marden, nonetheless.

"If I need to give my blood to ensure that you're removed from the throne, then I'll gladly do so. Because that's what I want, Marden. That's what I want from you. I want to see you dragged from the Pit."

Having learned Marden's habits, Bryen concluded that now was the time to take control of this combat. Now was the time to show Marden that titles counted for very little on the white sand. King. Gladiator. Neither word mattered. The only thing that mattered in the Pit was who was still standing at the end of the combat, and a title wasn't going to decide that. Skill, practical knowledge, and strength of will would be the determining factors, something that Bryen had learned through hard experience. And now it was time for the King to do the same.

Feinting to his left with his spear, Bryen pivoted and turned, bringing his weapon back around. Marden identified Bryen's intended attack too late, trying to raise his blade in time, but failing to do so. The King hissed more in anger than pain when the Volkun's spear sliced through his leather armor and across his side, leaving a bloody slash in its wake that colored his white armor a bright red. But Marden didn't have time to ponder the severity of his wound, as the Volkun forced him to backpedal quickly, maintaining his attack, the double-bladed spear twisting and turning in a mesmerizing web of steel.

AISLINN WATCHED the first few minutes of the combat between Bryen and Marden with growing confidence, recognizing immediately that her Protector was the better fighter, just as she had expected. Still, worry plagued her. She worried for Bryen's safety, and she wondered why Marden would put himself at risk in such a way. Was it simply arrogance? Or was there something more to it?

She wished that she could go down to the white sand to help Bryen. But she couldn't. Aislinn could only watch as the two combatants moved around the Pit.

For several minutes, the combat reminded Aislinn of what it was like when she was first training with Bryen in the circle. Bryen moving easily around the ring while she tried to score a hit. She could see that Marden was growing more frustrated. His anger never far from the surface to begin with, he appeared to be struggling not only to gain a strike on Bryen, but at the same time to control his worsening temper.

Then in an instant, Aislinn sensed a change. She didn't know what had caused it, but rather than Bryen dodging easily out of the way of Marden's attacks, instead he began to use the haft and the blades of his spear to deflect what was clearly a much swifter assault by the King. The weight of his heavy sword didn't appear to be bothering Marden as it once did and his step was lighter, the King moving across the sand with just as much dexterity as Bryen.

What could be the cause of this? When she had dueled Marden, once in the practice yard, the other time on the white sand, he had never moved so easily or so well. Yet now Bryen fought desperately to keep the King's heavy sword from cutting into him, having little chance to attack as he understood the likely result if Marden's blade struck home just once.

"They started without us?" asked a familiar voice with a slight touch of humor from just behind Aislinn and her father. "They were supposed to wait for us to arrive."

"Noorsin!" exclaimed Kevan, who turned in surprise and then picked up the Duchess of Murcia, pulling her to him for a hug, his large arms wrapping around her thin frame.

"Kevan, you're crushing me," she whispered into his chest.

"My apologies," replied Kevan, reluctantly letting her go. But before he did so, he kissed her gently on the lips, his open affection shocking her and those watching, never having seen the Duke of the Southern Marches act in such a way before. "I am so glad to see you. I did not want to leave you in the library, but I had no choice."

"I know, Kevan." Her fingers brushed the black steel of the collar around his neck. "Tetric has much to pay for."

"Indeed he does," agreed Kevan. "I see that you've brought some friends."

Wencel Roosarian and Cornelius Stennivere appeared right behind Noorsin, both offering their hands in greeting to the Duke of the Southern Marches.

"If you don't mind, Kevan, I can do without the hug and the kiss," said Wencel with a chuckle, his comment setting Noorsin's face ablaze.

Kevan laughed as well, glad to have more allies in Tintagel.

"If you're here, what's going on in the plaza?" he asked.

"Everything is under control," said the Duke of the Three Rivers. He provided an abridged version of what had happened once the combined forces of the Southern Marches, the Three Rivers, Roo's Nest, and Murcia appeared in the square, the soldiers of the Royal Guard realizing that in a matter of minutes the odds had shifted against them. Rather than having to fight no more than a few hundred gladiators as had been the case when the day began, they now faced an opponent with twice as many soldiers as they did.

"Captain Tentillin has everything well in hand for now," said the Duke of Roo's Nest. "The Royal Guard will not be a problem. The soldiers loyal to Captain Klines did what little persuading was necessary. Most of the Royal Guard sensed the change in the wind and chose not to stand against it."

"Yes, Benin and my other Sergeants can be quite convincing when need be," said the Blademaster, who had been listening intently, though his eyes never left the Pit. "I will help you with the Guard once this combat is done."

"Are you all right?" asked Kevan, his worry revealed in his voice as he gazed at Noorsin. The last he had seen of the Duchess of Murcia, she was curled against the wall of his library, bleeding from her nose with a savage wound on her head, her breathing sporadic at best.

"I am," Noorsin replied with a smile. "Aislinn's young Protector healed me." Before Kevan could ask the questions that were on the tip of his tongue, she looked down at the combat, watching Bryen glide across the Pit, Marden Beleron in close pursuit, sparks falling to the sand every time one of the gladiator's blades parried the King's sword. "But that young man is not all right."

"What do you mean?" asked Aislinn and Sirius, both at the same time.

"Can't you sense it?"

Aislinn was the first to understand, realizing with a cold shiver of fear why Marden's ability to fight had improved so dramatically after struggling for so long against her Protector. Opening herself to the Talent, her senses becoming more acute, her stomach threatened to revolt when she focused her attention on Marden. It was the same rancid taste of evil that she had first experienced when she had fought the Elder Ghoule on the coastal road in the Southern Marches and then again at the Aeyrie. Dark Magic!

Sirius' face turned as dark as a thundercloud, his eyes so hot they could set a forest on fire.

"I will deal with this," he said harshly, "just as I should have long ago."

The old Magus turned and stalked toward the tunnel leading away from the Pit, heading directly for the source of the Curse.

At first, Bryen was surprised by the turn of events on the white sand. He didn't believe that Marden had been holding back at the beginning of the combat, but he didn't have much time to think about it, his focus instead on defending against the King's now freakishly fast attack.

So as Bryen fought based solely on instinct, not thinking, just doing, his body moving naturally in response to the cuts, slashes, and thrusts that Marden sent his way thanks to the hours upon hours of training that had been ingrained within him as a gladiator, he allowed his mind to drift. There had to be a cause as to why the King suddenly had become swifter in his movements, more precise, more clinical, more deadly. Somehow, Marden had become a better fighter in just an instant.

The grimace that had graced Marden's countenance since the beginning of the combat, when the King had come to the realization that he had badly misjudged his opponent, now twisted into a maniacal grin. What had happened to the King? How had the situation changed so drastically so quickly? Then Bryen saw it, and he couldn't say that he was surprised. Behind Marden's eyes, he glimpsed the tiny spark of black. The Curse!

It had to be Tetric. Somehow the King's Advisor had infused Marden with Dark Magic. Marden might not even know that Tetric had done it, and he probably didn't care at the moment, because the Dark Magic coursing through the King's veins had just made Marden a much more formidable adversary. One with a very real chance of killing Bryen.

Backing away from Marden as the King continued to attack him, Bryen raised the haft of his spear above his head to prevent Marden from bringing his heavy blade down onto his head and splitting it open like a melon, then glanced up into the crowd. He didn't see much beyond the gladiators lining the lip of the Pit, unable to take his eyes from Marden for more than a split-second for fear of falling victim to his next attack. But he did glimpse Sirius storming off, so hopefully the old Magus had reached the same conclusion that Bryen had.

There was nothing that Bryen could do about the deadly dilemma that he faced at the moment as he slid his spear across Marden's blade and then rolled to his right, gaining just a little bit of space before the King came at him again. He'd leave Tetric to Sirius. Now, Bryen needed to focus on staying alive, and that meant steering clear of the massive sword Marden swung through the air is if it was no more than a reed.

"STAYING IN THE SHADOWS," said Sirius as he placed himself in the middle of the entrance to the tunnel, nothing but dim shapes to be seen beyond the brighter glow that revealed the exit onto the main concourse at the far end. "Just as you did when we were growing up. Keeping everyone in the dark. Assuming that you could gain more for yourself by never revealing what you were doing. So that you could never be held accountable."

The old Magus only had to wait a few seconds for the hidden shape to emerge from the darkness of the tunnel, standing no more than a dozen feet away.

"Why do it?" asked Sirius. "I taught you everything that I knew. I tried to help you in any way that I could. We could have accomplished so much if we had worked together. You were a Magus. There was so much more for you if you had stuck to that path. But you couldn't, could you? Your greed and your envy got in the way."

Sirius would have continued his diatribe, but the words stuck in his throat. There was something about this encounter that sent a shiver of fear down his spine. In all their previous arguments, Tetric had never been able to stay quiet, always breaking in, defending himself, always attempting to justify his decisions and actions. But he hadn't said a word, Tetric only staring at Sirius, his body still in shadow, most of his face still concealed.

Then a strangled cackle erupted from Tetric, the King's Advisor taking a few more steps closer to the Magus. Tetric looked no different outwardly than he ever had before but for one feature, one key characteristic that revealed the depths for which the King's Advisor had sunk in search of more power.

Sirius stared into Tetric's eyes. The humanity was gone. Tetric's eyes were pure black orbs, the Curse swirling within them like a black mist that moved at the whim of the wind. In that instant, Sirius realized that his brother was gone, never to be seen again.

Feelings of rage and sorrow warred within the old Magus, but he pushed down both. Reaching for the Talent, he crafted a shield of white energy just as Tetric flung a bolt of darkness toward him.

"Is that the best that you can do, slave?" demanded Marden as he swung his ancestral blade down toward Bryen's neck. "Is this all that the famed Volkun has to offer? Will you continue to run from me? Will you not stand and fight? Will you not stand before me now and accept that your death is just moments away?"

Bryen ignored the King's running commentary, blocking Marden's long sword with the haft of his spear and then spinning away. As he did so, he brought the blade of his spear that was closest to the ground up swiftly in an underhanded blow, the sharp steel targeting Marden's groin. If the slash had connected, it would have meant an agonizing end for the King of Caledonia, but with an incredibly fast recovery Marden got his sword down just in time, parrying the deadly strike with a clatter of steel that echoed throughout the Colosseum.

"I thought that this would be much more difficult," taunted Marden as he strolled around the Pit, his words carrying easily to all the onlookers who still remained strangely silent. "But it seems that your reputation will precede you into the grave. You thought all of these people came here to see you kill me? They didn't! They came here to see me! Their King! They came here to see me kill the Wolf!"

Marden launched himself at Bryen once again, his heavy sword cutting and slashing through the air, Bryen dodging, ducking, and deflecting as needed, sparks flashing in the dying light of the day when steel met steel. Time after time the King tried to force Bryen back up against the wall of the Pit, thereby limiting his options for escape and allowing Marden to finish the gladiator more easily. But even though the King fought with an unearthly speed and strength, it still wasn't enough. It still wasn't enough to kill the Volkun.

Calm and focused, Bryen ignored the King's attempts to distract him, Marden's arrogance and spite barely a whisper in the back of his mind. Bryen saw nothing but his opponent and the heavy sword that he wielded, the Protector twisting and turning with an agility that reminded many of the spectators why they had named him the Volkun in the first place. In their eyes, it was as if the hunter pursued the wolf, but this wolf refused to go easily, evading every trap the hunter set for him. Bryen refused to give up. He refused to allow Marden to gain what he wanted. He refused to let Marden take Aislinn for his own.

But what was he to do? Whatever advantages Bryen had enjoyed had been negated by the Curse, the black spark pulsing behind Marden's eyes confirming the contaminated gift that Tetric had bequeathed to him.

He needed a moment to think, to consider his options, to find a solution, so Bryen slashed with his spear, the steel skittering across Marden's blade as he expected. But he wasn't finished. Instead of disengaging, he continued his attack, Bryen's spear slicing through the air for Marden's neck. The King responded with an almost inhuman speed to block the blow, but Marden realized too late that it was a feint, Bryen pulling back the spear and instead slashing across the King's thigh, leaving a long line of red that soaked into his white leather armor.

The King screamed in both anger and pain as he stumbled back, never expecting to have been wounded in such a way after spending so much time chasing the Volkun around the Pit. For just a few seconds the taunts and curses came to an end, Marden taking a few seconds to assess the wound. That gave Bryen the time that he needed to contemplate his next and most likely final step.

Because the Curse ran rampant through the King, Bryen realized that there was only one way to defeat him. There was only one way that Bryen could leave the Pit alive.

Reaching for the Talent, Bryen enjoyed the warmth of the natural magic of the world flooding into him. Then he did as he had done so many times before during the last few months under the careful eye of both Sirius and Rafia. He accessed the Seventh Stone. For just a split second, he almost lost himself within the immense power contained within the artifact that had merged with him, both the Talent and the Curse calling to him, wanting to be used, the Curse caressing the thin boundary of the Talent that Bryen always kept in place around that tainted magic so that he wouldn't be corrupted by it himself.

As the two opposing magics coursed within him, he knew that he could kill Marden with the power that he currently controlled in the blink of an eye. But that's not what he wanted. That would defeat the purpose of why he had returned to Tintagel in the first place. He wanted to show the people in the stands that the King was no more than a man, no better than them but for the privilege that he had been born to, and to do that he needed to kill him like he would any other man. With steel. Not with the Talent or the Curse. But before he could accomplish that task, he needed to do something first.

Exercising a very delicate control over the energy flowing within him, Bryen opened himself to the power of the Seventh Stone just as he did on the pier at Haven when he fought the Elder Ghoules. In his mind, what he was doing most closely resembled a physick inserting a needle to inject medicine, but in this case, he would be doing the opposite, seeking to extract a poison. And that's what he did now, latching the power of the Seventh Stone onto Marden, then allowing that ancient force to drain the Curse from the King. The task was completed in less than a second, but taking in the power gifted to Marden made Bryen stagger, leading to several worried gasps from the watching crowd. It took Bryen a few seconds more to become accustomed to the additional corrupted energy that had become a part of him, that had become a part of the Seventh Stone.

"What's the matter, slave? Can't speak in front of your betters?" Marden smiled grimly, ignoring the wound in his thigh and approaching the Volkun with an arrogance that was visible to all who watched the combat.

The King of Caledonia was going to say more, but the words that wanted to pour forth got caught in his throat as a sickening recognition hit him. Marden stared at Bryen in nauseating understanding. How it was possible, he didn't know. But that cold power, that energizing strength that he needed to fight and kill the Volkun, had vanished. And somehow it was the Volkun who had stolen it from him.

"I don't talk to dead men," replied Bryen, who just then saw the black spark behind Marden's eyes wink out.

The Volkun's eyes narrowed. He had suffered enough of the King of Caledonia. He had experienced enough fighting in the Pit. Now was the time to end it. Swinging his spear toward Marden's wounded thigh, the King managed to raise his sword just in time to block the blow that likely would have removed his leg. But Marden had focused so intently on that single attack that he failed to realize yet again that it was only a feint.

Before his spear struck Marden's blade, Bryen pushed in on the tiny indentation on the haft of his weapon, separating the Spear of the Magii into two blades. With the sword in his right hand, he continued his swing for Marden's leg, but with the sword in his left hand, he sliced deftly across Marden's throat. Marden blocked one blow with a desperate parry, but missed the other entirely. Then Bryen stepped back a few paces, sword in each hand, glaring at Marden.

The King was dead, he just didn't know it yet. For a moment, their eyes locked, the King and the Volkun staring at one another. The Volkun's gaze merciless. The King's shifting from menace to disbelief to fear as a stream of blood gushed from the terrible wound running across his throat, the dark red flowing down his chest and staining his armor. Marden remained standing for just a few seconds more, then wobbled, his brain catching up to his body, before he fell backward into the white sand.

There was nothing but silence for several heartbeats, barely anyone in the stadium breathing, as Bryen stared down at the King of Caledonia, the blood spurting from the slice across his throat coloring the white sand red. Then the quiet that had reigned for so long was broken as someone in the stands shouted, "Long live the Volkun!" That released the citizens of Caledonia from the shock of watching their monarch fall in the Colosseum, the crowd erupting into a chorus of cheers that shook the very foundations of the arena.

Bryen heard the roar, the name that the crowd had bestowed upon him echoing off the white stone. It was just a name. The Volkun. But over time he had realized that it was much more than that. He remembered the conversation word for word that he had engaged in with Corinthus Beleron more than five years before when he was brought to the Palace before his combat with the Champion from Sharston.

"The crowd seems to have certainly taken to you, what with the name they've bestowed upon you. The Volkun. A mark of honor."

Bryen had locked eyes with the old King then, his protest sounding weak to his ears. "It's just a name."

"Yes, but names have power, young man," King Beleron had replied.

"Maybe so, but it doesn't feel that way when you're looking out from a cage," Bryen had replied, at the time having lost faith in the world and himself after fighting on the white sand for half a decade.

Bryen recalled how Corinthus had studied him, and then finally said, "Yes, I can understand that. But I get the feeling, young man, that you will not always be in your cage. And if you do, indeed, manage to escape your bonds, remember what I have just said. Remember that you will always have your name and that your name gives you a power that you can exercise if there's need. You are the Volkun. No one can ever take that away from you."

"Volkun!"

"The Wolf!"

The shouts continued to reverberate throughout the stadium, Bryen barely hearing them now, his thoughts elsewhere, his eyes still fixed on the King's body. For a moment he wondered what the old King would think of him now that he had killed his son.

Bryen didn't lift his gaze until a hushed amazement once again fell within the Colosseum, this silence not one of anticipation, but rather of fear, as Sirius and Tetric swirled into the Colosseum, Dark Magic and the Talent flashing through the air.

AISLINN FELT as if the weight that had been crushing her chest had been lifted when the King of Caledonia fell on his back in the Pit, his life bleeding out onto the white sand. Bryen had done it! She knew his skill with a blade, but she had worried for him during the entire combat, particularly when it appeared that Marden was going to get the better of him, the King's impossibly fast attacks forcing her Protector around the ring as he struggled desperately to survive.

She smiled broadly when Noorsin gripped her arm warmly, the Duchess of Murcia recognizing the multiple emotions that had played across her face as her Protector fought Marden and sympathizing with the Lady of the Southern Marches as the tension of the combat became almost unbearable.

"It's done," breathed Aislinn in a sigh of relief.

"Yes, that was quite final indeed, child," said Noorsin matter-of-factly. "That's one problem we no longer need to address."

Giving Aislinn a moment to compose herself, Noorsin turned her attention to Kevan.

"The Protector continues to do you ... us ... favors," she said.

"Yes, an extraordinary young man," replied Kevan.

The Duke of the Southern Marches remained conflicted regarding his daughter's Protector. He knew that what he had done to the gladiator was wrong, but it seemed that though he regretted what he had done, the young man continued to demonstrate the value of the decision that he had made. Even so, he worried about what would come next with the thousands upon thousands of spectators filling the stadium and lining the streets surrounding the plaza as well as the Royal Guard, their King now dead. But he wasn't too concerned.

He knew that there was no love lost between Marden and the citizens of Caledonia, so a change in leadership probably wouldn't matter so long as the deteriorating conditions in the city and the countryside improved. And he felt certain that the Blademaster, who had exited the Colosseum to deal with Killen Sourban, would immediately take control of the Royal Guard. So his thoughts naturally turned to the many questions that had been rolling around in his head since Noorsin and the Dukes of the Three Rivers and Roo's Nest had appeared.

"How did you know what was going on in the capital?" asked Kevan, his arm comfortably around her shoulders.

"Your daughter," replied Noorsin with a smile. "Aislinn got word out of Tintagel to me. Then I did what was necessary. We can't have the Duke of the Southern Marches under the sway of the King. That would tilt the balance too heavily toward the Crown."

Kevan nodded, not surprised by his daughter's initiative. "My thanks to you, Noorsin. If not for you, this would not have turned out as well as it did."

"You're probably right about that," replied the Duchess of Murcia with a knowing grin. "But don't worry, Kevan. I'll be collecting on your debt later."

Before Kevan could respond several shouts drew their

attention to the only unblocked tunnel that led away from the Pit.

Sirius had just backed through the entrance. He stood with his back to the Pit, the gladiators standing there scattering right before a bolt of corrupted energy blasted into the railing, destroying it and sending shards of broken stone into the crowd. Another bolt of the Curse followed. This time Sirius bore the full brunt of the Dark Magic on a large shield of white energy that he held before him, the force of the blow so powerful that it knocked him over the splintered railing into the Pit.

Out of the shadows of the tunnel Tetric emerged, a ball of black mist spinning faster than a maelstrom above a staff of black ash, a black diamond affixed to the top of the twisted wood. Having eyes only for the old Magus, Tetric walked to the balustrade and looked down into the Pit. Then, upon seeing his adversary lying unconscious, Tetric smiled evilly before leaping over the barrier onto the white sand.

SHOCKED to see the old Magus fall into the Pit and lay unmoving once he struck the white sand, Bryen latched his two swords back into the Spear of the Magii, left the King's body where it lay and sprinted to Sirius, standing in front of him protectively as Tetric landed just a few feet away with an unexpected agility.

For a moment, the King's Advisor stared at Bryen, the Protector simply staring back, silence having fallen once again within the Colosseum. Bryen realized in an instant that this was no longer the man who he had confronted a handful of times in the past, the most recent being in Battersea. And it wasn't just because Tetric's eyes were entirely black, the white gone.

Bryen had sensed the power in Tetric once before, revealing to Sirius that he could judge the strength of someone with respect to how much of the Talent or Dark Magic they could control before burning themselves to a crisp. The power that Bryen detected now as he stood across from the King's Advisor didn't match what he had identified before. Now it was on a scale that he had never imagined possible, and the one tiny spark of white light that he had located initially within Tetric was nowhere to be found. A pure evil roiled within Tetric, or rather what Tetric had become, because Bryen was certain that the adversary he faced off against now was no longer human.

"Are you sure you want to challenge me, Protector?" asked Tetric, his voice a scratchy rasp and deeper than it had been before. "I know that you can sense the power that I control. You can't stop me. Better just to give in, boy. It will be less painful for you that way."

After the last few days, Bryen assumed that he was too tired to see anything with a humorous eye. His body was sore. He was tired. He was wounded in a half dozen places. His mind was exhausted. Yet now, standing in the Pit, the King of Caledonia lying dead behind him, and Tetric having become something else entirely standing before him, he smiled and then let out a laugh that rang around the Pit.

Bryen laughed even harder when he saw the effect that his reaction had on Tetric, the Advisor's face first one of surprise and then quickly twisting into a malignant fury.

"What would give you the idea that I would ever be willing to give you what you want, Tetric? I may just be a gladiator, a Protector, but I am not a fool."

"No, you clearly aren't, boy. But you would be foolish not to take my offer."

"Why is that? I have no reason to trust you. No reason to believe a word you say."

"Because if you give me what I want, I can give you what you want."

"What would that be?"

"Your freedom, boy. Give me what I want. Give me the Seventh Stone, and I can remove the Protector's collar from around your neck."

Once again Bryen burst out laughing, the stress of the last few days finally catching up to him. But there was more to his reaction than that, as the half-truths and outright lies led Bryen's mind down a frightening, pernicious direction that he couldn't ignore.

"I have my freedom," Bryen replied. "I have what I want. There is nothing that you can give me now that I can't earn on my own."

"You're being naïve, boy," said Tetric, who was quickly losing patience with the dialogue. "If you won't think of yourself, think of the girl and her father. The Duke wears a collar much like yours. If you don't give me what I want, I'll kill him with it."

For a moment, Bryen hesitated. But he understood that now wasn't the time to demonstrate weakness, because he had realized what Tetric had become, or rather who Tetric had become. He should have been shocked by his discovery. But he wasn't. It all made a kind of warped sense.

"We have faced each other before," said Bryen.

This time Tetric smiled, understanding that his charade had come to an end. "We have."

"In the Sanctuary."

"Yes."

"I thought it was a dream, but it wasn't."

"In every dream there is some reality. You can't have one without the other."

"I know that now," said Bryen. "And I know that you are not one to act honorably. You are not one to keep your promises."

"You are more astute than the others, Protector," rasped Tetric. "It's a pity that I will have to kill you."

"You can try," Bryen replied.

For a few seconds more, Tetric stared at the gladiator, then with a guttural scream he rushed forward, shooting a sphere of black energy from his staff directly at Bryen.

The Protector responded instinctively, reaching out for the Talent once again and infusing the natural power of the world into the twin blades of the Spear of the Magii. With a quick flick of his wrist, Bryen deflected the ball of tainted magic with one of the blades, the Dark Magic slamming into the wall of the Pit. And then once more. Then again. And again. Tetric's attack appeared to be a stream of tainted power, Bryen moving like a whirlwind, his glowing steel blades becoming blinding streaks of light that illuminated the falling night as he defended against the assault.

Through it all, Bryen could feel the pull of the Dark Magic within him, responding to the Curse that was being thrown against him. The huge amount of power that Tetric pulled on called to Bryen, but thankfully he was able to ignore it, the Spear of the Magii helping him to maintain control over himself. To keep him focused on the challenge before him. To keep the call of the Dark Magic to barely a whisper in the back of his mind.

After only a few minutes, Tetric's assault came to an end. Bryen welcomed the respite, sweat pouring down his body, his strength, both physical and with the Talent, waning. He had done all that he could to protect against the Dark Magic sent against him, and it had barely been enough, several of Tetric's strikes almost killing him. Even worse, he could feel the tremendous power that his adversary possessed, and he feared that even with the Seventh Stone eventually he wouldn't be able to stand against it. But then his natural stubbornness came to the forefront, giving him a needed jolt of energy. If he was going to die this day, it would be on his own terms. He would choose his own death.

"You are overreaching, Protector," hissed Tetric. "You still don't understand, do you? You cannot defeat me. You will never be able to defeat me. Even though you are the Seventh Stone, you can never defeat me."

"Maybe so," replied Bryen quietly. "But that doesn't mean I won't keep trying. Because I will never stop fighting you. I will never surrender to the Ghoule Overlord."

Before Bryen's adversary could congratulate him on discovering the truth of what had happened to Tetric, the gladiator stalked forward, the Spear of the Magii a twisting blaze of white light as he slashed and cut at his opponent, forcing the creature that had taken Tetric's body and essence as his own to stumble back to avoid a lethal strike. Knowing what he was truly up against now, Bryen pulled in more and more of the Talent, as much as he could thanks to the Seventh Stone, his spear becoming a blur of blazing energy that resembled the sun.

Despite the speed of Bryen's assault, Tetric responded to each slash, cut, and jab with his staff of black ash, a staff that had confirmed Bryen's suspicions when he had first seen it. And as Bryen continued his onslaught, he saw something that surprised him. A touch of fear appeared in Tetric's eyes. Bryen realized that he had infused the twin blades of the Spear of the Magii with so much of the Talent that it was breaking through the magical protections his adversary had placed around himself. Every time Bryen struck Tetric's staff with his glowing steel blades, he chipped away a small piece of wood. Each strike also did something else that he did not expect.

The huge amount of the Talent that Bryen used with the assistance of the Seventh Stone also sliced into the Dark Magic, long gashes now appearing in the disguise that had been Tetric, revealing a mottled green skin beneath and sharp claws grasping tightly to the black staff. After a few more cuts with the Spear, the Dark Magic began to fall away from the creature's face, allowing Bryen to glimpse the sharp serrated teeth beneath, Tetric also appearing to grow in size as his flesh was sliced away, the beast within freeing itself from its disguise with every cut that struck home.

Bryen realized that he should have been frightened. Strangely, he wasn't. He had suspected this. Some small part of him had already concluded that he would need to fight against the greatest threat to Caledonia, a creature whose sole purpose was the destruction of the Kingdom and the enslavement and killing of its people.

The creature who had taken Tetric smiled in anticipation. He had known for quite some time what the Protector had become. He had tried to use Marden to achieve his goal. But it was not to be. No matter. Now he could take what belonged to him. What he had been seeking for centuries. Kill the Protector and he would gain the Seventh Stone, and then nothing could stop him. The creature began to pull in as much Dark Magic as he possibly could, the ball of black energy spinning atop the black diamond affixed to his staff gaining greater clarity, the mist expanding and placing the Pit into an unnatural darkness.

But before the creature could release the Curse, kill the boy, and take his prize, he howled in anger. A stream of white energy blasted toward him, followed by two more, this new attack forcing him to jump back from his prey and use the Dark Magic meant for Bryen to craft a misty shield of black.

Bryen stepped back as well, adding the Talent that surged within him to the fight, directing the flow through the glowing blades as he spun the Spear of the Magii to his front, combining his strength to that of Rafia, Aislinn, and Noorsin. The coordinated assault placed the Ghoule Overlord in a glowing nimbus of white-hot energy, protected only by a thin layer of Dark Magic.

The cursed Magii had placed him in a dangerous position. If he weakened his hold on the Curse, the Talent would incinerate him. With a groan of frustration, the Ghoule Overlord realized that though he was the closest he had ever come to achieving his objective, challenging the three Magii and the Protector who had become the Seventh Stone would threaten the plans that he had put in place centuries before, plans that he needed to implement that could not be delayed. He would have to wait for a better time, because though he could defeat the Magii standing before him, he risked himself by also taking on the Protector who had mastered the Seventh Stone, and that was not a risk that he was willing to take. Not yet. Too much depended on him still.

As the Talent streamed toward the sphere of Dark Magic, the Magii watched in fearful anticipation the transformation that was occurring. The creature that had been Tetric continued to grow taller, his shoulders becoming broader, his skin sliding off to reveal what was truly beneath. The King's Advisor was no more, and in his place towered the general of the Ghoule Legions.

"This is only the beginning!" shouted the Ghoule Overlord. "We come! We come for blood and flesh!"

Then in a blinding flash and thunderous roar, the Ghoule Overlord disappeared into a hazy mist of black.

Sirius, though still a bit woozy, had come back to himself when the three Magii had joined Bryen in his fight against the beast that threatened the very existence of the Kingdom of Caledonia. A wave of sadness struck him as he contemplated his brother's fate, knowing that it had come upon Tetric because of his greed and desire for more power. But he was also angry with himself because he had failed to kill the Overlord. And, because of that failure, he knew what the future held.

Just then a hand appeared in front of his face, and Sirius gladly took it, Bryen there to help him to his feet.

"Can you do that?" Bryen asked.

"Do what?" replied Sirius, not understanding the question since he was still distracted by his failure to defeat his brother. To defeat the Ghoule Overlord, rather, and that bothered him even more. He should have realized what the Ghoule Overlord had done to his brother. He should have known. Then he could have stopped what was to come now rather than putting so many more lives at risk.

"Dissolve into mist. Can you do that?"

"No."

"You can't?" asked Bryen with some surprise. "You're the leader of the Order of the Magii, and you can't do that?"

"No, I can't," Sirius replied with growing irritation. With all that had just been revealed, with all that had happened in the last few days, why was the Protector so fixated on how the Ghoule Overlord had escaped?

"It really seems like you should be able to. I mean you've been a Magus for how many centuries?"

"Well, I can't." Sirius tried to take a step, but then he grabbed onto Bryen's arm to steady himself, the world around him spinning ever so slightly.

"It still seems that you should be able to."

"Well, I can't, dammit." Sirius was trying to hold back his temper. Why did this lad have such a unique ability to get under his skin? "Is there a point to this?"

"Yes, instead of standing here thinking about what you can't do, think about what you can do. And if you can't do something, figure out how to do it."

Their conversation was interrupted when Davin and Lycia rushed into the Pit. Davin clapped his friend on his back, smiling broadly, glad to see that he was still alive. Lycia pushed her brother gently out of the way and pulled Bryen into a hug, not letting him go without a kiss to his cheek that lingered for several long seconds.

Through it all, Aislinn watched from the stands above the Pit, proud of what she had accomplished in helping to drive away the Ghoule Overlord with the Talent, but uncertain of what to do next. She wanted to go to Bryen, to thank him, to make sure that he was all right. But, what did she have to offer him other than the constant reminder of his enslavement?

"You did it," said Rafia.

"Did what?" asked Noorsin, the two Magii still standing in the front row of the Colosseum.

Most of the crowd had filed out, stunned. There had been no cheers. No excitement. Just a certainty in purpose. A certainty that what needed to be done had been done. The Volkun had removed the King from the throne.

There had been a simmering undercurrent of fear as well. A myth had come to life. The people of Caledonia had seen it with their own eyes. They didn't want to believe it, but they had no choice. The world that they had known was not the world as it was, and that had proven to be a jarring proposition. The Ghoule Overlord was real.

"Overthrew the King," said Rafia.

Noorsin gave her mentor a thin smile. "Bryen and Aislinn did that. Even though they were apart, somehow they did it together."

"Nevertheless, they did well," said Rafia. "You realize that this is just the beginning?"

"I've suspected as much for quite some time," nodded Noorsin.

Ghoules in the Southern Marches. Attacks along the southern edge of the Shattered Peaks. Elders searching for the Seventh Stone. The Seventh Stone healing and then choosing to merge with an inexperienced Magus barely a year removed from the Pit. And now the revelation of the Ghoule Overlord here in the very center of Caledonian power. All these pieces of evidence and more pointed to the same thing.

"Why am I not surprised?"

"You taught me well, Rafia."

"I'm glad that I was able to teach you something," the Keeper of Haven laughed. "Most of the time that you were under my instruction I felt as if I was just along for the ride, you spending most of your time teaching yourself."

Noorsin chuckled at that, remembering how much fun she had while she had studied with Rafia on Haven. It had been a quiet time, a good time. She had been free from her responsibilities as the Duchess of Murcia. Free of the dangers, threats, and worries that plagued her now. That all boded ill for the Kingdom.

"If Bryen and Aislinn can take down the King, do you think that they can kill the Ghoule Overlord?"

Rafia stood there in silence for a time, giving Noorsin's question careful consideration. Her former student feared that she would never answer.

"I don't know," she replied finally, her voice tinged with worry. "But I do know that if they don't, the Ghoule Overlord will take Caledonia for his own and this Kingdom will cease to exist."

"Not very uplifting."

"No, but truthful, and in times like this that's what we need. The truth. Unvarnished."

Rafia looked down onto the white sand, Noorsin following her gaze. Bryen stood off to the side, many of the gladiators with him. Congratulating him on his victory. Thanking him for what he did for them.

Aislinn was there as well, offering her support from a distance. Not feeling comfortable enough to push herself into the mix.

Marden's body had been removed, though a streak of blood remained, coloring the white sand red. She was certain that before what came next was all over, a great deal more blood would be spilled, likely enough to fill the entire Colosseum.

"What was that?" asked Noorsin.

Rafia turned to Noorsin with a start, realizing that she had been mumbling to herself, a habit that she had fallen into after spending so much time on her own on Haven.

"You must do what you must do."

"Where did you hear that?"

"From Bryen," Rafia replied. "He learned it from the Master of the Gladiators."

"You must do what you must do," repeated Noorsin. "Certainly appropriate."

"Indeed it is," confirmed Rafia. "One chapter is done. The King is dead."

"But another is to be written," offered Noorsin.

"And we must do all that we can to ensure that the story ends the way it should. Because if we fail to do so ..."

"The Second Ghoule War will begin, the Legions coming through the Winter Pass to flood Caledonia with pain and death."

"Unfortunately so," agreed Rafia. "We must do what we must do, no matter the cost, to ensure that the bearer of the Seventh Stone has a chance to rebuild the Weir, and if along the way he can kill the Ghoule Overlord ..."

"Then so much the better," finished Noorsin, her voice hard, unyielding. "One way or another, that savage beast must die."

EPILOGUE

A New Chapter

"I thought I might find you here."

Declan stood in the cramped doorway to the cell that Bryen had lived in for a decade. Bryen sat on the cot that was too small for him, leaning his head back against the crumbling wall. He was hidden within the shadows, only revealed when the single torch that lit the long hallway of the gladiators' barracks flared at the touch of the brisk wind that found its way through the many holes in the walls.

After his combats in the Pit, he had used the Talent to heal as many of the gladiators who had been wounded during the uprising as he could, Rafia and Aislinn doing the same. Many of his friends and peers who would have died from their injuries under normal circumstances didn't thanks to their efforts. Once they were done with the gladiators, they had focused their healing skill on the soldiers of the Royal Guard, helping as many as they could. Many of the soldiers didn't expect such kindness, not after the bloody fight that had lasted for much of the day. But, as Declan liked to say, a touch of kindness went a lot farther than continued animosity.

In consequence, Bryen was exhausted. Mentally and physically. He didn't heal himself until every last fighter wounded in the battle had been cared for, something that didn't go unnoticed by the men who had tried to kill him.

So he had returned to his room hoping to find a few hours to think about what had happened and the conversations that had occurred after the combat. He didn't have the patience for all the issues that had arisen now that Caledonia no longer had a monarch. He would leave all that to Duchess Stelekel and the other rulers of the land. They could hash out what would come next. He had other challenges to consider, challenges that he wasn't certain how to address.

"Were you looking for me or were you trying to escape Rafia?"

"A little bit of both," Declan chuckled. "That Magus is very intense. She would make an excellent gladiator."

"That she would," agreed Bryen with a laugh. "In addition to being intense, she's also very persistent."

"I assumed as much," nodded Declan. He looked at Bryen for several seconds, realizing that the young man he viewed as his son was struggling with something. But it wasn't really his place to impose, not unless he was invited to do so. "I'll remember that."

"What's on your mind, Declan?" Bryen knew that Declan wanted to speak with him about something, the Master of the Gladiators just hadn't figured out how to start yet. So better to give him the opening that he needed so that Bryen could get some sleep.

"It's almost like your favorite book, *The Revenge of the Lost*

Count," began Declan. "You return to Tintagel, save Lady Winborne and her father, expose Tetric for what he really is, battle the Ghoule Overlord and send him packing with the help of your friends, and, most important of all in my opinion, you free the gladiators."

"I'm glad it all worked out," Bryen said with a small smile, never having believed that his mad scheme would prove so successful. "I was worried for a while."

"So was I," admitted Declan. "But where's the fun in life if you don't have a challenge now and then?"

"I can't even imagine," replied Bryen drily.

"Yet even with all that success, you have some decisions to make."

"I do."

"The Ghoule Overlord escaped, but he isn't gone."

"No."

"Those Magii want you to go after him."

"Not yet, but yes," admitted Bryen. "First they want me to try to repair the Weir."

"A challenge that," nodded Declan. "Maybe even bigger than the challenges you just overcame. Can you?"

"I don't know."

"Whatever you decide," said Declan, "I just wanted to let you know that I'll be there with you."

"I know, and I thank you," replied Bryen. "But I'm not worried about that."

"Then what are you worried about?"

"Whether I can kill the Ghoule Overlord. I have this sense that the combat in the Pit this evening was just a precursor for what's to come. And that's fine. I'm not surprised. I'm not afraid of dying. Not after fighting on the white sand for so long."

"You're afraid of failing."

"Yes."

"You can't fail if you don't try."

"I know, and it's not the failing that worries me so much as the consequences of the Ghoule Overlord winning," clarified Bryen. Then he grinned broadly. "You know it's in part because of all your sayings that Rafia is so intrigued with you. It's these aphorisms of yours that are getting you in trouble."

"Is that so? I'll have to start keeping my mouth shut then."

"Good luck with that," said Bryen with a raised eyebrow, "because even now you still have a thought to share."

"How did you know?"

"I know you," Bryen replied softly. "You raised me. You helped me become what I am."

"I'm sorry for that."

"Don't be. You gave me what I needed to survive. You gave me someone to look up to. You gave me a father when I didn't have one."

Hearing the honesty and thanks in Bryen's voice, Declan found himself at a loss for words, which was a rare thing. His eyes began to water, and he needed to take a deep breath to settle himself. He had never been very good at dealing with emotion, but Bryen's words struck him in a way that nothing else ever had.

"Thank you for telling me that, Bryen."

"It's only the truth."

"Nevertheless, the truth can be a powerful thing," Declan said, having to wipe his sleeve across his eyes so that the tears running down his cheeks wouldn't be visible. "I can't help you decide what you should do next, but I can offer one last piece of advice."

"What would that be?"

"You must do what you must do."

"You must do what you must do," Bryen repeated softly.

Declan was right. He had finished one chapter. It was time to start the next. Come what may. Because he was never one to

run from the next challenge, no matter how much it might
cost him.

THE END

Keep reading for the first three chapters of Book 4,
The Protector's Sacrifice.

BONUS MATERIAL

If you really enjoyed this story, I need you to do me a HUGE favor – please follow me on BookBub or Amazon. And if you have a few minutes, consider writing a review.

Keep reading for the first three chapters of Book 4 of *The Tales of Caledonia, The Protector's Sacrifice.*

THE PROTECTOR'S SACRIFICE

BOOK 4 OF THE TALES OF CALEDONIA

By Peter Wacht

This book is a work of fiction. Names, characters, places, and incidents are the product of the author's imagination or are used fictitiously. Any resemblance to actual events, locales, or persons, living or dead, is coincidental.

Cover design by Ebooklaunch.com

Published in the United States by Kestrel Media Group LLC.

ISBN: 978-1-950236-24-4
eBook ISBN: 978-1-950236-25-1

Library of Congress Control Number: 2022903166

1. THE TRUTH REVEALED

The Captain of the Royal Guard shook his head in resignation as he stepped out onto the plaza that encircled the Colosseum. If only the King had listened to him. If the stubborn ass had demonstrated even a modicum of judgment and reserve, this minor rebellion would have ended before it had gained any traction among the people. The King's rule would never have been put in such jeopardy. But Marden listened to no one but Tetric, and the King's Advisor had supported every single one of the King's decisions.

Now, King Marden Beleron, the last of a dynasty three hundred years old, was dead. Long live the new ...

Sourban wasn't certain who would assume the Caledonian throne. Yet, he was certain of the outcome of the combat before the King of Caledonia stepped onto the white sand. It was a given. There was no doubt. He knew this gladiator. He had seen him fight many times in the Colosseum. He had won several bags of golds by betting on him more times than he could remember. No matter what Marden Beleron and his fool Advisor believed, no one and nothing could kill the Volkun on the white sand.

Despite his repeated attempts to change Marden Beleron's mind, the King had ignored him and stepped out into the Pit. The King was so eager to prove himself. He was so eager to be what he thought his people wanted him to be, visions of the loved, benevolent lionheart dancing through his head. Those visions would do little for him when he faced the steel of the Wolf's double-bladed spear.

What a complete and utter fool, thought Killen Sourban. The King had never realized that he could never be anything more than what he already was. He had shown such promise when he had assumed his father's place on the throne. Intelligence. Drive. Cunning. Yet all for naught. Because of his arrogance and recklessness Marden was a failed king. And now Sourban suspected a dead king as well, because there was no way Marden was going to escape the Volkun.

Of course, Sourban was not a fool. He understood that the second that Marden died at the hands of the Volkun, his own time in the capital would be coming to an end. Fast. His enemies would be coming for him. With some justification, he admitted. So he had waited through several agonizing minutes until the combat between the King and the Volkun was well underway before sneaking out of the only accessible tunnel that led away from the Colosseum onto the square, his primary concern escaping Tintagel as quickly as possible.

The merit of his decision was confirmed when he saw the Guards from Murcia, the Three Rivers, Roo's Nest, and, of course, the Southern Marches lined up in formation across the plaza. The companies of Royal Guard he had dispersed around the square were nervous, perhaps even a little frightened, by the arrival of these soldiers because these troops from the Duchies outnumbered them by at least two to one.

So far nothing had happened, the soldiers of the Royal Guard eyeing warily and with a little trepidation these potential adversaries. Because Sourban could see it just as well as they could. The Captains of the Duchy troops had positioned their fighters in overlapping ranks, one company always in support of another, ensuring, right from the start, that any fight on the plaza ended rapidly and in their favor, assuming, of course, that any of the soldiers would be willing to risk their lives for the soon-to-be-dead King.

Sourban shook his head in resignation once again. It wasn't his problem anymore. The city was lost the second the Duchy soldiers passed through the gates, and the Crown would be lost in a matter of minutes as soon as the Volkun turned the white sand red with the King's blood.

Resigning the soldiers under his command to their fates with nary a feeling of remorse, Sourban started walking across the plaza in a small lane that separated a company of the Royal Guard from a company of the Murcian Guard and provided the most direct access to the alley that beckoned to him at the far end of the plaza. With all that was going on in the square, the tension palpable and intensifying, no one bothered him. No one really paid any attention to him. He was almost to the edge of the plaza, just a few dozen yards from the anonymity of the maze of streets that surrounded the Colosseum, when he heard a commanding shout at his back that sent an involuntary shudder up his spine and immediately brought back memories of all the time that he had spent in the practice yard in the Corinthian Palace.

"At least Marden had the good grace to fight in the Pit before he died, yet you would slink away like a coward? I can't say that I'm surprised. You always preferred the easy way out, didn't you, Killen?"

Sourban, his long blond hair tied at the nape of his neck with a black leather band, stopped short, then reluctantly turned back in the direction from which he had come. His ice-cold blue eyes, normally free of emotion, revealed a hate that he couldn't hide. The tight smile that he offered his former mentor was more of a sneer, his lips twisting spitefully.

"The tide has turned, old man," said Sourban, ignoring the insult even though it burned deeply within him. "It's time for me to move on."

"Yes, and you were always one to follow the whims of the tide, weren't you?" asked Jurgen Klines, Blademaster of the Royal Guard. Tall and thin, he appeared austere, almost ascetic when you took in his thin mustache and pointed beard, his cheeks free of whiskers. His thinning grey hair was pulled back behind his head and kept out of his bottomless green eyes thanks to a leather strap tied at the base of his neck that looked very similar to the one Sourban wore.

"I simply try to go in the direction of the current, old man, and right now the current is leading me this way," he said, motioning to the crowd of people at the border of the square and filling the alley just beyond. Many of those people, drawn to the Colosseum by the conflict between the gladiators and the Royal Guard, now had begun to take notice of the confrontation occurring right before them, as did the soldiers standing in ranks on both sides.

"That will have to wait, Killen. We have unfinished business, you and I."

"You were better than me in the practice ring, but that was years ago when I was young and impetuous. Time hasn't been kind to you, Klines. Older. Slower. More emotional if you're still holding on to your grudges." Sourban grunted in amusement. "Are you sure you want to do this, old man?"

"Dying to, Killen," replied the Blademaster. "You know that. You've known it ever since you took her from me."

"She chose me," Sourban replied heatedly, unable to keep the emotion from his voice.

"She didn't know the real you. Neither of us did. And we both paid for it, though her price was beyond imagining."

For almost a full minute, Sourban stared at the Blademaster, his escalating anger stoking his hate. Yet at the same time the voice in the back of his head that had proven so useful to him as a soldier, that warned him of impending danger, was telling him to ignore the old man, turn on his heel, and disappear into the crowd. The Captain of the Royal Guard considered that option for just a moment, then discarded it. He couldn't do that. He had never been able to step away from a challenge before, and the one that the old man offered to him now was too enticing to pass up. The old man was right. There was unfinished business between them, and this might be his only chance to close accounts with his former mentor and friend. It certainly would be a satisfying way to end his time in Tintagel.

Even so, he still appreciated the risk associated with this challenge. Yes, the Blademaster was older, probably slower, but he was still a dangerous opponent. So Sourban decided to take the most direct approach possible. Smiling, Sourban nodded his head, and then gestured in a way that suggested that he had something else to say.

Then, he launched himself forward, closing the twenty feet to the Blademaster in just three bounds, pulling his sword from the sheath at his hip as he did so and slashing through the air with a cut that would have taken the Blademaster's head from his shoulders. If it had connected.

It didn't. Klines sidestepped easily, assuming his former pupil would make such a play. When he ducked out of the way Klines gave Sourban a slight nudge with his hip that threw him off balance. Sourban fought to stay on his feet, fearing that he would fall to the cobblestones, ceding the advantage to his opponent. Still, that effort to recover gave the Blademaster the time to pull his sword from its sheath and face off against Sourban with an almost unnatural, definitely unnerving calm.

Growling in anger because of the ease with which Klines

had avoided his surprise attack, Sourban, his face red with rage, leapt once again toward the Blademaster. Sourban brought his blade above his head, thinking to cut down into the flesh between the Blademaster's neck and shoulder blade, but he realized mid-swing that his attempt would fail. The Blademaster already was moving out of the way. So Sourban turned the blade in his hand, instead seeking to slash his steel across Klines' hip.

That improvised effort at least forced the Blademaster to use his sword to defend himself, the ring of metal echoing in the plaza as the Blademaster parried Sourban's attack. The Captain of the Guard's assault didn't stop there, the clang of steel meeting steel sounding with a discordant tone as he tried to keep the Blademaster engaged and on the defensive, seeking even the slightest opening that he could use to slide his blade into Klines' flesh. He wanted to end this combat quickly, and he hoped that he could overpower the old man right at the start.

Sourban knew how good Klines was with a sword. The man wouldn't have earned the position of Blademaster otherwise. And he knew that the longer the combat continued, the greater the odds that he would be the one to die rather than the old man. He had experienced the Blademaster's skill with a blade firsthand many times in the past, having sparred with him for what seemed like endless hours in the training circle. Sourban had learned a great deal from the old man, and he had viewed the Blademaster as a mentor at the beginning of their relationship. But that all had changed over time. So much so that for the last several years Sourban had been seeking an opportunity to kill his former friend. He had spent most nights dreaming about it. About how he would do it. About the look on the old man's face when he realized that Sourban was the one who was about to punch his steel through his throat.

But as he continued his incessant assault, blade whipping through the air with a speed that would be the envy of most any other sword fighter, a touch of fear settled in his stomach. He was beginning to comprehend that turning his dreams into reality might prove impossible. The old man was defending his attacks with an irritating ease. It was as if the Blademaster could read his mind, his steel already occupying the space that Sourban's blade was about to before Sourban had even decided what he was going to do. That realization fed his fear, which quickly spiraled out of control when he concluded that the old man was simply playing with him. The Blademaster was older, more experienced, but he wasn't slower.

Sourban tried one more series of attacks, his blade a blur as it sought the old man's thigh, then shoulder, then hip, then hamstring. Despite his best efforts, Sourban's steel never scored the old man's flesh. It never even came close.

The Blademaster stood there calmly, barely moving his feet, oftentimes just flicking his wrist so that he could deflect Sourban's lunge or stab, tilting his body out of the way or pivoting to the side to avoid a slash or a cut, allowing Sourban to tire himself out while he conserved his energy. Sourban would have been impressed by the display if it wasn't his life that hung in the balance.

As his rising fear slowly turned to terror, Sourban sought desperately for some solution to his problem. It seemed that his impetuousness was still too much a part of his decision-making. Now, to counter that, he had to find a way to win this combat that he had so foolishly engaged in. He could have walked into the crowd and lost himself in the city. But he hadn't. Just like the King and his doomed combat with the Volkun, Sourban had fallen into the same trap, allowing his ego to reign. And now that hubris was going to cost him his life. Unless he could find some way to distract the old man.

Stepping back to catch his breath, Sourban wasn't surprised to see the interest the duel had garnered. The soldiers standing in formation on the plaza closest to them, those of the Royal

Guard and those of the Duchy Guards, watched the contest intently. Yet none demonstrated any desire to intervene.

For just a second, Sourban thought to order the soldiers of the Royal Guard to come to his aid. But he scrapped the idea immediately. He could see that wasn't going to happen. Not with the looks of contempt and disgust on the soldiers' faces. They sensed how the combat was going to conclude, and it didn't bother them in the least. Rather, they seemed to think that it was the right ending for this story. The deserved ending.

Realizing that he was running out of options, Sourban turned to the only other course of action that came to mind that might actually allow him to live through this combat. He needed to make the old man angry, because only then would he find an opening. Only if the old man lost his focus, even if only for just a heartbeat, would he stand a chance.

"You were right from the beginning," said Sourban with a malicious grin. "All those years ago, you were right. I killed Anna."

Klines, who had been preparing to launch his first attack of the combat, one that he suspected would end the duel, was stopped in his tracks by Sourban's admission. Seeing the effect that his revelation had on the old man, Sourban continued, hoping that he could use the truth that he had kept hidden for years to his advantage now.

"She thought that she could break it off with me without any consequences. She thought that she could embarrass me like that without paying a penalty." Sourban's voice was soft, then he chuckled with a quiet fatalism. "She was wrong. She was mine. She will always be mine."

"You killed my daughter because you didn't want to be embarrassed? Because she was smart enough to see you for who you truly were?"

Recognizing the anguish in the old man's expression, Sourban's eyes flashed brightly. It looked like his play might be working. His opportunity would come, he believed, so now he just needed to be ready. He took a few steps closer to the Blademaster, who had lowered his sword so that the steel tip rested on the cobblestones.

"Yes, I killed your daughter," he said, the malice clear in his voice, "but not because of how she saw me. I killed her because she didn't see me for what I could become. And she didn't realize what that could be until my dagger had slid into her heart and I watched the light leave her eyes. That's when she realized that she had made a mistake. But by then it was too late. She was gone, and she had gotten what she deserved."

Sourban struck when he recognized the look of devastation that appeared on the Blademaster's face, lunging at the old man, his sword aimed for his gut. But just as the Captain of the Guard had done so many times when he was younger and training with the Blademaster, he had miscalculated. His revelation had shocked Klines, but his admission also had been a huge mistake on his part.

Listening to Sourban's confession, a cold anger surged through the Blademaster, giving Klines a clarity and focus that for most was difficult to attain. It was as if Sourban attacked him in slow motion, and in response Klines turned on a heel and spun out of the way, Sourban's blade missing him by more than a dagger's length. But the Blademaster didn't miss. Unable to recover in time, Klines drove his blade backward with two hands, slicing through Sourban's back, the tip sliding out of his gut.

The former Captain of the Guard slid off the Blademaster's sword and landed in a sprawl, his dark red blood staining the white stone of the plaza, his face revealing his shock at failing to kill the Blademaster. He had been so certain that his ploy would work, just as he had been so certain about so many things, only now realizing when it was too late that there was little certainty in life, other than your own death.

Klines stared down at Sourban without remorse. He took no particular pleasure in killing the murderer of his daughter, but he did feel some satisfaction and vindication. His daughter's killer, as he had suspected but had never been able to confirm, had finally been brought to justice.

He watched the dying man try to say something with his last few breaths. He didn't care what Sourban had to say. Rather, in that moment Klines was thinking of his daughter. Of what she could have been if she had not met Sourban. Of how much he missed her. And of how much the Lady of the Southern Marches reminded him of her. He had lost his daughter, but he would not allow someone so much like her to be taken as well. He promised himself then that even though he had failed to do everything that he could to protect Anna, he would do all that he could to protect Lady Winborne.

Klines turned away from Sourban to go back into the strangely silent Colosseum so that he could keep his newly made promise, but instead found Benin and several other Sergeants standing at attention.

"The Royal Guard stands with you, Blademaster," said Benin, pulling his blade from his scabbard and touching it to his forehead in a sign of respect, the other men with him doing the same. "Your orders ... Captain?"

Klines smiled wistfully, then nodded. With Sourban dead, he was the only other Captain in Tintagel with the rank and authority to command the Royal Guard. It seemed that the death of his daughter's murderer had just given him an added tool that he could use to assist Lady Winborne and the Volkun. And he meant to do just that.

2. TOGETHER AGAIN

They stood no more than six feet apart. Aislinn Winborne, Lady of the Southern Marches, stared across the space at her Protector. She had not seen Bryen since she had freed him from most of the restraints of the silver Protector's collar that still circled his neck. Right before she had left the Southern Marches for Tintagel, intent on rescuing her father from King Beleron's grasp while avoiding her own planned nuptials to the man who had become her captor. The man who was now dead.

Somehow everything had worked out exactly as she wanted. Marden Beleron removed from the throne. Tetric gone, though not in the way that she had imagined. Her father safe. How much of a role she played in it all, she couldn't say for sure. Because from what she had heard the catalyst for the massive change that had swept through the Caledonian capital was the young man standing in front of her. Her Protector.

Bryen looked no different than when she last saw him. His prematurely white hair with just a few specks of brown left was a bit longer than it had been, now down past his shoulders. His grey eyes were just as sharp as always, though she did detect an unexpected spark there that she had never seen before.

He had walked up from the Pit, having cleaned the gore from his double-bladed spear, but the same could not be said for himself. His battered leather armor, covered in blood and nicked in dozens of places, testified to the brutality of the insurrection and the combat that he had just fought, and he carried at least a half dozen wounds on his arms and legs. She couldn't tell how many for sure because of all the grime and dirt mixed in.

Still, his injuries didn't seem to affect him. He was just as stoic and imperturbable as always. Aislinn had already dueled Marden in the Pit, so she hadn't been worried for Bryen during the combat. At least that's what she kept telling herself while she watched, her heart in her throat several times until finally the King of Caledonia crumpled to the ground, turning the white sand red.

Aislinn wanted to say something, but she wasn't sure what. She had never expected to see Bryen again. She had hoped that she would. But she had assumed that he would have taken full advantage of her having given him his freedom. He had spoken of wanting to see the Territories, of leaving Caledonia and the slavery that had been forced upon him and starting fresh where there were no expectations and memories were short. Yet here he was. Rather than leaving the Kingdom as he could have, as he said he planned to do, he had come here instead. But why? Why take such a terrible risk?

Needing time to gather her thoughts, she allowed herself to be swept up for a moment by the rush of activity all around her. Wounded gladiators and soldiers of the Royal Guard were being cared for by the physicks, Rafia and Sirius assisting. Noorsin Stelekel, the Duchess of Murcia, stood by the tunnel leading away from the Pit. From what she could hear, she was asking Cornelius Stennivere, Duke of the Three Rivers, and Wencel Roosarian, Duke of Roo's Nest, to work with the Blademaster so that the Royal Guard could leave the plaza and return to their barracks, escorted by the Duchy troops of course, to ensure that nothing untoward happened now that the Kingdom had lost its monarch.

Duchess Stelekel then asked the Blademaster to deal with the soldiers, not more than a few hundred, who had tied themselves to the King's Advisor. Tetric had been revealed for all to see while fighting Sirius. The man who he had been was no more, taken by the creature who had threatened the Kingdom since the First Ghoule War. Duchess Stelekel wanted to make sure that none of the soldiers who had aligned themselves with Tetric had been corrupted in a similar way. In a surprisingly subdued manner, the Blademaster already had confirmed that the former Captain of the Guard, Killen Sourban, and the greatest danger to maintaining peace in the city, was no longer a problem. So matters were proceeding apace.

Once the Royal Guard returned to their barracks, Duke Stennivere and Duke Roosarian were to position their troops around the capital in all the plazas and at other key locations in order to prevent any unrest, hoping to ensure that the riots of the last few months were a thing of the past. The Volkun's victory over the King certainly helped in that regard, sending a wave of jubilation through the city, the residents of Tintagel feeling as if a yoke had been lifted from their shoulders.

Nevertheless, the Blademaster also would ensure that his most trusted soldiers assumed responsibility for guarding the city wall and the gates. Then, the Blademaster would take several companies of soldiers to the grain silos and begin distributing what remained of that dwindling supply throughout the city. Duchess Stelekel already had put a plan in place for getting the bakeries started again, the cost to be paid for by the Crown. Such an effort should be enough to feed the city for a few days. By the time the grain ran out, more shipments of that and other needed foodstuffs would arrive when the first caravans began to appear in the next three days,

Duchess Stelekel having made the arrangements before leaving Murcia for Tintagel.

"You've been busy," said Kevan Winborne with a short laugh. The Duke of the Southern Marches had come to stand behind his daughter after speaking with Tarin Tentillin, Captain of the Battersea Guard, and providing assistance to some of the injured gladiators. Kevan looked across at Noorsin Stelekel who, having given all the orders that needed to be issued, had walked over and now stood next to Aislinn's Protector.

The bloody, gore-splattered young man who had played such an integral role in freeing him and his daughter remained a challenge for Kevan that he was not ready to address, so he focused his attention on Noorsin instead. The Duchess of Murcia was known for her keen mind, but she was also exceedingly beautiful. Stepping forward, Kevan wrapped her in a hug, then kissed her, ignoring the shock that some of the people around them demonstrated at such an open display of affection from the usually reserved, taciturn Duke of the Southern Marches. In that moment, he realized how lucky he was to have a second chance, and he was not going to let the opportunity pass him by. His time as a captive taught him how fickle fate could be.

"I couldn't just pine for you as I made my way here," she replied with a smile, once Kevan had reluctantly released her from his arms. "Besides, this uprising has been in the works for quite some time. Since I began receiving secret correspondence from your daughter, in fact."

Noorsin finally felt as if she could breathe once more when Kevan gave her a devilish grin that she never thought she'd see again.

"Yes, Aislinn has certainly demonstrated her very unique skills during my incarceration," replied Kevan.

"So I've heard," said Noorsin. "And I'm intrigued to learn more."

"You are being far too kind, Duchess Stele…" Aislinn started and then stopped, noticing Noorsin's raised eyebrow. "Noorsin," corrected Aislinn, remembering the Duchess' wish to remove the formality between them. "You are being much too kind, Noorsin."

"I'm being honest," Noorsin replied. "Don't sell yourself short, Aislinn. The information you provided was critical to our success, and you gaining the trust of the Blademaster and a good number of the Royal Guard proved invaluable by ensuring a minimum of bloodshed here and when we took the city."

Noorsin would have said more, but she could tell that Aislinn's thoughts were on other matters. "And congratulations to the Volkun," Noorsin said, turning to Bryen. "Well done, young man. Well done, indeed. You never cease to impress me."

"Thank you, Duchess Stelekel. And thank you for your assistance. Without your timely arrival, my gladiators would have faced a grim future opposing the King and his Guard on our own."

"I don't know about that, Protector. From what I've seen while making my way here, you and your gladiators were more than a match for the King and Tetric, even with the steep odds against you." Noorsin then motioned for Kevan to take her arm. "Would you please join me, Kevan? The next conversation is not ours to be had."

The Lady of the Southern Marches nodded her thanks to Noorsin as she led her father out of earshot, her eyes never leaving her Protector.

"Why haven't you gone to the physick?" asked Aislinn. There was so much that she wanted to say, but her anxiety led her to the most obvious topic. The safest topic.

"It looks worse than it really is."

Bryen's voice was quiet and unexpectedly soft for someone so tall and imposing. He smiled, feeling a warmth and a familiar sense of connection upon seeing Aislinn again. Anyone could tell that she was beautiful with her long auburn hair, quick smile, and captivating dimples, but he knew also that Aislinn's beauty hid the fighter just beneath the surface, as well as so much more.

"You say that every time you're hurt," Aislinn replied. "I know you have an incredible ability to heal but those wounds look like they might need a physick."

"I'll go in a minute. There are gladiators who are injured worse than I am." Bryen hedged for a moment, looking away from her to recapture his thoughts. Why was he so nervous? For more than six months, he had spent every waking moment with the Lady of the Southern Marches, so why did now feel so awkward? He turned his gaze once more to Aislinn and decided that there was no point in dancing around what he wanted to say. Better to just be honest. "I just wanted to make sure that you were all right."

Aislinn didn't know what to say upon hearing that. Her own emotions threatened to overwhelm her as she looked into Bryen's eyes, which were usually cold grey orbs, but now were soft, almost uncertain. She stepped forward and hugged him, pulling him in close and holding him tightly despite all the activity around them, then she stepped back quickly, suddenly uncomfortable.

Bryen didn't know what to make of Aislinn's action. Despite their time apart, there was still a closeness between them. Yet there also was an unexpected distance that hadn't been there before. Why that new, unwanted feeling had worked its way between them, he didn't understand. It didn't make sense to him. He could tell it didn't make sense to Aislinn either based on her next question, as she sought to avoid the subject that was on both of their minds.

"You came to have the collar removed?"

"I came for you," he replied in a moment of uncommon honesty.

Aislinn felt like all the emotions roiling within her caught in her throat, preventing her from responding. She didn't know what to say. She corrected herself. She did know what she wanted to say. She just didn't have the courage to say it. Not yet. And that's when she realized that despite the cool temperature that accompanied the falling night, she was starting to sweat profusely, so she decided to change the topic. Unwilling to reveal what was going through her mind, she tried for humor instead.

"It took you long enough."

Bryen smiled sadly, realizing that she wasn't ready for the conversation that they needed to have. So he looked down at himself, a few cuts here and there but nothing too deep or too serious. Most of the blood on him wasn't his own.

"It's been a long day. I'm a bit slower than I should be," he said with a tentative grin.

Rafia, who watched the entire exchange with great interest, nudged Sirius in the side. After helping with the wounded, the two Magii had come looking for Bryen. The capital was theirs, the gladiators were free, but there was still more to do.

"That was more awkward than when you found me naked in that swimming hole, Sirius."

"That was not my fault!" Sirius protested, grumpy after the stress and strain of the last few days, and his failure to kill the Ghoule Overlord on the white sand leaving him seething in anger. "I didn't know you were there."

"I'm still not buying it, Sirius, even after all these years. You knew I was there. You had no other reason for being there than to catch me like that. You could have joined me from the beginning if you had just asked."

Sirius groaned in frustration as he once again allowed the

Keeper of Haven to get under his skin. Why he permitted her teasing to affect him as it did, he couldn't explain, as it simply added to his already considerable frustration. She never failed to rile him up when she put her mind to it, and her latest comments forced him to look away. He was blushing profusely as he remembered that never-to-be-forgotten incident, and then his grimace turned to a smile as he recalled how much he had enjoyed it.

When he finally looked back at Rafia, her eyes said that she remembered how much she had enjoyed that experience as well, which made the old Magus blush even more. But then a shout from Noorsin drew everyone's gaze. The Duke of the Southern Marches had fallen just a few feet from the entrance to the tunnel, a spiderweb of jet-black veins sprouting from beneath his collar, turning his neck a ghastly color.

"It's the collar," said Noorsin, who knelt down next to Kevan and immediately ripped open his shirt to confirm her suspicions, Aislinn there in an instant on his other side. Both women gasped in fear and shock. The tendrils had already begun to spread up the side of Kevan's face and down his chest, the threads pulsing a deep black with the taint of the Curse. "With Tetric gone, the Dark Magic is forcing its way into your father. Killing him. We need to get this collar off. Now. It's his only chance."

Rafia knelt down next to Aislinn, placing her hand on Kevan's chest and allowing the Talent to run through her fingers and then into him. Her frown deepened as she sensed the evil flowing through the collar and consuming the Duke.

"I don't know how to remove the collar, and even if I did, he could still die."

"He'll die if we don't," whispered Aislinn, her fear for her father's life revealed through a shaky voice.

"I know, child. You're right. We will try to remove the collar, and we will do all that we can for him. But it will not be easy."

"Blademaster!" said Noorsin, who pushed herself up off the ground. Klines had come back into the Colosseum, several dozen soldiers at his back. He had gotten there right before the Duke of the Southern Marches had collapsed, and he understood without being told exactly what was needed.

"Six men and a stretcher," Klines ordered. "We need to get him to the Palace before he dies."

3. ON THE EDGE

Aislinn grasped her father's hand tightly, trying to will her own strength into him, her terror increasing by the second. As the soldiers attempted to lay the Duke onto a makeshift stretcher, he began flailing about, clearly in agony as the Dark Magic ravaged him. The web of black continued to spread up and down his body, strands of corruption now appearing on his throat and cheeks as well as his arms and abdomen.

"Please, we need to help him," begged Aislinn of anyone who might be able to assist.

Tears streaked down her cheeks as she stared at her father. She had reached for the Talent as soon as Noorsin had ripped open his shirt to reveal the expanding gossamer of darkness raging through him. Yet her attempt at helping him was short-lived. Her skill in the Talent lay in directions other than healing, but even recognizing that, the Dark Magic already coursing through her father's blood had repelled even just her light touch as she attempted to locate and destroy the source of evil. She had realized abysmally that to take the approach that she had in mind, fighting the Curse with the Talent within her father, would lead to only one result. Her father's death. He'd never survive the conflict. So she hoped that others more experienced and skilled than her could do something to help when she couldn't.

"This wound appears similar to the one your young Protector overcame after his fight on the coastal road," said Noorsin. "So let's see if an approach similar to what I did then proves effective now."

Noorsin reached for the Talent. Usually, when the power of the natural world filled her, she felt an exhilaration, a charge of invigorating energy cascading through her that offered greater clarity, the colors of the world brighter, the sounds clearer, the smells sharper. But not this time. Now, she felt only purpose as she stared down at the man she loved, something that she only just admitted to herself. Her failure to tell him her feelings bothered her greatly now, because she feared she might not be able to save him.

"But I must warn you," continued Noorsin. "When I helped your young Protector, I was only helping, not healing. He used the Talent that I shared with him to heal himself. This Dark Magic your father battles right now is more insidious, more pernicious, and I don't know that I can heal him."

"All I ask is that you try," whispered Aislinn, who continued to maintain a strong grip on her father's hand so that he would know that he wasn't alone.

With her training at the Royal Medical School and strength in the Talent, the Duchess of Murcia was likely the most proficient healer in the Kingdom. So she began to apply her knowledge and skill to the obviously worsening Kevan as the web of black continued to expand. She had never seen Dark Magic advance so aggressively before. Usually, it would take hours rather than minutes to reach this point of infection. Kevan's face had become paler in just the last few seconds, the tendrils of black reaching his neck, then his forehead, which coincided with him beginning to struggle for breath, his gasps for air now no more than a rattle in this throat. After a long wheeze, the Duke suffered a bout of choking that Noorsin feared would rip him in two. When he finally settled back on the stretcher, the shivering and shaking came to an end, but his skin had taken on a greyish cast and a thin stream of malevolent black fluid oozed from his mouth and his eyes.

The calm that was so much a part of Noorsin's character began to waver as she watched his struggles worsen. Still, she began her work, attempting to burn away the filth of the Curse by sending tiny streams of the Talent into Kevan, as if she were a physick seeking to cut away befouled flesh. Much to her disgust and fear, she learned within seconds that her approach wouldn't work.

Incredibly the Dark Magic defended itself, blocking Noorsin's efforts. It was as if someone or something was controlling the Curse from afar, fighting her with it, keeping her from doing anything that could remove the rapidly worsening corruption. And she realized, just as Aislinn had discovered, that to fight the Dark Magic as she wanted to would simply accelerate Kevan's demise.

So she tried a different approach, seeking to grab hold of the Dark Magic and draw it like poison from a wound. She focused her efforts first near Kevan's neck, where the source of the Dark Magic lay against his skin, but she failed to seize it with the Talent. The Curse dodged every effort she made to grasp it and pull it free. She decided to try the same approach somewhere else, selecting a tendril on his forehead. Yet again the Curse easily wriggled away from her. It was the most remarkable thing she had ever seen, and under other circumstances would have incited her intellectual curiosity and desire to learn why it was happening, but now all she wanted was to destroy the Dark Magic.

Nothing she tried was working, and she was quickly running out of ideas. It was as if the Curse was teasing her. It was testing her abilities and finding them lacking. Because of that realization her all-pervading calm began to twist into panic. Her composure threatened to shatter as she continued unsuccessfully to use the Talent to cleanse Kevan, the Curse immune to her efforts and now spreading down his legs, his heart rate increasing to a dangerous level as his body fought a desperate but losing battle.

"Rafia, I need your help. Now."

The Keeper of Haven knelt beside Noorsin, reaching for the Talent as she did so. "What is it? Can't you burn it away?"

"Nothing that I would normally do in a situation such as this is working," Noorsin explained rapidly in tight, clipped sentences. "The Dark Magic is resisting whatever I do to cure Kevan. It's almost as if someone is controlling the Curse from afar. I can't even destroy a speck of the infection. It's almost as if it's playing a game with me. This has never happened before. Yes, the Dark Magic has resisted when confronted with the Talent, but it has not actively escaped the Talent as if it has a mind of its own. Nothing I have tried has worked, and I don't know what else to try."

Rafia swept the Talent over Kevan, who was now completely unresponsive, sweat pouring from his body and mixing with the thin black streams oozing now from his nose and ears.

"I can see it," Rafia said through gritted teeth. "The Curse is coming from the collar. I knew it would be linked to him since this collar functions similarly to that of a Protector's, but this blasted metal is different."

Rafia pulled in more of the Talent as she continued to explore the Dark Magic that was trying to consume Kevan.

"The Curse is shielded somehow, and you're right. It appears to have a sentience tied to some other creature. I can only assume the Ghoule Overlord since he's the one who likely created this monstrous tool. That's why this is so difficult. The

Dark Magic in the Duke is responding to the commands of the Ghoule Overlord, which the beast may have set within the Curse when the collar was affixed around this poor man's neck. But that's only part of the story. The shield protecting the Curse is the main problem. We need to penetrate the shield to get through to the Dark Magic, but I worry that the Duke doesn't have the strength to survive a fight like that. He's been afflicted by the Curse for too long, and he's too weak."

"Try, Rafia," said Noorsin, tears beginning to stream down her cheeks as the full import of what was likely about to happen struck her a vicious blow. "You must. He dies if we don't."

Rafia simply grunted in response, seeking to find some crack that she could manipulate in the shield surrounding the Dark Magic. But she couldn't find a weakness. That wasn't unexpected considering the likely source of this Dark Magic, so she didn't allow that discovery to faze her. She then sent several concentrated streams of the Talent into Kevan, seeking to break the shield with a focused force, much like a miner who based on years of experience could identify the perfect place to strike a wall with his pick-axe and cause the entire face to shatter as a result. But again, nothing. The Curse was too strong within Kevan and too well guarded.

So she took the same approach as Noorsin did when she first tried to help Kevan, hoping that she would have better luck than her former student had. Using the Talent, she reached for the Curse, trying to grasp it as she would a loose thread and then pull it free. But it was like trying to grab onto a slimy eel. Every time she thought she had the Dark Magic between her fingers, the Curse simply slipped away. And through it all, as the seconds passed, Kevan's condition worsened, his breath becoming more ragged and weak, as if there was some tremendous pressure on his chest caused by the Dark Magic raging within him that was slowly but mercilessly crushing him.

"I'm not doing any better than you, Noorsin," grumbled Rafia in irritation. "This is not just the Curse. It's something more as you said. Something more powerful. Tetric didn't do this. If what we saw in the Pit was real, this evil was placed upon him by the Ghoule Overlord. It's like the Curse combined with the very essence of that beast, as if we're fighting him and not just the Curse." She looked up from Kevan to Noorsin, the look of anguish on the Duchess' face confirming her true feelings for the Duke of the Southern Marches. "I'm sorry, Noorsin, but I don't know how to combat this."

"Please, you have to do something," pleaded Aislinn, tears streaming down her cheeks as she watched quietly and with growing apprehension as the two Magii tried to save her father yet demonstrated little success. "You must. Please, you must."

Bryen had watched dispassionately as Rafia and Noorsin strove to help the man who had continued his enslavement by bringing him from the Pit to the Southern Marches. He had no love for the Duke, though the misery and fear that Aislinn was experiencing tore at him. As the scene unfolded before him, for some unknown reason, another of Declan's many, often irritating sayings kept playing through his mind: "You must do what you must do."

So rather than simply waiting for the Duke's inevitable end, from where he was standing Bryen used the Talent to study the collar encircling the Duke's neck. He could certainly appreciate the irony of the situation. The man who had collared him now wore a collar himself and likely was dying because of it. But rather than acknowledge the unbecoming sense of comeuppance that trailed through Bryen's mind, he began to think about what had been done to the Duke of the Southern Marches. He assumed that if this blackened steel collar functioned in a fashion similar to the Protector's collar around his neck, then proximity to the holder of the collar was essential.

With the Ghoule Overlord having disappeared -- and he

was certain that this was not Tetric's work after having judged the power within him, which didn't measure up to the strength required to do something like this -- Bryen assumed that connection had been broken, which in turn had released the Dark Magic that had been infused within the collar. He had read about something like this when he was in the Library of the Magii on Haven, so he agreed with Rafia's assessment that a hidden hand played a role in what was happening to the Duke. A final bad twist of fate, a poisoned pill essentially.

The collar was impressive in its design, and it demonstrated a knowledge of Dark Magic that was frightening when fully contemplated. Then Bryen realized the trick. Focusing on the person infected by the Curse, in this case Duke Winborne, would do little good. Rather, you needed to focus on the source, on what was guiding the Dark Magic. You needed to concentrate on the artifact that managed the flow of the Curse into the victim. The only way to overcome the Curse was to destroy the blackened collar or drain the Dark Magic from it.

That's when Bryen realized that he was the only person who might be able to help the Duke. He didn't hesitate, although he had every right to do so.

"Rafia, Duchess Stelekel, please move back."

Before either Magii could respond, Bryen knelt next to the Duke, Aislinn still holding her father's clammy hand, knowing with a growing certainty that she was about to lose him. Bryen gave Aislinn a brief nod, attempting to say with the gesture that everything would be all right, even though he wasn't certain that it would be. Then he placed his hand on the collar, which continued to pulse a deep black, as if it was feeding off of Duke Winborne, which Bryen believed that it actually was.

Recognizing the danger presented by the collar, Bryen took several seconds to confirm what he had thought he had seen during his initial examination of the artifact with the Talent. The collar crafted by the Ghoule Overlord was slightly different than the one he wore, as a tiny pin hidden beneath the front of the collar pierced the Duke's flesh, serving as the means by which the Dark Magic contained within the collar flowed into him. Ingenious in a horrendously malicious sort of way.

That was the key, Bryen realized. That was the weakness. Rather than having the Dark Magic continue to flow into the Duke, Bryen needed to give the Curse another outlet. So he did. Opening himself to the Seventh Stone within him, he used the Talent to latch on to that single sharp point that was hidden from view.

The depth of the Dark Magic that he encountered sent a wave of revulsion through Bryen, and he almost collapsed next to the Duke, never expecting so much of the Curse could be placed in such a small artifact. Before he dropped to the ground, Rafia grabbed onto his shoulders, helping to hold him upright, Bryen keeping his hand on Kevan's chest so that he could maintain the connection that he needed.

Once he regained his equilibrium, having mastered the skill of manipulating Dark Magic behind a thin layer of the Talent, Bryen did that now, allowing the Seventh Stone to pull on the Curse contained within the collar. At first, the Dark Magic resisted. But that resistance rapidly disappeared, even the huge amount of the Curse contained within the collar no match for the strength of the Seventh Stone, which once it had gotten a taste of the Dark Magic, drew on it hungrily, pulling it faster and faster into Bryen, who paid careful attention to ensure that the tainted power remained safely behind the barrier that he had built within himself to guarantee that he avoided even the slightest touch of the Curse.

As he did so, Rafia gripped his shoulder with a stronger hand, understanding the difficulty of the task that he was engaging in and how much of his own strength it required, while Noorsin stared in amazement as she sensed the tremendous amount of power that the Protector was exercising to drain the artifact of its tainted energy. Finally, after several long minutes, Bryen completed the first part of his assignment. He had extracted the Dark Magic from the collar, which had been reduced to nothing more than a cold piece of metal. But Bryen still had more to do.

He needed to remove the remnants of the Curse from within the Duke without killing him. But how to shatter the shield that protected the Dark Magic that had already flowed into Aislinn's father? Attacking it with the Talent had done nothing but provoke a response. So what could he do that hadn't been attempted already? After thinking about his dilemma for a few seconds, using the Talent, Bryen searched for the weakest point of the infection, much as he did when he healed Duchess Stelekel after Tetric had attacked her in the Broken Citadel. He scanned as quickly as he could, understanding that time was running out for the Duke. Thankfully, he found what he was looking for.

The newest strand that had appeared, running straight up the Duke's forehead. He had watched it spread. As the Dark Magic expanded, it stretched the shield, weakening it for a split second in the very space where it grew. So Bryen waited as patiently as he could for his chance, watching that same strand.

When that thread began to inch higher up the Duke's forehead, Bryen struck with a stream of the Talent thinner than that of a hair, shooting the needle into the strand and piercing the shield at its weakest point. What happened next was much like what occurred when a water bag was pricked with a pin, a tiny stream of water shooting out with great force. In this case it was the Curse that burst from the minute hole, the Seventh Stone within Bryen absorbing the tainted power greedily.

It didn't take long for Bryen to complete his work. As the Seventh Stone took in the Dark Magic, the web of black that had spread across the Duke's body slowly receded. As it did, the sable substance oozing from his eyes, ears, and nose dried up and flaked away, the Duke's breathing and color improving. When the last of the Curse had been removed, Bryen released the Talent and took his hand from the Duke's chest, satisfied that Aislinn's father was healed now that he was breathing regularly and a missing warmth had returned to his body.

As Bryen rose to his feet, feeling more exhausted than he did after fighting in the Pit for several hours, he caught the look that passed between Rafia, who remained at Kevan's side next to Aislinn, who hugged her father with unrestrained joy, and Sirius, who stood on the other side of their small gathering with a large grin on his face. Bryen sensed that the grin resulted not from the Duke regaining his health, though the old Magus was clearly pleased with the outcome of Bryen's efforts, but rather with what he had just demonstrated.

He couldn't say with any certainty what the look that passed between the two Magii meant, but he could guess. With Tetric no longer a concern and Bryen in better control of the Dark Magic contained by the Seventh Stone thanks to his acquisition of the Spear of the Magii, Bryen believed that their thoughts had turned to larger and more pressing issues.

With the Ghoule Overlord now revealed, no one had any doubt that his Legions would attempt to break through the Weir. The only way to prevent those attacks, which would threaten the very existence of Caledonia, was to repair the barrier created by the Ten Magii. Bryen had seen it in Sirius' eyes, having learned to read the old Magus quite well after spending so much time with him during the last few months.

He had used the Seventh Stone to heal the Duke of the Southern Marches, but he had also passed an unexpected test, at least in the eyes of Rafia and Sirius. The collar contained a large amount of Dark Magic, though certainly not what would be required if Bryen were to attempt to rebuild the failing magical barrier. Even so, they already knew his strength in the Talent, augmented by the Seventh Stone, and they had assumed that strength would transfer to his manipulation of the Curse.

No, what had impressed the two Magii was what would also be required if he were to reconstruct the Weir. A deft, light touch. Precision. Something that he had just demonstrated while saving the Duke's life.

"Why would you do this?" Aislinn asked, who could barely get the words out. "After everything he put you through. After he put a collar on you."

"He didn't deserve to die this way," Bryen replied simply, distracted from his thoughts by Aislinn's question. "Besides, it was the right thing to do."

With nothing more to say, Bryen walked toward the Pit and the gladiators' stockade where he could clean and heal his wounds and maybe find some clothes not covered in blood.

LOOKING FOR MORE …

I hope you enjoyed the first three chapters. To keep reading *The Protector's Sacrifice*, Book 4 of *The Tales of Caledonia*, order your copy today from my website www.PeterWachtBooks.com or from Amazon.

www.ingramcontent.com/pod-product-compliance
Lightning Source LLC
Chambersburg PA
CBHW070229200726
48293CB00005B/1538